THE
LIGHT
ON
FARALLON
ISLAND

THE
LIGHT
ON
FARALLON
ISLAND

A Novel

JEN WHEELER

LAKE UNION
PUBLISHING

Published by Lake Union Publishing, Seattle

www.apub.com

Amazon, the Amazon logo, and Lake Union Publishing are trademarks of Amazon.com, Inc., or its affiliates.

ISBN-13: 9781662508981 (paperback)
ISBN-13: 9781662508998 (digital)

Cover design by Shasti O'Leary Soudant

Cover image: ©Mary Wethey / ArcAngel; ©sociologas / Shutterstock; ©Amundsen Productions / Shutterstock ; ©seksan wangkeeree / Shutterstock; ©robertharding / Offset

Printed in the United States of America

*To Mom, for always believing I'd get the chance to
dedicate a book to her one day*

"Heaven have mercy on us all—Presbyterians and Pagans alike—for we are all somehow dreadfully cracked about the head, and sadly need mending."

—Moby Dick, *Herman Melville*

Prologue

FATA MORGANA

When she was little, Amelia Osborne saw a ship floating above the horizon. It sailed not high among the clouds but several feet clear of the deep, blue ocean that should have bound it.

She struck out as if summoned, at once up to her ankles in surf, soon swamped to the knees, skirts and petticoats heavy with the sea. How far out would she have to wade before she, too, could rise above the swells? She struggled on up to her waist, to her ribs, eyes fixed on that magic vessel, so she didn't even see the wave that slapped her face as if for impudence.

Amelia's feet were tugged out from under her, body yanked about, nose seared by salt water as she was sucked headfirst toward the ship. She fought against the current but sensed that it was useless. When she opened her mouth to scream, the ocean rushed in. Her mind went mussel-black, blue and silver at the edges before they clamped shut on consciousness.

And then her eyes shattered with sunlight, her lungs with violent coughing. A foamy bilge pumped from her chest, gushed from her mouth.

She was a palsied octopus upon the sand, sodden clothes pinning her down, long hair tangled like seaweed about her face.

"There she is," Mr. Henry cried. "Breathe, now."

Amelia pressed one cheek against the cold beach and expelled the last of the sea she'd swallowed. As she gasped and sputtered, Mr. Henry plucked wet strands from her face. His own coarse hair dripped down his jaw. "Shh, now. You're all right. Calm yourself."

She tried. She rolled her stinging eyes to the side, where her older brother knelt in tears. Past his shoulder, their mother stood with a faint smile on her lips, arms folded at her waist, eyes untroubled as two deep wells.

Her countenance anchored Amelia—and alarmed her most of all. She buried her head in Mr. Henry's soaked shoulder and tried to sob away the image of that placid face.

∾

Some years later, Amelia asked if her mother recalled that day, how she'd gazed so calmly at her half-drowned daughter. "Did you not care if I died? Did you want me to?"

"Do not be ridiculous, child. I knew thou would come to no harm."

"How could you? If Mr. Henry hadn't swum out to save me . . .'"

"Thou would have washed back to shore. For it won't ever be the water kills thee. It will be the fire. I have seen."

One

The Devil's Teeth

April 10, 1859

I sail for the Farallones this morning. San Francisco will be behind me before sunrise. It seems fitting to leave these rooms in darkness. They still smell like smoke.

Amelia stopped short, scratched out the last sentence until it was a black pall upon the page. Before the ink was dry, she closed the diary and tucked it away in her carpetbag. She finished dressing, slipped from the boardinghouse unseen, and descended the steep front steps to meet the hackney carriage that would take her to the wharf. Her trunk had gone ahead of her the previous afternoon and should be safely stowed, if it hadn't been stolen in the interim. She tried not to fret over it, clamped her bag against her waist to keep from bending to touch her petticoat hem. But when she shifted, she could feel the weight of the hidden necklace brush her ankle. No one would get that, at least. Or what she carried in her hands.

San Francisco was a far less lawless place than in the early Gold Rush days of a decade before, but even as an established city with a cosmopolitan veneer, it was full of people eager to take advantage. Amelia couldn't help but sense threats prowling the darker corners, shadows peeling themselves off from the gloom, fleeing the gathering light.

She nearly leaped into the carriage when it arrived, kept the shade drawn as the horses hurtled her away—from danger, from sadness, from old stories she already felt she'd only heard secondhand. This planned exit felt more like escape. Amelia's muscles were tense, her lungs breathless, until they made the waterfront and she relaxed somewhat.

~

From the dock her escort, Mr. Pollard, was peering townward, rust-colored walrus mustache intensifying his concerned frown. His face brightened when he sighted her. "Good morning, Miss Riley! Manage to get any rest?"

"A little, yes."

"Good, good. Brisk, eh? But the weather looks fair. We should have a tolerable ride out—though even on the best of days, it's rarely what you'd call smooth sailing. I don't want to be thought a liar, so I must warn you on that."

"I can handle a little chop. In fact, I'm looking forward to the journey. It's been ages since I've had the pleasure of a boat ride."

Mr. Pollard's mustache spread like wings above his grin. "Still, there's no shame in any seasickness, either; the waves get the best of many a seasoned sailor on occasion. Especially once you hit the Potato Patch."

"Well, I promise not to pass judgment if you are so affected."

He laughed, green eyes crinkling to slits in his fair, ruddy face.

Amelia closed her own eyes to magnify the sounds of creaking ropes and wood-lapping water, to separate them from the slapping footsteps on the pier, the shouted instructions and sudden crashes of cargo being loaded. At a particularly loud boom, a flash of flames behind her lids forced them open. She swallowed a surge of fear, reassured herself nothing was amiss in this moment, this place.

Gentle air currents ruffled the billowing fabric of her skirt and shawl, tickled the edges of her bonnet, carried the rich scents of mud and salt and creosote into her nose. She breathed deeply of the marine air and felt more at peace than she had in weeks, even despite the tingle of apprehension she did her best to banish, and the dull ache of grief she couldn't.

They stood clear of the two-man crew until they were welcomed aboard the *Alba*, a thirty-five-foot fishing felucca that often transported the lighthouse keepers to and from the Farallones.

"We did get a proper tender last year," Mr. Pollard said. "The *Shubrick*. Four times this size, steam-powered, copper-clad. Just missed her, in fact. But she's not as frisky."

"Here, signora." The black-bearded captain offered a rough, sun-browned hand to help Amelia onto his sleek wooden vessel. Its sharply canted yardarm listed like a giant's fishing pole above their heads. "You sit here. Hold on, *sì?*"

Maintaining her smile took some effort. The last oceangoing boat Amelia had been on—over a dozen years ago—was much smaller, yet it had a deeper deck, and proper seats, which made it seem marginally more secure. This one looked likely to bounce her right off its flat surface into the sea at the first jounce over a wave.

There was no turning back now, though, so she settled in and tried to imagine herself glued in place. At least this time she was not alone. And nothing chased her save memories, but even they seemed to belong to someone else.

~

When the sail caught the breeze, Amelia felt it in her own heart, suddenly full to bursting with pure joy. Her unease fled all at once. Slivers struck her at various points on the journey: silver-bright slashes of panic when the boat skipped over a swell; stomach-dropping fear when the pointed prow threatened to pierce the belly of a wave and plunge beneath the water; skidding terror when a massive shadow rippled below them and she could think nothing but *sea monster*, though it turned out to be a leatherback turtle, seven feet long. But even then, when Amelia's chest collapsed like a wind-forsaken jib, in the next instant the freewheeling glee of being on the ocean coursed through her. Her soul expanded beyond what seemed containable in a mere human body.

The morning brightened, lending a quiet beauty to the steely water and the woolly gray sky, with its molten pockets of diffuse sunlight. Amelia was wet with salt spray and her face was numb from the wind, but she could not stop smiling. Even when the sporadic flashes of panic made her gasp, it turned into a laugh. The men laughed with her. "*Sirena*," the captain said. "Signora *Sirena!*"

He sang arias with his rangy, wild-maned mate, their voices loud and lusty, if untrained. Mr. Pollard provided commentary on the weather, the turtle, the whales he thought they might see, the rabbits he'd acquired in the city. He peeked into the shallow hold and reported they seemed well.

Owing to the sheer number of them—eight in total, among four cages—Amelia should have known their intended fate, yet on the pier, she'd inquired if the bunnies were pets for the children.

They'd no doubt like playing with them, Mr. Pollard had said, but they were destined to add a little more variety to the island diet. Pigs and goats had been ferried out before, but rabbits were faster to raise and easier to butcher, and still a nice change from fish.

Amelia's stomach twisted at the idea of eating one of those velvet-eared creatures. Still, she was hungry after several hours at sea. She gladly accepted a wedge from the sourdough loaf passed around for lunch. The captain broke the wax seal on a jar and tossed its tin lid into the ocean, dipped his bread into the black-streaked, reddish substance inside, then offered it to her.

"Caponata," he said.

Amelia sniffed; a pungent note of vinegar stung her eyes and made her cough, which also made them laugh. A more cautious whiff brought the scent of mellow garlic and concentrated tomatoes. She dipped her bread in, nibbled.

Perhaps because she hadn't eaten since the day before, it was the most vibrant thing she'd ever tasted. Rich and savory, with sparks of salt and sweet, all but melting into the chewy sourdough. She flipped her bread around, scooped up a more generous amount of the caponata with the untouched end. "Delicious!" she told the grinning captain. "*Grazie!*"

Mr. Pollard leaned away from the proffered jar, waved in dismissal. "If this fog holds up," he said, "you'll smell the islands before you see 'em. And that slop's a little preview for you."

Amelia was both intrigued and a trifle wary, not to mention impatient to get there now, her lower half numb from sitting, even after altering position countless times. But she had the caponata and bread to console her.

And soon, the day began to clear. Shades of blue revealed themselves both above and below the boat, a simple cornflower sky and a more complex swirl of colors washing around them, a sea of sapphires glittering into gray and black, then sparkling silver. She could lose herself in the shifting hues of the waves as happily as some could in the flames of a fire.

For a time, there was nothing else to see, save other vessels on their own courses, and a few distant spouts. Mr. Pollard spoke of whales gliding beneath the boat on previous trips, breaking the surface mere inches from the bow, allowing their great scarred heads to be stroked like dogs, even leaping clear of the water. But though Amelia held her breath at the thought of such an encounter, no whales approached.

She speculated she was the reason none came near. Silly, but it was hard not to indulge the thought, considering her history with the sea. Yet it wasn't worth dwelling on, and in some sense, Amelia's past was not even her own any longer. She was someone new now—and would be changed again once she reached her destination, she was certain.

Trepidation threatened to seep in at the thought, so she tried to clear her head, concentrated on the monochromatic kaleidoscope of the sea. She believed she'd made the right decision, after all.

$\sim$

In the seventh hour of their journey, when Amelia was fully entranced, the Farallon Islands finally appeared. At first, they looked like nothing more than a handful of dark stones dropped in the middle of the water, pebbles tumbled from Poseidon's pocket.

They were nicknamed the Devil's Teeth, in part for their jagged appearance, like a colossal carnivore's rotten jaw jutting from the waves, and in part for the way they chewed up vessels unlucky enough to founder on them. The square-rigged ship *Lucas* wrecked just the year before, twenty-three people dead out of two hundred on board. The islands were a grim hazard best avoided, yet there were those who made an unlikely home there. She would soon be among them.

The closer they sailed, the larger the Farallones loomed and the clearer their craggy details came into focus. There was not a smooth plane anywhere. The surf bashed itself to pieces at the islands' calloused feet, the rocks above speckled white with gulls and murres, thick as barnacles on the hull of a boat several years out to sea.

Half a mile from that teeming land, as foretold, Amelia could smell it. It was nothing like the caponata, though, unless the jar had been forgotten in a warm place all summer: a sharp cloud of ammonia underscored with a musty note like wet dogs or lathered horses, and salt, and flint, and mildew. The stench was so powerful it momentarily took her breath.

"You'll get used to it," Mr. Pollard proclaimed. "Quicker than you'd think!"

And then the sound, unlike anything she'd imagined. From a distance, it was the murmur of a crowd, but it grew into a far more complicated din. Thousands of avian throats shrieking and screeching, beaks chattering, cackles and squeals giving it the air of an asylum. Sea lions bellowed and barked in counterpoint. It was an overwhelming cacophony, like every sound she'd ever heard replayed all at once, filling her ears faster than her mind could process them. She placed a hand on her bonnet as if to hold in her wits. "Do you get used to *that*?"

Mr. Pollard laughed. "If you're lucky! The rest of us stop up our ears at night."

The other nickname Amelia had heard for the Farallones was the Islands of the Dead, yet how shockingly ill-suited that seemed as she beheld them.

Two

Arrival

Her insides lurched as the boat maneuvered toward a narrow inlet where waves crashed upon the rocks to either side—though she gathered conditions were as close to ideal as they ever got in this place. The motion of the open sea made the mouth of the cove jig in Amelia's vision, but the aperture appeared to widen as they approached, and the felucca sailed into the pocket of calmer water without striking stone.

There were no docks or piers on Southeast Farallon, the only one of the Devil's Teeth inhabitable by humans. Instead, atop the cliff some ten or fifteen feet above them, there was a derrick used to haul up supplies and smaller boats and sometimes people. Mr. Pollard gestured to it. "You can ride up on the dory with the rabbits and your trunk. Otherwise, it's a leap for the stairs and a little climb."

He indicated a set of wooden steps that looked more like an immense ladder propped against the rock face, its bottom awash so Amelia couldn't tell how much farther the rungs extended under-water. It must be safely fastened to the island, but if she missed it in her flight off the felucca, she would be submerged—or at least humiliated.

Neither derrick nor ladder seemed a desirable option for getting ashore, but in hopes of making a good impression, she said, "I could stand to stretch my legs."

Mr. Pollard beamed. "At low tide there's a bit of beach to walk on, but I'm afraid you'll have to get your dress wet today."

"It's already soaked through anyhow."

She wasn't certain she could even stand after sitting so long on the hard deck, legs both stiff and sea-wobbly. With the slick sea spray, she feared her feet would slide right out from under her when she tried to jump.

But with Mr. Pollard's help, she managed to rise and fling herself onto the stairs. She doubted there was a graceful way to do it, though the more experienced might suffer fewer bruises than she expected to find on her ribs and elbows come morning.

Amelia's hands cramped as she pulled herself up, but she dared not loosen her grip. A deranged gull darted perilously close as if intent on knocking her off. The wind plucked at her too, threatening to tangle her skirt about her legs and whip her soiled shawl off her shoulders.

She'd been warned to wear outer garments about which she was not too precious; Mr. Pollard had encouraged an oilskin if she had one, which she didn't. As they neared the islands and the gulls began to swoop over their heads, she understood why. The rocks were streaked and spattered with noxious guano. Soon enough she was too, but it seemed the least of her worries.

Why was the pull to look down as strong as her resolve not to?

When she finally reached the wooden platform at the top of the stairs, she crawled forward a few inches before she pushed herself to stand at full height. With nothing beneath her hands to steady her, she nearly swooned, the breeze buffeting her with fresh force.

From the corner of her eye, Amelia caught a dizzying glimpse of the other surf-skirted islets, one with a rectangular notch punched through the top. She wanted to gaze through that portal but thought it best not to turn her head yet, to keep her eyes fastened on the boathouse before her.

She tried not to toddle too drunkenly toward it and directed what she hoped was a composed but friendly smile at the two women standing there, holding back their children from rushing her.

The mothers looked to be roughly the same age, barely older than Amelia—in their midthirties, she supposed—though their established families gave them an air of even greater authority. They were lovely, she thought, even more so in contrast to one another.

Constance Pollard was tall—she had an inch or two over her own husband, in fact—and pale, save her glossy chestnut hair, which made her freckled skin and limpid gray eyes seem even more delicate. The undefined sweep of her features suggested a face rendered in watercolor.

Abigail Clifford was perhaps four inches shorter. She had luminous, dark skin and broader yet sharper features, lofty cheekbones, and large, striking eyes with heavy lids. Her tightly coiled, ink-black hair was fastened at the nape of her neck, but stray tendrils frizzed free at her temples.

During their interview, Mr. Pollard had mentioned the Cliffords' race, in case it might be an issue. "Not at all," Amelia had assured him, though in truth she was surprised. *We believe every man is equal,* she'd almost added. *Every woman, too.* But she'd been unsure how he would receive that. And she hadn't wanted to clarify which plurality she referred to: *we* as in Quakers. It seemed safest not to mention, a thing Amelia hadn't spoken of in years.

Now, she approached the group—six children between four and ten years old among them—and hoped she didn't look too bedraggled or smell too awful. As Mr. Pollard predicted, the insidious acrid odor and animal musk of the place had already started to become familiar.

Now that their father had gained terra firma too, Mrs. Pollard released their children to swarm him. Meanwhile, she commenced introductions, beginning with herself and Mrs. Clifford before indicating two men busy at the derrick. Percy Clifford spared a nod. Elijah Salter kept his broad back turned. Then the children were presented: Joy, Phyllis, and Samuel Clifford, and the Pollards' Claire, Fiona, and Finn. Amelia repeated each name as she shook each small hand to help herself remember.

"Now, let us show you to Stonehouse," Mrs. Pollard said. "You must want to freshen up and have a moment's rest on solid ground!"

In fact, she would have liked to watch the operation of the hoist. Mr. Pollard, having shaken off his children, had joined the other men at the derrick. Boats didn't linger in the cove, so the sooner they got the felucca unloaded the better. They had the assistance of a mule to turn the windlass that would tow up Amelia's trunk and carpetbag, and the rabbits, and whatever else Mr. Pollard had secured in the city. She was glad she'd chosen the stairs—yet fascinated by the alternative method of coming ashore.

The other islands, the broken triangles and spires of stone thrust up from the sea, also vied for her attention. But there would be plenty of time to study them, and she was not about to oppose the ladies who had brought her to this place. So she dipped her head and followed them across the relatively flat expanse between North Landing and Tower Hill, the highest point on the island. The lighthouse topped it like a candle on a misshapen dome of cake.

As they went, Mrs. Pollard played docent. "The summit's so narrow, the keepers' house wouldn't fit at the foot of the light, so they built it at the bottom of the hill instead. Which means you have to climb three hundred forty-some feet to get there! Switchbacks all the way. Still, it's worth doing at least once for the lens alone. If you're lucky enough to have a clear day, the view is marvelous."

Mrs. Clifford added, "Mind your footing and it's not so bad, though when it's windy you'll be bent double trying to make any headway. And not get blown off the path."

"Sometimes the men go up on hands and knees," allowed Mrs. Pollard, "or so they say, in the worst of the winter storms. But that won't be for a long while yet! Spring has sprung, and isn't it lovely?"

It was. Though Amelia had expected a barren landscape of naked rock, and indeed there were no trees or grasses, a thick carpet of green-stalked yellow flowers—goldfields, Mrs. Clifford told her, or, less poetically, Farallon weed—spread across the marine terrace. The color crept up the hill in places, a few last dabs from a meandering paintbrush.

"We have daisies, too," Mrs. Pollard said. "Harder to find, but it always cheers me to spot them on the rocks. Now, here we are!"

∾

Stonehouse was a simple, flat-faced structure made of a variegated mosaic of irregular granite blocks quarried on the island. Its patchwork facade recalled a fairy cottage, but its form reflected perfect symmetry. A chimney capped each end of the gabled roof. The front door was precisely centered and flanked by two pairs of tall windows. From within, twelve panes in each frame divided the view into a seascape stitched from glass postcards.

In the entryway, Amelia hung her bonnet and soiled shawl from the coat hooks.

A central hall divided the main floor into a kitchen and a parlor, which also served as the schoolroom. The children gyred through it, skirting every familiar obstacle just before the moment of collision.

Stairs at the back led to a half story tucked beneath the sloping roof, two bedrooms mirrored across a landing. Each had a fireplace, as did the parlor. The furnishings were plain, yet comfortable.

More than enough space for one soul, but less than ideal for three families, which was why two larger dwellings had recently been erected a few hundred yards to the southeast of Stonehouse.

"Of course, you're welcome to visit with us anytime," Mrs. Pollard said. "I imagine it could get lonely in here, though I daresay you'll be glad for some respite from the children!"

The little ones continued to run amok around the women; good-natured shouts and squabbles resounded. The crash of waves and the clamor of seabirds were muffled in the house, owing to the fact that the walls were three feet thick.

"We usually cook and eat together," Mrs. Clifford said, "so you're welcome to join us at mealtimes too."

"Yes, of course," said Mrs. Pollard. "Though if you prefer to eat alone, we won't take offense!"

A bit ruffled by their solicitous chatter and acutely conscious of the fact that she herself had said so little, Amelia answered in an overly cheerful voice, "Thank you; I admit, I haven't done much cooking, but I certainly don't expect you to cater to me—I'm no guest. I'm happy to help wash and chop, at least. I'm not sure I'm good for much else, but I can learn."

They smiled and assured her one more mouth to feed was nothing, and new company was always welcome. They didn't say outright but implied that it was the least they could do to offset the pittance they'd be able to pay her. Amelia didn't care about the money, but that, too, wasn't the sort of thing one could announce.

Mrs. Pollard clapped her palms together. "Now, we have a fine feast planned for tonight!"

"As fine as the Farallones allow," amended Mrs. Clifford.

"A welcome dinner. In your honor, of course."

"Oh, you shouldn't have gone to any trouble—"

"No trouble at all!" said Mrs. Pollard.

"There's a cake," her green-eyed girl declared as she twirled around the room and out again.

"We helped!" the slight-boned Clifford son added as he tore through after his playmates.

"Well, I thank you, truly. All of you! I do feel very welcomed already." And slightly flustered from the sustained attention.

"We're just so happy you're here," Mrs. Pollard said, and Mrs. Clifford nodded. Her smile was restrained compared to the other woman's keen expression, but an overeager glint in both ladies' eyes set off another wave of jitters.

Three

FIRST IMPRESSIONS

Mrs. Pollard stepped to the door to open it as voices became audible outside. Mr. Pollard and Mr. Clifford each had one end of Amelia's steamer trunk, which they carried inside and set gently on the floor.

"How do, Miss Riley." The first assistant keeper, taller and a little older than any of the rest of them, was clean-shaven, with an oval face and pointed chin, skin that gleamed a few shades lighter than his wife's—Amelia made her quick study as she shook his hand.

"Pleased to meet you, Mr. Clifford."

"Likewise. Looks like you've pretty near gotten acquainted with everybody else already, save the Salters."

"I think so, yes." *And the egg man*, she thought. Preceding her interview, Mr. Pollard had sent a letter naming the Farallones' year-round residents: his family, Mr. Clifford's, Mr. Salter's, and a singular Mr. Sisson, caretaker for the Pacific Egg Company. Amelia felt a tremor of unease at the thought of him now but only said, "And I haven't met the mule."

"She's called Mary," the stocky Pollard boy said. "She's been here longer than any of us!"

Finn's father confirmed, "She helped lug the supplies up that hill to build the first lighthouse in fifty-three. And the second one too, after they had to tear the first one down."

"Oh? What happened?"

Mrs. Pollard answered, with no small amount of glee, "They had it built up pretty as you please before the lens arrived—all the way from France, no less—and it was too big to fit in the tower! So down the whole thing went! They rebuilt it from the ground up, the right size this time around."

"No easy feat, you can imagine," her husband said. "Hauling supplies up there, hefting them onshore in the first place. Before Mary, the men had to take a handful of bricks at a time on their backs, scramble up on all fours. No path cut in yet. And then the lens came in pieces, of course; seventy-three crates alone just for that and the housing."

"Goodness."

Mrs. Clifford shook her head. "Sure wouldn't have liked to be the person responsible for that mistake."

"No, indeed."

Mrs. Pollard broke the lull that settled among the adults. "Well, we should let Miss Riley have some time to recover from the journey. Give her some space to breathe. We so rarely have a new face around here; we tend to crowd in—do forgive us. Supper should be done by six, but come over to the house whenever you're ready. We're in the first one you'll come to. Let us know if you need anything, of course."

As they wrangled the children for departure, Mr. Pollard turned back. "Ah, and you haven't met Mr. Sisson yet. He's busy getting things ready for the eggers when they arrive in a couple weeks. But he'll come to dinner tonight."

"He was invited, anyway," Mrs. Pollard said. "He does tend to be rather solitary, though. I wouldn't expect to see him. Or the Salters. They like their peace and quiet."

18

"Well," said Mr. Pollard, "whoever doesn't come, you'll meet them soon enough. Only so much space for a dozen-odd people to roam around here without running into each other eventually."

Amelia's smile belied her unease.

~

During her interview, Mr. Pollard had furnished a few more particulars about the islanders, including the fact that, like herself, Mr. Sisson hailed from England.

Upon that revelation, Amelia had almost abandoned her hastily decided plan. But there were millions of Englishmen in the world, and plenty of them in the States. This one was unlikely to be noteworthy. She'd tried to believe that, at least, even when she'd found more evidence that probably should have derailed her. She'd felt compelled to make for the Farallones, no matter what. There had been no other option.

Now, she feared she'd made a grave miscalculation. She wished Mr. Sisson had shown up with the rest, tried not to wonder why he hadn't. She didn't like to think of any unknown quantities lurking about this unfamiliar landscape.

But it was an unreasonable fear, Amelia told herself. She was the only true stranger on the island.

~

She could still hear the birds, faintly, when the last of her welcoming committee slipped out the door and pulled it shut. For a piercing moment, she felt utterly forlorn.

With nothing else dividing her attention, she drifted around the space—her own. It would take some getting used to, but she'd found herself quite malleable lately, claiming ownership of all sorts of things she'd never imagined. She kicked her foot out to feel the tap of the necklace in her hem, a solid thump against her ankle. Still there, then, but she'd have to be careful as she walked about the island; the sharp-edged rocks could unpick her stitches when she wasn't paying attention and claim her treasure.

Trailing her fingers over surfaces, as if to better commit their contours and textures to memory, Amelia inventoried details. A blackboard hung on one parlor wall, a basket of slates and bucket of chalk below, ready for classes to resume under her command.

Someone had wound the brass ship's clock before her arrival; at least, it seemed to note the correct time, nearly three already. A rank of bird skulls sat beside it on the mantel, fragile little things interspersed with shark-teeth fossils, smaller still, though one overspilled the confines of her palm.

She tested the weight of it and wondered at the scale of the animal it came from. Surely something extinct, or might its ilk still ply the fathoms? A fleeting thought of her mother, who prayed to such grisly gods, but Amelia put the tooth down and turned her back on those notions.

A more cheerful study: the bouquet of goldfields, picked just that morning, placed in an amber bottle upon the walnut table, alongside a handbell.

She noted a frayed spot on the braided rug in the parlor, the creak of a certain board beneath her tread, both of which she imagined she would cease to notice in time.

Upstairs, in the bedroom she'd been informed got the best morning light, the porcelain ewer had been filled with water. A soft cloth lay folded beside it on the washstand. She bathed the salt and grime from her face and neck, peered at herself in the spotted looking glass. She was either slightly burned or chapped from the wind and spray. The redness in her cheeks made her eyes look bluer, wilder. She couldn't hold her own gaze.

She unpinned her bonnet-flattened hair and finger-combed the tangled waves, a dull, tarnished gold that only sparked to life in the sun.

She made simple side rolls and fastened it all behind her head, slid the tortoiseshell comb back in place.

While she was tempted to sprawl on the spool-frame bed, she knew she ought to bring her clothes up and place them in the wardrobe, arrange her books, jot another note in her diary.

But the mattress was a more appealing prospect. A second after she sat, though, she heard a knock below.

She rose and trotted down the stairs, expecting perhaps a Salter emissary, but the man outside was not the brawny one she'd glimpsed at the landing.

"Oh," she said, "hello." She steeled herself. "Mr. Sisson?"

He regarded her with confusion, as if he, too, had expected someone else. Belatedly, he said, "Yes, Will. Lucy?"

Amelia smiled, nodded, tried to ignore the bobbing sensation in her stomach. "Lucy Riley. Pleased to meet you."

The furrow deepened between his brows; hazel eyes searched Amelia's face as if it were a mask he could peer beneath. She found herself struck mute.

Abstractedly, he stammered, "I just—I wanted to say hello. See you arrived safely."

She tried not to appear rattled, but his demeanor unnerved her. His accent was different from hers, some of his vowels broader, some shorter, others rounder. The smooth, rich tone of his voice, too, seemed to resonate in Amelia's marrow.

There was also the alarming fact that she found him handsome, despite—or perhaps in part because of—the intensity of his gaze, the gauntness of his tanned face and tall frame. He was older than she, although, as with those who lived largely outdoors, it was hard to say by how much; perhaps a decade, perhaps less.

As she groped for something else to say, Mr. Sisson shook his head. "Sorry. I seem to be a bit—scattered."

"Yes, I heard you're quite busy, readying the way for the egg-plundering horde."

He chuckled, barely, unable to stop his eyes flickering again across Amelia's face. "Indeed. Where are you from?"

A simple answer, yet her mouth did not want to speak it. "I've been in San Francisco nearly six years. In America more than ten, now. I almost feel as if I always was."

He allowed a hint of a smile, something harder just behind it. "But originally? Where were you born?"

She trusted the smile she gave in return appeared perfectly blithe. "Sunderland. You?"

"Very near there, in fact. A little fishing village just down the coast. Staithes?"

It meant nothing to Amelia, yet her throat still felt on the verge of sealing itself shut. She managed to say, "How funny," in a normal enough tone of voice.

Something closed off in him then, though an observer would have been hard-pressed to call him anything but polite. "Well. I'll leave you to get settled, then."

Amelia watched him stride down the steps. She should have been glad to shut the door and have a moment to lean against it, catch her breath, but she chirped, "Will I see you tonight? At dinner?"

Mr. Sisson paused, glanced over his shoulder with a calculating look—and was there something else? A measure of discomposure, or fear, or was it just Amelia's imagination, making his eyes a mirror for her own emotions?

All he said was "Perhaps."

Four

Fortress

With shaking fingers, she busied herself putting away her things. She didn't have much, so she drew out the process, fussing over every fold and drape of fabric and the precise placement of each object. Books composed the bulk of her cargo; she added them to the collection on the parlor shelves, which included several workbooks and teaching-oriented tomes her predecessors had left behind.

Two instructors had come and gone over the past eighteen months, Amelia knew. Mr. Pollard had warned her, "It is a very isolated existence, and it doesn't suit everyone."

It would suit her splendidly, being among only a handful of people, not cut off but protected from the greater flood of humanity. Unobserved, unknown, nigh unreachable. The idea—the opportunity—of securing the position had made her almost frantic. All she'd said, though, was "I don't believe one can ever be truly isolated if they exercise the power of their own imagination. And I have enough books to keep me company, besides."

"That's the spirit!" he'd said, and offered her the job.

Amelia knew, too, that eggers would swarm the island between the months of May and July. Their exploits made the papers every year: *The*

Farallone egg season has commenced, as we saw the parti-colored fruit in market a day or two ago; price six bits the dozen.

With the Gold Rush, the population of San Francisco had exploded. There were not nearly enough chickens to keep up with its appetites, so enterprising souls turned to the Farallon Islands' murre colonies. For the past ten years, intrepid men had raided the rocks and reaped great profits every nesting season, their mother lode continually replenished, even as the gold itself disappeared inland. Schooners still returned to the city laden with three hundred dozen or fourteen hundred dozen or other such mind-boggling quantities of eggs.

Before her arrival, when Amelia imagined herself in the milieu, she assumed the eggers would be naught but figures in the background, inconsequential to her own existence, gone almost as soon as they arrived. She hadn't thought of them at all as her interview with Mr. Pollard approached, focused on convincing him she was the right person for the post—though most likely, she was also the only applicant.

She hadn't been particularly curious about the caretaker, *who keeps things in order for the egg company throughout the year and helps us with odd jobs from time to time,* Mr. Pollard had written.

Until she'd learned Mr. Sisson was British. Then Amelia had been mildly terrified, though not enough to change her mind. She'd convinced herself she was being ridiculous, and she tried to do the same thing now.

But what if her initial fears had been justified? Were Mr. Sisson's origins significant, not a mere—a mammoth—coincidence? Had Amelia blundered into something far stickier than what she'd left behind?

If Mr. Sisson suspected anything, though, surely he would have accused her, demanded an explanation.

She'd been unsettled before she even opened the door. He must have noticed, must have wondered what was wrong with her. And now wasn't she just being more paranoid, grasping at straws, even knowing how fiercely they'd prick? Yet Amelia feared his provenance couldn't simply be happenstance—which didn't mean she had any notion of what the true implication was. There was more than one way to interpret the few vague clues she had. She couldn't be certain this wasn't pure coincidence.

Harebrained and bullheaded as she might have been, there was no easy way out now anyway—Amelia couldn't slip away again, self-marooned as she was. Nor could she hide. She had to believe she was letting her imagination get the better of her. It wouldn't be the first time.

While Mr. Sisson's presence was remarkable, then, it didn't have to be unnerving. Amelia would become accustomed to it.

Just as she would become accustomed to the racket; knowing what she did about the volume of murre eggs, she might have expected the babel of the birds themselves (though most of the raucous calls she heard now were gulls). Then again, the ad in the paper—*A teacher is wanted in this queer school district*—had also said: *Here is a chance for anyone who can appreciate the majesty of the ocean and who covets a quiet place in which to read and reflect.*

A quiet place! Amelia scoffed, though without rancor. It might have been noisy, but the island was quiet in other ways, far more important to her sense of security. She couldn't allow her equilibrium to be shaken already. Then she'd have to console herself, and that would mean admitting she was only jumpy because of what she'd done, reminding herself no one else here knew she was getting away with anything.

Unless one person did.

If Amelia were to thrive, she would have to smother that ember of fear, of guilt, of the certainty that she could never keep it up or pull it off.

When she judged herself as settled as she could be for the moment, she wandered out and scanned the landscape: rocks and sea and sky, and nothing else. An illusion of infinite space beyond the stronghold of granite on which she stood, simultaneously exposed and tucked away.

The island was a fortress—*or,* Amelia's mind whispered, *a trap.* She tightened her arms around herself and stared out to the blank horizon. The endless, empty view would be the same on every side.

Still, she would have liked to explore farther afield. But it wouldn't do to seem unsociable, nor did she wish to encounter Mr. Sisson again, so she continued to the keepers' quarters.

∽

The pair of clapboard-clad homes, situated perhaps two hundred feet apart, were far larger and finer than Stonehouse, complete with upper balconies. They could have been plucked from any city street and seemed fantastically out of place stranded on this feral rock. As Amelia approached them, she spied a pale face behind a window in the farther building. When she lifted a hand in greeting, the figure ducked away. Embarrassed to be caught spying, or simply shy?

Amelia studied the curtains for a moment in case they might part again. They remained closed, so she mounted the steps of the nearer house and knocked on the door.

One of the girls opened it—Fiona, Amelia thought. But when she chanced to use the name, the soft, round face clouded with indignation. "No, I'm *Claire*."

"Oh, I'm sorry. My brains are still a little wobbly from bobbing on the waves all morning. Will you forgive me?"

The two boys—the ten-year-old with his freckles and thick limbs, the willowy brown four-year-old with his elfin smile—both giggled behind Claire, but she only nodded and stepped aside to let their new teacher in.

"Then you're Fiona," Amelia said to the smaller, gray-eyed Pollard girl sitting shoulder to shoulder with the younger of the two Clifford sisters on the rug. "And . . . Phyllis?"

They both grinned and nodded.

Phyllis, lisping through a missing bottom tooth, said, "You're Miss Lucy!"

"Miss Riley," Fiona whispered.

"Either one of those is fine," Amelia assured them, then turned to the boys. "And that makes you Samuel and Finn."

They smiled and nodded too.

"Then we're just missing Joy."

Claire looked freshly affronted that she had been the only one misremembered but took it upon herself to say Joy was with her daddy, looking at the insides of a carriage clock. "It wasn't even *broken*."

"They do like to tinker!" Mrs. Pollard laughed, emerging in the doorway from the kitchen. "Welcome; please, make yourself at home. All settled in at Stonehouse?"

"Yes, thank you. It's very cozy. I found some rather good books in the schoolroom."

"Oh, good! We can send for any more supplies you need—of course, it won't be quick to get them, but just let us know if there is anything and we'll send a list when the next boat comes."

"I think we're fairly well set, but I'll keep that in mind." Without meaning to, Amelia said, "I met Mr. Sisson."

Mrs. Pollard's eyebrows rose. "Oh?"

"He stopped by to say hello."

The woman's brows ratcheted even higher. "Really? And how did you find him?"

"A bit—strange, to be honest. He seemed . . . preoccupied."

"Well, he is at his busiest just now, cleaning up the barracks and checking all the equipment and what have you. He can brood at times, but he's a very decent man. And a fellow expat, like yourself. He must have been eager to meet another Brit!"

"Yes, apparently we're from the same general area." She hoped the fresh discombobulation when she said it aloud wasn't evident in her face.

Mrs. Pollard only beamed brighter. "Imagine that!"

"Mm." Why was she still talking about him? "May I be of any help in the kitchen?"

"Oh, no, we're fine. Not long now! But would you like something to drink? Mr. Pollard has a lovely mead, or we've cider, or sherry."

"Just a glass of water, thank you."

When she went to fetch it, Claire announced, "The water from Amber Spring tastes like lemonade without any sugar in it."

"Like *vinegar*," Fiona opined.

"And where is Amber Spring?"

"At North Landing," Claire said.

"Mama gives it to us when we're sick," said Finn.

"It moves things along," added Phyllis, and every child except imperious little Claire giggled.

"You'll have to show me all around the island," Amelia said, addressing all of them but looking first and last at Claire so she might feel especially important. "I expect you all can teach me as much as I can teach you, for you must be experts in the secrets of this place by now."

"We are!" Phyllis agreed.

"Except Gertie," Claire countered. "She hardly ever goes outside."

Before Amelia could ask about that, Mrs. Pollard returned with the water. "Don't let them drag you down to one of the caves!" she cautioned. "Or go near the staircase at the landing; they're strictly prohibited from going within twenty feet of the top. And they'll likely turn your ankles trying to get you to run up Tower Hill, but don't chance it; the rocks are terribly loose. And when the fog comes in, stay close to the houses; it's easy to lose a sense of distance—you might find the edges of things closer than you expect."

The woman's wild eyes belied the static smile pasted to her face. Satisfied with those warnings—or thinking better of dispensing any more just yet and putting too much fear into the new arrival—she nodded and swept back to the kitchen.

"The seagulls will try to peck your brains out too," Finn added.

Fiona shuddered. "They peck all the other poor little birds to death."

"I believe it. One was having a go at me when I climbed up from the boat today, in fact. I nearly fell off! Right into the drink." As punctuation, Amelia took a gulp of water.

More giggles except from Claire. "Mama means it about staying away from those stairs," she said. "She always did, but especially since Serena fell down and drowned."

The matter-of-fact way she said it was almost as disconcerting as the news itself. "Serena?"

"She was our sister."

"I don't remember her," Fiona murmured, frowning.

Finn watched the toe of his shoe as he ground it against the carpet—Amelia wondered if that explained the frayed spot on her own parlor rug—but he didn't comment.

"Our mama doesn't let us go there without her either," Phyllis said.

"Well, that's very sensible. We shan't go near the landing, then; I've seen enough of it already, anyway."

"But when it's nice and the tide goes out, we can go out on the beach!" said Finn.

"And in the rowboat," Samuel added.

"Well, we'll make an exception on those days only, and we'll all go down together very carefully and stay safe."

"But I don't like the boat," Fiona fretted.

Phyllis pursed her lips but patted her friend's thin shoulder. "We can stay inside and play paper dolls."

∼

Before dinner, Amelia had a brief tour of the house. The Pollards lived on the upper floor, while the Cliffords claimed the lower; each level was the other's twin. The Salters had the second home to themselves, although they were the smallest family. She wondered why that was but didn't ask. She recalled how Mr. Pollard had first described them during her interview: pious, private folks who wouldn't be sending their daughter to school. Still, Amelia hadn't expected them to be so thoroughly sequestered, to not even say hello.

Everything inside both houses was identical, Mrs. Pollard said as they continued the tour, down to the parlor sets. The furniture was all newer and nicer than any in Stonehouse, to match its surroundings. Here, there were turned banisters, elaborately carved moldings, and wallpaper and wainscoting in place of bare plaster. If Amelia faced away from the windows, she could almost forget where she was.

Soon, they were all packed around the dining table, the younger children squeezed beside their parents at the corners.

As predicted, the Salters didn't come. To everyone's surprise, Mr. Sisson did. Amelia couldn't look at his face and so wasn't sure if he peered at her or she only imagined it, simply felt the sense memory of his inquisitive gaze from earlier. In any case, her cheeks were flushed, and she hoped the sun- or windburn hid it.

She stared intently at a platter of what she first thought was poultry. She wondered if they might have slaughtered seabirds for dinner, but the spindly leg bones betrayed their rabbit origins. The jumble must have represented at least half the bunnies who'd joined her on the boat. She blanched but accepted a serving and found it delicious enough to put the image of those sweet, quivering noses out of mind after the third bite.

Roasted turnips with their sautéed greens and a fluffy cornmeal pudding made a feast as fine as the Farallones allowed, indeed. It was more than adequate, and Amelia enjoyed the food as well as the companionable chatter, for the most part.

Naturally, she was asked a barrage of questions she didn't think she would have been so nervous to answer if Mr. Sisson hadn't been at the table. He said little himself, as if he'd only come to be polite— yet she sensed he absorbed every word she spoke.

Five

STRANGE BIRDS

The wives wouldn't let Amelia help clear the dishes, though the older children were pressed into service. Claire carried in the cake: three layers of golden sponge striped with raspberry jam, finished with a dusting of snowy sugar and a couple of the precious daisies Mrs. Pollard had mentioned earlier. "We were so fortunate to find enough eggs so early in the season!" she said as she carved the first slice.

Mrs. Clifford said, "Otherwise it would have been a cowboy cake. Full of raisins." She smiled at Joy as the girl wrinkled her nose.

"It's a good omen," Mrs. Pollard said, handing another filled plate over to be passed down the table.

"We're lucky Will isn't so jealous of his treasure as some of his men," said Mr. Pollard, with a sly grin at the egg-company caretaker, who smiled.

When Amelia glanced up, a feather brushed her heart. An infinitesimal tremor that nonetheless knocked her further off-kilter.

"There are plenty to go around, I think," Mr. Sisson said.

"And no one wants an old murre egg, anyway," said Mrs. Pollard.

"Fishy misery," according to her husband.

"They say it takes three months to get the taste out of your mouth," said Mrs. Clifford.

"But the ones in the cake are fresh as the daisies!" Mrs. Pollard assured them.

Through a mouthful of crumbs and jam, Claire said, "If you look long enough, you can find your name written on one."

"On an eggshell," her mother clarified. "They're covered in scribbles and splotches—no two alike. They say if you *do* see your name on one, it means you've been here too long. Personally, I've never made out any words among all the scratchings."

Mr. Clifford said, "If anybody has, it must be Mr. Sisson."

"I make it a point not to look too closely."

"How long have you been here, then?" Amelia said, almost aghast that she'd addressed him, if only because it meant he looked directly at her, and she couldn't very well avert her attention then.

"Eight years."

"Oh."

"And nearly all of that on the island, too," Mrs. Pollard exclaimed. "I've never met someone less interested in taking shore leave."

"You were even here before Mary," Fiona said.

"I was," said Mr. Sisson. "I saw the poor beast scramble ashore. Turns out, mules get seasick too. But she seems to have adjusted well since then."

"So have you, old man." Mr. Pollard grinned. "But you would've been a happy hermit save three months of the year if it hadn't been for the damn Lighthouse Board, eh?"

"Oh, I don't mind you lot. The early years were a bit less agreeable."

General chuckles rippled around the table and left Amelia feeling even more alienated, but Mrs. Pollard explained: "The first few keepers who had this post were . . . *eccentric*, if you want to use a kind word to describe them."

"They all went crazy!" Finn said.

"Not *crazy*," his mother corrected. "Not *all* of them."

"And one got swept away," said Samuel. "A giant wave washed him right off the tower one night!"

"*Allegedly*," Mrs. Pollard said, catching Amelia's look of consternation. "We haven't seen anything like that since we've been here. Over two years now. But there was all manner of trouble until they decided to post families on the island instead of single men. To keep them sane, you see. And civilized."

"And I'm certain I've benefited from that decision too," said Mr. Sisson.

"Oh, you can keep yourself in check," said Mrs. Pollard. "You're a gentleman at heart. Just look at your nails. More than I can say for some of your eggers, but that's not your fault."

"Nor are they *my* eggers, precisely."

"Wait till you see them," Mr. Pollard said, "scaling those rocks like mountain goats, shirts stuffed out to here, gulls squawking around every man's head. It'd drive anyone mad. Or you'd have to be mad to try it in the first place."

"One slip and they can just . . . disappear," his wife said, with a shudder much like Fiona's. "The birds peck their hands bloody too."

"No reward without risk," Mrs. Clifford commented.

"Speaking of, how many eggs do you reckon they've taken since the beginning of it?" Mr. Pollard asked.

Mr. Sisson leaned back in his chair, studied a corner of the ceiling as he calculated. "Our best year was five hundred thousand, and our worst was still close to four, so . . . well over three million by now."

"It's a wonder there are any murres left at that rate," Amelia blurted.

"We couldn't possibly rob them all."

"Though they try," Mr. Pollard said.

His wife frowned over her cake, having finally served herself the last sliver. "Then the poor little fledglings that do make it have such a rough start; you'll see. The chicks get marched to the edge of a cliff and sent tumbling off straight into the sea. If they're lucky, they manage to figure out what to do before they hit the water. It *is* a wonder any make it. And the gulls must kill hundreds more each year."

Mrs. Clifford glanced at Joy, who seemed to have lost her appetite for dessert at the mention of such unpleasant things. "But they come back in great flocks again every spring," she said, with a smile for her daughter.

"Life goes on," Mr. Clifford affirmed.

With a child's unconscious knack for saving a conversation, Fiona trilled, "I wish we would see a hummingbird again!"

"We may yet," said Mrs. Pollard. "Fall will be the best chance. We get lots of other visitors once the seabirds leave. Not in any great numbers, but you never know what you'll see."

"The gulls *never* leave," Finn groused.

"Not all of them," said his mother. "But that's to be expected; this is their home too. Now, you wouldn't expect to see a songbird in the middle of the ocean, but then sometimes you do. Last year we even had a pair of great blue herons show up in September."

"And the red-throated loon," said Mrs. Clifford. "It cried out and gave us such a fright. This *piercing* wail; it sounded so unearthly. We were almost sure it was—"

"A ghost!" Finn cried, which earned him another sharp look from his mother.

"Well, until we saw what it was and had a good laugh," Mrs. Clifford said.

"I expect a flamingo one of these days," Mr. Pollard crowed. "A penguin! A dodo!"

Even Mr. Sisson smiled. As if he knew Amelia had chanced another look, he met her eyes. "All sorts of strange birds get blown off course."

Again, she felt her stomach sway as it had on the felucca, even before she caught Mrs. Pollard shoot Mrs. Clifford a conspiratorial look.

∾

After dinner, Mr. Sisson excused himself, and Mr. Pollard had to prepare for the night's watch. He'd climb Tower Hill to set flame to the oil lamp and tend the wick and the clockwork mechanism. Every four and a half hours, it was wound again; every eight minutes, the lens completed a full revolution; every minute, the brilliant white beam flashed into the darkness and could be seen, on a clear night, slicing the sky over twenty miles away.

Mr. Clifford explained the workings of the mechanism and the lens, the chariot wheels and rollers, the hand-cut prisms, the counterweight, the vents to help adjust the flame. Amelia found herself eager to see it all up close. He promised to take her on the next fair day.

Over the past few hours, the wind had picked up. The glass rattled in the panes as they finished their cake. He predicted fog tomorrow. "Surprised you had such agreeable weather for your first day, truth be told."

"Another good omen," Mrs. Pollard said.

"Well," Amelia answered, "tomorrow will be for getting down to work anyway. Fog might be better for keeping me inside."

Mrs. Clifford smiled. "Never as cozy indoors as when it's dreary without."

"Indeed. I absolutely adore a rainy day. Fog's almost as good. I must be in the right place, then."

"And you must be ready for a good night's sleep!" said Mrs. Pollard when Amelia stifled a yawn. "It's been such a long day for you, too. Don't rush yourself getting acclimated. Sleep in as long as you like. We're rarely in any hurry around here."

She should have demurred, but the thought was tantalizing. In fact, Amelia's head had started to ache with a pulsing thrum, and the motion of the boat still echoed faintly in her body, a sort of sloshing in her blood. It might rock her to sleep in her dining chair if she lingered, despite the throbbing behind her eyes.

～

She politely declined an escort and stepped out into the gusty twilight alone. The gulls and murres still brayed from the surrounding rocks as the waves ceaselessly crashed against their foundations. Closer, storm petrels darted and jabbered through the gathering mist; the swift motions and shrill cries of the little birds spiked Amelia's pulse. Creepers of fog unfurled around her ankles. A sense of unease slithered in with them.

She glanced back at the Salters' house, but no faces peered from their windows. Nor had any figures emerged from either home. Yet Amelia felt followed.

She sped up to outpace the disquiet—*a ghost*, she heard Finn exclaim—though she told herself she just wanted to escape the chill, damp wind, the petrels like fairy goblins swooping through the occluded air. She rushed up the front steps of Stonehouse and flung the door shut behind her, hurried to light the candle in its holder on the table.

The pool of warm illumination in the dim, unfamiliar space was welcome, though it also accentuated the shadows licking the edges of things. The eye sockets of the bird skulls flickered.

Amelia walked upstairs with the flame held far from her, peeked into the empty bedroom just to be certain it was, in fact, unoccupied, and closed herself into her own room. She set the candle squarely in the middle of the washstand, pitcher and cloth removed to the floor so the pewter holder sat in the porcelain basin, just in case, though it seemed nothing short of a deliberate hand could tip the taper over.

She loosened her hair, shucked her boots, shed all her tedious layers: skirt and bodice; outer petticoat; enormous bell-shaped cage crinoline; the petticoat beneath that, its hem still holding its small, secret weight; corset; chemise; stockings; knee-length drawers. Refreshing to exchange all those for a single piece of fabric, a long nightgown she couldn't bear to button all the way up to her throat once freed from the rest of her garments.

She'd not yet used her chamber pot; she'd barely had anything to drink that day. She should fetch a glass from the kitchen and fill it from her pitcher, but couldn't bring herself to open the door, much less face the dark stairs, a black throat that would swallow her.

With wind whistling and birds murmuring and surf shushing from every side, Amelia turned back the covers, blew out the dancing wick, and slid into bed.

She hadn't slept so far removed from other people in years and was surprised to find herself so unsettled. The loneliness was to be expected. The fear was perhaps not unfamiliar, yet Amelia had trusted it would diminish in this remote place, not mushroom into something even more sinister.

She heard Finn's voice again: *They all went crazy.* She could easily believe the Farallones played tricks upon the mind of even the most imperturbable person, but sanity was a matter of pushing back, wasn't it? Staunchly refusing to believe that which couldn't be possible. And all current residents seemed fine—even Mr. Sisson. She would be too.

Rolling over to face the wall, Amelia pulled the blanket up below her eyes and placed a hand over her semi-exposed ear. Told herself nothing was sneaking up behind her, refused to turn around when she felt the filaments of hair at the nape of her neck prickle upright. It was just a draft, she reasoned. Nothing else.

She was alone, and she was safe. She repeated those words to herself through her exhaustion until they finally pulled her under, to sleep.

In her dreams, she saw flames and fists and blades and blood, but she'd expected them to follow her, the specters that haunted one's mind not so easily escaped.

Provided they were all that troubled her, Amelia could bear them. She had no other choice.

Six

DISCOVERY

Her second afternoon on the island, after a successful first day of classes, Amelia decided to greet the Salters. She knocked at their door and was met by a disconcerting pair. Elijah Salter, weather-bronzed and burly, scowled out of a mane of black hair that converged with a prodigious though not unruly beard. Up close, the very sight of him shrank Amelia's skin. He could have stepped out of her nightmares, a darker version of her fair-haired, blue-eyed father. Salter's bearing was equally imposing and his gaze just as trenchant. The way he looked at her conveyed not only judgment but understanding, it seemed. She feared he knew, somehow, not just who but *what* she was—a fraud, a sinner, an unnatural being.

Minerva Salter, stationed behind him, was small and pale. Her bleached-wheat hair was severely parted above a penetrating gaze and a full, immobile mouth. At first, Amelia hadn't been certain if she was the wife or the daughter, but then Gertrude peeked out from the parlor doorway.

She had her father's dark hair and her mother's pale eyes. She looked to be about twelve. Minerva's age was harder to guess, but she was surely not yet thirty. Amelia introduced herself and welcomed Gertie to attend classes, but before she could quite finish her sentence, Mr. Salter said, "No; she's needed at home. And there is nothing more she requires to know than what she learns here."

Amelia managed to maintain her polite expression, despite her instinctive irritation at his scorn—and the frisson of fear that Salter's New England accent triggered in her. She redirected her gaze at Gertie, said, "Well, even if you'd only like to come and borrow books, or—"

"She has her Bible," Salter interrupted. "That will be sufficient."

When Amelia offered no immediate reply, he said, "Good day to you, Miss Riley," and shut the door.

Thus dismissed, she stood faintly trembling on the stoop. Part of her wanted to knock again, even if she had to screw on a smile and speak pleasantly. She could address Minerva this time, invite her to visit. But Amelia sensed it was best not to make Mr. Salter angry.

She hurried back to Stonehouse and found she couldn't suffer solitude just then. When she returned to the keepers' quarters, she found the Pollard and Clifford children arrayed around the downstairs parlor, their mothers already making supper. She offered to help and was relieved to be refused. Casually, as if she were only curious, she asked if the Salters ever joined them for meals.

Mrs. Pollard scoffed. "Not even at Christmas." She nodded at her friend and added, "Not even when they all lived together."

Mrs. Clifford glanced over her shoulder at Amelia. "We used to be on the top floor in the other house. And it's true, we barely ever saw them then."

"Why did you move?"

"Oh, Mr. Salter wasn't fond of all the noise the children made overhead. We were happy enough to leave."

"And we're happy to have you here," Mrs. Pollard said. "It's nice for all the little ones to be under the same roof."

Amelia spared a thought for Gertie. "Do you know where they're from?"

"Somewhere in New Hampshire, I think," Mrs. Clifford said.

"No, New Bedford," said Mrs. Pollard, "wasn't it? Massachusetts? But they've been in California for years now. Amos said Mr. Salter's been posted all up and down the coast."

Amelia didn't hear their following comments, her focus turned inward again. New Bedford was famous as the whaling capital of the world, having eclipsed Nantucket some years ago. Both places were thousands of miles from her, here beyond the western edge of the country, yet she felt as if she'd been harpooned, yanked back into a past she wanted no part of.

She was afraid her voice would break if she dared ask any more questions, so she held her tongue. Eventually, her nerves settled somewhat.

As she returned to Stonehouse, well after dusk, Amelia forced herself not to look back at the Salter abode's glassy eyes. Still, she felt them watching.

～

Within the week, she established a schooling routine of history, geography, arithmetic, reading, and writing, including spelling, grammar, and penmanship. They also delved into natural sciences and poetry and even what passed for philosophical digressions. Amelia tended not to rein her pupils in too severely because she wanted to keep them interested, and in truth, she worried she had no clue what she was doing. She seized any chance to expound upon a topic or even a distracting sight that caught their interest.

They would count how many eggs were visible through each window whenever the fog lifted and track how the number fluctuated with the depredations of the gulls, or discuss why rainbows appeared and what created their vivid colors. Amelia often needed to consult a book to be sure she got certain facts right but considered it another good lesson: one never stopped learning. And if she couldn't find an explanation, she made a note to request an addition to the library when the lighthouse tender made its next visit. They'd have to wait months to get their materials, but answers would be forthcoming.

Of course, their parents would expect incremental improvements in their letters and sums, so they worked at rote learning for some part of every day, save Sunday.

The children cheered when she sent the paper dunce cap wheeling off on the wind. Their prior teacher, Mr. Wines, had made Finn wear it almost every day. Amelia assured them they wouldn't be needing it any longer.

"What about the ruler?" Phyllis said, and drew her dimpled knuckles toward her sides.

"We'll keep that, but only for measuring things."

She rang the little handbell at nine every morning, a formality everyone seemed to enjoy. By the appointed hour the children were always at Stonehouse anyway, marched over by Mrs. Pollard or having walked there with their teacher after she'd joined them for breakfast in the keepers' quarters.

They broke for lunch, which was laid out in the Cliffords' dining room as though it had appeared by magic. Lessons ended by three every afternoon, but often as not they remained together on through dinner.

Their mothers urged her to send the children away as soon as she liked once the school day was over, but she didn't mind their company. In fact, Amelia cherished it, if only for how it kept her attention focused away from other things.

While the Salters remained obscure, she got to know the others better, and the island itself. The adults imparted their knowledge, but her true orientation was conducted by the children on her fourth day in residence.

Fog had shrouded most landmarks in the intervening days, turning the windows into clouded mirrors. When Amelia stepped outside, the same pearlescent haze hung about her. She hugged the outer walls of buildings and only walked the short path between Stonehouse and the keepers' dwellings, head down, hands clasped in a long line with the children when they accompanied her. Alone, Amelia gripped her skirts, fearing the brush of invisible fingers otherwise.

When the fog cleared, she was happy to postpone lessons and be led about.

The Farallones were strung over twelve miles of open ocean; the unoccupied Middle and North Islands were far enough from the southernmost cluster that Amelia often forgot about them. Although Southeast Farallon's outlying sea stacks huddled close, they, too, were essentially inaccessible: Eye of the Needle, the broken-shark-tooth rock with the window-shaped hole near its apex; Finger Rock, a thin pinnacle rising like a bony pointer from the ocean; Sugarloaf, a two-hundred-foot dome whose top was still sometimes anointed by spray. Birds and sea lions were the only living things above the waterline on those outposts. The way the sea crashed around them, according to its own whims and with such tremendous power, Amelia couldn't picture anyone ever landing a boat in one piece on any of them, but apparently it happened on occasion.

The uninhabited western end of Southeast Farallon was cut off by a foaming chute of sea called Jordan Channel. Finn described how the eggers crossed it by dangling from a breeches buoy, like spiders walking along a strand of web in the air. He pledged he'd go over one of these days. Amelia swore to never let him out of her sight, especially once the harvesting commenced and the rope was rigged. Perhaps it was for the best his mother seemed so anxious to always keep one eye on him. She must be relieved Finn's sisters showed little inclination to roam.

For the time being, there was nothing spanning the gap, but Amelia still wouldn't let any of them wander from her side. Even if Mrs. Pollard hadn't ticked off her list of dangers that first afternoon—and added new ones every other day, reiterating the old in the interim—risks revealed themselves every moment on the island.

The rocks liked to shift underfoot, unsteadying ankles, apt to send one sliding into the sea if they strolled too near its margins. The waves surged up and grasped for purchase, crashed over the edge of the marine terrace at high tide. Amelia could believe a particularly ambitious breaker had struck the lighthouse a time or two.

She tried not to venture too close to the edge, yet the pull of the water almost overpowered her apprehension. Even from what seemed a safe distance, flecks of foam swirled like spring petals on the breeze and speckled her skirts. Salt spray misted her cheeks, cold as the breath of a spirit.

There was stark beauty in the Farallones' very bleakness. In an odd way, it seemed more menacing when the fog cleared and the ocean calmed, glimmered a dozen different tones of blue. It was easier to gauge the distance from any hope of outside human contact then.

On one hand, a comfort, but should help—or escape—ever be needed, that profound separation was a frightening prospect.

~

In an attempt to bend the island's wildness toward protection, a fog signal comprised of a whistle-topped chimney had been constructed over a natural blowhole. It harnessed the power of rushing waves as they forced air and spray up the narrow channel, but it remained silent as often as it sounded during fog, and sometimes keened madly during clear weather when the wind and surf were up.

The buildings were more successful achievements. Around the curve of Tower Hill, fashioned in the same style as Stonehouse, though smaller, was Mr. Sisson's dwelling. Attached to it was a bunkhouse where the egg-stealing men would sleep once they arrived.

Nearby were heaps of rubble, the remains of huts abandoned by Russian sealers nearly two decades earlier.

There was even a small stone chapel, set close to the easternmost edge of the marine terrace. The island's first lightkeeper had built it, driven by passion or boredom or fear for his mortal soul, stranded so far from God.

It was a squat structure without a steeple, though a wooden cross canted from the roof; the worm-eaten planks might have been salvaged from a shipwreck. Inside, six crude pews suggested the architect anticipated a congregation, though he'd only had his assistant keeper for company before he left—stark raving, according to Mrs. Pollard, who looked as if she wished she could swallow the words as soon as she'd spoken them.

The children said they read from the Bible at home, but no one used the chapel anymore—except the Salters. Amelia wasn't surprised, and didn't blame the others for shying away, damp and dim as it was, even in the daytime. Not to mention the listing pews looked sure to give you splinters the moment before they collapsed beneath your weight.

She kept her charges from darting into the mouth of Skeleton Cave, even before Finn explained how it got its name: from the long-dead woman found in its depths by none other than Mr. Sisson, who carried out the bones and buried them beyond the entrance.

"I think she's a *different* ghost than the one in the veil, though," Finn went on. He attempted to launch into an account of the *Lucas* shipwreck, which, Amelia gathered, had greatly increased the island's incorporeal population. She steered the talk in another direction; Fiona and Joy were clearly uneasy, and Amelia wasn't sure she wanted to hear more herself. Claire simply looked as if supernatural things—and even death—were beneath her.

As for Mr. Sisson, though he came to no more dinners, Amelia saw him occasionally, going about his business. They first crossed paths in the open during her tour, when a shaggy, piebald collie mutt galloped over; Amelia braced herself for impact.

"Banquo!" Mr. Sisson called. "Ha'way!" He whistled sharply.

The dog didn't jump up, only panted at Amelia as the children jostled each other for optimal petting position. After a moment she scratched Banquo's neck too.

Mr. Sisson approached, sighed over his dog. "He's a good listener until his flock of admirers comes in sight. Then he goes deaf to me."

Amelia smiled. He didn't quite return it but gave her a probing look that sent another jolt through her. Again, she struggled for words, though he seemed content with silence. Anyone else might have asked how she was finding the Farallones. He only watched her watch the children worship Banquo.

Glad the dog was there to divert her attention, she fell back to petting him too.

~

Her first full Sunday on the island came cocooned in more fog. She'd wanted to visit the lighthouse and considered making the trek anyway, if only to see the lens. The path up Tower Hill began right outside Stonehouse. It might be easy enough to follow even if Amelia could only see inches in front of her. But she remembered what Mrs. Pollard said about loose rocks and the edges of things rearing up in such conditions and thought she'd better not. The moisture-laden air only made things more slippery, besides. Made Amelia jumpy, too, and that wouldn't serve her well on a steep path.

Her restlessness didn't serve her well indoors either, so she dusted her furniture, swept her floors, washed her cataractous windows, beat her rugs on the doorstep, pulled her sheets tight and even. Finally, she sat in a wingback chair to read while the muted sunlight was at its strongest, bare feet propped on the crewelwork ottoman, hidden necklace hard beneath her heel.

When her eyes began to tire, her mind once more wandered to places she didn't want it to go, and her chest began to ache. She laid the book aside and made another circuit of Stonehouse.

The only room she'd ignored was the bedchamber across the loft from her own. It had been emptied of furniture, but there was a closet she'd never opened. Now she did—it was empty too, save a lidless orange crate with a folded quilt obscuring its other contents. Amelia knelt before it, lifted out the quilt, and gasped, nearly falling back as she recoiled, a sharp strain in her thighs. When nothing leaped out, she leaned forward again.

There was a massive skull, from what sort of beast she wasn't sure. In the center of the bony face, a gaping pit suggested a cyclops. What looked like short horns curled up and outward on either side. Sharp incisors as thick as Amelia's thumb curved down over its lower jaw. Matching tusks spiked up. Smaller but equally pointy teeth bristled in both directions around them. A mouth made for tearing.

Silly to be afraid to touch it, but she hesitated. When she did pick it up to examine it from other angles, she realized what she'd thought were horns were in fact the flaring ridges of eye sockets positioned on the sides of the head. The central pit, then, must have been where a nose would be. Some gargantuan seal, perhaps? It still looked deformed, demonic. Of a piece with the strange specimen that had adorned the parlor hearth of Amelia's childhood: a curiously twisted sperm-whale jaw that curled in upon itself at the narrow end. The broad, forked base joined into a spar that spiraled like a tentacle frozen mid-undulation, studded with teeth—six-inch-long ivory spikes instead of suction cups. But she dared not think of that now. Nor the immense shark tooth just downstairs.

The other detritus in the trunk was less exciting: spare candles; old linens; a mother-of-pearl dip pen with a broken nib; and an empty porcelain hair receiver patterned with violets, a chip in its rim.

Amelia returned the skull to its place beneath the quilt and hoped she wouldn't have difficulty sleeping now that she knew it was there in the next room. She'd finally gotten used to the hollowness of the house around her, and the constant noises of the birds and sea outside, so she succumbed to troubled slumber not long after touching her pillow.

It still felt strange to be without a warm, deeply breathing body beside her own, a heavy limb thrown across her side, soft skin radiating life and peace, to instead feel only emptiness, both surrounding her and within. And once she did drift off, her old phantasms plagued her, as if they knew Amelia no longer had someone there to guard against them. They came to torment her, compound her despair. Or perhaps they only meant to ensure she didn't truly forget who she really was, where she'd first come from.

~

At the keepers' quarters before that evening's dinner, Amelia visited with the children as usual, then left them out of earshot to stand in the kitchen doorway. She inquired—as lightly as she could—about the skeletal artifact she'd found.

"That sea elephant!" Mrs. Pollard answered. "Monstrous thing. The last teacher found the head on the rocks and decided to keep it for some strange reason. It was still rotting then."

"He cleaned it up for the classroom," Mrs. Clifford added. "It still disturbed the children."

"I can imagine." It would have upset Fiona and Joy, at least.

"I told Amos to throw it back where it came from," said Mrs. Pollard. "I can't fathom why he saved it instead!"

"Well," Amelia said, "it is rather interesting."

"I suppose. In a terrifying way."

"Don't worry, I'll keep it hidden. Is anyone missing a set of linens? Or a pen? I found those too."

"A mother-of-pearl pen?" Mrs. Clifford said. "I thought I lost that outside and it was gone for good. But—how did it end up over there?"

From behind Amelia, where he'd sidled up to eavesdrop, Finn said, "Maybe a ghost did it?"

"Or some fibbing, thieving little boy," his mother answered, fists planted on her hips.

Amelia blushed. "I'll go fetch it—before it's spirited away again."

Mrs. Clifford said, "Oh, just bring it by in the morning."

"But I might forget by then! I'll only be a moment."

Hurrying away from Mrs. Pollard's and Finn's rising voices, Amelia scampered back to Stonehouse. She was halfway up the stairs to the loft when a faint noise halted her.

Though she strained to make out another groan of wood, or swish of fabric, or human—*or inhuman?*—breath, whatever exactly it had been, she heard nothing but the muffled chorus of cackling birds and whispering waves and her own rushing blood.

As stealthily as she could, she climbed to the landing and crept across. A tall, shadowy figure stood in her room. Enough light came through the windows to reveal the planes of Mr. Sisson's face, and Amelia's diary splayed open on her nightstand, beneath his hand. Her heart skipped a beat, no spark of pleasure in that sensation now.

He uttered a low burst of breath that could stand for laughter, or disbelief, or perhaps even scorn. "Back so soon?"

Seven

THE LIE

Amelia almost explained why, until a flare of fury made her dart forward and snatch the notebook from the table. "Give me that!"

In a disturbingly conversational tone, Mr. Sisson said, "It isn't yours."

"Of course it is," she said, but her legs felt terribly weak as she backed away, holding the diary behind her.

"Well, the handwriting's different in the last few entries, I noticed."

Outrage seemed Amelia's best armor. She drew herself up and said, "What do you think you're doing here?"

Mr. Sisson's face was stone. "That is precisely the question I must ask you."

She swallowed against the catch in her throat, took another step back as he approached.

"Who are you," he said, "and why are you here?"

Her throat closed now; no begging his pardon or how-daring him. Amelia only inched backward into the hall, clutching the diary.

He continued to advance, in no hurry. "You're not Lucy Riley."

She replied in a whisper that seemed to come from far away, "Why on earth would you say such a thing?"

"Because I know her."

Her knees almost buckled. Yet what could she do but deny, deflect? "I'm sure it's a common enough name."

"Perhaps. But Lucy Riley from Sunderland—yet no trace of the north in that dodgy accent of yours—and a teacher too? And"—he reached into his pocket and Amelia held her breath, certain he was going to pull out a knife; indeed, the glint of silver in his fingers made her vision darken, but it wasn't a weapon, which she only realized as he finished—"*my* watch in your nightstand, when I have never seen your face before."

He bore down on her, still in slow motion, until she was backed up to the head of the staircase.

"This is patently ridiculous," she scoffed, and grabbed for the hand-rail, turned to flee back down the stairs. "I don't have time for the mad accusations of some—"

He seized her wrist, pulled her closer, away from her only route of escape. "I suggest you make time." A muscle jumped in his jaw, and though he loosened his grip on Amelia's arm, he did not let go. "I've lived with these people for years now; they know me. They trust me. And if I tell them they have an impostor in their midst, even without any concrete evidence, they'll have a great deal of questions for you. I wonder if you'd have satisfactory answers for them."

Finally, he released Amelia's wrist but held her gaze, his eyes several shades darker than before. There was black ice in them, and in his voice when he said, "However, I'm perfectly willing to keep this between the two of us. If you like. The choice is yours."

She was drawn so taut the cords of her neck ached; her eyes could barely blink, fixed in trepidation on his face. Her fingers hurt from pressing the diary so close. "Fine," she breathed, hating the falter in her voice, fighting to make the next words firmer. "But I have to get back now. They're waiting for me."

51

"Meet me tonight, then. Nine o'clock. At the barracks." A sardonic half smile twisted his mouth when Amelia blanched. "Or the chapel, if you prefer."

"All right. The chapel, then." She stood tall and stared back at him for another moment before she broke. Her voice was savage, but in the manner of a cornered animal frightened out of its mind, when she snapped, "Now get out!"

He didn't flinch, only said, "I'll hold on to this, though." He raised the watch as if in a toast, then sauntered down the stairs and out.

Amelia stood staring at the empty space he left behind, her body trembling, breath wavering, tears wobbling in her eyes. She collapsed into a crouch and dropped the notebook. Skirts and crinoline pooling around her on the floor, one hand braced on the wall, the other covering her mouth, she struggled to control herself, not to cry.

She had to wipe herself clean, a blank slate. She knew how hard it was to get the remnants and residue off; a ghost of what was written before always seemed to show through. If anyone looked closely enough, they could see some intimation of it. Best she could, then. She had to make the effort.

With a deep, steadying inhalation and a matching breath measured out, Amelia swiped her wrists against her cheeks and stood. She practiced the easy smile she would wear into the keepers' house as she moved to descend the stairs.

At the last second, she remembered to grab the pen from the trunk in the empty bedroom. When she moved the quilt aside, the huge, fanged seal skull didn't faze her.

~

No one seemed to sense anything amiss at dinner. They talked as voluminously as ever, asked how she'd enjoyed her first full week in the middle of nowhere. Amelia managed to smile and say, "It's the most extraordinary place I think I've ever been," which seemed to satisfy them.

She took her leave after a bit more postprandial chatter, though she mostly listened that evening. As she said good night, she almost wished someone had seen fit to ask if everything was all right.

She didn't know what she might have said had they expressed concern. In fact, she was certain she would have pretended nothing at all was the matter—but there was a chance she might have denounced Mr. Sisson. Warned them he had insane notions about her, might be suffering delusions. Taken an offensive stance against potential slander. But it would have been an act of desperation, likely futile, and certain to have a negative outcome one way or another.

With her silence, her pantomime of placidity, Amelia feared she'd sealed her doom. There was nothing she could do but accept it.

When she left to return to Stonehouse, Elijah Salter was on his way toward Tower Hill. Amelia froze on the keepers' stoop, considering letting him go by so she wouldn't have to turn her back to him and feel him following. But she couldn't bear the thought of Salter swiveling his head to peer at her as he passed, so she hurried in front of him like fleeing prey and shut Stonehouse's door fast behind her.

By the brass ship's clock, it was barely eight. She didn't know how to fill the amorphous minutes remaining until she must strike out for the chapel.

Her overriding impulse was to run, but there was nowhere to go, unless she cared to plunge off the edge of the earth, be swallowed by the sea. Would it even take her, or had her mother been right, all those years ago? Would she bob along like an unsinkable bit of cork? Glance like a feather off the serrated rocks and end up washed back onto land? Could she swim for San Francisco without being savaged by a shark? Absurd, but the images flashed in Amelia's mind as she paced the schoolroom, necklace swinging against her ankle as if urging her on.

No way to even launch a rowboat by herself, though, not from this formidable island, not at high tide.

The bird skulls stared at her from the mantel. Their living kin carried on calling and guffawing from the cliffs beyond the thick walls and fragile windows. Pitch-black outside the panes, except for the ghostly swaths and swirls of fog that pressed close to breathe upon the glass.

Amelia ought to think how to defend herself from Mr. Sisson. If she had time to craft an effigy and black ribbon to bind it, and could remember even some of the words her mother once intoned, perhaps she could effect some protection. But she didn't really believe in that, did she? She'd never seen it work before. Magic always miscarried. And, ultimately, there was no defense against Mr. Sisson's charges. There was only the awful truth, and a faint hope for clemency.

~

She lit a hurricane lantern and donned her shawl before she set out. The keepers' homes were dark when Amelia passed, save a faint glow from one of the Salters' windows. She hastened by and hoped no one glanced out. If they did, the fog might hide all but her flame, make her no more than a will-o'-the-wisp. She imagined Gertie clutching her collar, murmuring a prayer.

Fear pricked at Amelia, the heavy dread of confrontation like the point of a saber at her throat, and the airier, needling panic at the thought of being intercepted by something worse on her way—a wraith or revenant—or of simply veering off course, stumbling off the crumbling shelf of land beyond the chapel. Even if she might survive the water as her mother foretold, the rocks would crack her bones and cut her to pieces before she ever hit the waves.

But she managed to find her way, unmolested save by the chittering shadow-scraps of petrels streaking through the night, and the wing-churned fog itself. The hunchbacked chapel with its derelict cross shouldered out of the murk. Amelia glimpsed a flickering orange light in its depths.

He was there.

This was it.

Eight

The Truth

Mr. Sisson had set his lantern on the stone altar at the back of the blessed hovel. He stood facing the entry, arms folded over his chest. Only the firelight moved.

Amelia made herself walk down the aisle between the rough-hewn pews without hesitating, though she stopped short of the altar, perhaps two feet from Mr. Sisson, not quite out of arm's reach but almost. She placed her lantern on the floor. The wavering glow of their warring flames washed their faces in warm tones even as it cast eerie shadows around them.

He waited for her to speak, but she couldn't.

Finally, he deigned to begin, undisguised ill humor in his penetrating voice. "Well, who are you, then? And why did Cathy send you? Or does she even know you're here?"

Amelia frowned. "Cathy?"

"Or Lucy, whatever you call her. Are you here to spy on me, or—I don't know what. I'm at a loss, quite frankly."

Amelia's stomach knotted, then her throat; her jaw opened but her mouth was an empty cavern. When she could finally speak, she didn't bother with the put-on accent. She looked down and let the words fall at her feet. "She's dead."

"What? When? *How?*"

When Amelia glanced up, she saw such a change in Mr. Sisson's face: raw confusion, and fear, and pain she felt rack her own body. "Tell me what happened," he implored.

She looked at the ground again. "About three weeks before I came here, there was an accident. Lucy fell asleep with a candle burning and . . . it must have tipped over. She didn't wake up in time."

Mr. Sisson's features contorted, his anguish exaggerated by the shifting shadows. He turned his face, but it was not enough to conceal the emotion that rippled through him.

"I'm sorry," Amelia said. "You were close."

He scoffed, but she thought it might have been to stave off a sob. "Once," he said. "I haven't seen Cathy, or heard from her, in years. I'd no idea she was even here—in America, let alone San Francisco. I don't understand. I reconciled myself a long time ago to the fact that I'd never see her again. And then they tell me a new teacher's coming here, and she's from England, and she's called Lucy Riley. And *then*. You."

Amelia cringed. "I didn't know. I would never have come if I knew—"

"Then why did you? Why do you have her name? Her things? Who are you?"

She considered where to start. The beginning, she supposed—of one story, at any rate. Her heart ached so deeply she didn't know if she could speak, or breathe, but she made herself respond. Carefully, slowly, yet once the first thorny words were wrested free, she could not have stopped the rest even had she wanted to.

"I met her in Chicago, eight years ago." She couldn't speak of the circumstances, how she'd been so upset Lucy had pulled her aside on the street to ask if she was all right, how she'd walked Amelia home and calmed her down. And stayed with her, was still there when she woke in the morning. "We were fast friends," Amelia said. In fact, they'd never been apart after that.

"We went to St. Louis—we both taught there for a few years. And then she wanted to come out west. I was terrified. But I would have followed her anywhere. Because she was the best friend I ever had." And more than that, too much for Amelia to say, though she tried. "She was so kind, and brave, and so much fun, and she knew exactly who she was. And she made *me* so much . . . better, than I was before. More hopeful, and happy, and . . ." More alive, more real, than she had been in years.

Amelia shook off the thought of the time before she'd met Lucy—it didn't exist—but she couldn't shake the notion that whatever brightness she'd possessed had only been because Lucy shone so intensely. Amelia feared her own joy had only ever been a reflection. Losing someone she'd loved was devastating enough, but to think she'd also lose the person she had been with Lucy was unbearable. How to say that to someone else?

"After Lucy died, I just wanted to trade places with her. I wasn't really thinking beyond that. And they'd already mixed us up; our landlady said it was me—because normally I never went out at night, so they assumed it was me in the room—and then, when I went to the police . . . I didn't tell them the truth. I said I was her, and she was me. It was easier that way."

Amelia ground the heels of her hands across her cheeks and heaved a harsh, shuddering sigh. "I suppose I thought it was a way to keep her with me, keep her in the world somehow. I don't know. I was just too afraid to let her go. I didn't know who I'd be without her. How I'd survive."

Mr. Sisson studied her the entire time she talked, though she'd only let herself look back at him in glances, not wanting to see what his shifting expressions might evince. It didn't matter what he thought of her, only that she told him what he deserved to know.

But when she lifted her gaze to his, he was the one to look away, a terrible blankness on his face. He looked lost, and Amelia was overwhelmed with regret for infecting him with her own bewildering grief. "I'm sorry," she said again.

He turned with a grimace of not only pain but anger. "And now you're here because—?"

She shrank slightly but held her ground. "Lucy had the newspaper clipping, for the teaching post. She showed it to me, months ago, and we talked about it, what it would be like, but . . . I couldn't understand why she was interested. I never thought she was serious; she would have hated it here. I thought it was just a daydream. She had a lot of those. And then she said she had an interview scheduled, with Mr. Pollard—"

"And then she died, and you decided to go in her place?"

Shame coursed through Amelia, but she answered, "Yes. I was trying . . . to do what she would have done. And to be brave. But also to not have to be, in certain ways—to not have to be my old self and be afraid to walk down the street alone again. I couldn't imagine Lucy here, but from the first time she showed me the ad . . . I did think it sounded like a place that would suit me. I never felt at ease in the city, not really, not completely. I mostly always stayed inside. When I did go out, it was with Lucy. Because she could make the crowds seem to disappear. Or I could be part of them, for once. But without her . . . I knew I couldn't really *be* her, but . . ." Amelia emitted a huff of grim humor. "I suppose I felt what she felt. 'The hand of fate.' I thought I could be her, here."

Mr. Sisson's searching look made her feel piteously exposed. His voice rang in Amelia's bones when he said, "How can I believe you?"

She shifted her weight and felt the necklace tap against her ankle like a fingertip. "Maybe you can't. I wouldn't blame you. It sounds crazy. It probably is. But it's all true."

"Even if it is, it isn't all the truth, is it? I mean, who *are* you? And why was Cathy coming here?"

"To see *you*," Amelia said. "Obviously. But I didn't know that. She only said it was too exciting to pass up, a chance to see a place most people never even knew existed. It would be *such* a good story." Once she'd found Lucy's diaries, of course, Amelia had suspected that wasn't all—yet she'd still convinced herself she was wrong. She'd tried to, at least.

Mr. Sisson shook his head. "But that doesn't make sense. Why go through the keepers if it was to see me?"

She'd wondered the same thing, but he didn't wait for an answer before he reeled off another question: "And how would Cathy even know I was here?"

That, Amelia could answer. She felt a rush of humiliation at having to admit it, because it proved she was an utter fool for pressing forward to the Farallones. "She paid someone. An investigator. I found her notebooks when I was packing. I'd seen them before—she started a new one every year—but I'd never read them. And when I finally did, most of it didn't make any sense. They were more account books than diaries. Full of expenses and reminders. Almost everything was in shorthand anyway; you saw."

"Hardly anything. But—I'm in there?"

"Not this year's, but yes. Just the letter 'W.' Almost always next to the initials PD and a dollar amount. Sometimes with a city name, or a note that there was no news."

"How far back?"

"Eighteen fifty-one. In fifty-two, she wrote, 'W in SF.' That wasn't long before we set out for California."

The knowledge was a blow to Mr. Sisson. "All that time . . . she knew? And she didn't—"

Amelia fought a sympathetic twinge at the way his voice broke. "Why is that? If she knew you were here for that long—if she followed you all that way—then why would she wait *years* to do anything else?"

He slashed at his cheeks. "That's not in the books? That she hated me?"

"No. Why?"

He took a trembling breath. "Because I abandoned her. I left her to—"

"I don't want to know," Amelia interrupted. "I'm sorry, but if you tell me, it'll strip away something else, and . . . I can't lose any more of her." Yet she could not stop herself from saying, a moment later, "You called her Cathy?"

A sort of incredulous amusement seemed to move through Mr. Sisson, which at least momentarily eclipsed his sorrow. "Since that was her name, yes. Lucy Riley was a friend of ours. Catherine started using her name quite a long time ago."

"Why?"

"You need to ask that question? She was tired of being herself, I suppose."

He watched Amelia take this in, turn it over. His voice was surprisingly gentle when he said, "You're disappointed, aren't you? In Cathy, I mean."

"No." Amelia frowned, swiped tears from her cheeks, went on with some deliberation, "It's just . . . I always knew there were things she didn't tell me, but . . . I thought the things she did tell me were true."

Mr. Sisson sighed. "We never want to doubt the ones we care for, do we? We'll do everything we can to believe them, twist ourselves into knots to think well of them at all costs. It's so crushing when they let us down. But they always do."

"Always?"

"In my experience."

Amelia felt a jagged stone in the pit of her stomach, another in the hollow of her throat; she pictured a miniature Sugarloaf, an Eye of the Needle, the Farallones having already worked their way inside her. "You must try not to care, then."

"Only for blameless creatures," he said. "Of course, even the best of them will still break your heart. But at least they'll not deceive it."

She nodded, wrapped her arms around herself. "So, will you tell them?"

He stared into his lantern's flame as if the answer lay there. Finally, he said, "What would be the point?"

Uncomprehending, Amelia blinked at his shadow-painted face.

"You seem to be getting on well," he said. "With the children. And their parents. If they've no complaints, I suppose that's all that matters. You're here for them, after all. They don't care about your name."

It didn't make sense, but Amelia still couldn't speak, and then he was brushing past her anyway. She turned to watch him, desperate to ask if he truly meant it, and if so, *why*. Didn't he want her to leave immediately? Didn't he want to drag her out of the chapel by her hair and cast her into the maw of the ocean?

But she couldn't find her voice, crushed beneath that stone. And in a moment, he was gone, the last orange flicker of his firelight melting into the mist.

Nine

The Light

Amelia passed the next week in a personal fog; even on the clearest afternoon she felt shrouded in a thick yet intangible grief, or perhaps she was becoming misty herself. Transforming day by day into a living ghost. She half expected to begin gliding in and out of doors without having to open them, to reach for a book and watch her fingers pass into its depths, to sit at the keepers' table and be seen straight through.

There were moments when she slipped into a sort of stupor, brought back only by the children's probing voices or the unexpected blast of the fog signal, another demented gull swooping at her head or stones skidding away beneath her foot. Then fear slipped in to underscore her sorrow, twist it into doubt.

She didn't see Mr. Sisson save a handful of times at a distance, or for a few seconds as they passed in opposite directions. Although he did no more than nod in terse acknowledgment, Amelia struggled to believe he was done with her.

She struggled, too, with the fact that he'd known Lucy—in another life, by another name—yet Amelia still had no notion of exactly how, or when. Or even who he truly was.

She pored over the notebooks again for clues she'd previously missed or been unable to decipher, but Lucy hadn't been one to write at length. Most of her thoughts had stayed locked in her own head. In her entries after they'd moved to San Francisco, "W" appeared at least once a year, every July or August, along with a pair of dates. Before, Amelia had wondered if they'd marked meetings, but from Mr. Sisson's reaction in the chapel, she believed that he hadn't seen Lucy in some time. She'd covertly kept track of his visits to the city, then, but why?

The only answer that made sense to Amelia was that Lucy had loved him. One uncommonly long entry from August 1856, a few days after "W" appeared that year, read: *At work, I look up at the door every time it opens. It's never him. I never know if it's relief or disappointment I feel. I suppose I'm a coward, in the end. I've crept up behind his back, but I'll never tap his shoulder. Because shouldn't he sense me there?*

In late 1858, months removed from any mention of "W," she'd written: *Bulletin ad—teaching post on the Farallones. How can I possibly deny the hand of fate? I've applied.*

Amelia felt sick to think that Lucy had been secretly pining for some long-lost beau all that time. She'd claimed not to even like men. She'd always worried Amelia might want a husband one day, a genuine concern couched in jokes. Maybe that fear had been based on a kernel of Lucy's own hidden truth. Yet Amelia knew Lucy had unreservedly loved her too. Perhaps that was the simple reason why she'd never tried to contact Mr. Sisson—until she saw the teaching post, a sign from the universe.

That was the likeliest theory Amelia had devised after finding the journals, anyway. There'd been no definitive evidence that "W" was actually on Southeast Farallon, but of course she'd wondered— particularly since she'd just learned from Mr. Pollard that Mr. Sisson was British.

And yet, the very fact that Lucy had secured the teaching post seemed proof enough that "W" must not have been related to that decision—that Amelia must have been drawing wildly irrational conclusions in her emotionally fraught state. Because if all Lucy had needed was a nudge, then why would she have applied for the job? If she'd only wanted to reunite with Will, why not approach him directly?

Amelia still had no good answer. Mr. Sisson himself said Lucy—Cathy—had hated him, and what if that was true? Could her mission have been one of ambush, perhaps even revenge? Did he have something Lucy wanted back, or had she nursed some grudge she'd meant to settle? Every possibility seemed equally implausible, equally inevitable.

By forging ahead to the Farallones, Amelia had mired herself in complications and thrown Mr. Sisson into obvious turmoil. And now, seemingly, she'd been forgiven for her trespass. That could not be.

He would be angry, Amelia was sure. Once his shock wore off, he would begin to seethe. She couldn't forget the way he'd grabbed her wrist when she'd tried to flee from him in Stonehouse.

When the wind shook the glass in her room at night, she woke with a start, certain someone had pounded on the door, the echo of it quavering in her veins with every heartbeat. Then she heard a floorboard squeak, and knew it was only a matter of moments before someone stepped into her room. Yet nothing materialized.

At dinner, where she fought to at least appear present, she was further distracted by the fear that Mr. Sisson would stroll in and sit down with them, lean forward over the table and reveal her secrets and her truths to everyone assembled—the ones he knew, anyway, which were enough.

They'd be incensed that she'd lied. They'd have every right to be, to never again trust her with their children, to send her off on the next passing tug in disgrace. And back in San Francisco, other people who had known Lucy had surely marked her absence by now. One of them had given her the necklace that Amelia had taken. And maybe they'd discovered some hint of her deception too. She couldn't possibly return to the city, not to stay—nor did it seem she could remain on the island.

But perhaps she invested undue significance in the dreadful press of the darkness and the malicious clawing of the wind. Mr. Sisson didn't look at her with anything but slight confusion when they crossed paths. Still, he saw her, if not for what she was then for what she wasn't. Amelia's sense that Elijah Salter recognized her was heightened now too. Whenever she happened to encounter him scraping moss from his roof or leading Mary down Tower Hill, she felt caught out again.

~

Another Sunday came swathed in fog. Amelia rose and dressed but couldn't bring herself to open her bedroom door. Nothing absolutely required her attention, so she lay back on her mattress and watched the morning gradually clear through the window.

An hour passed, at least. Breakfast in the keepers' house was well over and done with. She tried to rouse herself, get up and go out, make something of the day.

The sky was an eye-aching, heart-wrenching blue; the water must be as well. The less Amelia looked, the less it would hurt to leave when she had to. The unreliable fog signal keened as if in sympathy. Or perhaps to taunt her.

Then, as if in answer to a prayer she hadn't lodged, a knock came at the front door. Amelia swung wooden legs onto the floor. She felt a sort of perverse relief in the arrival of a summons she had been so relentlessly dreading, yet her body quailed.

She neither hurried nor hesitated on the stairs. She opened the door with an impassive face, ready to take whatever was coming to her.

But it wasn't Mr. Sisson. Mrs. Clifford stood on the second step, smiling expectantly, Joy at her side. "Good morning. I hope we're not disturbing you."

"No—though I'm afraid I overslept."

"We brought you biscuits," Joy mumbled.

Amelia took the napkin-wrapped parcel with sincere thanks, noticed them both glance at her darned-stockinged feet and tried to tuck them beneath the hem of her dress.

Mrs. Clifford's smile redoubled. "I thought since it's so fair, you might like to take a look at the light today."

Amelia hadn't thought anything could cut so sharply through her fretful melancholy, but the invitation sent wind into her sails. "That would be lovely! I'll get my things."

Not wanting to waste time, she ate the biscuits on the way, which only attracted more seagulls. When she'd bolted her breakfast, at least she had the cloth napkin to whip about her head and deter them from coming too close.

"We'll be donning our miners' helmets any day now," Mrs. Clifford laughed. "We have a spare one for you too."

"Miners' helmets?"

"They get even more aggressive, so it helps to have a harder layer between them and your head. It looks queer, but it works a charm. Last year, one flew so hard into Mr. Pollard's hat it broke its neck. Hate to think what might have happened to him without it."

"Goodness gracious." Another outlandish danger to make Amelia wonder just what kind of place she'd come to. The climb up the hill was even steeper than it looked. Soon they couldn't speak for exertion, save in brief, winded snatches.

"Slow and steady," Mrs. Clifford panted.

"This must be . . . impossible . . . in storms."

"No nights off. They manage."

The rocky ground was ever loose and uneven, the footing precarious, yet they all managed to stay upright, despite a few slips and slides. They stopped periodically, to catch their breath and gaze over the indigo ocean, grateful for their vantage despite their searing lungs and twitching calf muscles and aching feet.

"Blue whale!" Joy yelped.

They followed her pointing finger and, in a moment, saw a white spout plume from the water, then another near it.

"Well spotted!"

Joy tried not to smile. "They're the biggest animals in the world," she confided. "But they don't have teeth, so they couldn't eat you."

"Well, that's a great relief. I'd love to see one up close in that case."

"You can," Mrs. Clifford said, "if we take the boat out. You can get right up alongside them—close as you please. To be honest, it always scares me a little, but at least they don't jump out of the water."

"Like the humpbacks!" Joy said. "They spin like ballerinas in the air." She demonstrated with one arm, still too shy—or sensible—to twirl her entire body in reckless imitation.

"I'd love to see them too."

They shared a smile as they continued their climb along the switch-back path.

∾

The lighthouse was faced in brick but built from the same Farallon rock as Stonehouse. A window high in its base let in enough sunshine to delineate the spiral staircase; it was a short climb along that tight whorl to the balcony and the watch room it encircled. By means of a slanted iron ladder that led up from there, they gained the lantern room itself, although that topmost part of the tower, with its walls of glass, was dark just then.

Mrs. Clifford opened a couple of the shades to better reveal the first-order Fresnel lens. Perched upon a pedestal that sprouted from the level below, the finely faceted dome was twelve feet tall. Its graceful curves and frilled ridges made Amelia think of a giant, frozen jellyfish shorn of tentacles. Rainbows shone inside the undulations of glass.

"It's beautiful," she breathed, as if they stood in a museum, or a church.

"The flame inside only rises about two inches tall," Mrs. Clifford replied in a similarly hushed tone. "But the way the lens magnifies it, it shines out across the ocean for miles. It's a miracle, isn't it?"

The normally reticent Joy pointed out its other features at length. She was recounting how Mary carried the oil up for the lamp when the happy satisfaction faded from her face. "It's made from whales," she said. "The oil."

"Not humpbacks, though," said her mother. "Or blue whales."

That clearly didn't matter to her daughter.

"It's for the greater good," Mrs. Clifford added. "And remember Genesis."

"God blessed them," Joy dutifully recited, "and said unto them, 'Have dominion over the fish of the sea.'"

Her mother cupped the back of Joy's head and kissed her temple. "All according to His plan," she said. "Now, shall we see the view He's wrought?"

Ten

REASONS TO STAY

Joy preferred to gaze into the complicated clockwork of the mechanism that turned the lens, so they left her to her solitary contemplation in the watch room.

"She's so tenderhearted," Mrs. Clifford said as they clanged out onto the balcony, into the wind.

Amelia smiled. "And so smart."

Mrs. Clifford's mouth quirked, her eyes on the horizon. "Sometimes I worry both things will be a burden. But that's the life of a parent: worry about everything, no matter what. Hope they don't know that, of course."

"They're lucky to have you," Amelia said. "And Mr. Clifford."

"We're the lucky ones. But we do our best. Try to, anyway." Mrs. Clifford leaned her elbows on the railing and sighed. "Sometimes I worry it's not fair to have the children here; it seems cruel, even, in certain ways. But then so is the rest of the world, and most times, even when this feels like the loneliest place on earth, I think they're safer here."

"You know precisely what the dangers are," Amelia said, without thinking.

"Yes. Although it doesn't mean you can avoid them all the time. I don't know if you've heard about Serena yet?"

"Claire mentioned her, yes. That she drowned at the landing?"

Mrs. Clifford nodded. "She was only four years old. Fell down the stairs about thirteen months ago. It only took a second."

"Poor thing. And the Pollards stayed?"

"I think for the same reason I would've gone," Mrs. Clifford said. "They don't talk about her anymore, but I know Constance thinks about her all the time—she sees her everywhere."

"Sees her? You mean, like . . . ?"

"Oh, no. No, those ghost stories are just that. But memories . . . I think she can't bear to leave because she's afraid she'll lose those too."

Amelia murmured sympathy. "Is that why the Salters keep Gertrude inside? Because they're afraid?"

"I'm sure that's a big part of it."

She hesitated, then said, "When you lived with them—what were they like?"

"Quiet, mostly. They're not the cheeriest bunch. I feel sorry for Gertie—I think she'd like friends. But my children weren't the right sort. Honestly, I doubt her father approves of many people."

When Amelia didn't answer, Mrs. Clifford straightened up and shook her head. "I'm sorry, Miss Riley; I shouldn't talk that way."

"It's all right."

"But I mean to make you like this place."

"I do."

"We've been worried," Mrs. Clifford admitted. "Connie—Mrs. Pollard—didn't want me to say anything, but . . . this past week, you've seemed quieter. I know it's a big adjustment, living here, but you seemed so enthusiastic at first. So different from the other teachers. You're the only one who didn't even get seasick. She thought that was another good omen. And I just wondered if there was anything we could do—or anything we have done. We want you to be happy here."

"I am. I do like it here, truly. I just . . ." Amelia couldn't think of a decent excuse, so she said, "I lost someone too, not long before I came here. I thought it was getting better, but . . . she's been much on my mind this past little while. That's all."

"I'm sorry. Grief comes and goes, but it never abandons you."

The words landed squarely in Amelia's chest. "Is that from something?"

"A poem." Mrs. Clifford looked away and hunched her shoulders, much like Joy had earlier. "Just something I scribbled down."

"You write poetry? Could I read it?"

"Oh, I don't know. I don't really show it to anybody. Even Percy. But I could give you a copy of that one. If you like."

"I would. Very much. If you don't mind."

"Of course not. I don't know if it would be much comfort, but—you know we read from the Bible on Sundays. You're welcome to join us. The Salters have their chapel service, but—well, you don't have to be alone."

Amelia measured her response before she voiced it. "That's very kind of you, but I think the poetry would do me better just now."

Evidently, Mrs. Clifford wasn't offended. She only smiled, and it seemed genuine.

They stepped back into the watch room to collect Joy. Before they descended the nautilus spiral of the staircase, Mrs. Clifford said, "Please do let us know if there is anything you'd like—to make things more comfortable for you here. We'll do whatever we can."

Amelia wished she could assure her, and Mrs. Pollard, and all of them, that she didn't intend to go anywhere. But she knew she couldn't make a promise that wasn't entirely hers to keep.

As they picked their way back down the hill, Joy and her mother spoke about other things in store: more stray birds they'd seen and hoped to spy again that fall; the bats that sometimes circled the lighthouse beam at night; the green flash that lit up the horizon at sunset when conditions were just so.

More reasons to stay, Amelia thought, whether that was what they intended them to be or not.

~

At the foot of Tower Hill, they saw Mr. Sisson and Banquo coming round from the direction of the egg-company property.

"Hello there," Mrs. Clifford called.

"Afternoon." He stopped, one hand on the dog's neck to prevent him streaking over. Banquo sat, but not without a great deal of writhing, haunches not quite touching the ground.

Amelia only realized Mr. Sisson was looking at her when he said, "Finally been up to see the light, then?"

It was discomfiting to stand so near and speak to him with other people witnessing the interaction. She thought she answered easily enough, though she was terribly self-conscious about having to use the accent they all expected now. "Yes. It's a work of art as much as a scientific marvel."

He allowed a hint of a smile, or maybe it was that he could not suppress it. "It always reminds me somehow of a cathedral. That's where the keeper should have made his chapel, I think."

Amelia glanced up at him but couldn't answer.

"Well, excuse us," Mrs. Clifford said. "I hope I'm not too late to see if Mrs. Pollard needs any help with lunch. You're both welcome to drop by, of course. Good day."

She and Joy bobbed their heads and veered off toward home before there could be any thought of tagging along with them, though it was tempting to invent a reason to run after.

When they were out of earshot, Mr. Sisson said, "I'm glad I caught you. I mean, I've been wanting to speak with you."

"Oh?" Amelia pushed down her panic, but surprise bubbled up in its place as he said:

"I'm sorry. I had no right to lay a hand on you. Or to threaten you. I should have apologized, before."

"Oh. No. It was nothing, really."

Though there still seemed to be confusion in his regard, it was altogether softer now. "It isn't what I'm like."

Foolish, perhaps, but she was inclined to believe him. All she could say was "If you want me to go, I will. The next boat that comes—"

"No. If you want to stay, then stay. If you go, it shouldn't be on my account."

The wild relief that gusted through Amelia couldn't be given in to; she couldn't quite believe he meant it, or fathom how. "You're not angry?"

"Only at myself now."

"But—it won't bother you? Seeing me? Knowing . . . ?"

"In the long run, no. It's been strange, coming to terms with the truth. Not terribly easy. But I suppose I'm getting used to it, by and by. Frankly . . . I mourned Catherine once already. And you're the last chance I have to know anything about what she'd been up to all these years. The last link I have to her at all. When I thought there was none. So—I'd like to talk with you some more. I've so many questions, about how she was, and . . . You knew her better than anyone, it seems."

Reflexively, Amelia scoffed. "I'm not sure that's true. But yes, of course. I'll tell you what I can."

"Thank you." Mr. Sisson touched his hat in farewell for the time being, then strode off toward North Landing, whistled for Banquo to follow. As was ever the case, Amelia felt slightly disconcerted by their meeting, though less so than before.

She returned to Stonehouse, let herself become reacquainted with its details, as if it were her first day all over again. By the time she went to the keepers' quarters for the evening meal, Amelia felt thoroughly anchored again, although even moored, boats bobbed with the currents, never wholly at rest.

At dinner she felt, if not entirely untroubled, at least solid again—and clearer, brighter; she could participate in the amiable chatter, follow all the conversations' threads and weave her own within them. She thought she saw Mrs. Clifford and Mrs. Pollard exchange meaningful looks a time or two.

As Amelia was fastening her cloak in the foyer before leaving, Mrs. Clifford approached and presented a folded slip of paper. "It's not much, but . . . sometimes it helps me to get things down in ink. Like talking to myself. Or like my heart is talking to me—I don't know. Maybe something in it will speak to you. At least I hope it won't make you feel any worse."

"I'm sure it won't. Thank you for sharing it. And thank you for taking me up to the light this morning. That was just what I needed."

She clutched the paper as she hurried home through the wind, then lit the oil lamp at the table the moment she got in, eager to discover what Mrs. Clifford had to say. The poem was called "The Little Black Cat." It read in looping, pale-blue script:

> Grief comes and goes like a little black cat that on
>   the milk of tears grows fat
> Drapes its soft weight on the pillow where you lie,
>   nuzzles your cheekbone as you cry
> Then slashes at you with its sharpened claws, sinks in
>   the needles of its ferocious maw
> Even as you cradle it in aching arms; perhaps you
>   love it for how it harms

Then, tear-starved, leaner, less inclined to scratch, to
wander far from home, more apt
Grief strays for days but in the end steals back again,
a faithful friend
For if one thing in life is true, it is that—like that
little cat—Death will not abandon you
Yet the darkest scrap of night is always swallowed
by the light
Until then, let the feral thing lie by itself in gentle
warmth and perfect health
Seek not to shoo it, nor to hold it close, but let it
come and go like a beloved ghost
And grow accustomed to the haunting, till you be-
come the one leaves others wanting—
When Grief is snuffed right out with you and the
little black cat is born anew

The shiver of surprise that went through Amelia was not entirely unpleasant. She'd expected something more conventionally comforting, she supposed. But while the words themselves did not exactly attenuate her sadness, she felt less alone, and privileged that Mrs. Clifford had agreed to let her read her words.

The woman's heart spoke to hers, indeed, as did so much else on the uncanny island. And after such a tumultuous week of uncertainty, of oppressive regret for what she'd lost already and what she was about to, every fiber of Amelia's being was glad to stay. Especially because she could still imagine nowhere else to go.

Eleven

PLUNDER

The first egg pickers arrived during the last week of April, their coming much discussed in the preceding days. Even the clamor of the birds seemed portentous, as if they knew predators drew near. But that was just Amelia's own anxiety shifted onto the unsuspecting creatures so she could feel sorry for them instead of uneasy for herself. Who wouldn't be a bit on edge before a platoon of strange men came to invade their space?

She girded herself, devoured every morsel of gossip the keepers cared to share about the eggers to soothe the hollow ache in her stomach. Always better to know one's enemies—not that she should think of them that way. But certainly not as friends.

There were twenty-odd men in total, a rough-looking, rough-talking bunch Amelia would have avoided even without Mrs. Pollard's dire warnings. As a rule, the pickers didn't mix with the keepers or their families, though it was impossible not to occasionally encounter them as one made one's way around the island. And Amelia couldn't help but watch their work.

Their initial order of business was to prepare for pillage. They brought equipment out—baskets and wooden tubs, rope and tools—and constructed the insubstantial-looking swinging bridges and traverse lines that so fascinated Finn. They even built their own derrick opposite the keepers' hoist at North Landing so they could load their schooners when they came each week for the newest haul of eggs.

She didn't speak to Mr. Sisson at any length during this time, busy as he was, but on the few occasions they crossed paths, the nods they exchanged were no longer so tense and brief. Their smiles were easier, if still reserved. Sometimes they even traded pleasantries.

They were coming to an understanding, Amelia thought, or trying to. She grew less wary of him every day. There was still a shade of pain in his eyes that moved her to sympathy, allowed her to convince herself he was no threat.

Salter's gaze, meanwhile, remained disturbing, but at least it was easy to avoid. When she did encounter him—tending to the exterior of his home or walking to or from the boathouse—Amelia didn't bother to say hello. She saw even less of his family, occasionally caught glimpses of Gertie's face in a window, and once spotted her on the Salters' stoop, polishing a pair of her father's shoes in the sunshine.

"Good morning," Amelia said, and came closer to extend her hand. "We never have met properly."

"My hands are dirty," Gertrude mumbled.

"With good honest work," Amelia answered, "so I don't mind."

Gertie swiped her palms on her dark skirt and shook Amelia's hand. "You talk like Mr. Sisson—you came here all the way from England too?"

Amelia's smile faltered, but she said, "Yes. A long time ago now. Where were you before? I heard maybe Massachusetts?"

"I was born there, but we've lived in California since I was little." Gertie looked back down at the shoe in her lap. "We were in Crescent City last year."

"You miss it?"

Before she could answer, the door opened behind her. She flinched. Minerva, when Amelia said hello to her, only tersely nodded and told Gertie to come inside.

She wondered what they were like together when Mr. Salter was elsewhere. It was hard to envision them doing anything other than stoically persisting in absolute silence. But Amelia also remembered how everyone in her own household had become different people when her father was gone, when it had been safe to laugh and sing and dance behind closed doors. She hoped Gertie and her mother passed some happy hours in private, at least.

~

The next day, the pickers scaled the slippery rocks en masse to smash every murre egg they found. It seemed so grossly cruel, and counterintuitive, but it was to ensure each egg they collected in the coming weeks was fresh.

A delirious Banquo lapped up as many red-orange yolks as he could get to, snapping at the gulls vying for the treasure. The marauding men fought them, too; they beat the screaming birds back with clubs or caps, and they busted gull eggs—neither as large nor as sturdy as the prized murre eggs—with the express purpose of culling their future competition.

The seagulls were equally relentless. They formed cacophonous clouds around the pickers, darted in to snatch spoils and slash scalps. It wasn't unusual to see men with blood trickling down their faces to match their beak-pocked hands.

It was a wonder more of them didn't fall to their deaths. Even without the opposing army of gulls harassing them every inch of the way, it would have been dangerous work. The sheer rock faces regularly slid to pieces beneath their feet, the rope nailed to the soles of their boots for traction only so much insurance against slips. Strains and sprains and scrapes abounded; bruises and even broken bones were common.

The panicked murres plunged instinctively toward the sea to escape the approaching danger, so where the eggers could not steal upon the riches from above, they faced an aerial stampede of even more birds. When Amelia watched from certain angles, the storm of wings was so dense she could no longer see the men struggling below them.

All these hazards were worth it for the money the eggs would fetch as food, but each murre fruit was a rather remarkable object in and of itself: twice the size of a chicken egg and teardrop-shaped.

The shell was thicker, too, able to withstand rough treatment, patterned with abstract speckles and scribbles, like ink etched and spattered upon a blue-green or gray-brown or ivory background, sometimes pale, sometimes dyed by nature to a deeper hue. Each one distinct, and extraordinary. In Lucy's diary, Amelia fancied they were *as if someone had used bits of sky as scratch paper.*

The eggers wore billowing flour sacks atop their shirts, with holes cut out for heads and arms and the original openings cinched tight around their waists. A slit at the neck allowed them to deposit eggs in the bizarre garment and so continue collecting without the burden of lugging a basket along with them.

Their fully loaded egg shirts formed lumpy, distended bellies before them, the weight of their loot pulling them forward. The vigor of their exertions made them stagger, but Amelia suspected drink contributed its effects in at least some cases.

At night, after they'd washed that day's hundreds or thousands of eggs in buckets of seawater and stored them in the stone egg shed at the landing, she heard them carousing from the barracks on the other side of Tower Hill. The din sometimes blended with the sounds of the plaintive birds that cried all night, at other times rose above it and over the wind, in distinct snatches of human song or shouting.

At moments she felt as she did back in the city, pulse racing at every raised voice that carried through the window, even men's raucous joy always teetering on the knife edge of rage—and now no Lucy to hold her close and murmur reassurances against her neck.

Amelia felt braver, less herself, in the daytime.

⁓

One afternoon, she chanced upon Mr. Sisson in a moment of repose and asked how many eggs each man could carry in his shirt. "I have the children making guesses. And I thought we could turn the answer into math problems."

He almost smiled. "Well, it depends on the man, but a slim one can fit twenty dozen in at once."

"Have you tried it?"

He did smile then. "No. But they've held contests. Who wins yours, then?"

"Phyllis. Claire will be in second place. She'll be more put out than if she came in dead last."

At that moment, one of the pickers battering the air above his head with the club in his free hand connected with a gull; Amelia winced at the explosion of feathers. Mr. Sisson's face stayed impassive, perhaps just a touch amused. "Curious sight, is it not?"

"Barbaric. Comedic, too. But yes, altogether odd. When they come down, they all look as if they've gorged themselves on rocks."

Mr. Sisson chuckled. Amelia felt a disconcertingly pleasant reverberation of the sound in her own body.

"I always think of some poor production of *Henry VIII*," he said. "With an overabundance of understudies tottering about, half out of costume."

She laughed, then peered at him. "How did you end up here?"

He shrugged. "I looked for a place no one else wanted to go." He nodded toward the eggers. "They'll suffer it for a little while, and a great deal of money. But most of them think I'm mad for staying out here all winter. Eight weeks of this hellish toil seems preferable to sitting out the rest of the year in idle isolation."

"Well, it takes all kinds."

He smiled wider, and Amelia had to look away. "I don't suppose you'd be free on Sunday," he said, "for a proper chat?"

Her stomach flipped, but she'd promised to speak with him. And she wasn't scared, at least not of Mr. Sisson, though perhaps of what he might ask. She only said, "Of course."

"Shall we meet at the chapel again? The Salters will have left by nine."

"I'll be there, then."

"Much obliged."

~

During nesting season, breakfast always included murre eggs, which the keepers collected for themselves in far smaller quantities than the egg-company men.

Earlier keepers had made more determined efforts to harvest eggs to sell in San Francisco, which caused conflict between them and the self-sworn rightful owners of the nesting grounds. Now, the families left the profiteering to the professionals.

Some of the eggers didn't condone even that small-scale gathering for the keepers' personal use. In fact, some occasionally posted signs threatening death to any unauthorized persons crossing invisible boundary lines. But Mr. Sisson enforced the official position that they had a perfect right and reminded the pickers—who weren't exactly under his control, though most deferred to his authority on the island—that there were plenty to go around.

Other factions from outside did press their luck, ragtag crews of a few men landing on the more remote rocks at their peril to snatch as many murre eggs as they could in the time before the company came to stop them. The eggers weren't above brawling or brandishing guns to defend their treasure from interlopers, though Mr. Sisson favored strong words where they would do.

It was tempting, Mr. Pollard allowed, to think of loading up the dory with eggs and taking it into the city for a quick spot of cash, supplement their wages from the Board. Extra food and clothes and candles for the winter. A new chess set, perhaps. A healthy store of tobacco, a few tots of something warm to drink.

His wife gave him a censorious look at that. He only winked back at her.

"But it's a miserable business," he continued. "And there are two-bit pirates out there even now looking to hijack a shipment of any size, reap all the rewards without doing any of the work. I suppose I'd rather not risk life and limb for a little more snuff and bacon."

"Anyway," Mrs. Pollard said, dishing out another portion of scrambled murre eggs, "we do all right."

Her husband murmured assent as he poked the tines of his fork into the brilliant marigold-orange curds. He added in a wistful tone, "Doc Robinson only took in one boat haul—and lost half of it on the way back besides—and he still had enough to start his business. Grew a theatrical empire from one boatful of eggs. Never set foot on the Farallones again. Wise man."

"Or a lucky fool," said Mrs. Pollard.

Mr. Pollard filled his mouth with more fluorescent eggs.

The children had grown to accept the parent-instated rule that Miss Riley was to be left to her own devices on Sundays, without question or pleas. Unless she expressly invited them to follow her, they were to say goodbye after breakfast and let her go in peace wherever she wanted.

That morning, Amelia said her farewells and slipped into the fog to find the chapel. Now, she felt no trepidation—well, no fear, though something flittered gently near her ribs.

She passed the Salters returning home and nodded. Elijah was flint-eyed as ever. Minerva didn't look up from the ground. Gertie flashed a smile that reappeared and reached her eyes when she glanced back to see that Amelia had stopped to watch. The girl returned her wave, albeit with a mere flutter of her hand.

Twelve

CONFESSION

The subdued daylight filtering through the window notches made the chapel somehow less gloomy than the first time she'd peeked inside, under a harsher sun. And now that no firelight flickered, there was nothing sinister about the space. In fact, it felt poignantly familiar.

Amelia sat in the front pew on the right side of the tiny room. She shut her eyes and imagined the meetinghouse of her childhood, vast in scale yet no more ostentatious than this chapel—and, save for the presence of the altar, quite similar inside. Its plain wooden benches had been better made but equally without adornment, its windows set just as high so nothing of the outside world but sky could be seen from within, and it too had no stained glass or crucifix or other holy symbols.

The crowd-swell murmur of birds helped conjure the memory of walking up Main Street toward Pleasant as a child amid dozens of other people. The women's long black dresses swished and the men's long black coats flapped around her, their wide-brimmed hats and plain bonnets bobbing high above her head. Their voices mingled into an indistinct thing with a life of its own. And Amelia had been a part of it, a single cell within a greater body, a molecule within a meandering river.

But then her family had been unwelcomed from that community. Cut adrift. Her mother, at least, had had other gods and rituals to turn to.

Amelia felt curiously close to her in the Farallones' eldritch landscape. She could imagine her mother standing on the rocks, casting incantations out to sea, salt air whirling the dark hair around her shoulders, vapors swirling about her feet, as if she might glide unimpeded above the granite.

She wondered if this wild place might not be a portal, a gathering spot for any spirit who wished to step through the tattered fog from another realm. Might her mother yet appear to her, materialize from the mists, were Amelia brave enough to wander out one night?

And if so, might other souls pay a visit? If she asked them to? Did she have such pluck—such power?

∽

The scuff of footsteps pierced her reverie. She turned to see Banquo bound inside. He received his benediction of neck scratches and ear rubs, bestowed his own gracious licks upon Amelia's wrists, and gazed at her with beatific amber eyes.

Before she could decide whether to move down the pew as Mr. Sisson reached them, he sat at the end of the one on Amelia's left, just across the aisle. They faced the altar while Banquo lay down to watch the door behind their backs.

Presently, Mr. Sisson said, "What were your Sundays like in San Francisco? I don't imagine you went to church. At least not with Cathy. But then, I wouldn't know."

Time to confront one ghost already, then. It was easier than Amelia expected to answer. "No. She slept in on Sundays. I didn't have to work but I usually got up to read sometime in the morning."

"Were you a teacher there too?"

"I gave some piano lessons. But mostly, I worked in exchange for room and board in the house where we lived. A chambermaid of sorts."

"And Cathy?"

"I can't seem to call her that," Amelia admitted. "But she had no end of jobs. And little schemes. And clever ways to earn a dime."

She said it fondly, but Mr. Sisson looked sharply toward her.

"Nothing underhanded," she hastened to add. "Just always looking for an opportunity to exploit. Some days she'd go down to the post office at the crack of dawn and join the line so she'd be near the front but not too close. A little later, it would already be stretched clear down the block. Often as not, someone would be willing to pay to take Lucy's spot. You'd be surprised how much, sometimes. She always said if she didn't get lucky, at least she'd see if she had any mail without wasting the whole day."

He smiled.

"She served at a few restaurants," Amelia went on. "Shucked oysters for a little while. Stopped that when she sliced her thumb open and had to pay for all the ones she bled on. But she brought them home and ate every last one. I think it was pure spite that kept her from getting sick."

He chuckled. "She always was stubborn. But no more teaching, then?"

"No. She talked about looking for another post when we first moved, but . . . she was happier to wake up and decide for herself what to do with every day. Stay up all night on a Tuesday if she wanted. Have champagne for breakfast if she felt like it. No one else's demands on her."

Perhaps it was the way Amelia trailed off, or something she'd already said, that prompted his next question, in a delicate tone. "Anything else you don't want to tell me? You can. I want to know."

Amelia looked down at her hands in her lap, worried her thumb where the scar would have been on Lucy's.

"She dealt cards at a few of the saloons. That was her steadiest work. She was quick, and sharp. She could keep up a good patter. She always had a full table and more waiting in the wings. And the prettier you were, the bigger the tips. So. It was a lot of money."

She didn't need to say the rest, was discomfited when Mr. Sisson grimly took up the thread for her. "And pretty girls dealing cards rarely stop at that when the clientele is feeling flush."

They hadn't talked about it often or at length, rarely even in direct terms, but Amelia knew Lucy had joined some of the more generous gamblers in upstairs rooms after she was done dealing for the night. That was good money too. Some of the diary entries appeared to attest to that.

Mr. Sisson shifted in his pew to look at Amelia. She glanced over to see if she might gauge his mood, braced for anger, or perhaps disgust, but there was only concern on his angular face.

"Don't you think someone might have hurt her, then? I mean, if she was in that sort of business, she would have met no end of unscrupulous characters—made enemies, I'm sure. And it does seem strange, doesn't it? That she was all set to come here, almost made the interview, would have been on the boat in another week or so, and then—she died, so suddenly? And like *that*? What if it wasn't an accident? Doesn't it seem suspicious to you?"

"No." Amelia felt sorry for him; however awful it might be, he yearned to uncover a better reason than mere chance to explain the death of a woman he'd clearly loved. If someone were responsible, he might be able to bring them to justice, at least.

And then, because she knew exactly who was to blame, she felt sorry for herself—and scared. "It was an accident," she said. "But . . . it was also my fault."

"How do you mean?"

Amelia resettled herself in her pew, looked down at her lap. "Sometimes she would drink. Even at home. Sometimes so much she'd be out cold. Insensible. You couldn't shake her awake; you could yell in her ear and she'd do no more than mumble and turn half over in her sleep. And that night, that was when she told me about the interview. That she actually intended to come out here. To leave me, just like that. No warning. No good reason—not that she would tell me. And I was angry. But more than that, I was hurt.

"I felt like she'd lied to me, betrayed me, like she was abandoning me, and how could she do that if she really cared? So we fought. We never fought, not really. Bickered, a little, but we always made up in the very next second. We were always kind to each other. Always.

"Well, I wasn't that night. I said awful things to her, and I stormed out, and I made myself stay away until morning. Because I didn't want to face her. I didn't want to hear her excuses or her promises or her reassurances. Because I knew she could talk me into believing it was all right. So I didn't give her the chance. I left her like she was about to leave me. And . . . I guess she reached for a bottle for company instead."

Amelia drew a steadying breath. "I warned her not to come after me. And I think I waited for her to show up all night. If I'd just gone back sooner, even if she'd still . . . I would have woken up. But I never even saw her again."

"Then how do you *know*? Maybe she isn't even dead." The wild hope in Mr. Sisson's voice was more than Amelia could bear.

"Our sitting room was ankle-deep in ashes. Mrs. McGowan told me how they found her, curled up over the desk . . ."

Like she was only sleeping, the poor wee thing, so black you couldn't hardly tell she was a woman. Not a hair left on her bonny head.

She didn't repeat that part, just said, "No one else would have been in that room except Lucy. And I might as well have struck the match myself."

Silence swelled in the damp air like smoke, infiltrated her body too. She felt it stealing all the space inside her lungs and head and thought she might fall unconscious, which would be a blessing.

89

But then his voice, so low and gentle, broke the quiet's hold. Every time he spoke, still, it did something strange to Amelia. Each word was a smooth, heavy rock thrown into a pond; it sank straight to her depths and sent waves outward through her entire body. She felt as if ripples of refracted light shuddered just beneath the surface of her skin. She held herself as still as possible in case he might see the shimmer otherwise, detect the disturbance. Even now, as he absolved her.

"That isn't true," he said. "It was an accident, as you said. Terrible, but no one's fault. Certainly not your own."

She shook her head and tears fell on her skirt. "But if I'd been there . . . then—"

"Then you might have died too."

"Then maybe I should have. I was *always* there. I was supposed to be. Even if we'd both burned—"

"Stop it." Not gentle, those words, yet they, too, struck Amelia like a tuning fork.

She looked over, a thin smile of pity on her lips. "You don't understand."

"I *do*." The anguish in his voice matched that in his eyes. He looked just as he had the first time they'd met in the chapel, when he'd told Amelia that he'd abandoned Lucy—Cathy.

Still, part of her wanted to insist he couldn't comprehend. She was prepared to explain her mother's prophecy that she was doomed to perish in flames, even to tell him how she'd escaped fire now more than once—and yet, in another sense, had not. She'd chosen to let herself die in Lucy's place, the only way she could. Not that it was a selfless act. But it was devotional, in its way. An offering, though without any real sacrifice on Amelia's part. Not because she was not willing. She would have thrown herself into the fire if she'd gotten there in time. She wished she had.

But the sooty thoughts tangled too tightly in her head and crumbled like ash when she tried to unspool them. She turned back toward the altar in silence. More tears spilled down her face.

"I'm sorry," Mr. Sisson said. "Will you tell me another memory of her? A happy one."

"Those hurt too."

"I know."

She thought she should ask him for one instead but still wasn't ready to hear more of Catherine, a stranger to her. And perhaps it might help, to seize on something she and Lucy had shared, when they were blissfully ignorant of any trouble yet to come, when they'd allowed themselves the extravagance of not thinking about such things that always intruded upon reality. When they'd made their own world to live in together, and trusted they would never leave it, or each other. When Amelia had, at least.

"She liked to play a game where we pretended we were sisters. When we went out. She invented this whole backstory about our aunt Maisie sending for us as children after our parents were killed—by a runaway camel at the circus. And Aunt Maisie was a widow who'd inherited a diamond mine, so we were raised in the lap of luxury. But, being orphans, naturally we fell on hard times again. Eventually, we ended up with a leaky canoe almost drowning us on the Panama short-cut on our way to San Francisco. And when we rode through the jungle, we had to share a half-starved, smelly, swaybacked, flea-bitten old mule—with only one eye, and no tail."

Amelia found herself smiling. "We'd just pile on details like that, one by one. The more ridiculous the better. There was no point in it, really; we didn't try to swindle anyone out of anything. We just tried to make them believe us—or want to believe us. And they always did. Sometimes they'd buy us a drink in the bargain. But that was just a bonus."

She slipped tentatively back into her imitation of Lucy's voice. "That's why she taught me to talk like her. Not that I ever said much in mixed company. But perhaps that was for the best, since you say the accent is—dodgy?"

Mr. Sisson laughed. "Just a bit."

They looked at each other, more candidly than they had before.

"Actually," he said, "it's quite good. I don't think most people would notice."

"Well, Lucy was a good teacher, when she wanted to teach. You know, you said that day in Stonehouse there wasn't any trace of Sunderland in my voice. But I don't think Lucy had any either. Not when I knew her."

He sighed and nodded. "The last time I saw Cathy, she did sound posh. Like a stranger. That's not how I remember her."

"You don't sound all that different."

"Well, I cleaned up my own accent once I came over here, got into business. Got tired of being mistaken for a docker who'd wandered upstairs. Even once I could afford better suits."

Amelia narrowed her eyes at him, even as the corners of her mouth tilted upward. "Before the egg company, then."

"Yes. Quite a while before that."

"What business was it?" she ventured. She smiled wider at the eyebrow he arched at her. "None of mine, I suppose."

He looked once more toward the altar. "I went by the same name then, but I was a completely different person too. So let's just say it doesn't matter now."

While Amelia didn't think that could possibly be true, she'd be a hypocrite to say it, and she wasn't that bold besides. She only said, "Fair enough."

But part of her burned to know more about him, wondered what other secrets she'd be willing to divulge to learn any of his own.

Thirteen

SCRUTINY

All her clothes were now imbued with the scent of smoke and salt and rich marine decay, a heady perfume. It comforted her, even through the tang of guano, which she regularly scrubbed from her cloak and shoes and bonnet. She'd added a raincoat to her list of items she desired from San Francisco, something that covered her head to toe and was easier to clean. *Men's waxed poncho*, she noted in the margin, so there was no mistake she was after function over form. Most of the other items she solicited were books. She'd considered jotting down *caponata?* too. But Amelia wasn't certain you could buy it anywhere.

The lighthouse tender would make its next visit in June. A couple of weeks remained to think of additional requests.

Meanwhile, the egg-company boats came and went, sometimes two or three in one week, unloading the last shipment's now empty baskets before taking on fresh cargo. The speckled eggs were piled by the dozens in their woven nests, covered with weeds and stones to keep the gulls from getting at them on their way to market.

Three weeks into egg season, though the presence of the pickers had become commonplace, Amelia sometimes still paused to watch them scale the rocks and fend off the gulls. Even without the pickers, she liked to stroll to see the view, never tired of—nor completely used to—the way the vista constantly shifted in color and intensity and mood.

Mr. Clifford, equally enthralled, often sketched the islands, the ocean. He drew the egg pickers too, quick ink renderings of the men upon their mission, or more rarely, at rest. He even made portraits of the birds themselves, the despotic gulls and the long-necked murres in their black and white tuxedo feathers.

One late afternoon, Amelia strolled toward Sugarloaf and the Eye of the Needle, draped in fog like grandes dames in oyster-gray chiffon. Passing the landing, she found Mr. Clifford completing a study of the daily cleansing ritual: a group of men, with deflated, sagging shirts now empty of their plunder, crouched on the rocks to bathe each egg in a wooden tub of salt water before packing it in a clean basket to be stored in the shed. Salter was nearby, brushing a fresh coat of whitewash on the boathouse.

Despite his presence, Amelia stopped a moment to observe the eggers and the artist, noticed one of the pickers glaring back. When she chanced to look again, she saw yet another man had his eyes trained on them, though his expression was less severe. The angry one said loud enough for all to hear, "Ain't this like bein' at the circus, boys, but the trained ape's watchin' you?"

Most of his group snickered; a couple spat. Amelia opened her mouth before she was quite sure what she'd say, but Mr. Clifford drawled, without pausing in his sketch or glancing up, "Best ignore it. Nothing gained in paying attention to them."

"But there's absolutely no cause for such despicable behavior."

"Doesn't bother me, Miss Riley. If it did, I could just get up and walk away."

The churlish man on the rocks still glared, but there was a gleam of cruel pleasure in his eyes now too. "Say, you think this ugly monkey gets paid to doodle all day long?"

Amelia drew in a sharp breath that pulled her shoulders back, but Mr. Clifford spoke quickly this time, looking levelly at her. "Please, don't."

"Got somethin' to say, honeypie?" the man called across.

Amelia set her jaw to trap her words but trusted he could understand the contempt in her eyes.

"Wonder what she gets paid for," he said, earning another chorus of filthy laughter.

Her attention was diverted again by the other egg picker who'd been staring—not at her and Mr. Clifford, Amelia now realized, but only at her. He didn't drop his eyes even when the others looked back to their work. There was something unsettling about his expression, inquisitive and amused at once. It didn't seem as if it should strike such an ominous chord, yet Amelia couldn't shake the feeling of foreboding, compounded by the way he didn't utter a sound, or move a muscle except his hands, methodically turning eggs in the water.

She looked back at Mr. Clifford's tapered fingers with their pale, neat nails, the confident lines emerging from his pen. The pickers' faces reflected on the page in miniature were robbed of emotion. Amelia had no doubt he could have captured every nuance of derision and danger if he'd cared to. Instead, he made every haggard face look weary, half-dead.

"They're not worth committing to paper," she muttered. Mr. Clifford hummed in agreement, unruffled as ever. "At least they'll be gone soon," Amelia said. She swept away with one last sour look at the unconcerned eggers and a final "Good riddance."

As she passed Salter, he gave her a critical look tinged with amusement—always amusement in certain men's expressions, no matter how unfriendly. It made her want to kick his paint bucket into the sea.

~

Until that day, she'd paid little attention to the differences among the pickers. They worked in such tightly coordinated groups they seemed like disparate parts of the same organism. Even up close, they were hard to parse. All the men dressed alike, even under their egg shirts, and most had faces obscured by heavy mustaches and beards. Salter, if he abandoned his comb and scissors, would have fit right in with them. They were all begrimed and weather-beaten beneath their hats and facial hair. Only a few were exceptionally tall or short; some were burlier than others, but most were honed down to the same lean physique and stood at roughly equal height.

On top of that, she only ever looked at them for prolonged periods from a distance, tended to avert her eyes after a nod for politeness's sake when she passed at proximity. But now that she'd committed two of their faces to memory, Amelia couldn't help but search for them every time she walked out of doors.

The angry one was elusive, or perhaps there were just too many others like him. But the one who didn't scowl, the one who only smiled beneath a shrewd, impertinent gaze, suddenly seemed to be everywhere she went. He never spoke or nodded, only leered. He didn't look away when Amelia inevitably had to, unable to endure his examination, feeling a desperate need to shield her face though it was far too late for that.

She did what she could to avoid him, and the eggers in general, but one evening, on her way to dinner, Amelia found him behind Stonehouse, availing himself of water from her cistern pump. She was incensed to see a stranger using it, letting it gush onto the ground. She was ready to upbraid the thief when he lifted his dripping face and she recognized it.

In that moment, she was convinced he recognized her too, though she didn't know how. Her voice snagged in her throat. Rather than attempt to unravel it, she turned and hurried to the keepers' quarters, where she said nothing about it, still silenced by that knot of fear.

~

She was restless all night, once more attuned to every jarring sound, no matter how small or indistinct. Unable to stop staring at the door, convinced any second the knob would slowly begin to turn—or the whole thing would burst off its hinges—she only looked away when she thought she saw the shadows writhe in the corners of the room. When her gaze landed on them, though, they were still, and empty.

Tired and ill-tempered in the morning, Amelia tried not to show it. She released the children a little early. The stiff wind helped hasten them home. As soon as they disappeared inside, she bundled up and headed out to find Mr. Sisson.

Not spotting him anywhere outside, she approached his house, closer than she'd ever ventured. Banquo barked before she even reached the door, and just as Amelia raised her hand to knock, it opened.

Mr. Sisson seemed surprised to see her, but welcomed her in.

She hesitated, but the wind was fierce. After a moment, she stepped inside. Banquo thumped his tail at her feet as she loosened her bonnet strings and unfastened her cloak. Mr. Sisson took them from her, though the wall pegs were right there.

His parlor was even more austere than hers, but he had a pea-green velvet chaise before his fireplace, and a Persian rug. His bookshelf was full, she noticed. His curtains were a surprisingly delicate lace. At a large, bare table on one side of the room, he'd been writing in a logbook much like the keepers' own, a blue floral teapot steaming beside it. He invited her to sit. The rush-seated ladder-back chairs were plain at first glance, but another revealed their finials and slats were finely carved to look like wave-bound mermaids. A whole school of scaly-tailed women swam around the table.

Amelia traced their fins and flowing hair with her fingertip. "Did you do these?"

"I did," he said as he fetched another porcelain teacup and filled it.

"They're exquisite," she said, and they both sat, smiling.

He closed his book. "So, to what do I owe this thoroughly unexpected pleasure?"

Amelia felt her smile widen, then fade. "I wanted to ask about one of the eggers. He's short, with curly dark hair, and a scar through the end of his eyebrow? He slouches, and barely ever blinks."

"Sounds like Achilles. He's new this season. One of the quieter ones. What about him?"

"Well, he was gulping water from my pump yesterday, and letting it spill all over the ground while he was at it."

"Oh. My apologies. I'll have a word with him. Remind them all to keep clear of your property. They should know better."

Amelia nodded, toyed with the handle of her cup.

"Is that all?"

"No. He didn't say anything himself, but the other day, he was at the landing with a group that was extremely rude to Mr. Clifford, for no reason. Other than the obvious."

"Hmm. I'm sorry for that, too, but I can't very well sack someone for speaking their mind. Abhorrent as it may be. Much less for happening to be in the same vicinity."

Amelia crimped her lips to tamp down her irritation. "Well, anyway, the main thing is, I don't like the way he looks at me. He stares."

Mr. Sisson barely suppressed a laugh. "Surely you must be used to that."

"No." Tea sloshed over the rim of Amelia's cup. "He looks at me like he knows me. It's prying. And, frankly, unsettling."

"And you want me to have a word with him about that too?"

"No. I just wanted to know if you knew anything about him. I was hoping you'd say he was a little odd, but harmless."

"You're worried about him?"

She studied the table. "Maybe. A bit."

A familiar furrow between his brows, Mr. Sisson regarded her through a scrim of steam as he sipped his own tea. Mildly, he asked, "Is someone looking for you?"

Fourteen

Suspicion

A hot glitter of nerves made Amelia twitch. "What? No. Well, how would I know? Why would you ask that?"

He gazed into his cup for a long moment before he offered his carefully measured reply. "You say Achilles looks at you as if he knows you. It seems to upset you out of all proportion."

"In your opinion. It's incredibly impolite."

Mr. Sisson's voice remained calm, considered. "I suspect becoming Lucy Riley wasn't a simple matter of paying tribute to a friend."

"I never said that was all it was," Amelia lobbed back.

"I know. You said you didn't want to be yourself, that you were afraid to walk down the street—"

"But it wasn't to *hide*. Not like you think."

"You don't know what I think."

"I can guess."

"Perhaps you shouldn't. But I don't suppose you'll tell me who you really are?"

She didn't answer.

"Not even a name?"

"My name doesn't matter."

"Then why not say it?"

"Because if you knew, it would only complicate things."

He gave an exasperated laugh. "We're well past that point, aren't we?" As he studied Amelia and mulled over his private thoughts, he began to frown again. "You said you were certain Cathy's death was an accident, but *are* you? Or do you think someone's looking for her? With no idea she's actually—gone? If she even is."

"Of *course* she is. We've been through that. And who would be looking for her?"

"I've no idea. But from what you've told me, I wouldn't be surprised if she ran afoul of someone. Owed them money, or perhaps one of her little schemes went bad. Maybe that's why she was coming here—for help. Because for *years*, she did *nothing*, and then just before she could get here . . ."

"No. That would be too much of a coincidence. For everything to work out that way. If she needed help, she would have hopped on a pilot boat to bring her out here right away. She was coming because she saw the post, because she thought it was some sign from the universe. As for why she wanted to come through the keepers, I suppose you'd know that better than I would. But no one was *after* her."

"All right. Then if someone's after *you*, who is it?"

"I didn't say anyone was after me."

"But you seemed to think they might be."

Amelia fidgeted with her cup. The exasperation in Mr. Sisson's next words made her flinch, but he saw and modulated his tone in the middle of his sentence: "If you want my help, you have to tell me what exactly it is we're dealing with. If you're in trouble . . . If you're putting the Cliffords and the Pollards in danger—"

"They are not in danger. Not because of me. *If* someone is looking for me, then . . ."

"Then what? What do they want?"

She stared into the tepid tea, heard her voice like it was an echo of someone else's. "To take me back."

"To where?"

Three beats of silence, and he sighed, rested his forearms on the table, bowed his head. When he looked back up, they locked eyes. "Did you give a jailer the slip?"

Amelia didn't dignify that with a response.

His tone softened. "Run away from a husband?"

Hers sharpened. "No. Never had one of those, thank God."

"Your family, then?"

She looked away in confirmation.

He leaned back in his chair. "And I suppose you're not some heiress, fleeing her golden cage or abdicating a throne, eh? Nothing so nice as that?"

Again, Amelia answered with silence. But she couldn't keep quiet for long; the thoughts churning in her head demanded expression.

"It almost doesn't make sense. It could just be that . . . Mr. Salter . . . he reminds me of—someone else. If they were looking for me, it would have been for a long time now. But if they *were*, they'd never stop. And maybe they had people looking out for a certain name. The papers published the wrong one, of course. Mrs. McGowan, our landlady—she thought it was a misprint. She was so appalled on my behalf. I didn't correct her, obviously; no one besides the police and the coroner knew I'd said I was Lucy. But if someone saw it, the other name"—the one Amelia never should have been foolish enough to use, even if it hadn't ended up in print—"then maybe they came by to confirm it, and maybe Mrs. McGowan told them . . . I didn't tell her where I was going, just that I was moving on. But she would have said, 'Ach, no, it was her roommate, Lucy Riley, that actually . . .' and then they would have had another name to look for. The fastest way out of the city is by ship, so if they went down to the wharves and asked around . . . maybe somebody else remembered."

Amelia thought of the *Alba* captain's laughing bestowal of the mermaid nickname, Signora Sirena, and his enthusiastic approval of how she'd devoured his caponata, and the way he'd shouted "Brava!" when she'd leaped for the ladder from the boat.

Even if he'd forgotten about her, there were probably official logs. "It would have taken them a while, I assume. To get the news, and then to come out here. Or send someone else."

Mr. Sisson considered it. "And this seems more likely to you than someone having a good old-fashioned grudge against Cathy?"

"Yes."

He leaned forward, his calm steadily eroding. "But there were other things you didn't know. And you weren't there. What if you're wrong?" He ran his eyes over the tabletop like he was reading it, his words increasingly quick. "Maybe with your name in the paper, as you said, someone thinks they got the wrong person—plenty of people send someone else to do their dirty work for them; mistakes can happen. If they saw the article—checking up to make sure the deed was done—then they'd want to find out why it said someone else was dead. So then they make inquiries and find out 'Lucy Riley' got on a boat to the Farallones. Whatever the landlady said to the contrary, if they even talked to her, they'd at least be suspicious enough to check. So—Christ, maybe that is what's happened with Achilles; someone sent him and now that he's found you, he's stumped."

Amelia shook her head to hide the tremor that went through her. "That's absurd."

"Why?"

"Because—no one ever would have killed Lucy! Besides, I don't think anyone else even knew where she lived. We never had visitors. She went out to see people. And Mrs. McGowan would have known if someone came into the boardinghouse."

"So maybe it was someone else who lived there."

"Absolutely not."

"Then maybe Cathy just made it *look* like an accident, and—"

"There was a body! She certainly wouldn't have killed someone else. And if she *had* staged it, she would have taken certain things with her. Nothing was missing." Including, of course, the expensive necklace that Mr. Sisson didn't know about. Amelia thought she felt it tapping against her ankle through her hem but chalked it up to the pulse galloping through every artery and vein.

"I keep thinking about those notebooks," he said. "Have you gone through them for clues, just in case—?"

"A hundred times, yes! There's nothing there that points to any kind of trouble." Even as she said it, she felt a flood of doubt and fear. She might have been trying to convince herself as well as him when she said, "Lucy didn't make enemies; everybody wanted to be her friend. And she could talk her way out of any mess she might have gotten into. But she didn't seem worried at all. Up until that last day . . . when we fought . . . she was as happy as usual. Maybe more so."

He seemed not to hear her, or not to care. "If I could just see the journals, then—"

"*No.*" Amelia stood so abruptly the tea things rattled.

"All right." Mr. Sisson stood too, but made no move to detain her, only saying, "Wait, please. I'm sorry." He raked a rather elegant hand through his dark hair and gestured to the table. "Will you please sit back down?"

She took a deep breath and sat, carefully. He did the same, topped up their teacups.

"I'm sure you're right," he said. "That it was only an accident. It's just hard to accept. You know that, of course. And I know you must be anxious, because of all that's happened. I don't mean to make it worse. Add Salter . . . he isn't the friendliest chap; even if he didn't put you in mind of someone else, he'd throw anyone off their footing. And honestly, this place . . . it breeds all sorts of mad ideas. So I think with Achilles, the simplest explanation is the right one too. He's just some poor prat who's taken a fancy to you and hasn't any idea how to express it. No cause for concern."

Amelia huffed. "I still might wake up to find him looming over me with a club in hand."

The alarm in Mr. Sisson's eyes made her look away. "I'll give you Banquo, then," he said. "Until the season's over. He'll spend the nights with you, won't let anyone get within five yards of the place without barking his head off."

She glanced at the dog, curled before the hearth. "Really?"

"Of course. If you like, I'll give you my gun as well."

"I wouldn't know what to do with that."

"Care to learn?"

"Not particularly."

"All right. So. Starting tonight, I'll bring Banquo round to you after dinner. Shouldn't seem odd if anyone notices. You are alone in there, after all, with a bunch of strange men practically right next door. That'll give us a moment to speak, if you have any more concerns. If Achilles says anything, or shows up near your house again, then I'll deal with him. And in the morning, just turn Banquo loose. He'll find his way back to me. We'll keep that up until they go in another month."

Amelia nodded, somewhat reassured by the plan, by the easy confidence with which Mr. Sisson laid it out. "Thank you." She drained her cup and rose to go. "And thank you for the tea. Almost as good as Lucy's."

He stood to see Amelia out. As she finished tying her bonnet beneath her chin and reached for the doorknob, he said, "You know, sooner or later, I would like to learn a bit more about you, whoever you may be. If we're going to be friends."

Quid pro quo ran through Amelia's head. He was still largely a mystery, though part of her preferred that. She only said, over her shoulder as she stepped out, "Later, then."

Fifteen

GHOSTS

"You're sure he won't mind?" Amelia nodded at Banquo, half inside Stonehouse, back legs still on the front step, Mr. Sisson one stair below.

"He'll be delighted for a change of scenery, I imagine. All sorts of new things to investigate in there. Won't wreak any havoc, though. He's housebroken, and he doesn't chew. Not furniture, anyway. Shouldn't have to go out until the morning. You might leave a dish of water for him, though."

"Of course." She ruffled the dog's black-and-white shag. "I don't mind sharing with you."

"Feel all right, then?"

"I do." It was mostly true.

"Then I'll see you both tomorrow. Good night."

Amelia let Banquo into her room, grateful for the company, especially since he seemed so pleased to be there, fully at his ease. She left the door open just a crack, wide enough for him to nose it open if he wanted. He lay on the braided oval rug and sighed as Amelia climbed beneath her covers.

Strange dreams flitted through her brain that night but didn't wake her. No old apparitions—no boy with the crimson gash in his egg-white forehead; no man reaching for her from his cloak of seething flames. No lovely Lucy, either. Only the already familiar Farallon phantom that now regularly shook Amelia's slumber: the sea elephant skull, looming even larger than in life—or death. A bright-white beacon shining from the deep pit in the center of its face. Unblinking, blinding her, as its shadowy jaws opened below, about to roar.

It never did, though. It only mutely gaped as the wind rattled bony fingers against the glass panes. Disturbing, but less so than some other figures that frequented Amelia's nightmares. Less personal.

~

When she stirred, she smiled to see morning light washing the wall. Banquo had guarded even her unconscious mind, kept the worst of its ghosts at bay. But when she rolled over to see if he was still curled on the rug, electric fear raced through her.

In the center of the room, the dog stood stock-still and silent, staring at the door, which was open much wider than when they'd gone to bed. Through it, Amelia could see only a black murk of shadows.

"Banquo?" she whispered.

He did not react.

She eased herself out of bed and took a few steps toward the door, made her voice ring louder when she said, "Hello?"

No one answered. Banquo remained frozen.

Driven by a flare of courage, Amelia jerked the door open all the way, thrust her head into the hall. Nothing there. She turned back to Banquo, who finally looked up at her, his enchantment broken.

"What are you doing, you crazy dog?"

He nosed Amelia's knee and wagged his tail. She scratched his ruff, only a little nervous to have her back turned toward the door.

She dressed quickly, let Banquo dart off on his own as she left for breakfast in the keepers' quarters. Silly as it was, she felt braver with the children following along behind her on the way back to the parlor for school. With their warm bodies and vibrant voices filling the space, Stonehouse didn't seem in the least unnerving, nor as if it could ever be. Yet when they left, Amelia found herself looking over her shoulder again, cringing from an anticipated finger tap that never came.

~

When Mr. Sisson returned Banquo after dinner, they chatted as before, Amelia in the doorway, him still almost at eye level even standing on the second step below. The dog heeled, awaiting a proper invitation inside.

"How was he last night?"

"Seemed content. And I slept soundly enough."

"Good. Any new encounters today?"

"No. But I've stayed close to home." She paused a moment before she prodded out the words hiding beneath her tongue. "You said he'd bark if anyone came near the house, but what if . . . Well, would he bark at a ghost?"

Mr. Sisson laughed. "I'm not sure. I don't know if he believes in them."

"I know it's silly, but—he was staring at something this morning. Through the bedroom door. Only there was nothing there. It was like he was transfixed. I spoke to him and he didn't seem to hear me."

"Strange."

"It was. And despite my best efforts to deter him, Finn's already told me about all the ghosts on the island. Twenty-three dead from the

Lucas alone, wasn't it? I knew about that, of course. But that keeper? Swept away?"

"Staggered out for a drink, most likely. Over the edge."

"And what about the woman you found in Skeleton Cave? Is that even true?"

"It is. Hence the not terribly clever name."

"Well, who was she? How did she die?"

"I don't know. I think she must have come here with the Russians. One of the Aleutians, maybe. No marks on her, but there wasn't much left either. I haven't seen any evidence of her save the bones. Nor any other spectral visions."

"I didn't *see* anything either. But it felt . . . odd."

He assessed Amelia with a twinkle in his eye. "I probably shouldn't say this, but . . . I heard the first teacher left because she saw a ghost."

"Really?"

"Oh, she was ready to go the moment she came ashore, I'd say, but according to Mr. Pollard that was the last straw. She wouldn't stay in Stonehouse by herself after that night. Slept in the Cliffords' parlor until the next boat came. She nearly leapt for it before they could even get the davit fixed. Asked for her things to be sent back to San Francisco, didn't even take the time to pack."

"What did she see?"

"Amos only said it was a woman, dressed in black. That's all they could get out of her, anyway. But she was jumping at shadows and fog from the moment she arrived. Silly girl. High-strung. Mouse's heart."

"So you weren't friends with her, then."

A smile stole onto his face. "Oh, no. She avoided me and Banquo quite religiously from the start."

Amelia flushed and hurried to change the subject. "What about the last teacher, Mr. Wines? Did he see anything that you know of?"

"No. Pompous prig. We avoided each other too. He seemed to find this place quite distasteful, but not frightening, as far as I'm aware. He had his appointed shore leave after the first four months and decided not to come back. They shipped his things off after him, too. Perhaps you should start packing now."

She raised her chin. "I'm not going anywhere. Even if I do see something strange. I'd just like to know what I'm up against. If anything."

"Afraid I can't help you there. But—do you really believe in ghosts?"

"I'm not sure. I believe in bad dreams." *And bad people*, she thought, but didn't add; instead, she just nodded at Banquo. "And he seemed to help with those. So I'm glad to have him."

"Good. Sleep well, then. See you both tomorrow."

～

That night, Amelia shut the bedroom door and induced Banquo to jump onto her mattress, his warm weight nestled by her feet. She still lay with her face to the wall. Tried not to think of disturbed bones and black dresses melting into shadows. Nor of little lost Serena or yawning seal skulls spilling forth a piercing beam, much less living men stealing through the night.

Naturally, the more she tried to deny them, the more insistently such ideas and images pressed against the backs of Amelia's eyes, like the fog pressed upon the window glass. But she wouldn't crack her lids in case her visions also swirled within the mist.

Soon enough, darkness overtook all else. She only dreamed of mundanely awful things—blood, and fists, and blades, and flames—and once more managed not to wake until morning.

This time, Banquo was still snoring at the end of the bed, and the door remained latched.

Perhaps a draft had pushed it wider the night before. Obviously, it was something so simple. And Banquo had heard a distant sound he then strained to hear again, something perfectly natural: a shout from one of the men that he might have mistaken for his master's, or a particularly obstreperous sea lion defending his morning perch. Perhaps it had woken Amelia, too, without her being aware, and that was why they'd both ended up staring into the dim wedge of hallway beyond the room.

Because there were no such things as ghosts, except the ones trapped in living heads, haunting beating hearts. That was what she'd chosen to believe.

Sixteen

FIREWORKS

Amelia looked forward to the solid, shifting presence of the dog at her feet. Even on those nights she startled awake, she found Banquo still settled there upon the blanket, and took comfort in the steady rise and fall of his ribs, his snuffling snores.

She looked forward, too, to seeing Mr. Sisson every evening. They usually spoke no more than a few brief words before he walked back around the hill. Yet Amelia was sorry to think she'd have to give up their regular exchanges once egg season ended. That wouldn't be for over another month. But then she'd catch an egger staring or be certain she'd felt someone's eyes on her, even if when she turned no one was looking—or it was only Salter again—and she'd will the days to hurry onward.

The first Friday evening in June, feigning nonchalance in the presence of the pickers, Amelia strolled past the egg shed. A sudden gust of wind filched her bonnet and sent it tumbling across the rocks. She made no move to chase it, but several of the nearby men leaped up in pursuit, like a pack of dogs after a rabbit. It was just her luck that the quickest of them was Achilles. He brandished the bonnet in one grubby hand

and grinned as he picked his way over to Amelia. She stood gripping her skirts, not smiling.

When he presented the hat, she took its edge in her fingertips and said, "Thank you," but he didn't release it.

A flush rose in her face as she tugged at the bonnet and Achilles tugged back. He chuckled at her. Several of the other eggers chuckled too. Unwilling to play such an inane game, Amelia let go and turned to walk away.

"Wait," Achilles said, and touched her shoulder—gently, but Amelia spun around and gave him what she intended to be a warning look. It felt more like naked fear.

"Don't you want it?" he said.

Not now you've touched it, she might have said, but once more couldn't speak.

Achilles's smile wilted. "Here." He extended the bonnet, pressed it closer when she made no move to take it. "I was only kidding."

Amelia grabbed the hat, but Achilles still didn't release it. Instead, he leaned closer and said, "You won't go tell on me again?" Then he let go.

She whirled away and was followed by fragmentary comments from several men. They didn't shout, but didn't mutter either: *ingrate*; *stuck-up*; *bitch*.

She said nothing about it to Mr. Sisson when he brought Banquo later, although Amelia wondered, not for the first time, how closely he associated with such men beyond what the job required. He didn't seem overly fond of them.

But if she had relayed what happened, would he have thought it harmless?

And wasn't it, after all? She'd dealt with far worse. Aside from the insults lobbed behind her back as she left—without so much as cracking a smile for them, when all they'd done was rescue her bonnet and joke with her—what had transpired that was so terrible?

Amelia felt strangely guilty, yet still unsettled. She curled up next to Banquo and cried into his fur, even as she felt foolish for being so shaken.

~

The next day, one of the eggers slipped and tumbled farther than normal, landed harder than luck usually had it, and cracked his head on the rocks below. Amelia didn't see it, but from the schoolroom they heard the clamor of the immediate aftermath, and she barely corralled the children from rushing to see.

She'd had to restrain herself too, certain it was Achilles, desperate to know. If it was, then she'd marked him, even unwittingly. The old temptation to believe—and the terror of suspecting—that perhaps some latent power ran in her blood seized Amelia. Her mother might have passed on some of the magic that had trickled through her own veins—or the madness. Or both.

As soon as she got the children back into their mothers' care, Amelia went to find Mr. Sisson. She could tell from the look on his face that she was right; she began to shake even before he confirmed her suspicions.

"Oh, God," she murmured. "I didn't mean to . . ."

He frowned. "What?"

"It was my fault."

"Don't be absurd. Were you up on that rock with him?"

"No, but—"

"These things happen. It's dangerous work. And he was new at it."

Amelia shook her head but knew better than to say more.

The pickers retrieved Achilles's body and placed it in the stone storage shed to wait until the next egg boat came, at which time the corpse would be loaded alongside the full baskets and taken back for burial in the city.

Amelia barely slept that night. Banquo's rest was disturbed too; he studied her with a look of anxiety as she watched the bedroom door. She waited for a cloaked figure to materialize from the shadows, so intently she expected to conjure it. She almost hoped to, even if the thought did terrify her. She would fall to her knees and ask it what to do, then wait in dread for it to answer. But nothing came save unconsciousness.

In the light of day, Amelia could entertain the possibility that Achilles's death had simply been another coincidence, not her own doing, intentional or otherwise.

~

Although Achilles's was the first human death that had occurred since she'd been on the island, feathered corpses had begun to pile up. Miraculously, some eggs managed to survive the plunder long enough to hatch. While the plush newborns were of no interest to the men, the gulls evinced great pleasure in impaling their tiny skulls with their beaks.

If they could have managed, Amelia had no doubt they would have harpooned thicker human heads as well. She was grateful for her miner's helmet, just as Mrs. Clifford had predicted.

She tried not to look at the bloody, limp bodies speckled all about, at first because it distressed her so greatly, and then because it failed to any longer.

It was the same with the thought of Achilles's death.

A happier occurrence came shortly after, which helped distract the children—Fiona and Joy from their worry and sadness (which only seemed compounded by the poor little birds strewn about), Finn from the macabre fascination of the event (though he never tired of examining all the brain-damaged avian corpses he came across), Phyllis and Samuel from a more generalized anxiety (not helped by the rampage of the murderous gulls), and Claire from the boredom that set in once the body had been removed from the island: the lighthouse tender paid one of its quarterly visits in the second week of June.

The general air was of jollity. Amelia couldn't help but be taken in by it, though some deeper emotion burbled up at the plaintive moan of the steamship's whistle.

She expected no correspondence but joined the throng, excited to read the latest newspapers for the sheer novelty of freshly printed words. Even Elijah Salter came to the landing, though he expressed no pleasure. His family remained cloistered.

The *Shubrick* was far too large to maneuver as close as the felucca had, so it anchored farther out, then sent a small skiff into the cove with supplies and mail and other sundries. The captain came ashore to visit, as did some of the officers and crew.

While Mr. Pollard bundled away a cache of fireworks as a surprise for the Fourth of July, his wife sorted the mail. It was a shock when Mrs. Pollard held a sealed square of paper aloft and called, "For Miss Riley!"

Heart thudding in her throat, Amelia took the letter. It was from the storage company where she'd rented a unit before she left San Francisco.

The fire hadn't spread far beyond the parlor of the modest suite she and Lucy shared, so most of their clothes and personal items stored in the bedroom had survived.

She'd packed some of Lucy's smaller possessions, the most precious stowed in the carpetbag she'd carried with her: the engraved pocket watch, now in Mr. Sisson's possession; a silver comb figured with birds and flowering vines, a few strands of gingery hair still caught between its teeth; a bottle of perfume Amelia only unstoppered to catch the scent of Lucy's shoulder; a porcelain pot of rose lip salve, its soft contents still stamped with Lucy's fingerprints. And she'd squirreled away the jewel-laden necklace just in case. She'd locked everything else in a storage compartment at Waldham Warehouse. Of course, she'd rented it under the name Lucy Riley.

She'd prepaid for an entire year and didn't know why they'd be contacting her now.

Luckily, boat days were unofficial holidays, so there were no classes. Amelia was free to be preoccupied with what would surely be unwelcome news. She carried the letter off to read.

The storage company regretted to inform her that someone had gotten past the night watchman on duty, broken into her compartment, and rifled through all her crates. It appeared several items of jewelry had been taken—an emerald ring, a diamanté brooch, and matching earrings—but nothing else on the manifest was missing. Those paste pieces weren't worth much money besides.

It set off a skittering dread, yet theft was a constant in the city—any city, Amelia supposed. She could almost convince herself she was simply the unlucky victim of a random crime. At any rate, she was separated from San Francisco by thirty miles of open sea, so there was nothing she could do about it.

If someone had spoken to Mrs. McGowan, perhaps they'd also already discovered more information at the docks. Or—another thrum of fear—at Waldham Warehouse; naturally, they had a record of Lucy Riley's current address.

Still, those thirty miles. No one could easily cross them to get to Amelia, even if they did know where she was.

She shut the paper in a drawer and went back to join the rest of them, eager for distraction to dull the edge of panic.

Lunch took full advantage of the murre eggs: a quiche, a cake, cornmeal muffins. The women also dispatched another few of the rabbits, which had multiplied since their arrival and more than replenished their original numbers. Unchecked, Amelia thought they might one day outnumber the birds.

Before the *Shubrick* men returned to their ship, the captain received the islanders' lists of requested items, to be brought back in a few months' time when the tender made its next visit. Meanwhile, if there was an urgent matter, they could potentially hail a passing tug or fishing vessel for assistance, but the *Shubrick* was their only regular and official link with the outside world.

Amelia stood with the children and their parents at the landing to watch the steamship go. The timbre of its breathy, wailing whistle stirred a yearning in her breast, intensified by the sliver of trepidation already embedded there.

Mrs. Pollard mistook her sigh and patted her arm. "You'll be due for shore leave next time around."

"Oh, I don't think I'll go."

"Afraid you won't be able to bring yourself to come back?" Mr. Pollard cracked, though not unkindly.

"No. I'd miss this place too much. Even just for one day. I've seen all I want of the city in the papers."

He laughed. His wife allowed herself a hopeful smile that didn't erase the doubt on her face. Mrs. Clifford, when she turned and caught Amelia's eye, looked as if she understood.

～

The next few weeks, at least for the stretches when Amelia was able to stop fretting over the break-in back in the city and what it might portend, were peaceful, save the screaming seagulls. Even the egg pickers seemed quieter than usual at night.

Independence Day revived them. They worked through the Fourth of July, ten hours of intrepid toil. Yet they could not ignore the jubilant air around the rest of the islanders.

While the eggers traversed the rocks, Mrs. Pollard and Mrs. Clifford prepared a supper complete with pies. Mr. Pollard had paid one of the egg-boat men to bring him fresh berries the preceding day. His wife kissed him as lavishly as if he'd given her rubies and sapphires instead of fruit. She guarded the treasure as vigilantly, too, but shared the remaining spoils once the pies were filled.

The children played on the flat expanse of land before the house, rolling hoops with juice-stained fingers, calling through berry-painted lips for Amelia to join them. She found herself swept up in their frenetic joy. When Mr. Clifford brought his fiddle to the front steps, they all dropped their sticks to dance.

Amelia knew she would draw more attention, but the pickers were far enough away that she couldn't make any of them out, and she didn't care—even when Mr. Salter passed by and glared pointedly in her direction.

She did falter when, a moment after he went inside, she saw Gertie vanish from the window where she'd been watching. He must have barked at her, Amelia thought, or perhaps physically jerked her away, grabbed one of her thin arms or yanked the thick braid that hung down her narrow back.

~

Later, once the sky turned velvet dark, Mr. Pollard set off his fireworks, delighting in the shimmering explosions almost more than Samuel and Phyllis and Finn. Joy and Fiona covered their ears and looked ready to run if a stray spark should come their way but clapped all the same. Claire seemed to find the noise annoying, the colored lights not terribly impressive.

Gertrude and Minerva stood just outside their house to watch from afar. Gertie returned Amelia's wave, which helped abate her earlier worry that the girl might have been manhandled. If she had, at least it hadn't cast a pall over Gertie's evening. Maybe she was used to rough treatment. But Amelia tried to push that thought from her mind.

Most of the eggers drifted around from their side of Tower Hill to observe, though they kept their distance from the families. She couldn't help but look for Mr. Sisson. She saw him at the margin of the group of ragged men. A fiery glow briefly illuminated his smile. By the time Amelia craned her neck to catch the glimmering burst of color, only its smoky afterimage remained.

He brought Banquo to her later. It was the fortieth night in a row they'd spoken to each other on her doorstep, which sounded both significant and oddly inconceivable. Amelia couldn't imagine the end of the ritual, though she knew it would come soon. And then what spell might be broken?

What enchantment was even now being cast?

∼

That night, she listened to the eggers revel in their barracks but fell asleep soon enough.

She woke sometime in the still-dark to Banquo barking, straight-legged and stiff-tailed before the door. Heart hammering, Amelia rose to open the latch. The dog shot into the hall and down the stairs. She peered into the tar-black shadows below but saw only the last streak of white in Banquo's fur as he disappeared.

Amelia heard no sounds of footsteps or floorboards or thumped furniture, no voices raised or muffled, no front door slamming or catching quiet as a whisper. Only the dog's harsh barks and nails scrabbling on the floors—then utter silence.

She waited, stared down into the well of shadows that obscured the stairs. Finally, Banquo appeared and trotted up as if nothing had ever been the matter. He jumped on Amelia's bed before she could even close the door to her room.

She went to the window and peered out. It was impossible to be certain, but she thought she saw a compact black shape among the jumbled rocks.

The darkness made it impossible to discern any revealing features, besides the fact it was someone short. Perhaps a child, or a smallish man. She could almost perceive a suggestion of curls, or maybe it was only the nooks and crannies of deeper shadows in all the surrounding craggy rocks. *Achilles*, Amelia thought, before she remembered that he was dead.

She didn't wish to see whatever might happen next, whether the figure would vanish like dissipating smoke or simply amble away on legs of muscle and bone.

She slid back in bed though she didn't think she would sleep, patted Banquo. "Good boy."

Idly, half-dozing as the adrenaline rush of fright receded, Amelia told herself that, whoever it was—and she couldn't say for sure, could she?—perhaps he'd only gone for a stroll, or gotten disoriented during his celebrations. He hadn't tried to come in, anyway.

Before she drifted off, she decided not to say anything, since she wasn't even sure now if she'd been awake. It could have just been a convincing dream.

Still, it turned out the daylight was not as safe as she'd surmised.

Seventeen

Confrontation

The following Sunday, on a pre-dinner stroll that took her near the egg shed, Amelia heard angry voices, one deep, two others high and childish.

She lifted her skirts and hurried toward them, found the glaring egger with Samuel's reedy brown arm tight in his huge, filthy fist, Finn looking on with desperate fury. A few other pickers stood by, simply watching.

"Let go of him!" she called. All faces turned to her as she advanced. Finn's was blotched with impotent outrage, Samuel's tear-streaked, his assailant's obscured by a bristling beard and the shadow from the brim of his hat, all frenzied eyes and bared teeth.

Amelia froze for a moment. But when the egger wrenched Samuel's arm and the boy cried out, she swept across the final distance and grabbed the man's collar with a vicious yank. "I said let *go!*"

He did, seemingly out of sheer surprise at being accosted himself.

"Run!" she told the boys, even as the egger recovered from his stumble and backhanded her, then seized her with thick fingers that dug as deep as they could go. He flung her as if he meant to pitch her off the cliff completely. Maybe he did, but she was too far from the edge. Still, she landed hard, bones jarring, sleeve tearing, face scraping against the loose rocks. She felt a warm prickle on her forehead. Heat seeped down her cheek.

Finn and Samuel were pelting toward the house, the egger in pursuit, the Cliffords coming in the opposite direction to meet them. Mr. Clifford had a garden hoe and Mrs. Clifford had their girls pressed behind her.

The other pickers on the rocks finally moved from their fixed postures. One offered his hand to help Amelia up, but she shrugged him off. When other fingers brushed her elbow as she stood, she pulled violently away. Belatedly, she realized it was Mr. Sisson, having just arrived on the scene.

"What happened?" He beheld her face with a look of shock that made Amelia's own heart stutter.

She gestured toward the houses. "That man—attacked Samuel."

Mr. Sisson hesitated only a moment before he ran toward the fray. Mr. Clifford had raised the hoe against the egger, while Mrs. Clifford had retreated, all her children tucked close now.

The Pollards had appeared too; Finn gesticulated and shouted up at his parents. Amelia limped in the direction of the fracas, touched her fingertips to the burning, bloody wound on her face as she went. As she drew closer, she made out more distinct words. Every third one of the egger's seemed to be a slur.

"He's a *child*," Mr. Sisson said, having inserted himself between the two other men, his back to Mr. Clifford. "Whatever he may have done, you have no right to lay a *finger* on him. Much less to bloody an innocent woman. You're on the next boat tomorrow, and if you try to set foot on the Farallones again, you'll be shot—you're lucky I don't do it now."

"Goddamn this place anyhow!" The egger spat for emphasis; the glob landed a centimeter from Mr. Sisson's foot. "Damn you all to hell! But you're already here."

He stalked off toward the barracks and cast another dark look at Amelia as she passed him to join the others. He spat again.

Mrs. Pollard rushed to tut over Amelia's injury, but she wouldn't be led inside until she found out what had happened. "It was *my* fault," Finn insisted to his father. "I drew a treasure map, and I hid a clue in the egg shed—but Sam didn't bother anything!"

Treasure map. Amelia felt a pang of guilt—they'd drawn maps as part of a lesson just the other day. "Is he all right?" she said to Mr. Clifford, who delicately manipulated his son's arm.

"Nothing broken," he said.

Samuel took a hitching breath as he used his free hand to smear the tears from his cheeks. "You're b-bleeding."

"Just a scratch," Amelia assured him, though she could feel her ear and collar were now sodden, and the pain in her knee throbbed harder.

"It needs tending," Mrs. Pollard said, and took her arm to gently tug her toward the house.

"I'll get the whiskey," said Mr. Pollard, and hurried inside ahead of them.

Amelia heard Mr. Sisson speaking to the Cliffords as she was led away. "I'll make sure he doesn't leave the barracks until it's time to put him on that boat. He won't be back again, I promise."

She saw that the Salters had come out but kept their distance; Gertie looked horrified, her mother concerned, Elijah rather supercilious. Amelia fixed her gaze on him until a drop of blood rolled into her lashes and momentarily blinded her.

In the kitchen, Mrs. Pollard dabbed Amelia's face with a wet cloth. "Gracious, what a mess. What a horrid brute."

"I shouldn't have grabbed him," Amelia murmured. Yet he might have broken Samuel's arm if she hadn't.

"He deserves a smack in the face with a frying pan," Mrs. Pollard said.

Mr. Pollard entered with his bottle, nudged his children out of the way. He handed the whiskey to his wife, who used another cloth to apply it to the abrasions. Amelia drew air in over her teeth. Mr. Pollard sucked his own in sympathy. "Percy should've split that pigeon-livered shit sack's skull in two."

"*Amos.*" Mrs. Pollard pursed her lips and shook her head. "Just imagine what the rest of them would have done to him if he had. Maybe you should have stepped in . . ."

"If he'd laid a hand on my boy, I would have. Would've laid him out flat."

"Well, good thing Miss Riley was the one who came across them, then."

With an indistinct mutter, Mr. Pollard left the room, scattering the children again as he went. Mrs. Pollard mustered a smile. "I don't think you'll have any scars; head wounds bleed like the dickens, but the cuts are all shallow, more scrapes than not. But you were limping too."

"Oh, just a bumped knee."

"Does it hurt?" Fiona piped up from the doorway.

"Only a little," Amelia lied.

"I should have kicked him," Finn declared, and everyone in the room looked round at him. "I should go *kill* him."

"Finn Patrick Pollard! I don't ever want to hear you *say* a thing like that again."

"But Dad said—"

"Don't listen to your father. A bunch of foolish bluster and nonsense."

"But *you* said he should've—"

"Do you want me to get the rug beater? Keep talking!"

Finn clamped his mouth shut and crossed his arms, left the room in a huff while his sisters looked after him, Claire with a roll of her eyes and Fiona a furrowed brow.

Mrs. Pollard sighed and pressed another clean cloth to Amelia's head. "Now hold this for a little while until the bleeding stops, and you'll be right as rain." She poured a slug of whiskey into a glass, handed that over too. "For the pain."

"Thank you."

She poured another for herself. "For the constant headaches."

As they shared a smile and threw back their drinks, Mrs. Clifford came into the kitchen. With a rather guilty glance at her counterpart, Mrs. Pollard spirited her empty glass into the sink and excused herself to go sort out her son. Her daughters trailed after her. Joy and Phyllis took their place in the doorway, Samuel apparently with their father for the time being.

"Good Lord. I am so sorry, Miss Riley. But thank you, for intervening like that."

"Of course." As if she could have done anything else.

Mrs. Clifford fetched a crock of honey from a cabinet and gestured for Amelia to take the cloth away from her temple, then smoothed the sticky golden goo onto the scrapes. "My mother used to do this for all my cuts. Helps them heal faster."

"Mine used yarrow," Amelia said. "Thank you."

Mrs. Clifford spoke as though to herself. "You'd think we'd be safer out here, so far away from other people. Don't have to worry about being snatched out of our beds and sold to somebody down south, maybe—but it doesn't matter if we were never slaves. We've never really been free, either. Even here, my babies still have to find out how much ugliness there is in the world for them."

Amelia knew there was nothing she could say, so she only listened, watched the girls move closer together in the doorway and Mrs. Clifford's expression shift from grim to grieved and then composed again. She shook her head and put the lid back on the honey. "I don't mean to complain—"

"No. The world is full of awful people."

"Well. But there are good ones too. And it could have been worse, right? It could always be worse. And it can always get better. Got to believe that. Or else what are we doing here?"

"Indeed."

~

Amelia excused herself from returning for dinner later, so Mrs. Pollard sent her off with a ham sandwich bundled in a damp linen napkin. Mrs. Clifford added the honey crock.

In Stonehouse, Amelia sat before the cold parlor hearth and sank into memories that made her numb, yet also made her tremble. Even before she'd been attacked, she knew the way the egger had slammed her into the ground, in her very bones. It was the same way her father used to hurl her mother to the floor, like he wanted to smash her to pieces.

On occasion Amelia had gotten a shove or a slap to the cheek. Her older brother, Nathaniel, had been pulled off his feet, had a hand twisted behind his narrow shoulders. Their younger sister, Polly, once received a pinch that left two bruises as if her chubby arm had been squeezed in a vise. But whenever their mother could intercede, she'd offered her own body to be brutalized instead. Little Jonah was the only one of them Amelia's father never touched, even in anger, until that last day. It revolved in a fiery vortex in her mind now. How she hadn't helped her baby brother. How she'd drawn Mr. Henry to his doom. How she'd seen her mother finally destroyed. And had almost died herself.

Perhaps she should have, Amelia thought, not for the first time.

A knock on the door startled her from her grim trance. She found Mr. Sisson on the second step. She instinctively turned her face to hide her abrasions and her haunted aspect.

"I'm so sorry," he said. "I can't believe that—" A muscle twitched in his jaw as he clenched it around what Amelia assumed were some choice words that he thought would offend a lady.

"I'm fine," she said. "I'm more worried about poor Samuel's little arm. Mr. Clifford said it wasn't broken. But that beast looked like he was trying to tear it out of its socket."

"Hateful bastard," Mr. Sisson spat. "They hadn't even touched anything, not that I could see. Might've moved some of the coverings around, but nothing was gone, or broken. I wish I could have put him out to sea. Or just thrown him into it. Half your face was red with blood."

Amelia's cheeks burned now. "It's just a scrape," she mumbled.

"Well, I could have killed him."

Something flared in her chest. She couldn't tell if it was more panic or some strange gratification. She made herself meet Mr. Sisson's eyes. "I'm glad you didn't. I'm glad he'll be gone soon, too."

"First thing tomorrow. I'll bring Banquo round in a bit. But you're sure you're all right?"

"I will be," she said.

When he delivered her sentinel later, Amelia fed the dog her sandwich, which she'd been unable to eat, the ham stringy shreds in her teeth, the butter an unpleasant film on her lips. She scrubbed her mouth and hands and changed into her nightgown, washed her wound again, smeared another thin layer of honey on it before she got in bed.

Banquo settled himself at her feet, and she lay staring at the ceiling, listening to the seabirds' racket. The men seemed quiet on the other side of Tower Hill, but as usual, Amelia heard oddly human voices in the hubbub of the birds, a whole theater crowd in hysterics at some dirty joke, punctuated now and then by a hoarse scream as if a fight had broken out in the pit.

She was careful not to think of vengeance or retribution, determined not to picture any scenes of calamity, even those that had already happened in her past. Nonetheless, they tried to insinuate themselves into Amelia's consciousness.

Eventually, she knew, they would win out.

Eighteen

Departure

After the murre eggs were exhausted, the remaining pickers armed themselves with burlap sacks and shovels. They collected all they could of the seabird guano, valuable as fertilizer in San Francisco and beyond. When they finished that harvest, at the end of July, they would leave.

In those last two weeks, Amelia's abrasions healed to barely noticeable pink marks, and her limp resolved itself. The remaining eggers steered well clear of her and averted their eyes when she passed. Mr. Sisson must have warned them all to leave her be. It was almost unnerving, how little Amelia seemed to exist to them. But she walked tall and pretended not to see them either.

While her wounds had still been fresh, Mr. Sisson's demeanor had been even gentler than usual. That had been unnerving too: his sudden sincerity, his unwillingness to tease her. Amelia had made enough jokes that he'd finally relaxed, relented.

As she strolled past the landing one evening, she saw him coming in her direction from the egg shed and let him catch up. When she commented on the impending departure of the company men—not caring if the elation was evident in her voice—he mentioned he'd go on the last boat with them, pay his annual visit to the city, conduct the necessary business.

"And as soon as I'm able, I'll catch the next passing ship so I can escape back here to . . . relative solitude."

She tried to sound neutral when she said, "How long will you be gone?"

"Probably not more than a week. Two at the outside. Why? Will you miss me?"

She felt a rush of warmth that she knew reddened her face, so she kept it turned away. "I'll miss Banquo."

"Keep him for me if you like. He hates boats. And it can be difficult to find lodging with him in tow."

"But then he'll pine for you. And I'd have to feed him and let him out. And I already have my hands full with the children."

Each indulging a small, private smile, each aware of the other's, they walked in easy silence for a moment, watched the wheeling birds and thin ribbons of fog blowing in.

"Wish you were going?"

"No." Amelia examined the assertion for veracity and decided it was true, but admitted, "I will be envious of you getting to take a warm bath, though—that's the only thing I really, truly miss about the city. Sometimes I heat up a bucket for the basin, but it's not the same as soaking in a tub. All the way up to your neck."

He laughed. "I'm surprised no one's hauled one ashore yet."

"Well, it would be a waste of water. And firewood. And a pain to fill."

"True. But when you get your leave—when is that? Soon."

"I'm not taking it."

"Really?" When she didn't answer, he said in a soberer tone, "Because you're worried about who might be keeping an eye out?"

She shrugged. "But I also prefer it here."

"Despite the lack of bathtubs."

They'd slowed their ambling steps as if to prolong their meeting by unspoken agreement, but finally reached Stonehouse. Amelia hesitated before wishing him good evening, thought she might ask if he'd join them for dinner later. Instead of saying any such thing, though, she blurted out that she'd gotten a letter from her storage company. In a rush, she explained the situation in its entirety, and summed it up with another twitchy shrug:

"I don't know why I mentioned it, really. It isn't as if there's anything you could do; I don't even care about the things that were taken. They weren't worth anything. Sentimentally or otherwise. I don't want them back."

"But you don't think it's a coincidence, do you? You think this adds credence to your theory that someone's looking for you."

"Or to yours, that someone's looking for Lucy."

"Or something of hers. You said nothing was missing from your rooms and there was nothing valuable in storage, but was there anything of more worth you brought with you?"

Amelia nudged at a loose rock with the toe of her boot; the concealed necklace brushed her ankle. "She had money, of course. Cash. I brought that here. I did spend some of it on the burial. And the storage. And a little for the damage, to the house. But I haven't touched another penny."

"It's no matter to me. But—how much? Do you think someone could be after that?"

"Possibly. It's about three hundred, so no small thing. But it was all savings, built up over the years, not something someone would have known about unless she told them. It wasn't as if she suddenly came into it . . ."

"But?"

"There was a necklace too. She hardly ever wore it. The first time I saw it was about a year ago—a little more than that. It's dripping with diamonds, and about a dozen rubies besides. Even though red was never Lucy's color. I thought it was best to keep it close, so I brought that too."

"Any idea what that's worth?"

"Maybe as much as the rest of her savings? More? Assuming it's real, which I think it is."

He raised his eyebrows. "Well, there's still a chance the break-in was just a random act. How would anyone have known 'Lucy' even had business there?"

"Mrs. McGowan. Waldham brought the crates to the house; I packed them up with a list of the contents; then they came back and took them all off to the warehouse. That wretched woman had her nose in the whole business, of course. If anyone asked, I'm sure she'd tell them."

"So, you want me to go and inquire if they have any other information? Whether any other lockers were looted, if anyone saw anything, et cetera?"

"Only if you want to. If you don't mind."

"No. I'm curious now myself."

"I'd better give you the letter, as proof you know me."

He waited at the bottom of the steps while Amelia ran inside to retrieve it. She brought two of Lucy's notebooks back out with her too, opened one to a specific page, and showed Mr. Sisson: *2/15/58—Saw E. Wore my collar like a good little pet. Would like to strangle her with it. Mad, to think I was ever fond of her.*

He looked up at Amelia in alarm.

"I don't know who 'E' is," she said, "but she must have given Lucy the necklace."

"Are there other references to her?"

"Here and there, but not usually in any detail." Amelia paged through the other journal and showed him another entry: *10/24/57— Saw E on Baker St.—thought horrid hallucination. The devil thinks I'm in England; must keep it that way.* "That's the first mention of her."

"You'd read this before? You said there was no sign of trouble."

"And there isn't. Not really. Lucy saw 'E' plenty of other times, and there's nothing else like those two entries. However she felt about her, Lucy wasn't hiding from her. Or running." Before he could spout more wild theories, Amelia said, "I only showed you because I thought it might be relevant to the break-in. I think after Lucy died, 'E' didn't see her for a while and wondered what had happened, so she went looking for her own answers. That's all. But I'd like to know for certain."

Mr. Sisson peered at her as she averted her eyes. "You think 'E' sent Achilles after you? For the necklace?"

"No." Amelia unfolded the letter and passed it to him, watched him read the date.

"May fourteenth," he said.

"Written after the pickers already got here."

"So Achilles was just some poor prat. Simplest explanation, after all."

Unless someone else sent him, Amelia thought, but bit her tongue.

"Well, I'll see what I can discover." Mr. Sisson slipped the refolded letter into his pocket. "Anything else I can do for you while I'm there?"

She shook her head, then said, "Take a bath for me, I suppose."

He grinned. "Gladly. I'll take two or three. Every day, perhaps."

Relieved by his ease, Amelia felt herself loosen. "Now you're just being cruel. But I will watch Banquo if you want."

"I think he'd prefer it. I'd certainly appreciate it too."

"An exchange of favors, then."

"Yes. Thank you."

"My pleasure, of course. He's a capital houseguest."

~

The day the last egg boat left, Amelia stood at the landing to see Mr. Sisson off. She raised an arm at the top of the cliff and waved as they sailed away, glad no one else had joined her so she had the moment to herself. No steam whistle, yet that same tidal tug at her heart.

While he was gone, Banquo stayed close, though the dog often went to double-check his usual quarters by day. Finding them empty, he returned to the schoolroom, much to the children's satisfaction. Amelia's, too.

~

In the second week of August, Finn celebrated his eleventh birthday. Practically a man in his own eyes. His father had saved a few fireworks for the occasion, and his mother baked a cake.

Accepting her plate from Mrs. Pollard at the dinner table that evening, Amelia said, "I never expected to eat so many sweets when I came here!" They all laughed.

Since she'd arrived, three of the other children had already had birthdays; Samuel turned five in the middle of May, his sister Phyllis turned seven in mid-July, and poor Fiona's sixth birthday fell in early June, the very day after Achilles plummeted to his death. She'd poked at her cake without much appetite, but at least she got to fully enjoy her brother Finn's birthday dessert two months later.

"Who's next, then? Joy or Claire?"

"My birthday's on December twenty-first," Claire announced. "Almost Christmas."

"Mine's September seventh," said Joy.

"Does anyone know when Gertrude's is?"

"No," Mrs. Pollard admitted, and Mrs. Clifford looked equally chagrined.

"When's your birthday?" Phyllis asked.

Amelia froze for a moment, unsure if Lucy had given her birth date in her letter when she'd replied to the newspaper ad. Even if she hadn't, that seemed the more appropriate answer, so Amelia smiled and said, "June sixteenth."

There were general murmurs, but Fiona gasped most dramatically. "We missed it!"

"That's quite all right."

"Oh, I should have put it on my calendar," said Mrs. Pollard.

"No, really, I've never liked to make a fuss."

Which was true enough, though Lucy herself had enjoyed as much attention as anyone cared to give. Her loosely bound, madcap coterie of misfits and merry rogues were happy to oblige. She was the sort of person who didn't simply absorb adulation but radiated goodwill back upon all well-wishers until they felt they had been the ones feted.

That was how Amelia had felt, at least. Just to be in Lucy's presence had been a gift. Every day a grand occasion in its own way, even when they did nothing but loaf about at home and laugh over trifles or luxuriate in their limp, tangled sheets. Whatever secrets Lucy had kept, nothing changed that unadulterated joy, or the pain of losing her.

When June sixteenth had dawned on Southeast Farallon, Amelia had passed the day as usual; it had been a Thursday, so there was school. The only concession she'd made to the significance of the date was to anoint herself with Lucy's perfume, a sweet swirl of almonds and jasmine with a whisper of clove. A trace of orchids, and vanilla, and a bright note of orange.

As she dressed that morning, she'd brushed the smooth curve of the glass bottle with her fingertips, a totemic action, then picked it up to remove the stopper and barely breathe it in. Amelia hesitated a moment before she tipped a drop onto her finger and touched it to each side of her neck, where the pulse beat just beneath her skin. Lucy had dabbed it there for her some nights before they went out, then kissed her there when they returned.

Amelia caught faint traces of the heart-rending scent all morning, but thought it had faded away by dinnertime, which she was both grateful for and saddened by.

Yet when Mr. Sisson arrived to transfer custody of Banquo that night, he'd stopped short. His expression was so much like that of the first day he'd regarded Amelia from that doorstep, she might have fallen back through time. "You're wearing her perfume."

She'd felt her stomach drop. "I'm sorry."

He'd shaken his head with a half smile, as if to dispel the notion. "It's just—you never have before."

"No. But I thought, since it was her birthday . . . Well, was it, really?"

He'd frowned, then looked surprised. "Yes, it was. That's right."

They'd said nothing else, only stood together in a wistful silence while the birds clamored from the rocks all around them. Amelia had barely seemed to hear them in that moment.

~

She missed him. While it was not a shock, it was somewhat distressing. She thought she understood, perhaps, why Lucy had been so magnetically drawn to him. Disconcertingly, he even reminded Amelia of Lucy at times—his sly streak, the way it was so easy and enjoyable to talk with him now. Even his smile, when he didn't try to restrain it, recalled Lucy's sunny grin.

Amelia chose not to think of it, or of him, as much as she was able. With Banquo in her care, it was difficult. But at least she kept herself from commenting when Mrs. Pollard wondered aloud how Mr. Sisson was getting on in San Francisco. Not that Amelia's reserve deterred the woman.

"I always imagined him gritting his teeth through a visit to the city, but I wonder if he'll enjoy it more this time around. Because, I must say, he's been *much* more sociable than I've ever seen him since Miss Riley arrived. He certainly didn't come to Miss Webster's welcome dinner."

"Well," Mr. Pollard said, "she *was* a cold fish."

"Amos! That's unfair. She was *delicate*. She had a nervous disposition."

"And a plain, pinched face," he added, with a wink across the table that Amelia studiously avoided, though it was hard not to laugh when Mrs. Clifford almost spluttered on her cider.

"I'm not sure Mr. Sisson ever even spoke with Mr. Wines," Mrs. Pollard mused.

"Wines didn't make friends with anyone," her husband said. "Except that old seal head."

Amelia did laugh then.

"But Mr. Sisson's always been polite," Mr. Clifford said.

"Oh, as far as that goes," said Mrs. Pollard. "Politeness can be the coldest thing you've ever weathered. The thinnest skin over contempt."

"You make him sound like a misanthrope," Mrs. Clifford interjected.

"No," Mrs. Pollard countered, "only a recluse. But have you ever seen him stop to talk so much? And always smiling. Except when he told off that filthy lout—who knew he had such a heroic streak? But he's become positively congenial! I might have even heard him whistle the other day. It suits him. There's a color in his cheeks."

"I oughta be jealous you spend so much time studying the man," Mr. Pollard teased.

Amelia had never seen Mrs. Pollard blush before. "Oh, there's little enough to look at out here. But I won't deny he's handsome."

"Neither would I," her husband agreed.

"But is he to *your* liking?" Mrs. Clifford said to Amelia, who was genuinely stunned, if not a little betrayed, but then Mrs. Clifford added dryly, "Is what dear Mrs. Pollard means to say."

"*Abigail*, I don't appreciate you putting words in my mouth. But since you have, we may as well have the answer."

Amelia chuckled, not without a trace of panic. "I feel I've been ambushed, a little."

"Just glad it isn't me for once," Mr. Pollard said.

Mr. Clifford spoke again: "I thought we wanted to keep Miss Riley amenable to staying here. Might this not be a bad tactic in that case?"

She gave him a look of gratitude, but managed to keep her smile and, for the most part, her wits. "No, no, it's all right. I find Mr. Sisson quite pleasant in every aspect," she told the table. "But I think the thing I like most about him is his undeniably charming, really rather handsome . . . dog."

That earned her more laughter, a toast from Mr. Pollard, and a reprieve from the subject for the time being.

Nineteen

RETURN

Two weeks at the outside—though Amelia didn't mean to count the days, they steadily amassed. She began to worry, in no small part, about whom Mr. Sisson might have met in the city.

She'd said she didn't think the mysterious "E" was responsible for anything worse than seeking her own answers. But Amelia also knew Lucy hadn't liked the woman—*the devil*—who'd given her the necklace. Beyond that, "E" was only a figment of her imagination. And she couldn't be certain that "E" had been behind the break-in. There was still a chance—however unlikely—that it was Amelia's father, or someone he'd dispatched. Someone who'd gone looking for Lavinia Henry—another monumentally stupid alias to have adopted—and only learned the name Lucy Riley in pursuit.

Amelia shouldn't have told Mr. Sisson about any of it—especially not about the necklace. What kind of danger might she have led him into—and might now be on her trail too, if it wasn't already before?

Even if he hadn't encountered trouble while hunting information on her behalf, what if the egger he'd banished from the islands had lain in wait for him?

Banquo calmed her as best anyone could, and Amelia was glad she'd kept him. Mr. Sisson would have to return, she told herself, if only for his faithful companion.

~

Her frayed nerves were further tested when a round of gunshots fractured a Tuesday morning. They were practicing simple division. Amelia ordered the children to stay inside while she ventured forth. The Pollards and the Cliffords were drawn by the commotion too. They shared a communal flinch as another barrage of reports rang out.

They sidled out to the edge of the marine terrace and saw Mr. Salter amid a cluster of dead and dying sea lions below. Bright-red blood sluiced off the rocks around his feet. He'd exchanged his Colt repeating rifle for a knife and bent to the nearest animal. He grabbed a handful of whiskers and braced his boot upon its head as he lowered his blade to its face.

Amelia was amazed—aghast—his footing was so firm. She pictured the granite crumbling beneath him, tipping him into the thrashing sea. A dangerous thought, perhaps, but it flashed through her head unbidden.

"What the hell are you doing?" Mr. Pollard called, and she startled.

Salter grunted with the effort of butchering the animal. The soft, sucking thwock of the knife parting dense flesh and blubber under velveteen skin made Amelia's stomach roil.

"Chinamen pay good money for the male parts," Salter said. "And the whiskers make mighty fine pipe cleaners. Surprised the egg company hasn't tried to corner the market on pizzles too."

He lined them up to dry in the intermittent sun and left the patchwork carcasses to rot or wash away. The rest of them tried to ignore the carnage and the gunshots, but it cast a pall.

Amelia's slumber was once more fitful, her dreams even bloodier than before. In them, Salter stood in the prow of a small boat and hurled a harpoon through the heart of a whale-sized seal, its dark eyes soft and sad. When he turned his head, he had her father's face, which was so much like her own. In the morning, Amelia covered her mirror with a dark kerchief.

At dinner that evening, she asked if anyone knew whether Mr. Salter had ever been in whaling, since New Bedford was known for it, and he seemed to have experience with butchery.

"Matter of fact, he said he'd been on a couple voyages," Mr. Pollard affirmed, "before he was married. Gave it up to start a family."

More's the pity for them, Amelia thought.

She wondered if Salter had in fact been a harpooner, or at least an oarsman. He might have been a mere crew hand, left behind on the ship when the whaleboats were lowered, as green with envy as with lack of experience. She doubted he'd been an officer, much less a captain, not with only a few voyages behind him. Yet he'd probably thought he deserved to be at the helm before he'd even boarded his first vessel.

Amelia wondered, too, if he'd ever sailed with her father. Improbable. Not impossible. If he had, perhaps that was why he looked at her so intently, trying to pinpoint whom she reminded him of. But she was confident that anyone who'd ever met Captain Osborne would not soon forget him. Maybe Salter knew precisely who she was, then. Maybe he'd already dispatched a letter to his old acquaintance . . . but that was ridiculous, Amelia decided.

Salter seemed quite content to have no contact with the outside world. She'd never seen him send or receive mail when the *Shubrick* came, though he attended the landing. Amelia's origins were surely an uninteresting mystery to him. He only cared that she was a woman, with the audacity to exist unaccompanied, yet not unconnected. Although, just then, she felt terribly alone.

~

Eleven days after Mr. Sisson's departure, the *Alba* brought him back. Amelia had no clue he had returned—until Banquo perked up and sprang off the rug to dash for the door. She went to look and saw nothing, tried to calm the dog. When she couldn't, she let him out and he galloped away in the direction of the landing. Her heart lifted, but she went back to the children and tried to concentrate on their lesson on homophones.

After she'd dismissed them, she sat at the writing desk by the window to make notes for upcoming classes. The day was overcast, rather warm and still, a knife-edge horizon where the mercury sky met quicksilver sea. Every ten seconds, Amelia looked out again and set down her pen, paper a mess of ink blots, fingers spotted.

Finally, her vigil was rewarded: she saw him, coming from the east end of the island with an empty wheelbarrow and Banquo at his heels. Mr. Sisson had divested himself of his jacket, rolled his shirtsleeves up over wiry forearms.

She didn't think of stopping to put on her cloak or bonnet but went outside at once and hailed him. He grinned, and she felt his gaze, even from that distance, like a dart in her sternum.

Banquo barreled over as if he hadn't just seen Amelia an hour ago. She stooped to tousle his ruff, then straightened and closed the distance between herself and Mr. Sisson at an easy saunter.

"You spoil him absolutely rotten? Feed him nothing but table scraps before you let him sleep on your pillow?"

"No. He's been miserable. Cried every night at the door. Scratched it to splinters. Even howled a time or two."

The dog panted up at them and they laughed at his fool's face.

"How was the city?" she said as they continued toward the landing.

"Crowded. Filthy. Noisy. Hazardous to life and limb, not to mention sanity."

"So, much the same as here."

"Oh, much worse. The baths were quite nice, though."

Amelia gave him the requisite withering look, unable to completely hide her smile, though it slipped off in the next second. "You missed Mr. Salter's rampage, at least. He shot about half the sea lions we had."

"Why?"

"Profitable parts." Amelia hurried to change the subject. "So, did you play detective?"

With a quick glance around to ensure no one else was out, he said, "I did speak to the storage-facility man, but unfortunately he'd very little else to say. Just: it was only your locker that was broken into, and allegedly, the watchman was overpowered from behind by a blow to the head. I rather expect someone paid him to look the other way. At any rate, they sacked him, and I couldn't manage to track him down."

"Ah. Well, thank you for checking."

"It still could have been pure bad luck, you know. A random pincher, took whatever they could stuff in their pockets and that's that."

He ducked inside the egg shed, onetime crypt, empty of all but tools and baskets and other oddments now, to return the wheelbarrow to its place. Amelia stood just inside the doorway, peered down the length of the dim interior, scant sunlight filtering through. She didn't want to speak the words careening around inside her head, but they beat their way down into her throat and burst in a frenzied flock from her lips.

"That would be too convenient, though, wouldn't it? I think it *must* have been 'E.' And if it was, then she knows I took the necklace and that I'm using Lucy's name. So, she must think I did a lot worse than only steal from her. Because it does look terribly suspicious. And if she *did* pay the watchman to get in there, then why wouldn't he let her look at the account books too? They have my address. So even if she didn't send Achilles after me, that doesn't mean she won't send someone else, or come herself."

Mr. Sisson stepped closer, mere inches from where Amelia stood in the open doorway. His voice was calm, but she knew that was by design. "Even if that were true, even if someone did manage to come out here to find you, then you'd give them the necklace and that would be the end of it."

Amelia twisted her fingers together. "Unless it's nothing to do with Lucy after all. Or it *is* and they also want revenge—because they think I *killed* her."

"I don't believe anyone would be able to sustain such a notion once they met you. And you should keep your voice down, out here."

She stepped away from the shed and scanned the marine terrace behind them, still empty of other people, then hurried down the short path toward the far edge of the landing and the coldly shining sea beyond.

Mr. Sisson followed, stood a respectful distance from where Amelia leaned against the side of the boathouse with her hands knotted before her waist. He moved a little closer when she said in a soft voice, "Did you ever think that? That I might have . . ."

"No." He looked out at the gunmetal ocean, took a deep breath before he went on. "It may have crossed my mind just for a moment, when I first heard what happened—when I didn't know you—but I've never truly believed it, even for a second. I know you didn't. I know you couldn't."

"But you don't really know me. Even now. Not at all."

Now, the calm in his voice came naturally. "I know how you are— and that is who you are. Names and such are all but trappings. Hardly the most important thing. I know you have a good heart; I believe that with all my own."

Amelia had to look away, tears welling in her eyes, though she was determined not to let them fall. "But I've lied—to everyone. That's the only reason I'm even here. They've been *so* kind, and every time I open my mouth it's more deception. And the worst of it—if I'd told

Mr. Pollard the truth that day, he would have hired me anyway. I know that."

"But you didn't know that then. You only did it because you felt you had to. There was no malice in it. There isn't. That makes a difference."

Even if she believed it, it wouldn't matter. Even if she'd told the truth—to the police and the papers too, like she should have—Amelia knew she still would have taken Lucy's necklace, and "E" would have found out. At least then Amelia might have looked a bit less culpable, seemed not so deeply devious, when "E" came looking. Too late for that now.

Mr. Sisson's voice brought her back to the present. "I stopped by the *Bulletin* offices while I was in town. Looked at their archives."

Amelia couldn't take her gaze from the sea but felt him peering at her.

"Lavinia Henry," he said, and she felt the resonance of his words in her own chest. Felt his eyes on her still. "Is that you?"

She hesitated, then let out a rueful puff of air. "That's the name I was using before."

After a moment, he laughed, couldn't help but shake his head. "I say, the two of you were well matched, weren't you?"

Despite her heavy heart and the lingering shadow of worry, the sides of Amelia's mouth lifted. "Even more than we knew."

She dashed her wrists against her wet lashes and dredged up the courage to turn her face to Mr. Sisson, to tell him a little more of the truth. "Lavinia was my mother. She had a hard time of it, but she did everything she could for me. And Mr. Henry was . . . a very dear friend to us both. He saved my life more than once. Taught me to sail when I was little."

Mr. Sisson chose his next words carefully, as if afraid to spook her. "So you grew up on the water, then. Somewhere back east, I presume."

"On an island, in fact. Nothing like this one, though."

"I can picture you on a boat. But carved into the prow more easily than trimming the sails."

"Well, I was good at it, and I loved it more than anything. Until I came out here, I hadn't even been on a boat—not on the ocean—since I left home; thirteen *years*. I knew I'd missed it, but I'd forgotten just how much. We took a steamboat from St. Louis to St. Joseph and then a few river ferries to get out here on the trail, but that's not the same as sailing. That sensation, like soaring over the water. Until you hit a trough, and then you're bumping through the air. It's such a freeing feeling, isn't it? Untethered to the earth."

She glanced at the upturned dory beneath the overhang of the boathouse. "I'm sure I don't even remember the difference between the boom and the bowsprit anymore, much less how to handle the sheets, but—*oh*, I've been wanting to get out on this rowboat at least. They keep saying I can come along when they go fishing, but I haven't managed it yet."

"I'll take you." He cut his eyes away as if startled by his own intensity. "I mean, I'm sure Mr. Pollard or Mr. Clifford would if you—"

"No. I'd like that. To go with you."

He almost succeeded in subduing his smile. "Well, we're bound to have a good Sunday for it soon enough. Fall always brings the best weather. Clear and calm. And there should be loads of whales coming through."

"That sounds wonderful." And perhaps a little terrifying, but Amelia thought that was often the case with the things you wanted most.

They stood a while longer, Banquo snapping at the kelp flies, yet another prolific inhabitant of the Farallones; they swarmed everything on days when the wind died down. Where the flies freckled Mr. Sisson's exposed forearms, Amelia wanted to brush them off.

"I should let you finish getting settled in now." She turned back up the path, and he fell into step with her as she walked toward Tower Hill. "Thank you, truly. I do appreciate all your help."

"Of course."

"If you wanted to come to dinner tonight, I'm sure you'd be more than welcome. They'd be glad to hear how the city was, what you got up to. Well, maybe not all of it."

"Perhaps I will. Though normally I need at least a few days to shake off civilization before I feel up to company again."

Amelia thought of Mrs. Pollard's recent comments, imagined how avidly she would look between the two of them, how much she would read into his very presence at the table. "In a day or two, then. No one's going anywhere."

He stopped outside Stonehouse to see her go in. On the top step, Amelia paused. "I'm sorry to have kept you so long from returning to your . . . *relative* solitude."

His grin spread warmth across his face and throughout Amelia's body. "Don't be."

Twenty

THE FACE OF GOD

The remainder of August brought interludes of clear, windy weather, but two Sundays in a row—and several other days in between—the island was socked in with dripping fog.

There was no pleasure boating in that weather, and the keepers were on edge. The lighthouse beacon was powerful, but the beam only cut so far through the thickest haze. The *Lucas* had foundered on such a night.

On clear days, Amelia spent hours studying the ocean. Through an old spyglass, she saw whale spouts galore, even flukes and breaches. She preferred spotting those to ships.

All summer long, in fact, she'd observed a staggering number of dolphins and bigger creatures: blue whales, humpbacks, gray whales (though she wasn't always good at telling them apart on her own). But as exhilarating as every far-off sighting was, she longed to be out there with them, close enough to feel the spray and see the glistening of their skin. To touch one, even with the barest fingertip.

Now that she had a firm promise from Mr. Sisson to take her out, Amelia was impatient for the weather to cooperate.

That first Sunday following his return, he came by Stonehouse after breakfast. Amelia was sulking, resigned to yet another day of reading, but she brightened when she opened the door. She could see nothing but mist behind him; had he backed away a few paces, he, too, would have been obscured.

"It seems our excursion has been postponed," he said, hands outspread in the fog.

"I wasn't expecting it to be so soon, anyway," Amelia lied, and rose from where she'd bent to pet Banquo, who promptly trotted past to his place on the parlor rug. "Will you come in too?"

"Just for a moment."

"I'm afraid I don't have tea, but would you like some coffee?"

"No, thanks." He nodded at the dog, stretched before the unlit fireplace. "He's missed you terribly, you know."

"Feeling's mutual. It's so strange trying to fall asleep without him at the end of the bed."

"Would you like him back? For the nights, I mean. I'm afraid I can't part with him completely."

"No. I'm getting used to it. By and by. But he's welcome to visit whenever he likes. You can tag along, I suppose."

Mr. Sisson smiled, observed the parlor. Amelia wondered if he was recalling the last time he'd been inside Stonehouse—uninvited, picking through her things. As if on cue, he reached into his pocket and withdrew the engraved silver watch. "I wanted to return this."

The disbelief must have been evident on Amelia's face, because he continued, "It isn't mine. Hadn't been mine for an eternity—for longer than it was. It was Cathy's, and you should have it. Since it reminds you of her. It doesn't hold any good memories for me."

Carefully, she took it, cupped the familiar, smooth weight in her palm, ran her thumb over the scrolled letters: *WS*. She'd once asked what they stood for, but Lucy had shrugged and said she didn't know, that she'd found it in a shop and liked the look of it. Amelia felt a twinge at the memory.

"Thank you," she said. She thought to add that it meant even more to her now that she knew it had originally been his, but she wasn't brave enough. Still, she blushed as she slipped the watch into her pocket.

Mr. Sisson looked away in deference to her, but perhaps also to conceal the color in his own face. He seized on the nearest distracting object at hand. A dark-brown clothbound tome, rather thick, the spine embossed in gold: *Moby Dick; or, The Whale*. He laughed. "Are you sure this is what you want to be reading before we go out in a little boat one-fifth the size of such creatures?"

"Yes. 'Ignorance is the parent of fear,' after all. Have you read it?"

"Parts. I may have skimmed others."

"Well, I've devoured the entire thing at least once a year since it came out. I seem to find something new every time. What do you like, then? Shakespeare?"

"Who doesn't?"

"Is he your namesake?"

"No. My grandfather was William, and his father before him, and on back through the ages. But before Banquo, I had a Beatrice, a Prospero, and a Puck."

Amelia laughed. "Our cats were all named after Roman gods and goddesses when I was little. Mother's idea. Juno was the sweetest of them. And Lucy—she had a spoiled old Pomeranian for a while, but that Scottish witch wouldn't allow pets when we moved in, so Lucy gave him to a friend. Mozart. That was the dog's name, I mean."

Mr. Sisson smiled. "Catherine always did like animals. Tried to sneak home every stray she came across."

"I think that's what she did with me."

∼

Amelia wasn't so quick to succumb to a dour mood when the next Sunday was socked in too. Now she had a different sort of hope and was gratified when Mr. Sisson once again knocked on her door. This time, he carried a knapsack, full of tea supplies.

He set about filling the kettle and lighting the stove while Amelia dusted the kitchen table, which she never used. "I'm a terrible house-keeper! A terrible hostess too."

"That's not what Banquo tells me." Among his tea things, he'd even brought shortbread, precious cargo picked up in San Francisco. "I don't share these with anyone, as a rule."

"Well, I'm honored."

"There is a strict two-biscuit limit, though." He couldn't keep a straight face. "No, we should finish them before they go stale. When they run out, I'll make us scones."

"You will?"

"Mm-hmm, and you'll be terribly impressed. I've had to fend for myself for . . . quite a long time now, so I've learned a thing or two to make it more enjoyable."

Through a bite of shortbread, Amelia said, "I haven't. Had to fend for myself, I mean. Not for a long while now. I'd probably starve if Mrs. Clifford and Mrs. Pollard didn't feed me. I bet they'd clean for me too—of course I wouldn't let them."

"Right, weren't you a maid back in the city?"

"Yes, but I got paid for that. It's only this room I'm neglecting, any-way. Well, and the dust is probably an inch thick in the second bedroom by now. But I've never had so much space to myself. It still feels strange. Almost as strange as taking goat milk in my tea."

He smiled as he poured. "I have fantasized so many times about wrangling a dairy cow ashore, but this does the trick, once you get used to it."

"Mrs. Pollard said they're getting a new buck next time the *Shubrick* comes."

"Ah, yes, the sacrificial stud."

They only kept two milking goats on the island, bred them once a year to keep them productive, but preferred to roast the male once he'd served his purpose. Amelia didn't inquire about the kids.

"At least he gets to have a good time before he goes into the stew-pot," she mused.

Mr. Sisson chuckled. "All any of us can ask for, really."

And sometimes even that was too much. But just then, nothing else existed beyond the kitchen table and the tea and the two of them, and that nutshell universe was as big as Amelia wanted.

~

Finally, on the last Sunday of the month, they were favored with clear weather. When Mr. Sisson knocked at Stonehouse, he was alone— Amelia remembered what he'd said about Banquo hating boats—and he was in his rolled-above-the-elbows shirtsleeves again.

She nearly ran ahead of him to the landing.

His own boat was similar in size to the keepers' dory, sixteen feet long, equipped with oars as well as a jury-rigged sail. Amelia descended the stairs to the beach and waited while he lowered the rowboat. The urge to unlace her boots and yank them off, peel away her stockings, was almost overwhelming. It had been well over a decade since she'd last had sand beneath her bare feet, felt it shift her weight as the water undermined the malleable grains, reveled in the push and pull of chilly surf against her calves.

But she wasn't a little girl anymore, nor was she a man, and there were certain rules of propriety she supposed she ought to follow. She settled for bending over to dig her fingers into the wet sand and dabble them in the shallow water where it met the beach. At the lower portions of the rocks, revealed by the receding tide, she spotted flame-orange starfish and seaweed-colored crabs, amethyst urchins and emerald anemones. A trove usually hidden from human eyes.

Mr. Pollard was taking the keepers' boat out too; it was a fine day, after all, and they hadn't had fish for supper in some time. Mrs. Pollard, Finn, and Claire were going with him. Fiona stayed behind, playing paper dolls with Phyllis, maybe. Amelia wondered that Joy hadn't come along with them, worried she might not have been invited. She almost asked Mr. Sisson to wait while she ran back to see if the girl would like to go too. Pure selfishness stopped her. She didn't want to delay another moment, nor did she wish to share his company.

He extended his hand to help Amelia onto the boat. She didn't need the assistance, but took it anyway, let her fingers trail against his as she sat—conscious that he was complicit in prolonging the gesture, didn't pull away when he could have.

They pushed off while the Pollards were still up on the landing. Both parties waved to each other; Amelia might only have imagined Mrs. Pollard's movements were a little frantic.

"Keeping an eye on you?" Mr. Sisson said, and she shot back:

"Keeping an eye on *you*."

They laughed and Amelia felt the water move them forward, couldn't help but laugh some more.

He coaxed her to help trim the sail. She pulled in the sheet and watched the curve of canvas as it caught the wind, felt the closest she'd ever come to having wings.

A pod of dolphins—twenty strong—joined them not long after, sleek pewter shadows racing alongside the boat just under the surface of the sea, leaping from the waves for the sheer thrill of it, it seemed. Playing peekaboo, or tag, with them, with each other.

It would have been enough, but soon, the whales finally appeared. First, they spotted geysers of mist blooming from the ocean. Glistering patches of skin like India rubber coats appeared above the waterline, mere hints at the stupendous bodies still below.

Amelia gasped when a white flipper taller than the Fresnel lens rose toward the sky just beyond their bow, laughed when it slapped the surface with a great shower of salt water that speckled everything back to the stern. Then a pointed head emerged, a warty-nosed giant with a thickly ridged throat. It stood proud of the waves like another small island before sinking back out of sight.

And at last, a creature the size of a train car launched its entire body straight up out of the ocean, an unfathomable power paired with an unlikely, seemingly incompatible grace. It leaped again and sent its huge, hulking frame into a spiral like a pirouetting dancer, like Joy promised.

It was a thing of bewildering, impossible beauty. It crashed back into the sea with a cloud of spray that pattered upon Amelia's face, already wet with tears.

She was mesmerized, enchanted. Yet slightly unnerved. It wasn't only the sheer size of the animals; these unlikely creatures—or their cousins—had plied Amelia's nightmares long before she ever read Melville.

Her father told gruesome fairy tales about killing the mammoth things. They'd harpoon a beast twice the size of their twenty-five-foot whaleboat and be zipped along at fifteen or twenty knots on a Nantucket sleighride. Their teeth clacked in their heads and their arses bounced off their seats while the very nails holding the boat together flew from the boards.

The hooked whale would sound; they'd pay out while it plumbed the depths, but eventually it would surface, and tire. Then they'd haul themselves in alongside. Sometimes they'd have to stab it ten, fifteen, thirty times before finding its huge, throbbing heart beneath all that hard fat and tough skin. When the gyrating blade found its home, it was to the cry of "Chimney's afire!" And a prodigious spout of blood and gore rained down upon all and sundry as the whale's lungs flooded.

The wounded creature would thrash in circles like a one-winged bird, churning up the water. Meanwhile, it disgorged chunks of squid and fish and the most fetid fluids from its spike-toothed jaw. Its gushing blood stained the whole sea red. Then, all at once, the throes would cease, its sudden silence and stillness profound. Naught but a boulder of dead flesh they towed back to the ship.

Then came the flensing. Her father told of knives and hooks and winches tearing strips of blubber off the unwieldy carcass, like peeling the thick rind off an orange. But it was a reeking, strange-shaped fruit leaking oil and blood instead of juice, befouling men and timbers alike. The hacked-up blubber was rendered in try-pots, iron cauldrons that billowed enough greasy black smoke to obliterate the moon above.

Below, the bloody decks and fat-smeared men and lofty rigging were all lit red with flames like the whole ship was afire, like Satan himself was sailing out from hell and they were his demons.

But sometimes, her father warned, the whale was not the only victim, or even a doomed figure at all. Men drowned in the oil-sloshing pits of cut-off whale heads, were pulled out slippery and limp as stillborn babes, lungs full of the precious fluid of the spermy fish, a waste on all accounts.

Forked tails broad as wagon sides smashed whaleboats and bodies both, thick wood and sturdy bones breaking with resounding cracks as easily as matchsticks snapped betwixt thumb and finger.

And once, a God-sized beast with teeth like ivory daggers and a bluff-like head with a malevolent brain buried deep inside it stove the whaling ship itself to kindling.

Her father and other men scrambled into lifeboats, crumbs floating on the water, left adrift to suffer for nearly one hundred days and nights. Blistered and blinded by the sun, skin corroded from the relentless salt, reduced almost to groaning skeletons as they were forced to eat the only meat left once food was gone, only eight of them had survived, Amelia's father among them.

This poetry, this litany, of violence and terror had infected her young mind and never left her, no matter how far from it Amelia ran.

But she tried again to push it all from her head and her heart, to let them be filled by the spectacle of the gentle humpbacks instead.

～

That whole week, she was buoyed by the memory of those living whales she saw with Mr. Sisson, untroubled even in slumber.

Then, on Friday, a red waver through the window woke her at midnight. Amelia's first thought was fire; her breath turned to hot ash. But there were no flames, no plumes of smoke—instead, huge ribbons of vermilion light rippled across the sky. Undulating curtains of scarlet luminescence bathed the island in a ruddy glow. The ocean glimmered as though molten.

Amelia could conceive of no earthly explanation. She cowered in fear of the world combusting at any second. Surely this was a sign of her own impending doom. She was too petrified to leave her bed.

But she pressed her forehead to the window and saw a dark figure near the edge of the rocks, its back to her, its face raised to the crimson glow, like a man on the prow of a massive ship cleaving the bloody sea. It was Salter; the bulk of him was unmistakable. Amelia strained to hear the prayers she was certain poured forth from his lips but took no comfort in the notion that he too might think it the end of the world. For him, it would be a rapture. His posture was proud, even ecstatic. She wondered if Gertie cowered at her own window and watched him too.

～

The next morning's sky was unblemished, but the blazing streaks that lit the night were all anyone could speak of. Even Mr. Sisson came to the keepers' breakfast table.

The younger children clung to the possibility of invisible dragons breathing fire, but Mr. Clifford thought they'd seen the aurora borealis.

"Aren't the northern lights green?" Mrs. Pollard said—as if seeking reassurance, for she had been disturbed by the vision too.

Of course, it was silly to think the trembling lights had been anything supernatural, much less meant only for Amelia, any more than they might have been meant for Salter. Still, it was difficult to shake her apprehension even after the matter had been dissected over oatmeal.

Long life to the killers. That was what they used to say on Nantucket. A hearty toast. A wish for good fortune and success.

Her father, a thoroughly fishy man with great greasy luck, had enjoyed both, and the killing itself. The hunt for prey, the promise of dominion. Even having finally given up the water and left the dwindling whales to other men, Amelia did not believe he could ever abandon that quest for vicious glory. And she was the only quarry he had left.

It had been hard to see the hellish glow of phantom try-pots in the sky, the rippling currents of red light like bloody tendrils spreading through black water, and not think them a portent. To see the ocean burning and not see her past, repeating. To see Salter and not see her father himself.

~

On Sunday, Amelia swallowed a lingering bubble of fear and went out again with Mr. Sisson.

They saw a blue whale, less showy than the ballerinas but even more incredible: thirty feet longer than the tremendous humpbacks, truly gargantuan. Like a small steamship gliding underwater—yet incomparable to any man-made object, dwarfing anything so new and trifling as human invention. An immense and ancient presence, a being like no other thing on earth, beholding it an experience of the soul more than of the eyes or the mind. At least as powerful as that strange red aurora, and equally explicable—just like the floating ship Amelia saw as a girl, the day she'd nearly drowned. Later, she'd learned that fata morganas were fairly common optical illusions, but it had still felt like magic, terrifying and thrilling in equal measure. There were innumerable things like that in the world, she supposed. She felt herself begin to grow preternaturally calm.

"Did you know Mr. Salter used to be a whaler?" she said.

"I hadn't heard that, no."

"My father was, too. A captain. Hard, from heart to hands. He was gone two and three years at a time, only home for a matter of months before he left again. But we were all happier when he was away. When he came back, he told the bloodiest bedtime stories; I still have images in my head of horrible things I never even saw myself. When I was little, they were monsters to me, the whales. More myths than anything. I saw pictures and paintings, of course, even bones enough, but they were all fished far out to sea long before I was born. I used to hear older people talk about when the men would kill whales just offshore, drag them straight up onto the beaches. Yet I still couldn't quite believe they were real."

Mr. Sisson regarded her with a rapt expression but said nothing. Amelia stared at the whale.

"I see them now and part of me still can't comprehend it. Can you imagine the first person to throw a lance at one of these creatures? The sheer audacity of it."

"Hubris," Mr. Sisson said.

"Exactly. Some men would come face-to-face with God and the very first thing they'd do is try to kill Him."

~

Amelia benefited from the deaths of whales, of course, like everyone else around her. Steel and coal and kerosene were gaining ground, but whalebone still girded the corset and cage crinoline she'd worn for years.

The flexible, tough, and springy stuff was in her umbrella too. It was in the wool winder Mrs. Clifford kept in her sewing basket.

Mr. Pollard's backscratcher was made of whale ivory, as was his chess set—and Amelia's own knitting needles, too. Whale oil lit their lamps, fueled the very lighthouse beam they shone out across the sea, greased the gears of the clockwork mechanism that made the lens turn. It was even in the soap Mrs. Pollard used to scrub her children's hands and their dirty laundry alike.

Spermaceti candles burned clear and true, just like the one that shone the last light on Lucy's face. Ambergris lengthened the life of her perfume.

There was no escaping the presence of those great oceanic dwellers in the terrestrial world, the remnants of such mighty yet mortal animals underpinning so much of what Amelia touched. A truth not unique to her, but perhaps uniquely disturbing. And yet, something she could live with, let sink into her subconscious most of the time.

Twenty-One

An Unexpected Guest

Six days later, the *Shubrick* returned with a dowdy raincoat, new schoolbooks, the usual load of oil, firewood, and paint, stores of hay and onions and potatoes, and the ill-fated male goat.

The crew that came onto the island to visit used the stairs up from the sea. The captain, once he'd greeted his eager audience at the landing, announced a surprise. "We've brought a visitor for Miss Riley!"

Amelia's heart plummeted into her stomach. Crimson light pulsed behind her eyes.

"Who is it?" Mrs. Pollard asked when Amelia couldn't find her own voice.

"A Miss Price. An old friend, I gather. Look at her, she can barely speak!"

Though she wanted to sprint to Stonehouse and barricade herself inside, Amelia fixed her feet in place. She managed to keep some semblance of a smile on her face; her shock could be forgiven, she supposed, or conveniently misconstrued. The wait was unbearable, but finally, the first boatful of goods was hauled up the side of the cliff. Amid the cargo sat Miss Price, whoever she was. A beautiful woman, dressed in a frock far too fine for the occasion—candy-shop stripes of rose and mauve and cream—her crow-black hair coiffed neatly enough for a ball beneath a flower-bedecked green bonnet. Mr. Salter glared openly at her, of course.

She looked a bit disoriented as she was helped onto solid ground. She minced away from the edge of the landing. Her bright, dark eyes scanned the group twice, a hint of a frown beginning to shadow them, before she fastened her gaze on Amelia and fashioned a smile of her own.

"*Lucy*," she said, advancing in a confectionary flounce of satin skirts. "My goodness, pet, I hardly recognized you!" She swept Amelia into a lavender-scented embrace, murmured under cover of the cool press of her powdered cheek, "Play along, dear."

Amelia did, though she remained silent.

Miss Price beamed at their observers. "Please forgive us if we go catch up for a few moments, won't you; it's been so long. We'll join you all again in just a little while. We have *so* much to talk about!"

Amelia allowed her arm to be looped through this stranger's and her body to be towed off up the path, though she had to steer them toward the right house, which felt miles away.

As they went, she looked in vain for Mr. Sisson. He must have been on the other side of the hill, putting a fresh coat of whitewash on the barracks or scraping moss from his roof in advance of the rains. Or perhaps he sat before his hearth, Banquo at his feet. Amelia pictured it and felt wholly bereft.

～

Inside Stonehouse, Miss Price hustled her toward the stairs, then whirled Amelia about and pushed her back another few inches. Her heels knocked against the bottom step; she almost stumbled.

"Who are you?" the woman said, a new chill in her voice that raised gooseflesh.

With a deep breath and a decision not to bother with the put-on accent, Amelia managed an equally cool response. "Lucy's friend. Who are you?"

"The same. A *friend* of Lucy's. A very good one."

"Does your name start with E?" Amelia asked.

Miss Price ignored her. "You're that little cunt she lived with, aren't you? The one whose name ended up in the paper. Lavinia something. Henry?"

Amelia let Miss Price interpret her silence however she liked.

"What the hell happened to her?"

"There was a fire. It was an accident."

"*Liar.* If it was an accident, then why are you walking around pretending to be her? Why did you take all her things?"

"I didn't. And I'm not. I'm not 'walking around' pretending to be her; I'm barely living in public. I just wanted to remember her, to honor her. And I didn't take her things. Though if she'd had a will, Lucy would have left everything to me anyway."

"I'm sure," Miss Price sneered. "Where's her fucking necklace, then?"

Amelia made a face to indicate how tedious she found the woman's language; somehow, it made it easier to keep calm, or at least to pretend. "I put everything in storage. I only brought a few keepsakes with me. But someone broke into the warehouse and stole her jewelry."

"Not that piece. With rubies and diamonds?"

"What is your name?" Amelia said.

"Eva, Goddamn it. Now, where is it? I know you have it."

The necklace felt like a millstone sewn into Amelia's hem, but the lie came out shockingly swift and smooth. "No. Lucy sold that one."

Surprise softened Miss Price's aspect, but not her tone. "You're *lying.*"

Amelia shrugged. "She said she wouldn't need it anymore, out here. And she wanted money to get supplies, for the schoolroom and whatnot. So she sold it."

"She wouldn't."

The genuine hurt that undermined Miss Price's voice made Amelia pause, but only for a second.

"I assume you gave it to her, then? I do have the money she got for it. I'll give that to you, gladly."

When Miss Price didn't reply, Amelia steeled herself and turned her back, started up the stairs. The woman followed and grabbed her elbow. "If you're planning on going for a weapon, you'd better not."

"I'm going for the money. If you want it."

After a moment, Miss Price released Amelia's arm and shadowed her into her room.

"It's under the bed; I need to move it away from the wall."

The woman made no move to help, but stationed herself close to the washstand, seeming ready to pick up the porcelain ewer and smash it against Amelia's skull if the need arose.

She pulled the bed frame out of the way and crouched to pry up a loose floorboard, which concealed Lucy's old tea tin stuffed with a rolled wad of bills, permeated with the lingering scent of the smoky leaves. "It's about three hundred," she said, and held the tin out toward Miss Price, who took it, glanced inside. Amelia didn't intend to sound mocking when she added, "I hope that's at least what you paid for it."

Miss Price bared her teeth, slashed a finger at the bed. "Sit down!"

When Amelia hesitated, the woman reached into her reticule and withdrew a pistol—so small it looked like a toy, but it still sent fear thudding through Amelia.

"Wrap your arms around the post."

She did. Miss Price set down the gun and the tea tin, came over to tie Amelia's wrists together around one of the bed frame's spindles, with a ribbon she pulled from her own bonnet. The knot was tight, the silk cutting into Amelia's flesh. The sensation of the soft, strangling fabric frightened her more than anything had thus far. She couldn't have screamed even if she'd been brave—and stupid—enough to try.

Tied to the spindle, Amelia watched as Miss Price upended her room. She pulled out and overturned every drawer, searched the pockets of every dress, shook out every chemise and stocking—even the blood-browned cloth pouches Amelia stuffed with flannel and tied to the waistband of her drawers each month. Eva opened every small box she found and scattered their contents: hairpins, spare buttons, mending thread, assorted mementos that meant nothing to her. She flipped through the notebooks but tossed them aside.

With a warning not to move, she went to the bedroom across the hall.

Amelia heard her open the closet there, then a choked utterance that must have been triggered by the sea elephant skull before Eva pounded downstairs and rummaged through the parlor and the kitchen.

Crockery and cast iron clashed, cupboard doors slammed, slates cracked, drawers squeaked and squealed. Amelia had a ridiculous fear for the fragile bird skulls on the mantel, for the defenseless pages of her books. The fireplace tools were overturned with a windchime-like clinking of brass against the tiles.

All the while, the absurdly little gun sat just across the room where Miss Price had left it, but even if she could have broken free of her fetters, Amelia's legs were leaden. They would tangle like a lame fawn's and send her crashing to the floor; she had the sense she might shatter into fragments.

She knew no one would come by to bother them, unless—if Mr. Sisson went to the keepers' quarters and Mrs. Pollard cheerfully announced Miss Riley had a visitor, then he would race to Stonehouse to see what was happening. Amelia was sure of it.

Though he was her only hope, she despised the thought of him coming to her rescue. He could be harmed, or could harm this woman, and it would be Amelia's fault. It was all such ugly proof of her own idiocy, besides. She would rather face her fate alone. That was what she deserved.

Finally, Miss Price returned, flushed and out of breath.

Despite her burning-numb, discolored hands and the tears clotting her lashes, Amelia mustered a convincing facsimile of composure. "I told you, it's gone. Just take the money and leave me alone."

Miss Price advanced toward the bed. She brought her face so hideously close they could have kissed. "Kitty wouldn't even dream of leaving you. She said you needed her. Needed protecting. But I don't know about that."

The name *Kitty* sent an agonizing bolt of shock through her, even before Miss Price plunged her hand into Amelia's pocket and came up with the engraved silver watch. Eva looked at it for a gut-wrenchingly protracted moment, then tossed it on the bed. Finding nothing else, she seized Amelia by the collar as if she might rip her dress open and see what spilled out.

"So, what, did you poison her? Slide a knife between her poor sweet ribs before you set her on fire to make it look like an accident?"

"No. She got drunk and fell asleep with her candle burning. I wasn't there that night. I wish I had been. I'd give anything for her to be alive."

Miss Price's face wavered, as if she, too, might cry. But only for a moment. Then her well-mannered mask was back in place and she looked away, to the perfume bottle on the plain pine vanity. She'd passed over it before, intent on searching for the necklace, but now she went to it and picked it up, removed the stopper, and closed her eyes as she inhaled. Gentle as Miss Price was with the bottle, Amelia's urge to scream at her to put it down was almost impossible to repress. "Kitty always did like a good time," Miss Price said in a rather wistful tone as she replaced the stopper and the bottle.

When she looked again at Amelia, her eyes hardened to onyx; her voice, the set of her shoulders and her jaw, all likewise petrified. "She

should have just told me when she left New York. She should have
known I would have helped her, that I wouldn't have ever said a thing.
But she never trusted me. If she had, she'd still be alive, wouldn't she?
Even if you didn't kill her, it's still your fault."

More tears rolled down Amelia's cheeks, which seemed to make
Miss Price angrier.

"There's *something* wrong with you. Nobody in their right mind
would do what you did, would they? Nobody innocent. You must have
some reason . . ."

"Maybe I was mad with grief. Maybe I still am."

Miss Price's laugh was caustic. "You seem perfectly cozy here to
me. I should go over there right now and tell them all you're not who
you say you are."

"Feel free. They won't believe you. They know me."

"They *think* they do."

"Yes. And they'll want to keep believing that."

Eva came to lean close again. Beneath her lavender perfume wafted
the scent of sweat; decay tinged her breath. Through her teeth, she said,
"Then maybe I should just throttle you right now." She shoved her
thumbs into the hollow of Amelia's throat and said, "Maybe snap your
neck instead, get it over with quicker. Or shoot you in the temple."
She poked the side of Amelia's head with a sharp index finger. "I'd do
it against your pillow so it muffles the sound. Then I could tuck you in
and tell them you're sleeping when I go back out—just so overwhelmed
at the surprise of seeing me again. Be at least halfway back to San
Francisco before anybody even notices. Long gone before they can do
anything about it."

It won't bring Lucy back, Amelia thought. *You'd get caught. You
wouldn't even make it off the island. Go ahead; I don't care.*

Bluffs, all of them, wild hopes and diversion tactics and lies that
raced through her head, but she couldn't trust her voice to come out
steady. Besides, she understood the power of silence. Amelia focused

on making her eyes into tide pools, still water over dark stone, the intimation of strange and potentially dangerous creatures hidden there.

Miss Price straightened up with a bitter laugh. "You are crazy. You take a dead woman's name and all her money and then you go live on some desolate fucking rock in the middle of the ocean? It doesn't make sense. Unless . . . whoever you really are—oh, it must be bad, huh? You must be hiding from someone. Maybe someone just like him."

A tremor went through Amelia. "Like who?"

Now Miss Price was the one to leverage the silence.

Though she loathed the rising volume and jagged desperation in her voice, Amelia couldn't control it. "Like *who*?"

Her visitor smiled, a sadistic twist of her lips. "Kitty didn't mention him either, hmm? I'm not surprised. I should have told him the second I saw her, just like she thought I would. But I was worried he might do something rash. Like cut her heart out. Only way he could have ever had it for himself. Maybe he'll take yours instead."

When Amelia trembled harder, Miss Price said with a lilt in her voice, "Then again, I might not say a thing."

She tucked the tea tin and tiny pistol into her handbag, then reached into a pocket, produced a pearl-handled straight razor, folded into itself. As she crossed the floor toward the bed, she unsheathed the blade. Came to hold it so close to Amelia's face she could have pared off her eyelashes with a flick of her dainty hand. "But suppose I can find out who you really are, little Vinny Henry. See who's after you now that I'm done. Might be worth my trouble."

Amelia set her jaw and did not shrink from the weapon, nor from the threat. "No one's after me but ghosts."

"Maybe. For now."

Miss Price lowered the razor so quickly it wouldn't have surprised Amelia to look down and see her own intestines tumbling into her lap—but she only cut the ribbon around Amelia's wrists. It was so tight against her flesh, the blade nicked her skin. A thin, bright line of blood appeared like an arrow pointing to her thumb. They both looked at it with rather detached expressions.

When she slipped the folded razor back into her pocket, Miss Price pulled out a handkerchief and tossed it on the bed. "A little token to remember me by. Besides, you don't want to bleed all over that quaint dress."

The blood continued to well up in the cut; a moment before the surface tension broke and a bead of crimson rolled down the side of her hand, Amelia picked up the scented square of linen and pressed it to the thread-thin wound.

"You'd better stay in here for a while yet. Until you hear the ship sound off, at least. I'll tell them you're resting, not to be disturbed."

In the doorway of the ransacked bedroom, Miss Price looked back at her. "I hope you know how lucky you are. But don't forget, luck runs out."

Twenty-Two

PROSTRATION

It could have been hours or merely five minutes that Amelia sat there staring at the opposite wall. She hadn't heard the steam whistle yet, but she hadn't heard anything else either, ears full of an empty, howling desolation. Something beyond fear and past sorrow, colder and emptier, filled the space in her chest and sent its tendrils probing all throughout her body.

There was still wan sunlight in the room when Amelia heard the door open below, a voice call out "Hello?" Alarm in it, even before he would have had time to take in the disarray of either kitchen or parlor. A few beats of silence in which he must have done just that, then his footsteps thumping up the stairs.

Like a child who thinks the act might make them invisible, Amelia closed her eyes. She heard Mr. Sisson enter the room, stride across the floorboards—yet she started when she felt his hand cup her own. He knelt before her, plucked the handkerchief away. The blood had dried it to Amelia's skin, and the fabric pulled. He winced in sympathy, looked from the shallow cut to her eyes.

She slid her hand free. "It's nothing."

But he reached for her again, fixated on the bloody line, a seam that could have undone Amelia, that undid him.

"Oh, God," he said. It was so much like a plea, Amelia thought he might lay his head in her lap. She might stroke his hair and shush him.

"It's *fine*." She stood abruptly, brushed past him to her washstand and swabbed the flakes of rust from her skin, which tingled where he'd touched it.

There were still red lines around her wrists. They would turn to plum-blue bruises that she would have to make sure her sleeves covered, lest Mrs. Pollard or Mrs. Clifford notice. She would explain the cut by saying she'd tried to slice her own bread for toast. They would laugh; she would too.

Mr. Sisson stood several paces behind Amelia. "So that was her. Eva Price?"

Amelia glanced at his face in the looking glass and he rushed to clarify:

"Mrs. Pollard introduced us—and I came straight over. What did she do to you?"

"Nothing. She just came for the necklace." Amelia felt the air displaced behind her as he stepped closer.

"They haven't left yet. I can—"

"No. She got what she wanted. It's done."

"She hurt you."

This time, Amelia allowed herself to meet his eyes in the mirror for a longer moment. "It was an accident. It'll be gone in a week or two. I'll have forgotten all about her by then."

He ignored Amelia's lie, her affected calm, made no effort to disguise his own emotions when she wished he would. "I should have come to the landing when I heard the ship. But I didn't think . . . My God, what might have happened. Please, forgive me."

Amelia's tone was as sharp as his was gentle. "All of this was my own doing."

"No," he said. "I should have told you."

She turned with a rustle of skirts, a flutter in her heart. "Told me what?"

He hesitated but had the decency and strength not to drop his gaze. "That you were right. That 'E' went to your boardinghouse, and the landlady told her everything. Your name, how it was really Cathy that . . . about the storage compartment. All of it."

Wings beat harder in Amelia's chest. "You knew that?"

"The *Bulletin* article listed the address, so when I was in town, I went to the boardinghouse too—"

"What? *Why?* Because you didn't believe me. You wanted to see if Mrs. McGowan's story matched mine."

"No, because I wanted to know if anyone had been round asking before me. And I should have told you that they were—"

"But you didn't! You acted like I was still imagining things. You said it could have been a coincidence."

The guilt in his eyes almost made Amelia feel sorry for him, but her heart hardened, as if to protect itself, at the tenderness in his voice when he said, "I didn't want to frighten you any more than you already were."

In reply, she emitted a sound of pure scorn; she wished it had been enough to make him stop speaking, but he continued to attempt to explain himself.

"I didn't have any proof that she *had* gotten your address. The clerk at Waldham wouldn't tell me when I asked for it, said it was against their policy. And if she did turn up, I certainly didn't expect it to be on the *Shubrick*. I thought I would . . ."

With every word, Amelia felt more intense tremors in her body. As he trailed off, she bent to pick up her strewn-about underthings, as much to hide them from his sight as for some activity in which to redirect the nervous energy overwhelming her.

In her right and rational mind, she knew it was preposterous, but when Miss Price had referred to some mysterious *he*, it had occurred to

Amelia: she could have meant none other than Mr. Sisson. Amelia didn't believe it, yet her traitorous, inconstant heart flooded with dismay.

The lie of omission about going to see Mrs. McGowan was a comparatively small thing, but he had no right to hide the fact that someone else had come sniffing around the boardinghouse first. If she'd known, Amelia might have run.

Was that why he hadn't told her? And what else had he still not said?

She'd come to trust him implicitly at some point, possibly as soon as he forgave her own deception—but hadn't he done that far too easily and completely? Shouldn't that have made her more leery of his motivations, and not less concerned?

She couldn't justify her fear with logic; the idea that he was a danger to her made no sense, would crumble if she could only meet his honest, lovely eyes. She sank to her knees before the armoire, rumpled chemises wadded in her arms.

"Please," he said, and made as if to help her up, but Amelia turned her shoulder.

"No. You should go. You shouldn't even be in here."

When she chanced to look at him, the distress on his face was unbearable. She said the same words she'd spoken the first time they'd been alone in this place, though now they were without teeth, a whisper, not a hiss. "Get out."

This time, he did flinch—but again, he obeyed her command.

She wished, in some sick, shameful, secret part of herself, that he'd refused, that he'd grabbed her wrist again, shoved her back against the armoire.

If Amelia knew she should be afraid of him, then she could shield herself, and that might be easier, less terrifying than the abject adoration that threatened to fill her now.

She put Stonehouse back in order as the daylight waned, lit no fire or lamps or candles as night fell. Around seven, a tapping on the door gave her pause, but when she opened it a few minutes later, all she found was a covered plate of food on the top step. She brought it in and picked at it but wasn't hungry.

Later, nightmares reeled through Amelia's mind, though she barely slept. Her fingertip kept brushing the razored line on her hand. A little deeper, a little to one side, and she might have bled to death. It would have been all the same to Miss Price, she surmised.

Ruminating over her, Amelia realized she'd seen the resplendent woman once before. Roughly fifteen months before the fire, she and Lucy had been traipsing about downtown. Something had, just for an instant, stopped Lucy in her tracks. That was not an easy thing to do, which was why Amelia herself had stiffened and followed Lucy's gaze. She'd glimpsed that jet hair and refined brow and a similarly garish dress ballooning beneath that tidy waist—she was all but sure of it.

Lucy had barely broken her stride before she'd turned Amelia about, with a gay laugh and a proclamation of having just decided on some much better destination for them—Dawson's ice cream parlor. In another moment, Amelia had forgotten she'd ever noticed Lucy falter.

She didn't even think of it when, halfway through their ices, Lucy claimed to have forgotten some essential errand and begged off with profuse apologies. She'd kissed Amelia's cheek as she left, promised to catch up with her a little later. Not two hours hence, she'd come home, her manner so breezy, Amelia never doubted she'd gone anywhere other than the place she'd named.

Now, Amelia couldn't bear to imagine where Lucy might have hurried off to that afternoon, what she might have done once there. She refused to let herself be tempted into such torturous exercises. But she couldn't erase the knowledge that Lucy had spent time with that minacious woman and had cared for her once—or that she'd spoken of Amelia to that harpy, truthfully and perhaps tenderly, which seemed even worse.

Vinny. To hear that nickname on those venomous lips split Amelia's heart asunder, left a line of poison. *Kitty*, too. Miss Price had presumably known Lucy's real name and had her own pet version of it.

By comparison, it seemed, Amelia had known nothing. A fragile little thing that needed protecting, indeed. A broken bird that could never fly again—but, carried snug in Lucy's pocket or perched upon her soft shoulder, she would have never known the difference; she would have sworn she soared.

Twenty-Three

ABSOLUTION

The day that followed Miss Price's visit was a blur. Amelia taught lessons but remembered nothing of what they'd worked on. She ate meals at the keepers' quarters without tasting anything and frustrated everyone by brushing off their excited questions about her caller. "She said you used to know each other back in New York!" Mrs. Pollard beamed, hoping for more details, which Amelia didn't furnish. She barely slept for the second night in a row.

And then it was Sunday, but she felt impossibly distant from the previous week's end, when she'd beheld the blue whale, when Mr. Sisson had watched her marvel at the splendid creature, and in him, she'd sensed a kindred recognition of sublimity.

Why hadn't she been more cautious? How could she have let herself see only what she wanted to? A link, a lifeline, a way past the brick wall of death that had cut her off from Lucy. Why take him at his word when he was still, essentially, a stranger? Why not ask him—why not demand to hear—what his time with Lucy (*Cathy*, Amelia's brain interjected) had been like, and precisely how and when they'd parted?

Because she didn't want to know. At first, because it would have damaged her perception of Lucy. But then, perhaps, because it might have altered her perception of Mr. Sisson too.

He said he'd abandoned Lucy—Cathy—but under what circumstances? He'd admitted that she hated him, yet Amelia had seen no indication of that in the diaries. Confusion, yes, conflicted feelings, but no evidence that she'd borne him ill will.

Before, Amelia had assumed that Lucy held herself back from reaching out to him because she'd loved Amelia too, because they'd pledged to spend the rest of their lives together—until Lucy saw the teaching post and interpreted a different destiny.

But what if Mr. Sisson's suspicions were more accurate, and Lucy had only wanted him to help her out of a difficult situation with Miss Price? *The devil*, she'd written. A woman Lucy hadn't trusted and had wanted to strangle, the necklace a tether, not a token of affection. But then the question remained: why had Lucy not reached out to Will directly, immediately?

Was it for the same reason she thought he could help her? Because he was dangerous, had a capacity for violence? Hadn't he said he could have killed that egger? And blatantly threatened to shoot him in front of everyone? Even if it was partially in Amelia's defense. He'd told her once that he used to be a completely different person.

And while he hadn't known Miss Price, they'd both called Lucy by different versions of her true name. She'd known them long before Amelia ever met her. She'd seemed determined to leave them in the past—yet had been compelled to locate Mr. Sisson well before Miss Price found her. And even then, even if Lucy had thought he could help, she'd still hesitated to call on him. Either she'd been afraid to, or she'd been too proud. Lucy was always resourceful, fiercely self-reliant. She'd preferred to handle all affairs on her own. But then the newspaper ad for the Farallones—the hand of fate, nudging her toward him at last.

It sounded mad, but no less than other things Amelia already knew were true. Even if her conjecture was correct, she'd never know why Lucy had kept it all a secret. Perhaps it was because she hadn't wanted Amelia to worry or had been trying to protect her from danger herself.

It was useless to speculate, impossible not to.

It might all be over now, all crises averted, if only Amelia had come back home that night. She imagined Lucy would have apologized, would have told her everything. Amelia would have done the same. She would have helped Lucy out of whatever dilemma she'd worked so hard to conceal. And then she might be with her this very moment, and her heart would not be so irreparably broken.

~

Folded in a wingback chair, Amelia tried to read. But her thoughts kept circling back on themselves, until—as if she'd summoned him—she heard Mr. Sisson's knock on the door. By now, she couldn't mistake it for someone else's.

She waited until he knocked again, then went, opened the door only wide enough to form a wedge. His voice failed him, but she saw Banquo wasn't there. To forestall any awkward invitation, she said, "I'm staying in today."

"Of course. But—may I speak with you? Please."

Amelia kept her eyes on the threshold between them and said, "Not here."

Softly, she shut the door. Dawdled long enough with her boots and things that she wondered if he might be gone when she opened it again—but thought even if she waited until morning, he would still be there.

~

They walked east toward the unobstructed sea, until they turned around the curve of Tower Hill and continued to the chapel.

Amelia kept her head bent, bonnet obscuring most of her face, but felt his eyes on her.

"How are you?" he said, a strain in his voice she felt in her own throat.

"Fine," she lied.

"I'm sorry. I know there's nothing I can possibly say that—"

"I'm not angry with you," she interrupted, plainly, placidly. "Stop apologizing."

When he acceded with silence, Amelia glanced at him. There was nothing to read in his face but unendurable concern and affection.

She went first inside the chapel. As before, she took the end of the pew nearest the rough stone altar. Mr. Sisson hesitated a moment, then crossed in front and sat beside Amelia. Not too close, yet a mere two or three inches between them instead of the entire gaping aisle this time. Upon her lap, she clasped her hands as if in prayer, but her heart was as empty as her head.

They gazed at the bare wall, marked only by a square of sunlight unstained by any colored glass, a luminous window upon the white-washed stone. A shadow flashed across it, made it seem to waver, a magic portal on the verge of closing.

Presently, Amelia spoke.

"I did think for a moment she might really kill me. Miss Price. She threatened all sorts of things. And yet the worst of it, somehow, was that . . . she knew Lucy. And I didn't know *her*. I can't abide the thought of them breathing the same air. But most of all, I can't seem to come to terms with just how much I didn't *know*. More and more all the time. I imagine you could fill a book with things I have no earthly idea of about . . . Cathy."

The very name was a lamentation on her tongue. She drew in a deep, fortifying breath. "Will you tell me how you met?"

Mr. Sisson frowned. "How we met?"

"For a start."

He shook his head as if to dispel confusion. "Cathy was my sister."

Amelia's breath caught. How was it that such shocks were still capable of jolting her? She felt numb as she said, "Lucy told me, once, that she'd had a brother. But—she said he'd died when she was only young."

Anguish cleaved Mr. Sisson, fractured his voice. "It must have been easier for her to think of me that way. After what I did."

"Abandoned her," Amelia murmured, and waited for him to continue. When he didn't, she said gently, "What happened?" But there was a raw hunger in her question too.

He looked away. "I left home when I was sixteen. Catherine was only ten. We'd lost our mother, and our father was letting everything run to ruin. So I thought I'd save her—save all of us. Better, I'd elevate us. We were never poor, but I was determined I'd lift us up to a station we deserved. Dream far bigger than our father had.

"He was a sailor—he had been, and his father before him, and on back. Fishermen for generations. Then we moved to the city from Staithes; our father had a shipping firm. Cholera decimated that. But I could handle boats from the time I was a boy. And I knew I'd never find my fortune in Sunderland. So I got a place on a ship, going to Boston. It was horrendous, but I had free passage. That was all that mattered. I could come out here for nothing and make myself into a new man. A rich one, of course."

He spared a bitter chuckle for his childhood aspirations. "I was such a git, with such an empty head for all it was full of dreams. No grasp on reality. Our uncle, our mother's brother—he used to look in on us once in a while. Made sure we weren't starving or completely filthy or running wild. He said he'd look after Cathy. So I didn't worry; I couldn't. I had to go."

Mr. Sisson took a second to gather himself before he went on. "And then there was Lucy. Our Lucy. We grew up with her. She was only a year younger than me, but . . . several steps farther up the ladder. It's a wonder we ever mixed at all, but our fathers were acquainted through business, and our mothers were friendly enough. She loved Cathy like she was her own little sister. Said she loved me too—but I knew even then I'd never win her over in the end. She'd never marry me unless I could offer her a better life than the one she already had. So, two birds, one stone. Complete and utter selfishness under the guise of great nobility. I was hardly original in that."

He sighed and tilted his head back to the ceiling. "I remember Catherine begged me not to go. I felt terribly sorry for leaving her, of course, but I never considered staying. She tried to thrash me. Must have rained down a hundred blows with those soft little fists. And I laughed at her. Fondly, but I'll never forgive myself for that."

He had to stop again, swallow the sharp-edged lump in his throat. "Anyway, she had Lucy to look after her, and our uncle; that's what I told myself. She'd be fine. She'd forgive me. Eventually. Once I showed up with riches enough to buy her anything her heart desired. I would have put her in a castle if she wanted, a little princess. Naturally, Lucy would have been my queen. Christ. As if they would stay trapped in amber while I went off halfway around the world. As if everything else in my life would simply wait. It didn't, of course. They didn't. And I was away for so long."

"Where did you go?" Amelia breathed. "After Boston?"

"I managed to dig up a little gold in Georgia, at the tail end of their rush—nothing like what happened here, but enough to parlay into a string of businesses. Small things, begetting bigger things. Half ownership in a sugar refinery by the end. And all that time—nine years I was gone—I hardly ever wrote home. Just to keep them apprised; I never even gave them a return address. At first, I told myself it was because I'd never be in one place long enough for a reply to possibly reach me. But the truth was, I didn't want to hear from them. I didn't want to know if I'd missed anything important—and after a while, I knew I would have. I didn't want to get homesick. Didn't want to be diverted from my grand mission, but then it never seemed to have an end.

"And then one day I realized I had made a fortune. A modest one, as those things go, but more than I'd ever dared dream of. I could have offered them almost anything—not a castle, but an estate, certainly. A townhouse in London, too. Dresses and jewels and a life of luxury and leisure. If it hadn't been too late for that to mean something. Because by the time I finally came back, our father was dead. Cathy'd gone to stay with our uncle, after. Four years she was with that—vile monster. With the most innocuous smile. I never knew . . . I never dreamed."

Amelia saw how Mr. Sisson clenched his hand. She wanted to place her own upon it but didn't dare, held herself perfectly still.

He heaved another unsteady breath. "Then Lucy married. Quite well, in fact. She took Cathy in with her, as a sort of lady's maid, and then when the children came, she was their governess. She had been educated, so it wasn't only a favor to her. But then . . . our Lucy died too. The husband sent the children off somewhere, turned Cathy out. She found another job, teaching at a school in a town nearby. That's when she started using Lucy's name. But I managed to find her."

"And then?"

He summarized the rest of it as briskly as if he were recounting ordinary business; it was the only way to get through, Amelia knew. "She apprised me of all that I had missed, and she made it very clear that she wanted nothing more to do with me and she would never forgive me, and I believed her, completely. Didn't blame her, of course. I did hold out some hope, but eventually, I gave that up too. I came back to the States—I was on the East Coast then, but I didn't stay much longer. Sold my stake in the business and started looking for lonelier places. Ended up here after a while. Perfect spot to be in exile. And then . . ."

He looked at Amelia with an expression both quizzical and pained. "At first, when they told me about the new teacher, I did think maybe it was just a coincidence, a cruel little trick of fate. But I didn't really believe that, because what universe would take enough notice of me to align the stars in such a way? No, I *knew* she was coming. After all that time. I just had no idea why. Couldn't stop thinking about it, and I couldn't decide what seemed most likely. If she wanted to reconcile, or maybe ask me for something, or—bloody hell, even exact some sort of revenge. I was prepared to accept any of it. Just to see her again."

Though he'd managed to control his own tears, Amelia couldn't any longer.

"That whole first week," he said, "I waited for you to come to me, to tell me what it was she wanted. Racked my brain trying to work out what exactly she was playing at. Wondered again if it wasn't pure happenstance—because you seemed as confused as I was. Honestly, I thought it more likely I was finally going mad. But somehow it *never* crossed my mind that she was . . . That was a total impossibility. Even after everything else. Because even our own hearts deceive us, don't they?"

And in telling him the truth, she'd killed his hope. The death of his sister was the death of all the dreams he'd harbored for her happiness. No wonder he'd grasped at the awful, absurd possibility that Cathy might have staged the fire—or that he had wanted someone to have killed her, so that he might make them pay.

"I'm so sorry," Amelia said.

He shook his head. "You didn't know."

Which only served to make her weep more profusely. She covered her mouth with her injured hand, clawed her other fingers into the fabric of her skirt. With her head faced forward, her bonnet shielded her and served as blinders both, but it wasn't fair to cry so in front of him, and she forced herself to stop. She drew in a hitching breath and dabbed her sleeves against her cheeks, studied Mr. Sisson with the shade of a frown. "You do remind me of her, sometimes. Not in looks—except when you smile, but—I feel I should have known, somehow."

He shrugged. "I always favored our mother. Cathy took after Father."

Another wave of grief moved through Amelia. "I took after mine. I had brothers, and a sister, too."

It was all she could manage, but she thought he understood her offering. "Tell me about them," he said. "Next week, perhaps? If it's nice, we could go out again, in the boat."

"Yes," Amelia said, not without some desperation, her gleaming eyes searching his for more. Any lingering doubts she'd had about his character were obliterated, but in their place was a rekindled blaze of yearning to know everything else, no matter how sad or shameful. It was the unattainable wish to truly and completely know a friend, but also a desire to recognize even more of herself in him.

Twenty-Four

THE DEPTHS

The following Sunday, she woke to the usual sounds of surf and gulls—though their numbers were much diminished now, and one could no longer call their racket a din—with something else piping above it all. An ascending vibrato call of short, shrill notes that put Amelia in mind of a mechanical toy being wound faster and faster, then spinning away like a little top.

She found its source in a small, black-accented yellow bird perched on the water pump behind Stonehouse, as bright as one of the long-gone goldfields. The landscape of the island now was wrought in tones of brown and gray and black, except when the sea and sky showed blue, which happened less often as the days advanced.

That morning was overcast, though not foggy, and the yellow bird seemed the brightest spot for miles around. Amelia didn't recognize the creature, only knew it was far from home.

Over the past week, she'd watched her cut scab over and her thin bruises fade from grape-black to lavender before they mottled to their current chartreuse shade. They troubled her—as signs of violence in and of themselves and as everything else they represented—but so did Mr. Sisson's divulgence at the chapel.

Amelia's head had been too full of too many baffling things to concentrate on much of schoolwork or dinner conversation since Miss Price's visit. Mrs. Clifford's and Mrs. Pollard's attentive concern this time was not tinged with panic. She guessed that Mrs. Clifford had told Mrs. Pollard that she'd lost someone, and that they presumed her visitor had stirred painful memories. So they sought to soothe her, but didn't fear she might be thinking of leaving them.

Yet now an inner voice urged Amelia to flee. It had not stopped whispering since Miss Price left Stonehouse, no matter how hard Amelia tried to ignore it, keep it at bay.

She knew too well now she was not unassailable on Southeast Farallon. But even if Miss Price hadn't threatened her, she would have felt beset by troubles.

Lucy had slipped almost entirely from her grasp the moment Amelia learned she was dead. Every day without her further weakened her memory, or at least warped it out of true. Perhaps it would have happened even if she'd not met Mr. Sisson or Miss Price. But with each revelation they layered on top of what Amelia knew, or thought she knew—like so many coats of cloudy lacquer, each crystalline truth obfuscating rather than clarifying—it was more and more impossible to recognize the woman who remained in her mind.

Still, she couldn't imagine letting go. *If you had only told me,* she kept thinking, and kept hearing a contemptuous laugh in reply, unsure if it was Lucy's or her own. She had no right to pine for such transparency when she'd kept so many of her own essential truths concealed. She'd discovered too late that once you learn you don't need to lie to someone, the thought of telling them you've been deceitful is too terrible to bear. So you keep up the fiction and hope the love makes up for it, even as you hate yourself a little more every day. But Lucy never pried; she always understood the importance of leaving certain things buried, undisturbed. That itself should have been a clue.

❧

That Sunday, Mr. Sisson came to fetch Amelia as arranged. She'd meant it when she said she'd like to go out again, but that was a whole week ago, and now she was a different person.

Still, she held her shoulders back and offered a faint smile as she exited Stonehouse and walked with him to the landing. On the beach, she closed her eyes and felt Mr. Henry peeling sodden tendrils of hair from her face. Saw her mother's dark irises behind her own closed lids before flames forced them open. The sky was clear, but the ocean was black and opaque as smoke.

Amelia declined Mr. Sisson's proffered hand, stepped into the boat by herself, skirts bunched in both fists to lift her hem an inch. They pushed off and floated on a curiously calm slate sea.

He asked after her siblings—her fault, since she had mentioned them, but now she couldn't imagine how such words had ever passed her lips. She sketched them with the barest strokes. Nathaniel, older by five years, a serious boy who grew into a mournful man, a whaler like their father, though Nat had no violence in his heart. Polly, four years younger than Amelia, a quiet, peculiar little thing. And Jonah, the baby, twelve years Amelia's junior and full of light; she was sure she'd never heard him cry, not even at the very end.

As if they were the only other things that mattered, or perhaps to thwart any further questions, she offered up their deaths: Nathaniel lost in a shipwreck at twenty-one; Polly taken by a sweating sickness at five; Jonah gone even younger. "In a fire," Amelia barely managed to add.

"I'm sorry," Mr. Sisson said. Nothing else, and she was grateful.

There were no whales. Once more, Amelia wondered if it was because of her. There were no dolphins, even, but a strange sort of pull in the pit of her stomach made her keep scanning the flat horizon until she spotted a dorsal fin.

A small black sail above the water, a triangular notch of shadow like a miniature Sugarloaf. But there was something odd about it—there was no curve, she realized; the trailing edge was straight. And then it was nothing but a thin line, because the animal had turned in the direction of their boat.

She stiffened a second before she registered Mr. Sisson's own tension. The outsize tooth on Amelia's mantel sank itself into her mind. "Is that a shark?"

"It's all right," he said.

She scrambled as far back as she could from the edge of the boat and set it rocking.

"It won't bother us. Steady on."

"It's coming this way."

"They like to have a look, that's all."

Amelia drew closer to him but could not take her eyes off the fin, and the creature now drawing near beneath the water. It didn't even approach the size of the whales yet was far larger than she would have liked. Larger than their boat, or at least matched in length. Wider around than the boat, too, so it was nothing to imagine being swallowed whole—but Amelia knew sharks tore things to shreds first. She'd seen them from a safe distance, slicing through slicks of blood around headless sea lions almost hidden under clouds of cawing gulls.

It sank farther down and became a shadow that passed beneath them, only it had substance. She felt its back bump the bottom of the dory—not a jolt but a gentle brush that nonetheless sent her eyes squeezing shut, her body cringing into a smaller space between the benches.

Mr. Sisson's voice was still easy, soft. "It's all right. It's just seeing what we are."

Despite her trepidation, the urge to open her eyes was irresistible, and Amelia peeked, then peered out, even stretched her neck a little to keep sight of the shark. It was graceful, too, like all things underwater, and emanated its own primordial, implacable aura. It seemed to demonstrate more pointed interest in them than the whales, without any of the dolphins' playfulness. Not a blatant threat, per se, but not a benign presence, either.

Yet when Amelia's heart settled some, fascination overtook fear. She'd heard her father speak of great sharks ramming whaleships in a frenzy, biting them and leaving saw teeth embedded in their planks, even landing square on top of them and their crew after launching their thrashing bodies from the water. But that had been amid warm pools of whale blood sloshing in the cold ocean, inciting them to ravenous madness.

She chose not to think of the sharks he'd described circling the lifeboats, dogging them for miles, seeming at last to possess the souls of the men bobbing above them in their wooden cradles-cum-coffins, so that they began to regard each other with those same hungry, empty eyes. This beast, as Mr. Sisson said, seemed simply curious.

As Amelia satisfied her own curiosity, another shark appeared, out of nowhere—as if invoked by the blink of her lashes, the beat of her heart—and then a third. Her breath became shallow. The sharks swam around and beneath the boat with sinuous, silent movements. When she chanced to crane forward again, she lost sight of one. Mr. Sisson was just reaching for her, suggesting she not lean quite so far out, when the shadow came rushing up from below, its arrow-pointed head gashed with a goblin's rictus, snaggled rows of razor teeth bared. Its eye was a black scrying sphere, but Amelia could read nothing in it.

She shrank back as it broke the surface, turned her head into Mr. Sisson's shoulder, seized his arm. He held her close, murmured another stream of reassurances, gently chafed her sleeve. Amelia began to melt against him but tensed at the barest brush of lips upon her temple, the soft words, "I've got you."

She pushed herself away onto the opposite seat, looked down into the deep-blue fabric of her skirt, unaccountably ashamed as much as frightened. "Can we go back now, please?"

"Of course." He picked up the oars, pulled for the inlet at once.

~

Was even the water now unfriendly? Had Amelia made it so? She couldn't shake the thought—that she was affecting the very island again. How many coincidences could she brush off before she gave it proper consideration? If it was true, she must control her inner turmoil.

If it wasn't, it signified something perhaps even worse. Amelia's sense that her mother could reach her through this desolate place might have merit. Those vermilion lights she'd dismissed as a common enough phenomenon might have presaged the coming of Miss Price after all. Then what might the shark foretell?

No matter how vehemently Amelia wished to be free of her past, it shadowed her. Before, Lucy's innate brightness had seemed to eradicate every scrap of darkness; if Amelia ever saw a specter or a shade, she had only to blink and it became a flat, painted prop. Without Lucy's light, the darkness gathered and became harder to dispel.

For all Amelia tried to be like her, she was not. Learning Lucy had in some sense been a fiction made it even harder to pretend, made Amelia's own secrets start to rise in a flood tide. She felt like a dazed sailor who'd just climbed aboard an abandoned boat. It looked seaworthy, capable of carrying her even through turbulent storms, but a jagged crust of barnacles had grown beneath the waterline. If Amelia didn't face the accumulated burden, didn't scrape her consciousness clean, it would grow unbearably heavy, and she would be dragged into the depths.

Mr. Sisson had said that *how* you were was who you were, but it was undeniable that the past shaped every person; Amelia's character—now, and forever—was inseparable from who she'd been before.

Yet when she considered the same notion in Lucy's case, it didn't seem to matter that she had ever been anyone else. Because she'd made Amelia sore with laughter, delirious with adoration, and unafraid of so much. She'd been her home.

If she'd also been in danger, it felt apt that Amelia had taken on her plight, since she had not saved Lucy from it.

~

Soon enough, Sunday came again. She met Mr. Sisson with a stronger smile, no lingering fear over sharks, no bruises now on her wrists. She wasn't Lucy, or Cathy, or anyone he knew, yet Amelia hoped she was also not a stranger.

Naturally, she couldn't simply forget Miss Price's threats to summon someone else from Lucy's—Catherine's—past, or perhaps alert a figure from Amelia's own lost life, but she could choose not to fear them either.

She might be safer if she left the island, slipped on yet another name. The necklace hanging in her hem meant she could go anywhere. But she still had no notion where that might be, nor any sliver of desire to run, to be anyplace else. Not if it meant she would be alone, even farther from the last tangible traces of Lucy and the only living friends she had, Mr. Sisson chief among them.

Let fate find her where it may, then, and—Amelia thought as fervently as a prayer—let her enjoy her time here, however much was left.

She exulted in the stodgy balm of Mrs. Pollard's split-pea soup, in the melodies of other itinerant songbirds stopping by as September rolled into October. In the weight of her blanket as the nights grew colder, in the rainbow that shimmered in the fish-stinking mist of a whale's spout when the sun hit it just so one afternoon. In the crashing of the waves and the lowing of the wind, in the children's earnestness and antics and even their more dramatic sulks. In Mrs. Clifford's poems and Mr. Pollard's jokes and Mr. Clifford's unshakable calm. In the scent of Lucy's perfume and the roil of Melville's words, the feel of the thin pages and cloth-covered boards beneath her fingers. In the sudden pebble-scatter sound of raindrops striking the windowpane one morning. In Banquo's lolling tongue and bounding strides. In Mr. Sisson's smooth voice and warm regard. In every lovely thing about him.

Yet there was danger in comfort, too, the promise of pain in each pleasure taken, and it would be folly to give herself up completely. That was what the voice in Amelia's head told her when it realized it could not convince her to go.

Stay, then, but be cautious. Don't forget, luck runs out. Happiness, too.

Amelia did her best to tune the voice out, the way she'd almost learned to tune out the seabirds as they shrieked and cackled all night, but it persisted—some days stronger, others weaker. Like the fog signal, impossible to predict or ignore but not necessarily to be heeded.

Damned, delighted; Amelia wavered between the two, was both at once. Was, for the time being, alive. That would have to be all that mattered.

Twenty-Five

Storm Season

By November, they relinquished any hope of boating. The weather slumped into a surlier mood, as if in response to the shortening hours of sunlight. Nights were full of black-winged wind howling down the chimney and battering the panes, all hours thick with clammy-fingered fog.

Amelia dreamed her usual dreams—sometimes shrank from Salter or uncertain shapes in the mist even during the day—but one night, she woke from pure unconsciousness to a pounding she thought at first was in her head.

She groped for the watch on her bedside table. Not quite the witching hour, yet well after midnight. The pounding was most certainly coming from outside.

There were voices, too—none she recognized, though the wind and the late hour could have distorted them. Were they angry, or beseeching? Were they even real? She wanted to hide, but neither the black space beneath the bed nor the close confines of the armoire would truly protect her, and what if something terrible had happened that required her assistance? She had to move.

It took several shivering moments to make her legs obey. Then she went to the stairs and hurried down.

The second her foot touched the bottom floor, the pounding and the muffled shouting stopped, the abrupt cessation almost more alarming than the uproar. She stood and waited for it to begin again, skin prickling, mind swelling with all the awful possibilities that might await.

When she could bear it no longer, Amelia charged toward the door and yanked it open—and there was nothing but the night, alive with wind and thick with fog.

She had to squint as she walked down the steps, but still, there was nothing to see. Nothing emerged from the mist, though the beacon high atop the hill flashed in the belly of the fog above. Lightning without thunder. A fish that had swallowed a firefly.

Only the wind reached for her, tearing at her hem and hair. Still, she watched, and waited, until her terror and bravado both drained away with the last remnants of warmth from her bed. Only then did she turn and shut herself inside.

Nothing seemed to have come with her. But Amelia had the sense that if she'd stepped any farther into the fog, she would never have found her way back to the door. She would have walked into some other world entirely. Perhaps she should have gone.

∾

During daylight hours, at least, the rain and wind promised certain pleasures: a warm fire that set damp clothes steaming, their chairs pulled nearer to the hearth and, therefore, closer to each other.

Mr. Sisson still hadn't baked her scones, but the second Sunday of the month, he brought squares of parkin, a dense, dark spice cake so chewy and sticky it clung to teeth and fingers like fudge.

"It doesn't look like much," he admitted, "but it tastes as good as my gran's. If I say myself."

He set to work on the tea and Banquo took his place by the fire screen. Amelia opened the tin to a waft of nutmeg and ginger. "It smells like Christmas!"

"There's oatmeal in them. And black treacle—not molasses, mind."

"I wouldn't know the difference."

"You would if you tasted them side by side."

"I'll take your word for it." She got plates, put them and the parkin on the side table she'd already positioned before the fireplace, flanked by chairs even cozier than those at the kitchen table.

They settled with their cups and saucers and spoke of the preceding week. At the risk of sounding crazy—once again—Amelia said, "I know you don't believe in this sort of thing, but . . . I had the strangest night on Thursday. I was sound asleep, and then—almost two in the morning—I woke to this frantic pounding on the front door, like someone was trying to beat it down off the hinges."

She told him how she'd tried to convince herself it was just the wind, that the soughing accounted for the voices too, but she knew better. And how it suddenly stopped, the instant she reached the first floor.

"I opened the door anyway, and there was nothing there. I even went outside in the rain—barefoot, no cap, no cloak—to look, but there was no one. They couldn't have gotten clear of the house that quickly. So, in the end, I could only conclude that no one was ever there. Yet they were most certainly banging on my door."

He tilted his head. "Well, you know that was the anniversary of the *Lucas*, yes? And that was exactly how it happened last year—the ones who managed to claw their way ashore, they started pounding on the door, shouting for help. It was a nightmare. Didn't stop when we woke up."

He gazed into the fire. Amelia watched him as if she could see the images he replayed in his mind.

"Amos was in the tower. The fog was so thick, he'd no idea anything had even happened until morning. Meanwhile, the rest of us were groping about in the rain and the dark, doing what we could, which wasn't much.

The ship was broken apart on the rocks. Some people got caught between the two. They were swamping the lifeboats; other people were beating them back. It was bedlam. Mrs. Pollard and Mrs. Clifford had the fireplaces blazing, gathered up every spare blanket and cloak and sweater they could find—and it still wasn't nearly enough. The children were terrified."

"What about the Salters?"

"They weren't here yet. I'm sure they would have prayed. Maybe it would have helped. As it was, the twenty-three who died . . . only some of them could even be retrieved. Percy and I managed to fix a line to the mast at daybreak; people were still clinging to the rigging out there, only the topsails left above the surface. But that was the last of them.

"It was so strange; one hundred seventy-seven people made it onshore—so we were a ragged little metropolis all of a sudden, overrun with these poor beggars, these refugees. They weren't here long; the rescue ships came that same day. But it took hours to move everyone—a parade of dories back and forth. And then this place suddenly seemed so empty when the last one was gone."

He looked from the hearth back to Amelia, fully in the present again. "But you must have known that. That it was the day. I'm sure young Finn was spouting off about it, and I'd wager his mother said something at dinner. And then it *was* windy that night . . ."

Her cheeks flushed. "Yes. But—it wasn't even ghosts I was afraid of, really."

"No?"

"Well, not at first. I heard that pounding and I thought for sure . . . It sounded like someone was here for me."

Understanding washed any trace of amusement off Mr. Sisson's face. "But that's all over now."

Amelia sipped her tea, held it close as if for the extra warmth.

"You don't think so?" he said. When she didn't answer, he could not entirely conceal the incredulity in his voice. "You still think your father's after you, then?"

His eyes grazed the mantelpiece, where Amelia had moved her book when she cleared the table for their tea things. He tamped down a sigh.

"I suppose you can't avoid seeing Salter, but perhaps you should put the Melville away for a time."

"Perhaps you should refrain from patronizing me." The clipped stridency of Amelia's tone surprised them both.

Humor only tinged the first words of his reply before it slid into sincerity. "I'm sorry. But I cannot believe you have anything to fear from that quarter. Truly, I don't."

"But you can't know that. Unless you've seen his obituary, in which case, please, frame it for me for Christmas. Otherwise, it seems you'd do well not to make presumptions."

Mr. Sisson raised his eyebrows at the fire. "All right. I just—I wish I could ease your mind. That's all."

Amelia sighed apart the steam from her cup. "I wish you could too. And if it hadn't been for Miss Price, you might."

He answered with tender finality. "She isn't coming back. And she knew where to find Cathy. That's the only reason she found you. Your father doesn't have a clue about any of that. You're safe."

"Maybe. But Miss Price said there was someone else looking for Cathy too—except she called her Kitty. And . . . she said he'd be much worse." Mr. Sisson looked so horrified Amelia had to look away. "She couldn't have meant your uncle, could she?"

"No, he's dead, the bastard. But—why didn't you tell me this before?"

"What difference does it make?" Amelia couldn't possibly confess she'd thought it might be Mr. Sisson himself, even for a second. "You don't have any idea who else she might have meant, do you?"

"No." His saucer rattled faintly as he returned his cup. "Are you sure she wasn't just trying to scare you? She knows you're not Cathy. So, if she sends someone else after you, then—"

"If she makes them think I killed Lucy, they won't care who I am. I don't know why you can't accept that. And she did say she might try to find out. Where I came from. So then it could be my father yet. Either way, it doesn't matter. Because I'm not leaving this place. I don't belong anywhere else. So if someone else is coming, then they'll find me. And whatever is meant to happen will."

Mr. Sisson seemed almost offended, at the resignation in Amelia's voice or the cavalier attitude she evinced. "Nothing is going to happen to you. Even if someone else does come."

She focused on the leaping flames, as if she might see some harbinger there, but felt his eyes trained on her profile. He almost sounded perfectly reasonable when he added, "If anyone else comes, then I will do whatever needs to be done."

Amelia whipped her head around. "Don't talk like that. It has nothing to do with you."

"Of course it does. Don't talk like what? Like I care?"

"Like you'd do something foolish. Because I wouldn't stay if I thought it was putting anyone in danger, like you said before. I won't. And don't think I'd be grateful to you for killing someone on my behalf if that's what you're hinting at. We're not playing knights and dragons."

He let out a huff of breath. "So you'd rather I left you to your fate? Because *I* won't do that—"

"What say do you have in it?"

He was entirely earnest and didn't break eye contact. "I won't leave you alone again at all; that was my mistake in the first place. Not keeping a closer eye out. Nothing would have happened if I'd been there."

There was a shadow of a smirk on Amelia's lips now, but it trembled under threat of other emotions winning out. Skepticism was only a shield. She looked away. "So you'll simply never let me out of your sight, then?"

"No. I'd be happy not to."

Heat crept up her neck as she stared into the empty cup cradled on her lap. Eventually, she managed to say, "I'm sure I'll be fine. What are the odds of someone else showing up, anyway? If they do, maybe they'll end up in the ocean, on the rocks. Maybe it'll only be their ghost that comes banging on my door."

She placed the cup on the table and rose to poke at the fire. With her back to Mr. Sisson, she added, "I'm probably scared over nothing. You were right about this place breeding wild ideas. It's different in this weather, too. Spooky."

"And safe," he said. "From visitors, at least."

She glanced over her shoulder with a hint of a smile. "Live ones, anyway."

~

Conversation subsided, ceased. They listened to the crackling fire and pattering rain, Banquo's deep, drafty snores, the gusting wind, the eternal rush of the ocean all around them.

When he took his leave, Amelia stood in the front hall to watch Mr. Sisson don his coat and hat.

"Next week," he said, "I'll bring those scones. Currants, or no?"

She smiled again, but only briefly, looked down at the floor as her fingers squeezed the fabric of her skirt. "I'm not sure we should do this anymore."

He laughed. "What, have tea?"

"Yes. Here. Just the two of us."

"Banquo makes three." When Amelia failed to respond, his amusement curdled. "This is because of what I said? Because you're determined to keep me at arm's length even when—"

"It's because it isn't proper."

He scoffed; she raised her voice. "I don't want to do anything to jeopardize my position—"

"I doubt there is anything you could possibly do to jeopardize your position at this point. They adore you. You could waltz in there right now and tell them everything and they'd forgive you. As for propriety, I suspect they'd overlook a great deal more than your only chatting to me."

Amelia's eyes flashed up at him, then away; her cheeks flamed. He hurried to excuse himself.

"But—no, of course, I understand. I'm sorry if I've put you in an awkward position, or if I've imposed—"

"You haven't." She looked at him with distress she couldn't hide. It threaded her voice as well. "You should come to more dinners. We can talk there. They like your company too."

He was momentarily at a loss for words, and then only managed, "Right." He shouldered his bag of tea things and motioned Banquo to his side. They ducked out into the cold, blowing rain as Amelia stood in the door to watch them go.

She would call them back before they got too far. She almost believed Mr. Sisson could tell she wanted to, would save her the agony. He'd turn around himself, stride right up to the top step and take her by the elbows, look into her eyes.

But he never glanced behind him, and soon he disappeared around the hill.

He was a gentleman, after all, wasn't he? No matter how much it pained him, he would respect her wishes, without the impertinence of argument or the humiliation of supplication. He would leave her alone, like she tried to pretend she wanted.

∾

For five weeks, she barely saw him, even by chance. The weather kept everyone indoors. During the few breaks in the wind-driven rain and fog, sometimes Amelia walked around to his side of the hill. Still, she rarely happened upon Mr. Sisson. When she did, they exchanged a few words in passing, like they used to, but that was all. When he and Banquo were ensconced inside, she ached to go knock on the door, but felt she didn't have the right, having revoked it herself.

One afternoon when she sat polishing the silver with Mrs. Clifford just for the excuse of her company, he came round for a game of chess with Mr. Pollard. And on the occasion of the goat roast, he came to dinner when Mrs. Pollard expressly invited him. Both times he was cordial, and Amelia was flooded with felicity that tipped into a longing she hoped wasn't too plain on her face.

She was surprised—pleasantly—to see he was growing out a neatly trimmed beard, though apparently, he'd had one before; over the goat, Mrs. Pollard commented, "I see you've given up your razor again."

"Well, it is getting colder. Helps keep my face warm in the winter."

"But Miss Riley won't recognize you in another few days!"

I think it looks quite dashing, Amelia wanted to say, but only dipped her head and kept her eyes on her plate.

In fact, though she was the one who'd said he should come to more communal suppers, she found it difficult to speak at all, and not only because she was ashamed now to have him hear his sister's voice come from her own lips.

Twenty-Six

CELEBRATION

The *Shubrick*'s last visit of the year was delayed by the weather. When it came during the third week in December, its cargo included a scraggly pine tree they propped up in a crock in the downstairs parlor. No fireworks this time, but walnuts and oranges were hidden from the children until the holiday.

In the meanwhile, they helped tie ribbons and bows for decorations and string garlands of popcorn and murre eggshells Mrs. Pollard had washed and saved to festoon the tree. Claire, Fiona, and Joy tried their hands at tatting lace snowflakes with the women, and those were liberally hung about.

Amelia didn't go close enough to peer through the Salters' windows, but she imagined their rooms remained undecorated.

On Christmas Eve, Mr. Sisson came to dinner with multiple batches of his parkin for the dessert table. He stayed awhile afterward as everyone gathered in the parlor, crowded and hot, the fire blazing. Mr. Clifford played his fiddle and Mrs. Pollard her mandolin. They'd moved the furniture to the margins so there was space to dance, mostly for the children, though each of their parents took a turn. Amelia couldn't resist their exhortations either. But even the redoubtable Mrs. Pollard couldn't coax Mr. Sisson to join them.

Amelia was disappointed, denied the chance to brush his hand and meet his eyes so close. Imagining their bodies swinging away from each other was its own delight, as it would be the start of returning to face each other again, to steal a touch she felt tingle in her fingers.

But he kindly refused and excused himself to go up to the lighthouse. He'd occasionally stood watch before they were assigned an official second assistant keeper. Now Mr. Salter had come down with a bad cold, brought ashore by the *Shubrick*. Mr. Sisson had volunteered to take his tower duty and to go up on Christmas, too, to give the families a rare stretch of uninterrupted time together. Amelia felt a bit deflated by his exit. She didn't have the children's boundless stamina anyway, so she smothered a sigh and sank onto the sofa.

"It's so kind of him to stand watch," Mrs. Pollard said, fanning herself on the other end of the couch, in a bit of disarray.

Amelia tucked her own stray hairs back, the roots damp with perspiration. "But is that . . . allowed?"

"Oh, the Board would pitch a fit if they knew, but it's not as if it's *difficult*. If a man can read and row a boat, he can tend a light."

Mr. Pollard made a vague noise of mock offense but was too jolly to argue. Amelia suspected his flush was helped along by spirits; they'd all been drinking cider and wine to some degree, but she'd smelled something stronger on him when they'd whirled near each other in a Scottish reel.

Now, the adults were all sitting down, the children singing for them, Fiona with the most concentrated sincerity, Claire plucking at their mother's mandolin to accompany her little sister. Finn and Phyllis and Samuel and even Joy still twirled and jumped about the rug, their energy inexhaustible, and exhausting.

"And he's beyond capable, of course," Mrs. Pollard went on. "He could apply for a position if he wanted to, but I expect the egg company pays more. And asks less. But Lord knows we appreciate the help now and then. Really, we ought to have a third assistant keeper to help lighten the load full time, but—well, I suppose we mustn't get too greedy out here."

Amelia murmured a noise of agreement, and Mrs. Pollard stretched over to pat her hand. "How are you getting on?"

"Oh, I'm splendid. Stuffed. A little dizzy, but in the best possible way."

"I mean with Mr. Sisson, dear. You used to spend all your Sundays together. Not that I spy, but I did notice; I couldn't help it. Now you don't. But you still seem friendly."

"Oh. Yes. We are—friends. That's all. I thought it best we saw a little less of each other. Now I'm not sure why." Amelia blamed the last glass of cider for loosening her tongue, and for making her words sound so gloomy.

Mrs. Pollard patted her again. "Well, this can be a lonely place. If you found some good company to make it less so, then I'd be happy for you."

Perhaps that was the cider talking too. At any rate, Amelia squirmed, even before the well-meaning woman shifted closer to murmur, "You'll just want to be careful, of course," her breath a hot prickle that turned into a damp vapor against Amelia's ear. "A bit of sponge, soaked in oil—or vinegar, either one. Put it in place before—high up, I mean. Inside. Hasn't failed me yet."

She shot Mrs. Pollard a frozen smile that didn't reach her wide eyes and nodded like a marionette, then sprang off the sofa and across the room as if desperate to join the children in their new game of making shadow puppets on the wall.

～

That night, Stonehouse echoed with silence, even as rain beat upon the roof and wind whistled down the chimneys. Amelia's room was cold, but she never lit the fireplace in there. Her motivations were different from Ishmael's, but she did like the effect, as Melville wrote, of being "one warm spark in the heart of an arctic crystal."

She tucked herself up in the blankets to trap her body's radiant heat, listened to the wind, the rain, the waves, the lonesome quiet underlying and magnified by them.

She thought of the Salters sequestered in their cheerless home, and of Mr. Sisson aloft in the lighthouse, and of Lucy—Cathy—away somewhere further still.

~

She spent Christmas morning in the parlor, with coffee and a piece of parkin from the plate of goodies Mrs. Pollard sent her off with the night before. She made a small fire and gathered Lucy's notebooks with the idea of paging through to reread all the entries that mentioned her. Although in some sense, of course, Amelia never appeared. She was there as *V* for Vinny. It made her sad to see that lying letter now.

> *11/18/55—Raining cats, dogs, all Noah's ark! But V has off today, so we're stuck inside together. Forget why I ever want to go out . . .*

> *5/12/57—Nabbed the daintiest little rose meringues; told V they reminded me of her. Lovely, sweet, so delicate— and melt in the mouth. Her cheeks went as pink as the sweets at that. Am sometimes so happy it makes me ache, turns to melancholy, some strange sense of unfairness. Why couldn't I have always had her?*

Amelia set the books aside and held an orange to her nose. She scratched the peel with her thumbnail, wished she had cloves to push into the pebbled skin. Lucy loved making pomanders for the holiday. Their rooms would be so thickly perfumed with the sweet, spiced smell it used to make Amelia feel deliciously faint.

When they ventured out for sugared gin and loud music, Lucy would stuff extra oranges in a bag to give away, but first she would char a spare clove over a candle flame and rub the burnt nubbin on her lashes to darken them.

Amelia could almost see those merry eyes when she closed her own—gazing from just the other end of her pillow, sweat-smudged soot darkening the spaces beneath Lucy's eyes, her smiling cheeks and sleepy lids narrowing them to blue-green slivers. The candlelight danced there, warm sparks melting her cool gaze; it caught the ginger threads in her red-gold hair as it flared across the snowy linen and burnished her once-more naked lashes, limned her pink, parted lips, and made the very words that passed through them glow.

My little dove. How sweetly you coo.

The embers kindled by the recollection warmed Amelia—then burned—then began to fade until they were cold and dark. She struck the logs apart in the hearth and judged it time to seek the company of the Pollards and the Cliffords.

They would have welcomed her as early as she pleased, but she didn't want to feel she was intruding, and couldn't help it, ever the outlier observing their domestic bliss. She counted them all friends, yet still sometimes felt out of place among them. Part of it, of course, was the lie on which the very acquaintance was built. But even had she come to them as her true self, her own name and history intact, Amelia suspected she would have held herself at some remove. The loss of Lucy was still too raw a wound; she had to shield it carefully, and tenderness itself scraped most deeply if she let it close enough.

When she opened the door of Stonehouse to head for the keepers' quarters, Amelia saw a few strange rocks on the bottom step. She wondered who had put them there. But then they resolved into minia-ture sculptures, carved bits of wood, and her heart flew into her throat.

She descended and bent to gather them in her hands: a tiny sail-boat, a blue whale four inches longer but still pocket-size, and a hump-back to scale in relation to the other two. She laughed, cast her welling eyes about, but there was no one to be seen on the marine terrace. Even as she smiled, a lump formed in Amelia's throat—or perhaps it was still her heart lodged there.

∽

Fiona and Claire were down with sniffles. Their mother appeared to be suffering the after-effects of her unaccustomed bout of imbibing. Still, the mood in the keepers' quarters was festive, if subdued compared to the previous evening. There were games and gifts and a walk around the marine terrace since the sun was peeping out.

"Never had a Christmas so fair since we came here!" Mr. Pollard said. It was windy and cold, but mostly clear, mere wisps of cloud. A dry day, save the pools and slicks of spray that were always present, and the remnant puddles of rain making scattered mirrors on the rocks.

Had Mrs. Pollard felt up to the jaunt, she might have proclaimed it another good omen—or, as she'd taken to doing lately, eight months now after Amelia's arrival, ascribed it to "our good luck charm." It always triggered a pulse of guilt.

All the rain had brought fresh green to stipple the terrace, and there was other new life on the rocks: a few baby elephant seals, only days old. The adult males had arrived earlier in the month, far less monstrous than the naked skull still hidden away in Stonehouse had suggested they would be. Their ungainly bulk and pendulous noses were even humorous—at least until they brawled fiercely enough to draw blood.

They threw their heads back to roar and bellow, then smacked their teeth into each other's hides with resounding thwacks. Crimson tributaries ran down their massive bodies, their bristling mouths likewise red with blood. They sometimes charged each other off the rocks, into the sea.

The sheer size of the oldest males made Amelia nervous, especially since Mr. Pollard told her they sometimes made it all the way up onto the terrace, near the houses. If she were to stand next to one raised to its full height, she knew it would dwarf her—like a small, misshapen whale that could waddle on land.

She was anxious in a new way now whenever she had to walk through the fog. Mrs. Pollard, who despised the male sea elephants, advised her to carry a laundry dolly or rug beater just in case, though such implements seemed laughably inadequate protection. The way Mrs. Pollard spoke of the animals' unfortunate habit of crushing the babies beneath them as they fought made them sound like premeditating murderers that deserved the gallows. When she mentioned that they used to be hunted for their blubber but now there were too few of them for anyone to bother, her tone suggested she would not have stopped until they were exterminated. Amelia wondered that Mr. Salter hadn't tried to make a small harvest of his own.

For the moment, at least, the animals were peaceful—which didn't mean quiet. They made a bizarre array of noises, some of which sounded both eerily human and like the squawking seabirds, underscored by the rumbling vocalizations of the bulls. Amelia made out belches and strangled screams and hooting monkeys, the commingling of which was somewhat off-putting, but the children effervesced with laughter and exclaimed over the precious pups.

Everyone was in high spirits as they headed back to the house.

They passed Mrs. Salter and Gertrude out for their own stroll, their patriarch still abed. Gertie grinned. She and Minerva both returned Amelia's "Merry Christmas."

And then they met Mr. Sisson, on his way to join them for an early dinner, without Banquo, in deference to Mrs. Pollard's aversion to indoor animals. Amelia could only smile at him as they drew near each other, could not stop smiling at him all through that evening.

When he left ahead of sunset to make his way to the lighthouse, she said her farewells and Happy Christmases too. The ambiance in the keepers' quarters as they left was one of sated sleepiness. The boys were belly-down on the rug, Finn carving a bar of soap with his new pocketknife while Samuel watched, his windup tin frog forgotten for the moment. Joy and Phyllis flanked their father on the sofa, eyes sagging closed as Mrs. Clifford read to them. Mr. Pollard had stepped out for some air, which Amelia suspected meant whiskey; Mrs. Pollard had retired early, ostensibly to check on her girls. She'd allowed she might lie down for a little nap herself and never rematerialized.

Amelia was suffused with a sense of peace as she stepped out with Mr. Sisson. They'd spoken few words to each other all evening, but as soon as they were outside, she thanked him for his gifts.

He kept his eyes on the ground as they walked toward Stonehouse. "I thought about bookends—a humpback head and a tail—but you don't have the room on your shelves. Reckoned you could find a place for a few trinkets, at least."

"Talismans," she said, and pulled one from her pocket. "I might just carry them around with me all the time."

Amelia sensed his smile grow wider as he looked forward again. "Glad you liked them."

A few steps from Stonehouse, before Mr. Sisson could bid her good night, she said, "Can I come up with you?"

She looked away from the surprise on his face, too soon to be sure if there was also apprehension. "It seems so terribly sad to think of you sitting up there all alone on Christmas. But then maybe you'd prefer that. And I suppose you'll have Banquo anyway. I—"

"No. I leave the barracks door open for him, but he prefers sleeping on the rug to scrambling up at night. And I'd be fine on my own, but . . . You know I like to be alone with you."

Amelia glanced up at him as he stopped short.

"Erm," he said. "That is, I should greatly appreciate the company if you are so inclined."

She laughed. "I'd like to see it again, anyway. I haven't been up since the first time. Never at night."

"Good one for it. Best fetch your mac, though."

Amelia wrinkled her nose at the clear sky. "Really?"

"No chance this holds out for long."

She ran inside for her oilskin and grabbed her knitting basket too, dumped its contents on the chair. She threw in a deck of cards and the few bits of food left in her kitchen: a square of parkin, a pear, a handful of nuts, a sliver of hard cheese, the last of Mrs. Pollard's cookies. She left the thumb-scraped orange on the side table.

Twenty-Seven

The Lantern Room

The wind snatched at Amelia's bonnet, so she took it off and stuffed it in her basket. She wouldn't let Mr. Sisson take it, though she had to carry it in the crook of her elbow. She needed her hands free to lift her skirts as they luffed about her ankles and threatened to snag on the jagged rocks. Amelia thought they might yet have to drop to all fours to avoid getting blown over or off the hill, but they managed to make their way to the top without crawling or falling.

When they stepped into the dim enclosure of the tower, it was as still as the eye of a storm. Amelia's face felt slapped; she knew it must be florid beneath the wind-ravaged nest of her hair unraveling all about her shoulders, but she didn't mind. She unfastened her cloak as she followed Mr. Sisson up the short curl of stairs to the watch room.

He lit the lamp on the workbench that curved along one portion of the circular wall. All else that fit in the cramped space was a single chair, the metal stem that supported the lens one level above, the gearbox that made it turn, and the angled ladder stairs that led into the lantern room at the top of the tower. A few hooks were handy for hanging outer garments.

Amelia placed her basket on the workbench and tried to rearrange her hair by feel alone. He climbed up to uncover the glass walls and light the flame that would cast its beam out across the sea. While he worked, she leafed through a copy of the third edition of the Lighthouse Board's rules for keepers, just printed the previous year, 1858. Its eighty-seven pages dictated proper procedures down to the second and the tenth of an inch. Not difficult, perhaps, as Mrs. Pollard attested, but regimented in the extreme.

There were meant to be two watchmen in the tower every night, to share duties and ensure that neither man became incapacitated. As head keeper, Mr. Pollard had clearly dispensed with that stipulation. Which, Amelia supposed, was lucky for her.

The night's first round of tasks complete, Mr. Sisson sat on the workbench while Amelia took the chair. They talked of how he'd come to be a de facto lighthouse assistant: one of the early keepers taught him what he needed to know, he said, then paid him to stand watch in his stead while he went on a monumental bender.

She asked for more stories about those first men, before the families—she'd only ever heard them spoken of obliquely, but he was happy to fill in the blanks. Even the more unsettling aspects of their tales seemed less ominous the way he told them.

One keeper spent more time devising traps for mermaids than maintaining the lighthouse and Stonehouse. He shot an egger in the shoulder when they first set up on the island, not over disputed murre fruit but because he was convinced the man had let an elusive siren escape.

"Good thing he didn't see your dining chairs," Amelia said.

"I hadn't started on those yet."

The fellow who built the chapel had worn a string of seagull feet around his neck, for what purpose Mr. Sisson had no clue. But he'd never forget the way they clacked together, like the lightest wooden windchimes, or strips of jerky in the breeze. A far-off, dry sort of clapping every time the man moved about.

"At least he couldn't sneak up on you," Amelia said with a laugh.

A third keeper, according to Mr. Sisson, refused to leave the tower for days on end. He'd made Mary haul up whole hams and jugs of ale along with the oil casks but brought no food for her, so she would break her tether and wander back down the hill in search of sustenance. Once, she'd barged right inside Stonehouse and raided the keeper's store of breakfast oats, much to his fury when he finally returned home two days later looking for a morning meal.

"And I suppose she ate all his bacon too?"

"No. She'd already hauled that up here."

Yet another man had taken to wearing a beekeeper's hood to deter the kelp flies, which drove him mad. When they still found their way inside his armor, he ripped off every stitch of clothing and ran clear across the marine terrace, shrieking oaths the whole way. "But covered in enough kelp flies to protect his modesty."

Their laughter accumulated like a golden haze that warmed the space despite the cold gusts of wind whistling outside.

As darkness erased the two small windows in the watch room, the close, round space seemed even smaller. It was a castle turret, a secret place locked away in a fairy tale, where time might stand still, though every four hours the mechanism must be wound to keep the magic in motion. A paradoxical paradise.

They stepped onto the balcony to admire the stars, as densely clustered in the sky as the murres had been on the rocks six months ago. But blessedly quiet—or maybe it was only that the relentless wind and rushing surf drowned out their celestial music.

The sight reminded Amelia of the vast expanses of star-salted heavens she and Lucy had gazed up at from the California Trail as they'd traveled west. Nothing but empty plains around them some nights, the absolute darkness beyond the last circles of firelight too much to bear looking at for long. So they'd cast their eyes up and let their heads swim with delight that swirled in to obliterate the fear.

Despite the stories they wove for strangers later, no leaky canoes or pathetic donkeys or sweltering jungles featured in their journey to San Francisco. There had been other hardships: fierce storms, broken wagons, illness, death, sundry other bodily threats. Even the specter of the Donner Party's devastation some six years before, the tree stumps around their camp in the pass cut off at the level the snow had lain on the ground, well above their heads. All things they never spoke of once they were past, even to each other—but they'd recalled the stars often. They'd been able to see them in each other's eyes before Lucy's had gone out, black as char.

Amelia wondered if her own still held those lights anywhere in their depths, or if they only shone as reflections on their surfaces when she beheld a different sky, as now.

She sighed and Mr. Sisson looked over. "All right?"

"Mm-hmm. Just . . . reminiscing. Getting sentimental."

He bowed his head. "I'm sorry. It's your first Christmas without her in a long while. I didn't even think."

"Well, you've had more practice. Has it gotten easier?"

He waited a moment to reply. "It has. Sometimes it feels appalling that it has. But yes."

It felt appalling that Amelia wanted it to, as well, yet the notion of relief was dizzying; she gripped the railing at her rib cage and said, "I can't keep a hold on her anymore. Memories, even. I feel like I hardly knew her, but—God, I miss her so much."

Mr. Sisson laid one hand atop Amelia's own. It was a cautious gesture, a gentle weight and warmth that radiated up her arm and rippled outward. She closed her eyes and splayed her fingers, laced them with his own. When he caressed her knuckle, it set something fluttering inside her, yet also anchored her against the gale and the tide of grief, gave her the strength for another confession:

"I've missed you, too."

He faced her as the wind plucked strands of her hair loose again. "I've been right here."

A tear spilled down Amelia's cheek, and he brushed it away with his thumb. When she turned her lips into his palm he swallowed and tilted up her chin. "Tell me your name," he said, voice soft and frayed.

As she stretched her neck toward him, her mouth seeking his, he drew back, still searching her eyes, her parted lips. "Please."

She took a deep breath, then gave it to him, to the stars and the wind and the sea. "Amelia Osborne."

"Amelia," he murmured, and she felt something loosen and rise inside her. "Hello," he said.

Through their spreading smiles, they kissed.

∾

They were a wind-whipped flurry of skirts and shirtsleeves and eager limbs, all tangled up in each other as they stumbled back into the watch room, laughing and clumsily kissing as they went. They bumped past the chair and Amelia found her back against the angled iron stairs. She stood on her toes and used the highest tread she could reach as a seat, not that it was particularly comfortable. Not that she cared, not when a soft barrage of competing sensations made that hard metal melt away: breath, and skin, and lips, and hands. Tongues and teeth and formless utterances more than breath yet made of it, as full of it as sails with breeze.

There was only so much of her he could touch so she felt it. The hard carapace of her corset—over a linen chemise and under a wool bodice that came up to her throat—meant he couldn't get at her breasts or waist, but she wouldn't dream of undressing there, as cold and uncomfortable as it was. So she pulled him closer, plucked at the buttons of his vest. He helped undo them and shrugged it off, as he had his jacket, and then Amelia tugged the braces from his shoulders, brushed her way down the front of his shirt to the placket of his trousers, where she pressed more firmly, her body's hunger redoubled by the way he moaned into her mouth.

He moved her fingers from his buttons and grabbed her voluminous skirts in handfuls that caught most of the underlayers too, no delicate manner of getting everything out of the way. "You've got on enough bloody fabric to rig out a barque," he said, and they laughed again.

Amelia helped lift the cloud of crinoline and petticoats, her arms too full to touch him, and then she sucked in her breath at the brush of his fingers on her bare skin, the rumble of his words: "There you are."

One hand holding up as much fabric as possible, she curled the other around his arm, kissed him through her own sighs as he stroked her. She pulled at him again, one leg hooked around his hip. She buzzed at the reverberation of his voice in her body as he said, "You want me?"

"Yes," she breathed.

"Here? Like this?"

"Yes," she said, and then again.

Finally, he freed himself, and once more she hauled up her layers, feeling for a fleeting moment like a circus tent, but then all she felt was him—and herself around him, against him, her hips and mouth moving in a rhythm much like his own, like one of them was the bobbing boat and the other the lapping waves. Not in opposition, yet not quite in perfect sync; he began to get ahead of her and would crest before she did, but there was pleasure to be had for herself in his. Amelia drew in her breath as he slipped out of her, watched his face as he finished in his hand, the other braced against the metal stair above her head.

She kissed the inside of his wrist as his cries subsided into heaving breaths and he leaned his forehead into her chest. Her fingertips touched the soft hair and hot skin at the back of his neck. Her eyes closed, and she could still feel an echo of his movements, her blood beating heavily all throughout her body, a warm, wet pulse between her thighs. And then his lips were on her neck, her jaw, her mouth, his hand beneath her skirts again, fingers poised to slide inside her, which made Amelia gasp and open her eyes.

"Is that all right?" he said, and she nodded.

It felt like he opened something inside her, like a key smoothly turning in a lock.

With her eyes closed, Amelia could see Lucy, could feel her too. But that promised heartache, so she opened her lids and watched Will's face again, as he watched hers. She kissed him and clutched his arm and arched her head back against the stairs, cried out and quivered as he fastened his mouth to her throat. Pleasure surged through her like the surf and she let herself be racked by waves, until she had to still his hand because any more would be too much. Then the tide ebbed and Amelia felt as if she'd just washed up on a soft, warm shore.

She floated on dry land, or perhaps in the sky, for some indeterminate time, vaguely aware of soft, spare kisses on her neck, her temple, her lips, her cheek. And finally, with a great, shuddering intake of breath that only amplified the feeling of fullness even as she exhaled, she came back to herself, looked at Will again, struck by his beauty.

"Does this mean we can have tea again?" he said, and laughter burst from her, from them both. They kissed each other through it, and Amelia wrapped her arms around his neck as he circled his around her waist. He pulled her up from the stairs and held her close against him.

She wished he'd never let her go, but it was almost time to wind the clockwork.

While he was occupied, Amelia unpacked her basket, laid out the little feast. She sat upon the workbench while Will took the chair at her knee, produced a flask from his pocket. When she raised an eyebrow, he said, "Don't worry, it isn't goat milk."

They ate and drank and talked some more. He loosely clasped his fingers around Amelia's ankle through its salt-stained leather boot, his thumb upon the laces, a hair's breadth from the weight of the necklace hidden in her hem, yet she felt no concern at all.

Around ten o'clock, rain began to strike the tower—a patter that turned into a deluge that roared against the glass walls of the lantern room above them but did not douse the light.

~

They kissed away another hour but then, while Will was attending to the vents and gears and topping up the oil reservoir, the downpour lulled Amelia to sleep. When she woke, the world outside was already beginning to lighten. She hung her head so her hair might hide her face while she swiped at a mortifying slick of drool. When she asked if she'd snored, he said, "I could barely hear it over the storm."

She slid off the bench and peered out a window; the rain pelted still, and clouds hid the sun, but however muted the daybreak, it was proof the night could not last forever. Now Will would have to extinguish the oil lamp and clean the lens, a methodical process he allowed could be tedious or meditative depending on one's mood. He'd have to don a linen apron and roll up his sleeves so his buttons wouldn't scratch the prisms, swab every notch and nook of glass. She had to commence classes in two hours. He offered to walk with her down Tower Hill before he returned to finish his work, but Amelia said she'd go alone.

Swamped in her hooded raincoat, she executed a tight twirl and asked how she looked. "The very height of fashion, no?"

"I'd like you in anything," he said, gathering her in one last embrace, "but even better, I think, in nothing at all." He smiled against her neck as she laughed, nuzzled her cheek. "God, I want to see you. I want to feel all your skin against my own. Can I come to you? Tonight?"

"Let yourself in after eight. I'll lay a fire upstairs. But leave your shoes by the door if it's still raining like this."

"As you command." He kissed her again, let her oilskin trail through his fingertips, then lingered by the window to watch her go.

From the head of the path, he was blurred by the distance and the water running down the glass between them, yet never so bright or clear in Amelia's mind. Another undousable light.

Twenty-Eight

DISAPPEARANCE

She must have looked like a heavy-lidded lizard, yawning her way down Tower Hill, ambling inside Stonehouse. She felt strangely—yet not unpleasantly—indecent. Though there was no outward sign of what had happened, Amelia felt she should have glowed or given off a vibration like water in a glass when an earthquake shook the room.

That sensation vanished when she went to change her muddy skirts. The tattered, sodden hem of the dress was proof she'd been up in the lighthouse and therefore was not a bother. But when Amelia's fingers brushed the hem of her petticoat and felt no telltale weight, her heart went cold. She quickened her search around the perimeter of the garment and blanched when she found a ragged tear.

It was almost nine, yet Amelia went to retrace her steps at once—only to encounter Mr. Salter, almost upon Stonehouse. He was leading Mary, laden with fresh canisters of oil to resupply the tower storeroom atop the hill. Amelia stayed herself and weathered his foul, red-rimmed gaze as he passed. She watched him start up the zigzag trail and reluctantly returned inside.

Conducting classes was arduous. Amelia claimed a headache and dismissed the children early. She went immediately back up the lighthouse path. This time she picked her way to the top but saw no signs of the necklace. She shivered with more than cold by the time she came down again.

It had occurred to her—reoccurred to her throughout the whole interminable day—that perhaps she hadn't simply lost the necklace. She'd fallen so deeply, enchantedly asleep. Will's hand had been right there on her ankle, close enough he might have felt the subtle bulk of the jewelry against his thumb. What if he'd extracted it while Amelia slumbered?

She went around the hill to his house, barely felt her feet or face, might have been a gliding ghost for all the contact she seemed to have with the ground and air.

When he opened the door, he grinned. "Couldn't wait for me, eh?"

"Do you have something of mine?" Amelia said, and watched his expression shift into confusion, concern.

"What do you mean?"

Though she was certain there was no guile in him at all, her heart remained unsteadied. "The necklace," she said.

Will's frown deepened. "What necklace?"

"Lucy's. Do you have it?"

He shook his head, some tinge of anger seeping into his voice. "I thought you gave it to Miss Price."

Amelia raised her chin. "I gave her the money. I told her the necklace was gone. Already sold."

"What? *Jesus*, why? She—"

"Never mind why. Did you take it? Or find it?"

"No." He wasn't only angry now but offended, hurt. "You honestly think I would do that? And then lie about it? Now?"

Amelia looked away, overwhelmed by a welter of emotions.

"When did you lose it?" Will said, more gently. "Where was it?"

"In my hem. It was there last night. It must have fallen out this morning when I walked down."

"Well, Salter came up not long after . . ."

"I know," she said, and met Will's eyes again.

"If he has it, I'm sure he'll bring it back to you."

Amelia stifled a scoff, shook her head.

"We'll go get it, then," Will said.

"*No.*"

"Why don't you come in and have some tea and—"

"No. I have to go."

He came out and called after her. "Amelia!"

Even though no one was within earshot, she whirled around. "Keep your voice down!"

She left him standing there, staring, as she continued her march back around the hill, straight to the Salters' house. She knocked too hard but couldn't help it. When Elijah answered, Gertie and Minerva out of sight somewhere inside, Amelia squared her shoulders, leveled her voice. "Did you happen to come across a necklace on the path this morning?"

The hint of humor in Salter's expression made it all the more terrible. "Aye," he said, and stepped out, closer, shut the door behind him. "That harlot's hoard of rubies and diamonds. Yours, was it?"

"It is. Thank you for keeping it safe. I've come to take it back."

"Then I hope you can hold your breath, for you'll find it on the floor of the ocean yonder."

Amelia wavered. "What?"

"Lay up no treasures for yourself upon the earth, where moth and rust destroyeth, and thieves break in and steal. Repent, and lay yourself treasures in heaven."

"How dare you," Amelia said, voice trembling like her limbs. "*You* speak of thieves? That was not yours to take!"

"Nor yours to keep," Salter said. "The deceitfulness of riches chokes the world. Wealth is a snare, and harmful lusts drown men in destruction. Women too."

Amelia balled her fists to keep from shoving him. She hated the tears that spilled forth, almost more than she hated Salter, but she was powerless to do anything about either. "Goddamn you," she said, and blindly turned to stalk away.

He raised his voice so it would follow her: "Whosoever trusteth in his riches will fall, but the righteous shall flourish as a sturdy branch!"

～

A little later, there was a knock at Stonehouse's door. Amelia let Will in but didn't let him hold her. She stood apart, told him what happened, refused to let him go confront Salter.

"It doesn't matter," she said, clinging to Will's arm to keep him still. "It's gone."

Yet when he tried again to draw her close, Amelia pulled away. "I have to get ready for dinner soon."

"I'll come too," Will said.

"No—" She felt a rush of guilt at his wounded expression. "Don't feel you have to because of me."

"Amelia . . ."

Why had she told him her name? It seemed to have undone some tenuous charm, even as it had felt like a magic spell the first time he said it. She turned her back.

Will stepped closer, said softly, "What's changed here? Between us."

"It isn't us," she said. "It's . . . everything. That necklace was the only thing of any worth I had—in case I ever needed . . ."

He laid his hand upon her arm. "I have enough. I can take care of you."

Amelia spun around and clenched her teeth. "I don't want to be taken care of."

～

Dinner seemed stilted, or maybe it was only her. Mrs. Pollard took her aside after and asked if everything was all right. "Abby said she saw you and Mr. Salter earlier. He shouted after you?"

"A little misunderstanding," Amelia said, and declined to elaborate. "Nothing to worry about."

Mrs. Pollard smiled, though her manner was agitated. Amelia wondered what she thought but realized she didn't care. She couldn't.

That night, Will didn't come. Amelia laid no fire in her room. She lay and thought about the necklace, imagined diving for it, surfacing with it in an upraised fist. She pictured Salter scowling at her from the rocks, infuriated she hadn't drowned—and frightened too.

But it was gone, and it wasn't the first time Amelia had lost something precious. She sighed and turned over in her bed. She closed her eyes and tried to conjure the sensation of someone behind her, about to reach out and stroke her hair.

She dreamed her mother came to her, folded the noose of rubies and diamonds into Amelia's palm with her cold, skeletal fingers atop Amelia's own.

When she jerked awake, the room was still mired in shadows; she peered into their depths but discerned no figures there.

Her clenched hands were likewise empty.

∾

After classes the following day, Amelia went to Will's and embraced him in the doorway, flush with relief when he pressed her closer.

"Can we make a fresh start of things?" she murmured into his shoulder.

"I'd like that," he said against her hair.

"Come over tonight," she told him, and kissed him before they parted, not caring who might see.

Twenty-Nine

WHITECAPS

Amelia left the keepers' quarters only a little earlier than usual after dinner, not so much that it should seem suspicious. If that even mattered—which she didn't think it did. Even if she were wrong, it wouldn't have stopped her, a hopeful, happy defiance in her breast.

The necklace might be gone, but that did not mean all was lost. Nor did the fog seem to conceal anything that might perturb her as she hurried back to Stonehouse, rushing toward something, not away.

Rain thrummed on the windows and sloping roof. Amelia bathed as best she could with pitcher and basin. She unpinned and combed out her hair and built up the fire in her bedroom before she dressed in her nicest nightgown—collar, cuffs, and long row of buttons all edged in a subtle frill of scalloped linen lace. It made her look like a virgin bride, she thought, the spill of white to her ankles, the neck like an upright Elizabethan ruff that strangled a little besides. She unbuttoned it to her collarbone, then undid one more, just above her breasts.

And then she waited, each passing moment more excruciating, and more exhilarating, than the last. When she heard the front door of Stonehouse open, she stood before the fireplace, just close enough to feel its warmth against her back. She stayed still as Will walked up the stairs, even as he stepped into the room and stopped a moment to behold her—but when he came to kiss her, Amelia wrapped her arms around him like she'd been drowning and he could save her, or like she would pull him under too.

He was the one with too many layers now. She moved his fingers from the button between her breasts and began to work at his fastenings instead. When he was naked, she was too shy to look at him, so kissed him again instead. His urgency was not without gentleness as he helped Amelia shed her simple garment, and then the heat of the fire felt as if it were all around her.

They stood with their bodies just touching, lips barely brushing, hands unhurried, gliding down each other's arms and backs and hips. She fit her face into the curve where his shoulder met his neck and pulled him closer so the breath shuddered in his chest, and in her own.

He bore her backward—slowly, softly—and laid her on the bed. A brief flare of fear rose in her, but it was coupled with desire, which subsumed it. The firelight washed his skin, and Amelia felt her pulse flicker in kind. And when his mouth met the wetness between her thighs, she had the sense, again, of the sea, of rolling waves and buoyancy, but now she thought of liquid fire, too, or something molten, some transmutation of her self. There was no earth, no air, no distinction between their bodies.

≈

Every night that week he came to her, and every night she experienced the same preternatural phenomenon. The sheets foamed around them like whitecaps, yet in their midst, still they burned, an unquenchable ember even once the blaze at last subsided and the bed was becalmed.

Then Amelia would lay her head upon his shoulder, rise and fall on the swell of Will's breath. Sometimes they would talk, tease each other, or tentatively approach more serious topics; often, it all tangled up together, like when she moved his hand away as he reached for her knee again before she'd even caught her breath.

"See what happens when you spend eight years all alone on an island?" She laughed and rolled out of reach.

A thought needled her, not for the first time. Lightly, she ventured, "Although, I suppose you probably had company when you went on shore leave . . . Not that I care. I didn't have any claim on you then. Not that I have any claim on you now—"

"Oh, but you do." He moved closer and brushed the hair back from Amelia's brow. "You possess me completely." He was smiling, but as he gazed at her, he grew serious. "And I didn't see anyone like that the last time I went."

"Why not?"

"Because. My head was already too full of you."

"Your head, was it?"

He grinned, trailed his hand beneath the sheet. "Don't pretend you weren't besotted. You were already thinking about me in the bath."

A wild laugh bolted from her. "I was *not*. I was only thinking about baths in general!"

"Well, you certainly put a pretty picture in my mind."

Amelia pivoted onto her side and hid her face against his shoulder as her own shook with more idiotic giggles, but suddenly, the giddiness ebbed away.

She stilled. He pulled back to look at her. "What?"

"Nothing." She shook her head and nestled closer. It was just that this—this unfettered glee, this silly sort of joy—was exactly what it had been like before, the first and only time she'd ever fallen so heedlessly and haplessly into another, and she couldn't suppress a sigh, dismayed by the heaviness that settled on her.

"Do you ever think about her?" Amelia murmured. "Your Lucy?"

"Sometimes," Will said, after a moment. "But I didn't even know her. Not who she was once I left. We were only children. And then . . .

she was more like a saint in my mind. Not even real in some way, in the end."

He looked toward the bedside table. "You know, I gave her that watch, originally. To count the hours until we met again, or some such tosh. Christ. And when I went to see Cathy, once I came home—after she told me I didn't know her either and never would—I left a letter for her, with my address in the States. She sent it right back to the hotel wrapped up around the watch. I hadn't even known she had it until then. Almost threw it out. But I took it back to her landlady instead. Never knew she'd kept it until that day I found it here.".

Amelia raised herself on one elbow, touched Will's cheek. He turned his face and kissed her fingers.

～

He came to the keepers' quarters to celebrate New Year's Eve that Saturday. Mr. Clifford climbed up for the year's last watch while Mr. Pollard drank his assistant's share as well as his own. Amelia missed Mr. Clifford's fiddle music, but Mrs. Pollard played her mandolin. Her husband attempted to tap a rhythm with spoons while Finn blew on an empty jug, which at least made everyone laugh—even Claire—which only encouraged him to blow harder.

It was fun at first but became a torment to wait until midnight when they could escape. They feigned some reluctance to kiss when Mrs. Pollard urged them to it. Will only pecked Amelia on the cheek, though his hand rested on her waist. To her surprise, Mr. Pollard followed right behind with his own smacking kiss beneath his prodigious mustache, then assaulted Mrs. Clifford's cheek too. She seemed even less thrilled with the consolation than either Amelia or Mrs. Pollard.

They finished their glasses of champagne, another of Mr. Pollard's special orders relayed by the *Shubrick*, and said good night almost at once, hurried to Stonehouse, where they were barely through the door before they fell upon each other, showering kisses and shoving at clothes and laughing all the way upstairs.

They didn't bother to light a fire in her room, didn't need it once snuggled skin to skin beneath her covers. Amelia thought of Melville's arctic spark and felt herself not one of two but part of a larger, brighter, even warmer thing once more.

"It's Sunday," Will said as they drifted toward sleep.

She could only manage to murmur acknowledgment.

"So, I could stay," he said. "Unless you can't bear to see my face first thing in the morning."

Amelia smiled against his chest and murmured something else, but even she wasn't sure what it was. She might already have been dreaming.

~

When she woke, he was still there, illuminated by the silvered sunlight of another stormy day. They had it all to themselves, she realized, but she didn't care if they did nothing but lie there in the silence woven of wind and rain and breath, and the wash of the sea.

Thirty

THE FIRE

It was somewhat alarming, the things Amelia found she could say to Will now that he knew her name—and body.

Still not everything. Nothing about the other men she'd met after leaving home. In fact, little about the period between fleeing Nantucket and meeting Lucy at all. But other things she'd meant to let sink into oblivion began to float to the surface, and as she picked through the flotsam and jetsam of memories, there was much Amelia was willing to share.

"How did you leave home?" Will asked one night. "Sail away? Or stow away?"

Maybe it was because they were naked and tucked up in bed and in each other's arms that it seemed possible—even inevitable—to answer.

"I rowed. In one of the old whaleboats we used to play in when we were little."

Amelia burrowed into a more comfortable position and stared into a ceiling corner while Will stroked her arm, the motion like a metronome pacing the rhythm of her words. She let them float out as if picking random notes, the song taking shape as she played it.

"It was the middle of July. Eighteen forty-six. The thirteenth. The night the whole town burned."

The flames in the hearth danced in the corner of Amelia's vision, might have come from within her own head.

"I thought I would die. Mother told me, when I was little, that fire would kill me—I'd almost drowned, and that was her way of reassuring me. So, when it broke out, I was *so* certain, so scared. But she told me to run."

The motion of Will's hand slowed, but Amelia continued speaking at the same methodical pace.

"The fire spread so fast . . . It spilled down the streets like running water, leaped up into the ropeworks, breathed through the warehouses. And then the whale-oil barrels caught, hundreds of them. They started exploding—it was like a cannonade, and the flames . . . they rolled out into the harbor. All that burning oil, it set the very waves alight."

"My God." Will's hand stopped entirely, but Amelia's words flowed forth under their own momentum now.

"Two hundred feet from shore I could still feel the heat like a furnace; the stern blistered. I thought the whole sea would catch, and the ocean would burn me alive. I would have believed it was a nightmare if everybody hadn't been talking about it after."

"Jesus. And where were you, then?"

"Falmouth. A little town on the mainland."

At first, Amelia hadn't known where she'd come ashore. Beyond the crescent of rocky sand that finally stopped her blackened boat she saw nothing but dozens of sheep. She'd dragged herself over the gunwale and crawled a few inches across the deserted beach before she could stand, then wobbled up an incline and into the midst of the grazing animals. The scent of swaying pines had filled her head as hugely as the noise of their boughs stirring in the wind while Amelia walked beneath them, the landscape stippled with ponds.

"There couldn't have been three thousand people there. It's a wonder no one marked me. But I kept my head down, moved along quick as I could. Lucky for me, I knew how to hide my accent, too, when I had to talk. Listened to plenty of gossip, though, looked at the papers whenever I could. They said the fire started in Mr. Geary's hat shop, a stray stovepipe spark, but that was a lie. Or a mistake. Most of the rest was true; all the shops burned, most of the warehouses, the Athenaeum, all but one of the wharves, hundreds of homes—everything in that town was made of wood, and most of it was soaked in oil."

She closed her eyes and the flames grew larger, savage talons raking the night sky and stretching out across the water. When she opened her lids, the image was reduced again to the faint flicker of the fireplace on the edge of her vision.

"They said it was a miracle that despite all that, there were no casualties. Hundreds of people were homeless, had no food, lost their livelihoods, but at least no one lost their lives. That's what the papers said. But I know three people died in our house that night. So I know my father must have survived. Otherwise, they would have at least reported us missing. But they didn't. So Father must have said we all ran off together—me and Jonah and Mother and Mr. Henry. And they kept it quiet out of respect. And either he hid their bodies or someone decided to lie for him about that too."

"Christ Almighty," Will murmured. He pushed himself up on his elbows, dislodging Amelia.

She continued, "Or maybe he got lucky and there was just so much rubble no one ever noticed. Because it would have been obvious if they'd found them. Mr. Henry wouldn't have had any reason to be there so late. And a fire wouldn't have broken his nose anyway. Or my mother's ankle." To say nothing of Jonah's skull. And Amelia couldn't speak of that.

Will peered at her, stricken. "How easy would it be for Miss Price to find out who you really are? If she meant to. Could she?"

"I don't know. It wouldn't be easy. 'Lavinia Henry' wouldn't get her anywhere. But I'd never say she couldn't; I wouldn't rule out anything."

Will passed a hand over his face. "But if your father was after you, all that time, surely he would have found you by now. If he was ever going to."

"I don't know that either. It doesn't matter."

Will sank back onto the pillow. "Maybe they did eventually find out what he'd done. And maybe he's rotting in jail right now. Or maybe they hanged him."

Amelia resumed her place upon Will's shoulder. "I doubt it. He was charmed, in some sense. One of the most successful captains they'd ever seen. A shipwreck survivor twice over. And everyone knew about my mother and Mr. Henry, of course. Father already had their sympathy for that. We were read out of meeting for it before—"

"Read out of meeting?"

"Of the Society of Friends. Our church, essentially. Being read out is like . . . a milder version of excommunication. We weren't welcome anymore. People were willing to turn a blind eye for a while, but they couldn't once Jonah was born. Almost two years after my father left for another voyage. Eight months before he came home."

"I see. So that's why he . . . ?"

Amelia sighed, tucked her hand beneath Will's arm. "That was part of it, of course. But if it were only that, he would have dashed Jonah's brains in while he was still in his crib. Instead, he barely looked at him. He'd already known about my mother and Mr. Henry too. Before there was proof, I mean. But he didn't say anything. He might have beaten Mother a little harder when he came back that time, but nothing else changed. And then he went away again. When we heard the news his ship went down—I was *sure*. I hadn't seen my mother that happy, that calm, in years. Even though Nathaniel was on it too. And he didn't make it back. But our father did. *Again*. And he knew it was Mother, who tried to kill him. Who killed his only natural son. I suppose that was what he couldn't forgive."

Will frowned at her. "What do you mean your mother tried to kill him? It was a shipwreck."

Amelia hesitated. She should correct herself, pretend she'd misspoken, or he'd misunderstood. But she wanted to tell him, wanted to say it out loud, because it was a truth that sounded like the most absurd fiction. Giving it voice might make it both less horrible and more real.

"Before he got a captaincy, my father was on the *Essex*. The ship that went down, rammed by a whale. The one Melville wrote about. Well, Father survived it. One of only eight men who did. He married Mother not long after. And she spent years trying to fix fate's mistake, once she knew what he really was. I don't know if he was always like that or if it was the wreck that changed him. He had to do awful things to survive. But something made him a monster. So she prayed, to a power older and stronger than God. That's what she said. Never named it to me. I didn't want to know more. But the year before the fire, it finally answered her. You see, it was the same whale that stove the *Essex*—she called it up from the sea. Just south of the equator. It sank him again. But he still survived."

Amelia wasn't surprised Will looked confused—and wary—but her voice was not so even-keeled now.

"I know how it sounds. But she was different. Not everything she said or did could be explained. I never doubted she had something to do with that wreck, and neither did Father. So he burned her for a witch. And maybe the fire just got out of control. Or maybe she tried to take the whole town with her."

The shock on Will's face was terrible. "*Jesus*. Amelia . . . I don't know what to say."

She didn't either, or simply didn't want to speak the words that came into her head. But why not, after everything else?

235

"Sometimes I worry. That I'm like her, somehow. That I've made things happen, even when I didn't mean to. The fire, in San Francisco. I was so angry with Lucy for planning to leave me. And then Achilles . . . the day before he fell, he—he teased me, and all I could think was that I wished he was gone."

Will was too taken aback to console her, or refute her, as Amelia had expected.

"Do you think I'm crazy?" she said.

"No. I think you've been through so many terrible things I can't believe you're so sane. But all of that . . . hideousness, and death—that has to have changed the way you see things, how you remember them."

"So you don't believe me."

"I do—the important parts. That your father—"

"They're all important parts. They're all true."

Will looked into her eyes for a protracted moment before he said, "All right."

"Don't say that because you want to appease me."

"I'm not. If you say it's true, then it's true."

Amelia studied him, tried to decide if she believed him, if she could unearth any other intimations of thought or feeling behind his solemn face. She could barely raise her voice above a whisper to form her next words. She'd made a ruinous mistake.

"Are you afraid of me?"

"No," Will said, and leaned in at once to kiss her, her mouth, her cheek, her brow. "I love you. My God, I love you."

Thirty-One

Nesting Season

Easy as it was to say so many earthshaking things, *I love you* chief among them, it was no hardship not to talk at all, to simply be together.

They passed the rest of the winter toasting bread in the hearth for their tea and throwing crusts to Banquo, watching seal pups grow fat and play fight (ignoring as best they could the unlucky ones), trying to speak only of safer things, though nothing ever was, entirely.

One rainy night, Will sang a line of an old bawdy song—"The roads they are so muddy, we cannot walk about"—and Amelia joined him for the next: "So roll me in your arms, love, and blow the candles out."

He studied her face as he smoothed an errant wave of hair away. "Our father loved that one. I don't know if he taught it to us on purpose, but we picked it up when we were only little. Our mother was so terribly cross—but she tried so hard not to smile at the same time. We'd no idea what we were singing, of course, but we loved the sound of it. And how it made them both laugh."

They smiled, private smiles at different memories that commingled and grew into a shared thing, but stopped talking again, and spoke with their bodies instead.

～

Perhaps it was because he loved her that Will never so much as alluded to Amelia's romantic past, though she assumed he must be curious. Must understand, or at least suspect, the truth about her relationship with his sister.

If he did, he likely preferred not to think about it. And Amelia couldn't offer anything of her own on such matters. Nor could she speak of any of the other men she'd been with, even the ones she'd wanted.

The year before she'd fled her home, Benjamin Coffin brought Amelia flowers. She'd gone walking with him by the windmills on the hill where she'd so often strolled behind her mother and Mr. Henry. She'd let Ben hold her hand. Once, on the widow's walk of Amelia's house, he'd kissed her, his lips a butterfly lighting on her cheekbone as she smiled out at the harbor.

He'd been ineffably gentle, but he'd wanted nothing more than to be a whaling captain. She couldn't abide the thought of pledging herself to such a man, even if she knew he was nothing like her father. Ben would still have had blood on his hands; that would have been his glory.

Amelia's bosom friend, Hope Folger, thought Ben would stay sweet. She thought Amelia should marry him and be happy when he went to sea. She planned to wed an oceangoing fellow herself. With their husbands gone, they'd have years together, blissfully uninterrupted.

But then the fire had upended everything and Amelia had disappeared. She wondered if Ben had ever looked for her. If Hope had.

Alone and unmoored at sixteen, Amelia had been a shrinking, cringing thing with horse-wild eyes. But she'd quickly learned to put steel in her spine and remove everything from her gaze—even if her soul still cowered like a guttering candle flame within her.

Because she'd had to keep moving, she'd found work—cleaning, mostly, anyplace that needed help: bars, homes, stables, inns—and ferreted out whatever true charity she could. Still, the going was slow. She'd barely made it out of Massachusetts before a year had passed. Yet her father hadn't found her.

She'd avoided Boston and New York City and all such significantly populated places on the coast. Cities should have seemed ideal, filled with such an excess of people she could have disappeared in their crowds, but she'd feared those were exactly the places he would look.

Chicago, when Amelia arrived there four years later, seemed foreign enough, and far enough inland, to shelter her for a time.

But all along the route, from Falmouth onward, other men took liberties, or tried to. Their approaches and personalities varied—fulsome; pugnacious; oddly prissy, as if she'd been the one to make unseemly advances; even scornful. Salter was like that, she thought, without wanting to. He'd ravish a woman for pleasure and as punishment for her bewitching him.

While some made more serious incursions than others, all sought to take what Amelia never consented to give. She learned that some things could be stolen over and over again. And that sometimes it was easier, or at least more prudent, to acquiesce.

She'd done all she could to avoid unnecessary contact, although twice in four years, a glimmer of goodness and even attraction had moved her to offer herself—not for food or shelter or to avoid violence but for the comfort of a kind touch. She'd judged those men safe to spend a night with but stayed no longer. She'd given them nothing she couldn't spare.

But then she'd let Lucy in, and everything had changed.

Back home, Amelia had always been affectionate with Hope. As children, they'd sprawled and squirmed together like kittens from the same litter. In adolescence, they'd held hands, leaned their heads on each other's shoulders, and shared beds, still in perfect innocence. When they'd begun to speak of Ben's interest in Amelia, and the prospect of marriage, they'd practiced kissing amid debilitating fits of giggles that soon dissolved into warm, heavy silences. She'd barely begun to understand what she felt before it was ripped away.

In St. Louis, Amelia had kissed Lucy first—lightly, on the cheek, like Benjamin once kissed her. Then, more recklessly, and wonderingly, on the lips.

When Lucy kissed her back, something familiar had ignited inside Amelia. She'd had years to dwell in grateful awareness of their love before she lost Lucy too.

Will still didn't expressly remind Amelia of his sister—save that wide, warming grin and the way he loved to tease her, the way he made her so ridiculously happy—but she wondered if it hadn't had something to do with the pull she felt toward him from the start. As if a dormant charge in her blood had responded to an electric impulse in his, or her very soul had sensed he was not entirely a stranger.

When he moved in her, if he was not Lucy, at least he was also no other man. And sometimes Amelia could almost pretend nothing bad had ever happened to her, that nothing more would ever trouble her again.

～

Strangely enough, she felt less afraid of certain phantoms than she had in a long time now that she'd acknowledged them aloud. Speaking of them had once seemed the most frightening and impossible thing. But now that she'd done it, hauled them out of the dark, skull-bound sea of her own head, they nearly collapsed, deep-ocean fish that couldn't hold their fearsome shapes once pulled above the surface, into the light.

Other dangers she didn't know intimately enough to exorcise. Whoever might be after Lucy—and might be tipped off by Miss Price—was nothing more than a gleam of eyes and teeth in the darkness.

Still, Amelia felt as safe as she could be, hemmed in by rocky cliffs and screened by sea spray, wrapped up in fog and Will's warm arms besides.

One afternoon, he told her Salter had seen him come inside Stonehouse. "Looked quite grim, too. Yet perhaps . . . vindicated?"

"God, I hate him," Amelia said, then blurted another thing she'd never been brave enough to say before: "Do you think he hurts them? Gertie and Minerva?"

There was surprise on Will's face, she thought more for the bluntly stated question than the notion itself. "I couldn't say. He's strict, clearly. But I've never seen any obvious signs."

"Maybe he cares enough to make sure bruises don't show. Or does things that don't leave marks."

"I imagine we'd know by now," Will said, though with a tinge of doubt.

"People can know and not do anything," said Amelia. "And what *can* you do? Even with proof. He'd have the right to raise up his family as he sees fit."

Will answered delicately. "He might not be so like your father."

"Well, Gertie reminds me of myself too. How I learned to be so small, and still, and silent when he was around. I was just lucky he was away so much. She's trapped in there every day."

Amelia felt a gnawing guilt for not having spoken more with Gertie, for knowing that it hadn't only been an instinctive fear of Salter that stopped her from trying harder. She had wanted to spare Gertie and Minerva any misplaced punishment he might mete out, but she'd also simply wanted to avoid any trouble that had nothing to do with herself.

And Elijah had taken her necklace anyway, cast innumerable possible futures into the deep. Made an enemy he doubtless underestimated.

∾

In late January, Mrs. Clifford announced she was expecting. The dinner congregation erupted in congratulations. Mrs. Pollard was moved to tears. Mr. Pollard said, "A boy, I hope! Even out our numbers before we're completely overrun with women on this rock."

Finn and Samuel echoed the clamorous wish for more male blood on the island. Mrs. Clifford said, "We'll be glad for whatever blessing God sees fit to give us." Her husband smiled at her and squeezed her hand.

On Sunday, Amelia took out her knitting before the fireplace while Will made another attempt at *Moby Dick*. He took every opportunity to be distracted.

"What's that you're working on now?"

"A baby blanket—for Mrs. Clifford." She rushed the words together, so it was hard to tell if the surprise on his face formed immediately after the mention of the baby. Even when his features relaxed into a smile and he said how lovely that was, Amelia bent her head to her stitches to hide the color in her cheeks. Silly, but she was acutely conscious of the fact that they'd never spoken of babies before.

"It wasn't a secret, was it?"

"It couldn't possibly be at this point. Have you seen her lately?"

"No," Will said, in a teasing tone that made Amelia raise her eyes to his. "I don't think I've seen anyone but you lately."

She parroted Mrs. Pollard: "Well, you have little enough to look at out here, after all."

"It doesn't matter what I look at," Will said. "You're still all I see."

Amelia arched an eyebrow. "I'm not sure that's as flattering as you think it is. If you're including all the elephant seals and seagulls . . ."

He laughed. "See why I don't write you poetry?"

"I'll gladly take your pastries instead."

Upstairs, one blustery February night, she told him, "I think you should stay away for a while. Until the baby's born."

"Why?"

"Because what if it happens at night? And someone comes to get me while you're here?"

He chuckled in that way that still made Amelia quake. "You really think they don't all know by now?"

She rolled onto her stomach to hide her face in the pillow, but also so Will would stroke her back. After a few moments, letting her voice remain somewhat muffled, she confessed, "Mrs. Pollard did share some . . . interesting methods of preventing conception. Honestly, it sounded more like a salad-dressing recipe."

Will laughed a second after Amelia did, and then neither of them could stop. "When was this?" he said.

"Christmas Eve. She was drunk, I think."

"Christmas *Eve*. Do I have her to thank for the Christmas present, then?"

"No," Amelia said, and turned again, onto her back. "Thank the stars for that."

"I do," he said, and kissed her. "Every night."

～

Whatever the other islanders knew or thought, however much Amelia wanted Will by her side every second she could possibly steal, she pressed the point of his staying away from Stonehouse for a while.

She missed him, and never slept as well without him; the shadows seemed to stir more meaningfully when he was gone.

But she wasn't afraid until March, when the *Shubrick* made its first visit of the new year.

Thirty-Two

CONFINEMENT

Though it was Mrs. Clifford's last reliable chance to head into San Francisco for the birth, she didn't seem at all tempted by the possibility. She probably wouldn't have been able to find a doctor to attend her or a hospital willing to admit her anyway. It shouldn't have surprised Amelia, yet the thought hadn't occurred to her before.

Just as well Mrs. Clifford seemed confident in letting God's will guide the labor, then—and in having two women there to help it along. But what choice did she have?

~

When it came, the *Shubrick* brought nothing for Lucy Riley, for which Amelia was glad; the tender's appearance now made her nervous, just like it made Mary chafe. The mule had learned to associate the steam whistle with hauling heavy loads of cargo up the rocks in her winch harness. If she hadn't been corralled before the ship signaled its approach, she often needed to be chased down.

Amelia had to curb a similar impulse to bolt, easier to do now that Will joined the rest of them on the landing.

That cold day in March, Mrs. Pollard waggled a letter at him. "Mr. Sisson! All the way from New York!"

He managed to only look startled for a second. Amelia's shock felt frozen on her face. She watched Will read the address, felt her heart race faster at the way he wouldn't look at her. "Pardon me a moment," he said, and turned and walked away toward the other side of Tower Hill.

Amelia's mind churned with terrible notions. Miss Price had known Lucy in New York, of course. Will had never mentioned any connection to that city, yet clearly had one. The awful, obvious thought was: Could it still be possible that Miss Price had in fact been referring to him when she'd spoken of some sinister man who might have harmed Lucy?

It made even less sense than it had before, and Amelia didn't believe that Will had lied when he said he didn't know Eva Price. Yet an echo of his voice from one of their first conversations in the chapel came to her now: *I was a completely different person then.* So perhaps both things were true. Maybe the Will Amelia knew was once the man who'd wanted to hurt Lucy but had become a calmer, kinder person through the years.

She couldn't help but recall how he'd grabbed her wrist the first time they met in Stonehouse. Yet he'd apologized, and he'd only ever touched her gently since then.

She should go after him—she *must*—but she didn't move, and then Mrs. Pollard was ushering everyone except Mr. Salter to the keepers' quarters for lunch.

Halfway through the meal, Will reappeared, acting perfectly normal, though it wasn't customary for him to join them on these crowded occasions. Amelia studied him, neither soothed nor fooled by his calm demeanor, not least of all because he still avoided meeting her gaze.

She saw him pass a letter to the *Shubrick* captain as the men readied themselves to return to their vessel. She barely restrained herself from hauling on Will's arm as they all filed from the house. But as the others ambled to the landing to watch the tender depart, she did take his elbow.

"Who was that letter from?"

"My old business associate," Will said, eyes trained forward as he led Amelia toward Stonehouse. "Carmelo Ricci."

She frowned. "What did he want?"

Will didn't answer until they were inside. He removed his cap, stared at it as he turned it in his hands. "I lived in New York for a few years. That's where the sugar refinery was. So, when Mrs. Pollard said Miss Price was from there, I assumed Cathy must have gone to the address I'd left her. Beyond that . . . I thought she might have fallen in with a bad crowd, but not one I ever knew. Miss Price wasn't around the Riccis in my time, anyway."

He shook his head and chuckled grimly. "The funny thing is, I wrote to Carmelo last year, right after you told me what happened to Cathy. I thought maybe the letter never made it, or Carmelo decided not to respond. We didn't exactly part on the best terms; he wasn't sad to see me go anyway, miserable bastard I'd turned into, in his words. But when you told me . . . I wanted to know if Cathy had gone there."

"When did she?"

"Carmelo said she turned up back in forty-nine. About a year after I gave up and left. But he'd no idea where I'd gone, so he couldn't help her. She mustn't have had any other plan. I imagine she didn't have much money left. So I can see why she would have done it . . ."

"Done what?"

Will looked up and sighed. "He said she married his cousin, Giancarlo."

"What? No." A tremor of shock started in Amelia's body, spread to her voice. "Lucy was never married."

"Apparently so. I never dealt directly with Gianni, but he was always skulking about. He could be charming. If you didn't know any better. I suppose by the time Cathy did, it was too late. I'm not surprised she left him—only that he never found her, frankly. Or me. She managed to hide her tracks well, leave false trails—Carmelo said they found a record of two tickets booked to England under Will and Catherine Sisson. And she had a head start, too, slipped off while Gianni was away on business."

Will practically vibrated with emotion Amelia couldn't quite pin down. Fear, she thought, as well as anger. He looked about to tear his hat asunder. "If I'd thought she'd ever actually go to New York—if I'd had any *idea*, I never would have left."

Amelia understood what he was saying—and not saying—even as she resisted, brain operating independently of her balking heart. "So that's who Miss Price meant, then. Gianni. And that's why Lucy wanted to come to you—so you could explain things to him and help her shake Miss Price too. Because if *you* told him Lucy was in San Francisco, then maybe he wouldn't be so angry. And then Eva wouldn't have had any leverage left. Two birds, one stone."

A glaze of tears made Will's eyes shine bright in the dim room. "It makes sense. Except I still don't understand why she *waited*, why Cathy didn't just come straight to *me* . . ."

If it was fear, Amelia thought, it wasn't of Will's anger but of his pain. "She must have been worried you wouldn't see her. After what she'd said about not forgiving you. She must have felt so guilty. Maybe she was going to pretend it was a coincidence that she ended up here too."

The tears rolled down Will's cheeks.

Amelia wanted to hold him, but there was more to discuss. "And maybe she wasn't sure she wanted to get you involved either. How bad is this Gianni, exactly?"

Will appeared pained but didn't look away. "I tried to have as little to do with him as humanly possible. I never saw him do anything outright. But there were no end of stories—he didn't have too many enemies because everyone heard what happened to those. No one who knew him dared get on his bad side. But with strangers, even the smallest slight would set him off . . ."

"Tell me," Amelia said. "I need to know."

Will gave his cap another twist, smothered another sigh. "Allegedly, he broke some woman's ankle when she trod on his foot on the street and failed to apologize. And there was a newsboy who insulted him; so the story goes, Gianni pulled the lad into an alley and sliced out his tongue. That sort of thing. Half of it rubbish, I'm sure—"

"But easy enough to believe?" Amelia felt made of water, yet somehow remained standing. "Miss Price said whoever was after Lucy would have cut her heart out. That maybe he'd take mine instead."

Will expelled a harsh breath. "I swear to you, Giancarlo Ricci will never lay eyes on you. I just sent another letter off with Captain Harris, asked him to get it on a clipper if he can."

"What does it say?"

He shrugged. "The truth about Cathy's death."

"And you think they'll believe that?"

"Coming from me, yes. Carmelo will. So Gianni will too."

Amelia choked out a derisive laugh.

"Look," Will said, "we know Miss Price knew Cathy was in San Francisco for well over a year, yet she never told Gianni. If she goes to him now—with any story—he'll find out she kept that from him. He won't take kindly to it. So, if Miss Price is as shrewd as she seems to be, then she won't breathe a word. And she was only trying to scare you."

Amelia gnawed her thumbnail. "Well, even if she *doesn't* go to Gianni, he'll get your letter soon enough. And won't that sound like a tidy coincidence? His *wife* was here all this time and now she's dead? Even if he believes you, he sounds like the kind of man who'd want to see for himself."

"Then he can see." Will seemed suffused by a sudden calm. "He won't turn up here, though. Not in a million years."

"Then he'll send other men."

"Then he will. If he does, they can't come ashore without being seen, they can't do anything but assess the situation once they're here.

He may be ruthless, but he is not stupid." Will stepped closer, gently took Amelia by the arms. "If he sends someone, I'll speak to them. I'll go back to the city with them if Gianni's there, talk to him myself."

"*No.*"

"What, then? Do you want to leave? We can take the boat, sail north—away from San Francisco."

"No." Amelia disengaged and turned her back, her mind churning so violently she could pluck no single thought or feeling from it. She gazed out the window at the fragmented view of crenellated rocks and tumbling sea, the hazards that also made this place a haven. With a deep breath, she faced Will again. "If you're telling the truth, that he'll believe you, or he'll at least be reasonable if he doesn't, then we're fine, aren't we?"

Will waited a beat too long to say, "Yes," but his voice was still steady, so she nodded.

"Then there's nothing to do. Nothing's changed. We're fine."

~

She tried to believe it and sometimes succeeded, or at least managed to push the fear and doubt down deeper. Mrs. Pollard sensed Amelia's nervousness, assumed it was all due to Mrs. Clifford's confinement, rapidly approaching.

"You won't have to be there," she assured her. "Not in the room itself, if you don't want to be. But it would be a great help to heat the water and mind the children and all that."

"Of course. Whatever I can do."

She remembered her mother's delivery of Jonah. Amelia had been twelve, barred from the bedroom, but the entire house reverberated with rending cries; they rang in her ears even when Mr. Henry escorted her along Orange Street to try to take both their minds off it. By the time she'd been permitted to see her mother and meet her brother, the bloody sheets and afterbirth had all been whisked away, but a deep, metallic smell, not unlike the butcher shop's, lingered in the room.

As Mrs. Clifford's time grew nearer, Amelia couldn't help but fret on her behalf, as well as about the expectation that she would help with the delivery—but in an odd way, it was a comfort, a distraction from other worries.

She wished she hadn't banished Will from Stonehouse. But she was used to managing her own fears in the dark and suspected he was too.

Her resolve only wavered on the twenty-third, the anniversary of Lucy's—Cathy's—death. Amelia couldn't sleep at all. She thought she would put her cloak on over her nightgown and go to Will's, just to curl up in the space between his side and arm and let her tears run down his ribs, but she couldn't move.

She half hoped the knock would come that night, the summons to witness the arrival of a new life. But nothing troubled Amelia's door save the wind, and a soft, finger-tapping rain.

∾

Mrs. Clifford's labor began on the second Saturday in April, but the baby didn't come until Sunday. She mopped up her own water and went about as usual that first day, until the nausea set in and the pains became too great to ignore.

When the business of pushing began, Amelia rushed in and out of the bedroom on various orders from Mrs. Pollard—boiling water, cleaning basins, fetching brandied cherries and beef broth and fresh linens. She observed the proceedings, or fixed them in her mind at least, as vivid fragments: Mrs. Pollard's hands gently rubbing lard into Mrs. Clifford's nether parts, as she said it helped the passage; Mrs. Clifford's hands pulling on a towel knotted to the bed frame, the long tendons in her wrists standing out as a wrenching cry seeped from between her clenched teeth; the way the snowy sheets sucked up the bright outflow of blood, tide marks of brown and crimson spreading ever outward until the sodden mass had to be replaced; how when Mrs. Clifford got up to squat the bud of the baby's head appeared as if it would burst forth in a rush before retreating back into the body in which it had grown, as if reluctant to leave that shelter.

In between offering assistance and snatching such frightful and fascinating glimpses of the process, Amelia checked on the children. They were all meant to stay upstairs. Samuel happily slept in Finn's bed while the older boy himself sat staring—wide eyes fixed on the wall every time Amelia popped her head in. Phyllis and Joy sat on the staircase, ready to run to their mother's side if they were called or allowed. The older girl was fully awake, but her sister slumped against her, fighting sleep.

Mr. Clifford sat in a dining chair he'd dragged into the hall outside the bedroom door. He served as sentry when Amelia was dispatched to the kitchen or ran out back to draw more water. Every time she passed him, she gave an encouraging smile and said it was going well, wouldn't be long now. He nodded but never looked away from the pattern of the runner; his right leg never stopped jouncing.

At almost three in the morning the baby finally slid into the world. He was limp and wrinkled and didn't make a sound. He seemed a strange color underneath a greasy white film that put Amelia in mind of candle wax and sperm whales. She thought something must have gone terribly wrong and tried to keep her face from showing it. She held her breath while Mrs. Pollard briskly rubbed the tiny limbs and narrow chest with a soft towel and swished a fingertip into his slack, silent mouth. But then she thumped his back and his furious little face twitched and gaped in a shuddering cry that made them all laugh even as tears sprang to their eyes.

Mrs. Clifford held her arms open and received her son with a beautiful hysteria.

"Go ahead and tell the proud papa," Mrs. Pollard said.

Mr. Clifford was standing outside the door now, thumbs hooked into the armholes of his vest, a shade of expectation on his otherwise stoic face. He could hear the thin cries and the wild laughter and the sweet, murmured words of his wife, but he must also have heard the silence stretching before.

"It's a boy," Amelia told him.

He broke into a grin as a soundless laugh shook his shoulders. "Can I go in?"

"I don't see why not." As if it were her place to tell him, besides.

Mrs. Pollard looked like she wanted to fuss about Mr. Clifford entering the room but must have decided there was no point. The Cliffords were oblivious to everything save their new son and each other, so she only murmured a few last instructions to Amelia, said she supposed a clean shift could wait a little while. She swept the placenta into an enamel basin, the soft mass of dark tissue still attached to the baby by the ropy cord of flesh stretching from his swollen belly. His anchor, still fastened to his body though he was already unmoored from his mother.

~

As Jacob grew stronger and began to look less alien and less angry at being expelled from the womb, and as Mrs. Clifford began to heal, the last of the elephant seals left the rocks and the seabirds returned in increasing numbers. The goldfields bloomed and the islands of the dead once more teemed with life.

The eggers would return soon too; it would be a year since Amelia arrived on Southeast Farallon. How much had changed, and how much else had not—in such a cosmically short time so much had become constant, innately familiar, depended upon, even as new uncertainties abounded.

She tried not to think of the end of things, of things that had been or that might be in the future. Life would go on after she was there to mark it, and even she would live in the memories of others for a time once she was gone. Everyone and everything seemed, in some small way, immortal. Time did not pass so much as revolve. For now, it carried Amelia forward.

Thirty-Three

CROSSING THE JORDAN

With the arrival of the egg pickers, Amelia was once more without Will at night. He thought it best to sleep by the barracks, to keep an eye on things. She preferred none of the eggers know, anyway. Will asked if she wanted to resurrect the old arrangement in which he brought Banquo to her every night until the season ended. Amelia declined, only because she didn't want him to think he had reason to worry—at least not any more than he might already.

They both scrutinized the season's crop of pickers, absent the man who'd assaulted Samuel, of course. None seemed innately suspect or cause for particular concern.

Indeed, May and June passed rather unremarkably. There was another visit from the *Shubrick*, which brought nothing beyond the usual staples; it was far too early for Will to expect a reply from New York. They celebrated Samuel's sixth birthday soon after, and then Fiona's seventh.

Amelia took a plate of cake over to the Salters. She hoped Minerva and Gertie would be there alone, but Elijah answered her knock and refused her offering. "Let me make it clear," he said. "You are not welcome here."

"I know," Amelia said. "Yet here I am."

When he shut the door in her face, she barely flinched.

Then Lucy's birthday came. No one asked her age, of course, but Mrs. Pollard had marked her calendar after all. She made a cake with murre eggs and invited Mr. Sisson to dine with them that evening.

Amelia thought it might be awkward, depressing, but she didn't feel more than a twinge of melancholy, and Will seemed in similar blithe spirits. Perhaps there was effort concealed behind his smile too, but she only cared that it felt like grace to be held in his arms and kissed in the doorway of Stonehouse that evening.

She permitted herself to smell the neck of the perfume bottle in the morning, and again before she went to sleep. She wondered if Cathy had worn the scent when she was married to Giancarlo Ricci—in Amelia's mind, he was no more than eyes and teeth flashing like blades in the dark, shadowy hands wrapped around Lucy's throat.

That night, Amelia woke up choking.

≈

The first day of July was a Sunday, fair. Will came by to ask if she wanted to take a stroll on the beach, though it barely took two minutes to walk from one end to the other. They climbed down to the patch of sand. This time Amelia unlaced her boots, stripped off her stockings and left them by the bottom tread. She held her skirt and petticoats and crinoline up above her ankles to let the swash anoint her feet and squinted out at the blue reaches of the sea where they met the paler sky.

"End of this month," Will said, "the egg-plundering horde will be leaving again. It'll be time to make my annual foray into civilization. But I don't want to go. Unless you'll come with me."

Amelia was startled, but smiled, eyes still narrowed against the sun. "You know I can't do that. Honestly, the idea of walking down a street, with crowds of people . . . It seems too strange to be real anymore. Besides, I already sent Waldham another year's payment."

Will stood close enough that their arms brushed, lowered his voice though no one was anywhere within earshot. "Wouldn't it be nice, though, to spend a whole week together? Go to sleep in the same bed every night, wake up there every morning? You could have your bath. We could take one of those together too . . ."

Amelia laughed, leaned against him. "It's too obvious if we leave together. And then come back grinning like idiots."

Will drew away to look at her, semiseriously. "What if we come back married?"

Amelia's heart skipped a beat, but she laughed again. "Is that a proposal?"

"It would be a poor one, so no. But you might say I'm . . . testing the waters."

She smiled back out at the ocean, sunlight splintered all across the rumpled cerulean plain. "They look favorable to me."

Before he could reply, voices drifted down from the rocks; a group of eggers had arrived at their washing station.

Amelia made a mock curtsy at Will, bobbed her head. "Well. Good day, Mr. Sisson."

He watched her go toward the ladder, but obligingly turned back to the brilliant horizon as she bent to gather her boots.

That evening, all Amelia could think about was what he'd said. She'd rejected the possibility of marriage long ago and hadn't been sorry. The concept of becoming a wife to any man was repugnant. But now, she thought she might like to have Will for a husband. She certainly liked the idea of staying with him—or even of going somewhere else together.

Whenever she did leave the island, Amelia realized, she could no longer fathom going alone.

~

Next morning, daybreak woke her. Raised voices drew her to the window. She could see nothing, nor could she make out any words, but then glass shattered, a series of small explosions, each one splintering Amelia's nerves.

She dressed as quickly as she could, corset over nightgown. A gunshot propelled her heart into her throat, made her fingers fumble on the last few fastenings of her dress. A few moments later, a frantic knocking on the front door nearly made her trip headfirst down the stairs.

Mrs. Pollard stood outside, wringing her hands. "Have you seen Finn?"

"No," Amelia said. "What's happened?"

Mrs. Pollard glanced back in the direction of the keepers' homes, from which indistinct arguing still issued. "Someone smashed a lot of eggs in the shed last night. Naturally, they came looking for the boys—and one of those ruffians started pitching rocks through the windows. Of the wrong house, no less! He must have busted out every one of them before Mr. Salter fired that warning shot! I'm sure it'll take forever to replace them—and cost a fortune, too, not to mention what we're going to owe them for the eggs. But now I can't find Finn; I thought he might have slipped away in the commotion, maybe come over here."

Amelia frowned. "I haven't seen him. Maybe he went up the hill?"

"I doubt it. He couldn't have made it up to the top yet anyhow, and I didn't see him. Unless . . . well, if he smashed the eggs in the middle of the night—and I hate to think it, but he has held a grudge against the pickers since that brute hurt you and Samuel last year—then he would have had plenty of time to hide somewhere . . . Oh, but I don't want to have to check that horrid cave! He's run off there before in a sulk, but he knows he's not allowed!"

"I'll go with you." Amelia bent to retrieve her boots, deciding stockings could wait, but paused in pulling open one shoe and glanced up. The unease on Mrs. Pollard's face sharpened into fear when she saw the worry crystallize in Amelia's own eyes.

"What?" Mrs. Pollard breathed.

"Maybe he went across the bridge—over the Jordan." Finn's fascination with that narrow channel of rough water and the flimsy lines the eggers strung across it had never wavered.

"No." Mrs. Pollard swayed but did not fall; instead, even as two figures approached Stonehouse and one called out, "Any luck?" she turned and hastened toward the western part of the island, in the opposite direction from Skeleton Cave.

Another shout—Mr. Pollard, calling his wife's name—and Amelia hesitated only a second before abandoning her boots and running after, rocks jabbing her bare feet. She became aware of the men pursuing. Her fear fluttered harder.

Mrs. Pollard never broke her stride and somehow never stumbled. Amelia tried to simultaneously watch her, mind her own footing, and make out the landscape ahead of them with the wind whipping her loose hair about her face. A light fog wreathed the tops of the rocks like a haze of smoke from a doused fire. She strained to see the ropes that spanned the Jordan Channel materialize.

But as they neared the gap where the eggers had built their precarious bridge over the churning passage of water, they could see the misty space above the surf was empty—no hemp spider lines strung across the break in the granite hulks, though they'd been there the day before. She had a vivid image of Finn cutting them, or perhaps they'd simply given way in the dark.

Amelia pushed hard to close the short distance between herself and Mrs. Pollard, managed to say, "No, don't!" and grab for her, but the woman's sleeve slipped through her fingers.

She jerked to a stop at the edge of the land, peered over into the chasm, and screamed in a manner that pierced the marrow of Amelia's bones. Mr. Pollard sprinted past a second later and yanked his wife back before he looked over the ledge himself and uttered a ragged curse.

Amelia couldn't move, couldn't look.

Will was right behind Mr. Pollard and called, "Amos, wait—" as he began to climb down the rocks.

Mrs. Pollard dropped to the unforgiving ground and curled into herself as she sobbed. Amelia crouched at her side and touched her shoulder as they waited for the men to reappear.

When they did, it was only with Finn's knife. His mother keened not at the harrowing sight of his broken body but at his sudden, complete absence from the world.

Some of the eggers had gathered nearby; low murmurs passed between them. They parted as Mr. Pollard staggered through their midst, muttering to himself, "He nearly lost his damn knife on top of everything else. I'll tan that boy's hide when I find him!"

The knot of men reformed in his wake. One said loud enough for Mrs. Pollard to hear, "I'll bet that whole load of broken eggs he fell and got washed away. Serve the little bastard right."

Will spun and jabbed a fist that burst the man's nose, then tackled him and sank an elbow into the egger's ribs before he could even attempt a defense. Will grabbed the man's head to lift it and slam it back into the ground.

"Stop it!" Amelia shrieked, too afraid to reach out. *"Will! Stop!"*

He'd wrapped his hands around the egger's throat but released the man and leaned back on his heels, breath heaving through him. The bloodied man beneath Will breathed too, groaned faintly with every exhale, but otherwise lay motionless.

"Get up," Amelia said, and after another second, Will did.

No one else moved or made a sound. Even Mrs. Pollard watched mute and frozen, still crumpled on the ground.

"Help him," Amelia said to the other eggers, with a vague gesture at their battered workmate, and tentatively reached toward Will to lead him away.

But he resisted. "No—Amos is right. Finn might be out here somewhere. I'll go help him look." To the eggers, he said, "You lot get that bastard back to the barracks and start mending the lines. You've work to do."

They did as they were told, and Will set off to search for Finn. Amelia helped Mrs. Pollard up and led her to the keepers' quarters, where Elijah Salter stood surveying the gouged-out windows of his house. He turned to watch the women pass. Perhaps there was no schadenfreude in his expression, but neither was there sympathy. Amelia glowered, felt once more as if blood were in her eyes.

Mrs. Clifford opened the door, a question she didn't need to ask hanging on her lips. She stood aside to let a sobbing Mrs. Pollard pass. Amelia helped her upstairs, where the woman collapsed on the sofa and her daughters huddled in her arms.

In a low voice in the Cliffords' parlor downstairs, Amelia relayed what she knew.

"I should have heard him come down," Mrs. Clifford muttered. "I'm up half the night with Jacob anyway. I should have heard him open the door."

"He was determined. And he knew enough to be quiet. Mrs. Pollard didn't hear anything either."

"Oh, *God*, it's a wonder he didn't take Sam with him." The breath went out of Mrs. Clifford; she gripped the back of a chair, and Amelia touched her shoulder.

~

A somber atmosphere pervaded the house. Everyone was raw, as if their skin had been peeled back. The staccato reports of Salter's hammer as he nailed boards over his broken windows were nigh unbearable.

They did not find Finn, even when they took the boats out to see if he had somehow made it onto one of the other islets. The next time Amelia ventured into the Pollards' parlor, someone had arrayed the pocketknife and several crude carvings on the table: a bird, a boat, a seal, a rabbit, a dog, which she thought was meant to be Banquo.

"You should never have given him that awful thing," Mrs. Pollard snuffled from her perch on the sofa, bookended by Claire and Fiona, all their eyes fastened on the objects the lost boy had left behind.

Mr. Pollard only sighed, but a moment later said, "What I want to know is, how can they even prove he did it? Maybe one of those sons-a-bitches smashed the eggs and lured Finn out there last night. Maybe I oughta go over and break some more fucking heads in—"

"Amos, please." There was only weariness in Mrs. Pollard's voice. "It was an accident. Just another *stupid* accident in this *awful* place. And this time we don't even have a body. Not that it would matter, would it? We don't have any home where we could bury him—he'd be in San Francisco, just like his poor little sister, and then we'd be all the way out here or else moving on someplace else, *again*. Leaving them behind anyway. My sweet babies."

As if they could be any further gone than they were already, as if they could ever be excised from their mother's memory, wherever they were laid to rest, or not. But Amelia understood the impulse to cling to what remained, to want something to cling to. It still hurt, sometimes, to know she had nothing left of her own family to hold or look at.

Even with Lucy, there'd been so little to commune with afterward. The coroner had advised against seeing her body, yet Amelia had imagined it a million times. She could still hear Mrs. McGowan crooning about the charred, disfigured remains. *But she wouldn't have suffered, dearie. She wouldn't have woken up for the smoke.*

That claim was far less comforting than touching Lucy's combs and bottles and clasping the silver watch in her fingers; those were tangible things Amelia did not have to choose to believe, could not doubt.

261

She slipped her hand into her pocket as she regarded Finn's things across the room, felt the smooth weight of the watch in her palm, the way the metal warmed against her skin, its heartbeat ticking in her fingertips. She wished she could do something, anything, other than stand and share the family's pain.

But there was no taking it away, Amelia knew. No helping shoulder it, even. Like love, grief was boundless, and eternal. It flowed all throughout a body and flooded all the space around it, drowned you again every time you took another breath. Only time would tell how much the tide might ebb, but sure as the sea was ruled by the moon, it would roll back in again. You would be touched by its swash for the rest of your days. And no matter who stood beside you in solidarity, you were an island, in the end.

~

Even so, Amelia let Will and Banquo into Stonehouse every night after Finn's death. That first evening, she'd been slightly shy of Will. She'd instinctively tensed at his touch, although it was gentle. He'd stepped back from her, distress plain on his face, and said, "I know what I did was . . . excessive. Misplaced. I'm sorry I did it. And I'm sorry you saw it. You'll never look at me the same way again."

She'd immediately crossed the space between them and embraced him. He'd wrapped his arms around her in kind. He'd stayed until morning, held her while she cried, and while she slept. Amelia skimmed her lips around his grazed knuckles, the little one broken, judging by the way it swelled. Even when she exhausted her tears, and sobbed her brain and body to fatigue, her flickering panic would not subside entirely.

What if someone came for Will? If the battered egg picker survived and decided not to pursue the matter—and if none of the other men spoke up on his behalf—then maybe no one would care. But the mere possibility of Will being harmed frightened Amelia, even more than Will's own anger had.

Or what if she woke one night and saw the pale shade of a boy slip around the edge of the door, while Banquo stared from his spot on the rug?

Or if he barked at a solid black shape, and her father's boot—or that of some other man sent by Cathy's husband—splintered his jaw?

What if more of her own past insisted on repeating?

~

When she lay still in the dark and tried to be lulled by Will's steady breathing, Amelia saw the night of the fire again and again. Other things as well: the bloody whale battles her father had impressed upon her—murders, epic struggles for life even when all was lost; the toothy twist of ivory to which her mother prayed for ruin and release; the short, slender finger bone Amelia found once in her father's coat pocket, the top two joints of a pinkie, scored from where the meager flesh had been gnawed off it years ago, after his first brush with death in the *Essex* disaster. *To remind myself,* he said when he caught her staring, *to seize every opportunity God puts before me.*

If God had indeed protected him, what retribution might yet lie in store for her? The guiding light Amelia tried to keep and nurture within herself might only be an ember waiting to catch and burn her down from inside, take everything around her with it.

When she woke from a nightmare with a feeble cry and found Will smoothing her hair, telling her she was all right, Amelia clung to him and hid her face in his shoulder.

This stirring up of old things, however smooth-edged they'd become after years of being tumbled by the tides of time, was far worse than before. It was not just bits and pieces rising in a current before settling back down again, but an entire moon-dark sea of memories whipped into a whirlpool. It all revolved inside Amelia's mind as if it had only just happened, was still happening, or was somehow yet to come—and the eddy only slowed when she pressed herself to Will's warmth and let his heartbeat fill her head.

Even as her breathing calmed, she feared she was being foolish, selfish. She should let him go, and go herself, not endanger him with her devotion or her dependence. But it was too late for that now, Amelia knew. It would be too late even if she'd still had the necklace to fund an escape. She'd let Will fall in love with her. Worse, she'd let herself fall too. She'd likely doomed them both.

Thirty-Four

HOMECOMING

When they'd received the news of her father's rescue, Amelia's mother wept. Mr. Henry held her upright. Amelia peeped through the keyhole and listened with her ear to the wood, while Jonah occupied himself with a drawing Amelia had started and charged him to finish.

"He won't go back again," their mother said, "I know it. We must leave. We should have left already."

"We will," said Mr. Henry. "Anywhere you want—all of us, tonight."

"But he shall never let us go. He'll follow if we try. Hunt us to the ends of the earth."

"Then we can appeal to the authorities. God knows you have scars enough to show as proof."

A scathing bark of laughter thick with tears was Amelia's mother's reply. In the ringing silence that came after it, she strained to hear Mr. Henry make a promise she knew his gentle soul could never let him keep. Instead, all he offered was a different, less specific lie. "We'll find a way, my darling."

Even then, Amelia's own heart had sunk into her stomach.

∽

When her father filled the doorway of their home again two weeks later, he seemed to blot out all the light, undiminished by his ordeal. No one went to him or offered effusions of relief or gratitude.

"The sharks would have given me a warmer welcome into the brine," he jeered, and Amelia felt the ocean swell of her mother's rage from where she stood across the room, by the threshold of the parlor.

At the foot of the stairs, Amelia tightened her grip on Jonah's warm, damp hand, but her father only paused a moment as he passed the two of them. His cold blue eyes slithered like eels over Amelia, didn't see Jonah at all.

"You've grown some. Fairer face than your mother, but that same dark look. What else has she taught you, I wonder . . . Little witch."

He continued up the staircase and disappeared around the bend. His footsteps creaked above their heads, turned the house into an unsettled ship. Their mother crossed the floor but stopped short of caressing either child. Her expression was far from the calm gaze she'd fixed on Amelia the day she'd nearly drowned.

∽

Her father slept well into evening. Her mother disappeared into the cellar for a while, then laid the table for dinner, but no one disturbed him, nor did any of the rest of them eat, save a few morsels of Indian pudding for Jonah. None of them retired upstairs either, though the hour hand of the grandfather clock moved past nine, then ten. Night drew darkness across the windows even as the curtains remained open. Jonah's head drooped, as did his eyelids, but he never asked to go to bed.

When Amelia was only Jonah's age, her father had brought home the malformed sperm-whale jaw that took pride of place on their mantel. The whale it was wrenched from had been a bona fide adult, almost fifty feet in length, according to Amelia's father. It fought valiantly but succumbed all the same, a vanquished monster slicked red with blood that glowed like hellfire in the light of the try-pots.

That skeletal souvenir was a fearsome yet fascinating thing, a curio, a testament to both the wonders of nature and the supremacy of man. But when the great Captain Osborne was gone on subsequent conquests, Amelia had seen her mother treat it more like an altar, lighting candles and burning herbs around it, murmuring words into its whorl of teeth, even anointing it with her own blood when she thought no one was spying. Or perhaps she didn't care if she was observed. It never ceased to give Amelia shivers, even when there was no firelight to make the jawbone flicker and bristle with shadows and there were no crimson droplets running down its porous length.

That night, as they hunkered in the parlor waiting for a storm to break, the hot, dry wind picking up outside, the room dark except for what moonlight stole in, her eyes strayed back to it repeatedly. It made her think of a giant albino centipede that would writhe to life at any moment and scuttle over to pounce on her, pierce her with poison-tipped claws and suck the blood and fat and marrow from her body until only a brittle husk was left.

Sweat trickled down her back beneath the corset she'd only recently become obliged to wear; her clammy skin crawled, and her breath tickled inside her throat. She tensed in anticipation of any sound from above and started every time the wind gusted against the panes or rumbled down the cold bricks of the chimney, the sound like the ghost of fires past.

～

When her father finally stirred and came downstairs, they assembled again, trailed him into the dining room. Jonah rubbed a fist into his sleepy eyes.

"Did no one eat?" her father grumbled, seeing all the places still neatly set.

"We were hardly hungry," said her mother. "Wouldst thou like some ale? Or wine?"

"Cider."

"Amelia, fetch some for thy father."

She did as she was bid, did her best to ignore his smirking glower as he took his place at the head of the table and she slipped past to the basement stairs.

Her mother lit the tapers in their candelabras and filled a plate with cold beef and boiled potatoes.

When Amelia brought the cider to her father and filled his glass, he stayed her arm with an iron hand and peered up into her face, his eyes cradled in a webbed ropework of fine lines etched by constant squinting against sea glares and sea gales.

"Didst thou miss me, daughter?" He plainly mocked her mother's plain speech and Amelia's unease. "Didst thou lose thy tongue these past few years?"

"No, Father."

He let her go and she took her seat. She refused to look up from the table, until reflex made her do it when he said, "Pour yourself a glass, girl."

Amelia hesitated, and his voice hardened. "Have a drink with your poor father, little wretch. Raise a toast to his cursed good fortune and continued health despite all efforts to imperil it. Raise one to your dear, drowned brother, may God rest his watery soul. Even as the lobsters eat his eyes and liver."

Amelia took the bottle in one hand and her glass in the other, but paused when her mother said, "No."

"And why ever not, Lavinia dear? She's old enough. Should we not drink to our sweet, dead boy? And my own bloody luck?"

When she said nothing, he slammed his fist on the table; all the cutlery and glass and china rattled, the candle flames shuddered, his family shrank. He pointed at Amelia with a long-nailed finger. "Pour."

She did. He raised his glass and she raised her own, the amber liquid in it trembling.

"To cheating death and dealing doom. Long life to the killers, and long suffering to those who survive. Blessed oblivion to the ones who've lost."

As if a string were tied between them, or they were playing at being mirrors, their hands brought their glasses to their lips. But he did not touch the rim of his to his mouth, not quite, and before Amelia could tilt her wrist more than a millimeter, before more than a shallow swallow of cider touched her tongue, her mother sprang from her chair and dashed the glass from her fingers.

"Damn thee!"

Her father laughed, put his own glass back down, laced his fingers upon his stomach. "Is every bottle in the cellar poisoned? Every slice of beef? Would the little one like a potato, perhaps?"

Amelia looked between them, the front of her dress wet, her glass in shards beside her empty plate, some slivers having skated off onto the carpet. She tried to discern if there was a strange taste in her mouth, if the prickle at the root of her tongue was anything other than fear. When she saw her mother lunge across the table for the carving fork, Amelia only just managed to scrape her own chair back out of the way. But her father had time enough to move as well, and when her mother charged at him, he caught her wrist with one hand, the side of her cheekbone with the other. She dropped the fork and he sank his talons into her arms to help haul himself to his feet, then cast her down so she cracked against the floorboards, doused her with the cider from his glass.

Amelia stood frozen in old, familiar dread, but Jonah—who had been too little to remember ever seeing such a thing before—jumped up and rushed to their mother's side.

It was an accident, Amelia was almost certain, that her father dealt Jonah a glancing blow with the heavy wooden chair he'd picked up to break over their mother's body. One carved mahogany arm hit the boy's bony shoulder, and the force of the impact sent him spinning back toward the hearth. Its grate had been taken up for cleaning, the season for laying fires passed. Jonah's temple connected with one of the andirons as he landed. The look of surprise on his face eclipsed that of any pain he might have felt.

Amelia threw herself to the floor by his side but was afraid to touch him; blood began to run from his head, and she saw there was no way to hold it back.

She uttered a strangled cry as her father set the chair down, almost primly. "Bastard brat shouldn't have gotten in the way."

When she remembered it, along with mortifying guilt and grief, such corrosive fury coursed through Amelia that she marveled she'd not leaped up and torn him to pieces with her bare hands—that her mother hadn't either, that they had not transformed into a pair of wild panthers and rent him into gory shreds and splintered bones, a raw roast not worth eating. But neither of them had been able to look away from Jonah. Her mother rolled over onto hands and knees and shuffled to his other side, let her fingers hover over his quivering body.

As if incensed no one paid him any mind—or perhaps anxious some spontaneous cure might be effected by touch and words alone—Amelia's father grabbed a fistful of her mother's dark hair and yanked her back onto her feet.

"Foul pythoness," he snarled. "You'll reap just what you sow."

Without thinking, Amelia grabbed a piece of scrimshaw from the mantel, the nearest thing with any heft at hand, and swung it at her father's head. The yellowed whale tooth caught his temple and stunned him into letting go of her mother. A bead of blood rolled down his face, but the wound was minor, only enough to enrage him further. Amelia stared, aghast. But then her mother shoved her, said, "Go! Run." And before her husband could lay his hands on their daughter, she turned to hold him back, redirected his fury onto herself again.

Amelia bolted out the front door. Instead of going to the wharf, she turned in the opposite direction. Sprinted up Main Street, veered onto Pleasant with a stitch in her side, and pounded on Mr. Henry's door until the meat of her hands went numb.

Why had she not at least gone for the police? The notion never occurred to her that night. She'd barely been able to speak, but words were not required to make Mr. Henry understand something terrible had happened. In his dressing gown and robe and slippers, he followed at a fast clip back to Orange Street, outpacing Amelia at the end, disappearing through the front door a moment before she gained the steps.

The air inside the house was a roil of strange sounds, her mother speaking in tongues—a thing Amelia had only ever overheard before in whispers—bawling an incomprehensible language that sent an icy spike of fear through Amelia's gut, a different kind of terror than before, though one that burned right beside it.

Her father, meanwhile, grunted and growled amid blue curses and cries of witchcraft and wantonness. Both crazy; that was the simple thought that flickered through Amelia's mind when she beheld them. What hope did she ever have?

Blood trickled from her mother's mouth—he'd hit her again after Amelia fled. He'd also ripped down the curtain cords and knotted them around her to bind her to the banister. Though her skirts were too long to reveal any evidence, from the way she slumped to one side, Amelia had the sickening thought he'd hobbled her, broken an ankle so she couldn't run. And she saw that the fabric awash around her mother's legs was dark in patches—not with blood, nor could it possibly all be cider. From the overwhelming smell, and the sight of the wall sconce in pieces on the carpet, Amelia understood in a searing flash it must be oil; he'd cast the lamp aside and opened the reservoir, splashed the fuel all over her mother's navy dress. One of the brass candelabras from the dining room had been carried into the front hall and sat perilously close to those streaked skirts.

"What in God's name are you doing?" Mr. Henry cried.

"Putting an end to all this wickedness. This devilry!"

Amelia wanted to slip past them and check on Jonah, but she was too afraid—to risk being snatched up herself, to risk being noticed at all, but also to risk finding her baby brother not breathing, not blinking. She didn't hear any noise from the dining room, but then he never cried. Whatever state he was in, he shouldn't be alone. But she could not move.

Her father began to empty the nearby bookcase, piling the printed kindling at her mother's feet. Mr. Henry edged closer to them, said over his shoulder, "Amelia, go fetch the police."

"She'll be dead before you get back," her father promised.

She'll be dead anyway, Amelia thought. She didn't see any way her mother could survive—or any of them, really. She thought the best thing to do might be to twine her arms around her mother's waist, close her eyes as the fire caught and clawed through them both. Or perhaps her father would reconsider, if she fastened herself to her mother and refused to let go. She could be a shield, if only she could *move*.

"Just calm down," Mr. Henry said, in a reasonable tone that made Amelia want to laugh, the way a lunatic would gibber. "You've been through a great trial," he continued as he took another minuscule step toward her father. "You're not thinking rationally." Amelia wondered what he thought of her mother's glossolalia, if it frightened Mr. Henry too.

"Speak with me, Osborne," he pleaded. "Just give me a moment, man to man."

In response, her father charged at him and struck him in the face with the book he held. The corner split Mr. Henry's eyebrow open. Amelia danced back a few paces as he staggered to one knee and clapped a hand to his brow.

"You don't love her," he said, still in that reasonable, soft tone, now with a touch more fear. "You treat her like an animal. Worse than that. Why not let her go, then? We'll leave this place, and you can—"

Amelia wanted to warn him to stop; she knew he was only making her father more infuriated. But her throat was stopped by sheer horror, even as he reared back and kicked Mr. Henry's gentle face with his heavy boot.

She could only gasp, but it served to tear her mother's attention away from her arcane prayers or maledictions. She screamed Mr. Henry's name instead—*"Owen!"*—which snared Amelia's father's attention, though a second before he'd fixed his eyes on his daughter and looked about to lunge.

He spun back to the banister, against which her mother now struggled more ferociously. As she thrashed and Amelia's father fought to subdue her, she wrested one arm free. She shrieked again, "*Go*, now! Run! *Run!*"

But Mr. Henry was moaning on the floor in his nightclothes with a ruptured face, and Jonah was all alone in the dining room with a leaking head. Amelia was paralyzed by the inability to either help them or leave them behind. She was as mute and useless and immovable as the clock, simply standing witness, marking time, for all the good that did.

As her parents fought against each other and Amelia failed to do anything at all, the candelabra was knocked over. The tapers touched her mother's dress. The speed with which the fabric caught fire was astonishing.

"Go!" she screamed, again and again in an ascending pitch until it was not a word so much as the piercing, plaintive call of an unknown bird. The fire climbed up her skirts toward her face. It was hard to tell but Amelia thought her mother was holding on to her father as the flames unfurled in all other directions too; they covered the books, and crawled onto the carpet, and puffed up her father's sleeves.

At last, Amelia obeyed her mother's shrill command, stumbling over her own feet and the threshold of the door, falling and clambering up again, skinning her chin and the heels of her hands. She bruised her knees through all her layers of skirts, shouted—at least thought she shouted, shrieked in her head, "Fire! Help! Fire!" as she tripped down the narrow street. Her shoes clattered on the wooden sidewalk, and she didn't stop or look back until she reached the wharf.

It only took a minute; it seemed impossible that the fire could have spread so much, but other buildings were already alight. In between panicked glances at the burning town, Amelia searched desperately for a boat that would do, something small, something she had any hope of handling on her own. No sails, lest they catch like paper.

Lines kept slipping through her fingers, but finally, she cast off. Her oars knocked against other boats and the wood of the pilings, and all the while the flames spread with unbelievable speed, the fire ravenous, intent on consuming the entire island.

They couldn't have gotten out, Amelia thought—she *knew*—and yet she lingered, hoped to see someone appear through the pall of smoke and the orange glow of the flames coming ever closer. Mr. Henry, with her soot-streaked mother leaning on his shoulder, or with Jonah dangling in his arms. Or alone, even, because Amelia knew she could not bear to be.

∾

But none of them came—only other residents fleeing the rapacious fire. And because Amelia was also terrified to die, she pushed off too, even before she spotted Hope, or Benjamin. She ignored the pain in her scraped hands and swiped the blood from them on her skirt so the oars would stop slipping from her grasp. She rowed as hard as she could as the scorching wind blew ash and sparks out across the water and the black smoke burned her streaming eyes.

When the whale-oil barrels caught and burst and the waves propelled the burning oil out after her, Amelia felt her heart explode in kind. She pushed harder—arms burning, palms blazing—and did not stop until she was far enough away to see nothing more than a fierce glow on the horizon. The only sounds then were the slap and slosh of water against the hull and her own ragged breath thick in her ears.

She had done what her mother wanted. Escaped. But Amelia had no idea why, or what for. No clue what might come next, what she was supposed to do now. She'd felt so preposterously small and so completely severed from safety. She'd tucked herself into the bottom of the boat and let the waves take her where they would. She imagined being lost to the vastness of the ocean, wasting away as sharks circled her, or sinking when the boat took on too much water. If she was meant to drown, she would open her mouth to swallow the sea as she had so many years ago. And perhaps in her last moments, Amelia would see it again, that ghostly ship floating above the waves, come to welcome her aboard, with no one to pull her back this time.

Instead, she drifted far enough that she lost sight even of the firelight on the horizon, and the shimmering black sea stretched all around her. The slopping, sucking susurration of the hungry swells made Amelia afraid enough to row again, blindly and frantically, but she got nowhere save deeper into panic, and cried herself hoarse.

No ships passed; only the blind eye of the moon regarded her, marked her passage. At some point, she thought she dozed—slumped over in the boat and closed her eyelids when she couldn't move her stiff, aching arms another stroke. When the sky began to lighten several hours later, she blinked and saw land. She shoved her raw hands around the oars again.

The current helped carry her to Falmouth, where Amelia stumbled onto unfamiliar ground and walked toward her uncertain future, blank as an end page in a book.

～

The last time she'd seen her father was through a snarl of flames, yet he'd looked as formidable as ever, even with the fire licking at his coat. Under his incandescent gaze, Amelia had been shocked not to feel fingers tugging on her dress, or fists battering her face. Stunned by the utter freedom to stumble back and scramble for the door as her mother shrieked for her to run.

And though she got away—so far from there—she still had not escaped that night, nor any of what came before it.

He shouldn't have survived the inferno, she thought, and yet of course he had. Nothing else had managed to kill him; perhaps nothing ever would. It was easy to imagine him bearing down on her over the years, silently, invisibly, in no haste at all. Because he'd always had total faith in his own sovereignty and must have been confident he would catch up in the end.

Even if he didn't, his memory lived in Amelia's head. And the world was full of other men like him, always would be.

Will was not among their number, but perhaps he could hold his own against one if it came to that. Still, Amelia prayed it wouldn't.

Thirty-Five

DOMINION

During daylight hours, no one wanted to gather in the schoolroom, so Amelia spent long stretches of time in the Cliffords' parlor. She gave Joy assignments to distract her, since she was the only one who seemed eager for a return to normal routine.

Samuel had grown quiet and somber, and while he let Phyllis pull him into games of jacks and marbles, he showed little genuine interest. Fiona and Claire stayed upstairs with their mother.

Meanwhile, the eggers rebuilt their rope span across the Jordan Channel. As Amelia watched them traverse the chasm, a silly, ardent hope swelled in her breast: that Finn had gone across and back before he set to work with his knife. That he'd achieved a moment of triumph before he fell, and that he'd not been too frightened when the drop came or felt too terribly alone. With any luck, it had surprised him such that he never had time to realize what was happening at all.

That was the best anyone could wish for, she supposed, for themselves and for all those they loved.

$\sim$

Within the week following Finn's demise, the Pollards left the Farallones.

Mr. Pollard slurred an apology to Mr. Clifford for leaving him in the lurch, and gripped Amelia's hands as he thanked her for everything she'd done for them. His eyes were glassy, unfocused in a way that could not be put solely down to grief. The waft of liquor from his pores made it hard not to pull her head back, but Amelia embraced him and tried to say she was sorry.

Mrs. Pollard hugged her too, hard enough to hurt, but could say nothing through her stuttering breaths and sobs. Fiona cried into Amelia's shoulder when she crouched down to say goodbye, and even Claire squeezed her in a brief, almost furtive embrace before she took hold of her mother's hand again and led her away.

～

Not an hour later, as Will and Amelia sat at her kitchen table ignoring their cooling tea, the front door of Stonehouse burst open and made them both jump. By the time they gained their feet and went to the hall, Elijah Salter was right outside the room.

He spared a look of distaste for them both and peered past into the kitchen, then looked into the parlor.

"May I help you?" Amelia said, still more surprised than anything— she had the alarming thought that perhaps Gertrude was missing now. When Mr. Salter made for the staircase, she raised her voice to add, "Excuse me!"

She and Will trailed the man upstairs, watched him look into her bedroom, then the one across the hall. When he'd seen all there was to see of Stonehouse, Salter finally deigned to address Amelia. "I will be taking this dwelling, effective immediately. You will vacate the premises by this evening."

For a moment, she could only gape. "But—this is my home. I—"

"This structure was built by the order and labor of the US Congress Lighthouse Board for the use of the keepers on Southeast Farallon. You reside here without official permission or recognition from the Board. As head keeper in charge, I am well within my rights to evict you and repossess this house. If the Cliffords choose to retain your services as a private tutor, then you may remain in residence with them."

Amelia was unable to find her voice. Behind her, Will said, "This is utterly preposterous."

Mr. Salter turned anthracite eyes on him. "You are neither a relative of this woman nor an employee of the Board. So I might ask what business you have in here with her at all, let alone where you find the temerity to question my decision."

Will treated him to one of those breath-bursts of laughter, laced with scorn at this absurdity, but Amelia touched his arm to stop him from saying anything more.

"Remove your things posthaste, Miss Riley," Mr. Salter said. "Personal effects only; anything that was in this house before you arrived must stay." At the head of the stairs, he glanced back, lips twisted in contempt. "Take your bedding with you too."

They watched him descend and disappear, heard the front door open and shut again.

"He can't do this," Will said.

"Yes, he can." Amelia stood in the doorway to her room, her back to Will, and felt her heart contract. She struggled to keep her voice even. "No use fighting it. Would you mind going for one of the wheelbarrows for me?"

Will sighed in defeat. "Of course."

Alone, Amelia let herself take a deep breath and step across the threshold. Sixteen months ago, Stonehouse was a strange and slightly unsettling space that she had since come to think of as an almost sacred refuge, a place wholly and fully her own, though of course it never really had been. She'd always known, on some level, she would have to leave it, but certainly not so soon, and now the prospect gutted her—even if she was only relocating to another building, not yet banished from the island entirely.

There was nothing to be done for it, so she began to pack her trunk, pondering what else she would take with her, Mr. Salter's directives be damned. He didn't need the bird skulls on the parlor mantel, or the schoolbooks the previous teachers had left. He didn't know Amelia hadn't brought the threadbare rug with her, and if he challenged her, she was confident he'd be more than happy to take the newer floor covering from the Pollards' former parlor in its place.

∾

Amelia tried to sound bemused, not broken, as she explained to the Cliffords. She managed not to cry, at least. They were incredulous on her behalf, and offended on their own, though Mr. Clifford was equally intent on remaining stoic.

Mrs. Clifford, as she helped Amelia carry her things upstairs, said of Salter, "I suppose he *does* have seniority in the service, but not on this island. It should have been Percy who got promoted. Whoever they end up sending next, you watch—they'll be first assistant keeper, and he'll be demoted to second."

Later, as Amelia helped with dinner, a thought occurred to her, and she voiced it. "Don't worry about paying me anymore. Or half is fine. But I don't need anything if it's any trouble."

"Not at all," Mrs. Clifford said, rather sharply. After another moment, she sighed and set down her spoon. "We were the ones who pushed for a teacher in the first place—I was. But honestly, I don't know how much longer we'll be here either. All depends on who they replace Mr. Pollard with, I suppose. What else is open. How awful an overseer Mr. Salter turns out to be. All kinds of things. But I'll give you as much warning as I can. We won't pull the rug out from under you."

"Thank you." Amelia didn't know what else to say, or why it should come as such a surprise, or hurt so much. The slipping away of things, and people, was never easy to bear when you let yourself get attached to them. She should have better protected herself, she supposed, but in the end, she wasn't sorry she'd let her defenses down.

~

The Salters were already ensconced in Stonehouse by suppertime. Amelia watched them from the window of her new room as they moved their furniture from their blinded, boarded-over home—until Gertie paused and glanced up at her, as if she'd sensed her gaze. Although Amelia felt wretched for simply stepping back behind the curtain, she couldn't bring herself to return the girl's limp wave.

Will joined the rest of them for dinner that night. There were more bitter comments bandied about, though the adults didn't speak quite as freely as they might have, owing to the little ears in attendance. The little minds alert for every nuance of forbidden knowledge and grown-up secrets, even more so since things had already gone topsy-turvy, with their teacher now their upstairs neighbor.

Amelia helped clear the plates. In the kitchen, Mrs. Clifford said, "Selfish though it may be, I'm mighty glad you're here with us instead of the Salters. Still, I am sorry."

Mr. Pollard had been scheduled to stand watch that night. Elijah Salter went up instead. Mr. Clifford was surprised the new head keeper was prepared to continue his predecessor's routine of unsanctioned one-man watches, but then it was a treacherous climb up and down the hill, and close quarters for two men to share all night. Without a third, neither keeper would ever get to rest if they both went up every evening. Will said he'd be happy to help but doubted Salter would allow that any longer.

When he left, Amelia couldn't so much as touch his hand, only stood to say good night and felt her own muscles strain toward the door. It was so peculiar not to don her cloak and bonnet and bid the keepers' house good night as well.

Instead, she climbed the handsome staircase and drifted through the Pollards' flat, an ache in her chest as if something inside it had also been dislodged. She changed out of her clothes in the wrong room and slid into a foreign bed, though it had her sheets and quilt and pillows on it, so it smelled familiar, at least. A little like Will, too.

The wind sounded much the same, whistling around the eaves and rattling the window glass, howling and moaning down the chimney—and beneath it all, the pandemonium of the birds and the continuous rush of waves against the rocks. When Amelia closed her eyes, she could almost imagine she was still in Stonehouse, though her heart was far too wary to succumb to such trickery.

～

She missed her postcard mosaic view through the windows, the plain angles and furnishings of Stonehouse, even the way the sunlight fell on the walls. Of course, she also missed being able to welcome Will into her bed. She hadn't been brave enough to tiptoe out in the middle of the night yet, though the eggers had finally gone again. She'd offered the Cliffords the upstairs level only in part because it might have made it easier to slip away; it also had the balcony and the benefit of no footsteps overhead, which Amelia thought they more than deserved. But Mrs. Clifford politely declined. She didn't expect to be there long enough for it to matter anymore.

Between classes, Amelia walked around Tower Hill to visit Will and Banquo at their abode. She went on Sundays, too, sometimes early enough to hear the Salters in the chapel. Elijah preached as fervidly as if he had a whole congregation.

Amelia didn't think they marked her presence, though she didn't care. And she didn't think she and Will made any noise loud enough to carry all that way, though she almost wanted to try as an act of antagonism—let them hear her crying out to God herself. Give Mr. Salter more fuel for his fire and brimstone.

As they lay half-dozing, Amelia murmured, "When the Cliffords leave, will you let me stay here so I don't have to go live in Skeleton Cave?"

Will chuckled. "You know you can come stay here now. Just give the word. I'll get the wheelbarrow."

Amelia smiled and rolled onto her side to drape an arm across his chest.

"But maybe it's time we go too," he said as he stroked her shoulder.

"Do you really want to leave?"

"God knows I've been here long enough. I'm tired of being in such a ghastly business. And I'd certainly prefer not to have Salter for a neighbor." Will turned so it was easier to look at Amelia, tucked a strand of hair behind her ear. "I'd like to be someplace where no one calls you Lucy Riley. Where I can use your name, all the time. And we can be as free as we want to be, married or not. Where I can kiss you whenever I like. And I never have to eat another murre egg as long as I live."

Amelia's lips curved up beneath his own. "Where, then?"

"Where would you like to go? Anyplace at all."

She rolled onto her back again and studied the light on the ceiling, tried to imagine an ideal destination, nowhere she'd been before. In truth, Amelia would go anywhere with Will, but if she had to choose a place, she could only picture it in pieces. There would be trees—tall pines, that sounded like the sea when the wind filled them—and the ocean itself, of course, or perhaps a lake would do. A river. Open skies and wild spaces only lightly scattered with people. Different weather in winter, more than just rain and fog.

"Somewhere where the snow falls on the water," she said. "Canada? Or maybe Alaska?"

"There's an idea. We could learn to speak Russian."

"*Da*. I can't go until the Cliffords do, though. Don't want to desert them."

"Of course."

Amelia bit the tip of her tongue but then said what was in her head anyway. "Maybe we should sneak Gertie out with us."

Will's fingertips stilled against her arm.

"I'm worried she thinks I'm angry with her," Amelia confessed.

"Because her father tossed you out? She can't be blamed for that."

"She might not feel that way."

"Why not go talk to her, then?"

"Because I don't want to get her in trouble." Amelia didn't know for certain that it would set Salter off, much less what exactly he might do if it did. But maybe she was just making more excuses for her own inaction.

～

Salter stood watch every other night. He'd spend the hour after first light meticulously cleaning the lantern and lens. Amelia was certain his wife and daughter rose just as early.

The following morning, she went to Stonehouse on the pretext of having left something behind. Minerva was busy in the kitchen, only peeked out into the hall as Gertie answered the door.

"I'll just be a minute," Amelia assured Minerva, and though the woman looked doubtful, she let them go upstairs.

Mr. and Mrs. Salter had moved into the previously empty bedroom, Amelia saw. She stopped just outside and turned to Gertie. "I'm sorry I didn't wave at you the other day. I hope you don't think I'm cross."

Gertie tucked her chin against her chest. "I'm sorry you had to move."

"It doesn't matter."

"Father says it isn't good for a woman to live alone."

Amelia pressed her lips together. "I'm sure he does. How are you liking Stonehouse?"

Gertie shrugged, then stood straighter, as if she'd been reprimanded for the gesture before. "It's snug. I hit my head on the ceiling in my room all the time."

Amelia smiled. "I did that once or twice too."

Gertie smiled back, an evanescent thing.

"Have you found the hiding spot under the floorboards yet?" Amelia said, and Gertie's eyes widened.

She looked intrigued, but then shook her head, went serious. "I don't have anything to hide."

"No, of course not." Amelia faltered.

"Have you come by before?" Gertie asked, and Amelia was further flustered.

"When, dear?"

"At night. I thought I saw you."

"Here?"

"Outside, mostly. A few times. But once I woke up and I thought I saw a woman standing in the corner."

Amelia swallowed a fizz of fear. "Well, no, that wasn't me. Unless I've suddenly gotten awfully good at sleepwalking."

Gertie's laugh was like a sun-shower. But then a clatter from the kitchen made them both startle.

"Did you need to get something?" Gertie said with a certain urgency in her tone, and Amelia hesitated.

"Yes." She went into the Salters' room, opened the closet, and bent to the orange crate thankfully still at the bottom. She'd taken the sea elephant skull but left the chipped hair receiver, the quilt, the candles.

She settled on the receiver, since it was small and damaged, least likely to be missed. When she lifted it, it rattled. Amelia frowned, but before she could peer inside, Gertie said, "You'd probably better go now. I mean, we'll have breakfast soon. And you have classes, don't you?"

"Yes. You know you're more than welcome to come to them. Despite what your father said."

Gertie shook her head at the floor. "I have to help Mother."

"Of course. But you can come by anytime you like. Just to visit. Or read a book. You don't even need a reason."

The girl met her eyes for a moment. There was a shadow of dejection on Gertie's face, even as she twitched a politely indulgent smile.

On her way out of Stonehouse, Amelia looked into the kitchen and held the porcelain pot up to Mrs. Salter. "Thank you," she said, and the woman produced a smile even less convincing than her daughter's.

Amelia stepped outside feeling far less reassured than she'd hoped to be, but no more certain any of her suspicions of mistreatment were warranted. Abstractedly, she peered into the small hole atop the hair receiver and stopped in her tracks. There was an oceanic glimmer of diamonds, ruby sparks. Her necklace.

Thirty-Six

Fresh Blood

She told Will at once, breathless with excitement at recovering her treasure and flushed with indignation that Salter had kept it for himself.

"Bloody bastard," Will said.

Amelia felt her skin ripple. "It was like something led me right to it." She pretended not to see the wariness that flickered in Will's eyes. "But part of me thinks I should go put it back."

"Why? Because you think he'll come after it?"

"No—let him try. But what if he thinks it was Gertie, or Mrs. Salter?"

"I highly doubt that. They'll tell him you came by, won't they? I imagine he'll go check his hiding spot first thing. He'll know it was you."

Once, it would have frightened Amelia, but now she hoped it was true.

If Salter did check on the necklace that day, he kept it to himself. The following evening, though, Amelia made sure she was near the base of Tower Hill when he was due to climb up to the light again.

Salter startled when he saw her, and she drew some power from his surprise.

"Thou shalt not covet," she said. "Thou shalt not steal. Thou shalt not lie. I know you broke at least those three of your commandments. And I wanted you to know that I took it upon myself to help put you back on the path of righteousness by removing the thing that so sorely tempted you. Consider it divine intervention if you like. I certainly do."

Salter's fingers tightened around the handle of the unlit lantern he carried. His beard quivered as he ground his teeth. "You think you're mighty clever, don't you? But you're a blasphemous little whore who's bound to burn in hell."

Amelia chuckled, softly. "My mother thought I'd end in flames too."

Salter's expression slipped for a moment into discomposure. Before he could move, before his scowl was even quite restored, Amelia stepped past him and kept going at a stately pace, the necklace tapping time against her ankle once more.

At every subsequent encounter, Salter glowered at her more fiercely than ever, but now she smiled.

In August, he recommended shooting sea lions. Amelia avoided the bloody evidence as best she could, but the gunshots were audible from everywhere on the island.

She remembered how, the previous year, she'd instinctively envisioned him sliding into the sea—and how she'd felt a flare of panic, worried she might make it happen, as she'd worried she'd caused Achilles's fall. Now she let herself hold the image of Salter losing his footing, tumbling down the rocks, thrashing in the surf, slipping under. It was even more satisfying to envision a massive shark slicing through the water to seize him in its serrated snaggleteeth. She closed her eyes and breathed deep, slow.

Of course, Salter remained alive, unscathed. Amelia was almost disappointed.

Eventually, the rifle blasts ceased, and the crimson stain washed out of the water, but vermilion ribbons still waved behind her eyes some nights.

~

She no longer feared slipping out of the keepers' quarters to see Will for a few hours when she couldn't sleep, though she always crept back before the sun.

One night in late August, she left him sleeping and gave Banquo a farewell ear tousle on her way out into a wet fog. It was hard to see, but Amelia could have navigated the whole place blindfolded by then.

For once, the fog signal was in harmony with the weather. It sounded with every inrush of waves, but the dense air muffled its pitching moan, dampened the squalling of the gulls and the roaring of the sea itself. Still, Amelia thought she heard something else—a true human sound, not the deceptive mimicry of the birds or the otherworldly wailing of the siren. She tilted her head and raised her lantern, for all the good that did. Was it singing she heard, or sobbing?

She struck off in the direction of the chapel, from where she thought the noise emanated. Amelia shuffled carefully, despite her confidence a moment earlier. As she drew closer, she was sure the voice was human, and feminine. It rose and fell in prayer.

Could it be the elusive woman in black, at last? Would Amelia recognize the shadow's face when it turned toward her as her mother's—or even her very own, a reflection that had stepped through a hazy mirror?

With the lantern before her and her breath shallow in her lungs, Amelia saw the building emerge from the mist. There was the inky gap of the open doorway, and the faint glow of the freshly whitewashed outer wall—and on it, a bloody handprint, dripping down the stones with the condensation from the fog.

She held her breath and stepped into the dark interior, lit only by her little flame. "Hello?"

The voice stopped. But as Amelia stepped down the aisle, her flickering light revealed Gertie, on her knees before the altar, head turned to peer behind her shoulder, a claret patch on the back of her white nightgown where it touched the dirty soles of her bare feet.

Amelia paused a moment. "Are you all right?"

The girl stood and shrank back, stained palms leaving fresh marks on the altar behind her.

"Oh, darling, what happened?"

Gertie shook her head but answered in a tremulous voice barely above a whisper, "It was not Adam who was deceived, but the woman being deceived was in transgression. And I suffer the same wound as Eve, for I am as wicked. I tried to hold it in, but it keeps coming out." She offered her blood-smeared hands as proof, as supplication. "Am I dying?"

"No." Amelia set down her lantern and unfastened her cloak. "Here," she said, and draped it over the girl's trembling, scrawny shoulders. "It's all right. This is perfectly natural. It just means you're growing up. It's nothing to do with wickedness, and you're not going to die. Your mother doesn't know it's happening?"

The girl shook her head harder.

"Well, she can help you." Amelia hoped that was true. She picked up her lantern, linked her other arm through Gertie's elbow. "Let's get you back home. It's dangerous to wander around in the dark and the fog. The edge of the island is awfully close to here, you know. You must be careful."

She steered Gertrude back to Stonehouse. As they approached, she wondered what exactly she should do. Send the child back inside by herself, to sneak upstairs and bleed alone until her mother woke in the morning? Go in with Gertie and find some scraps of flannel to wad up for her? Or knock and risk the wrath of the poor girl's father?

As it turned out, the Salters were already awake, though by the looks of them, only recently. Elijah had pulled a coat over his nightshirt and perched a cap on his head. Minerva was in her wrapper and slippers behind him in the door. He'd just swung it open to stomp outside when Amelia and Gertie came close enough through the fog to glimpse him. He saw them a second later.

"Where the devil have you been, girl?" he snarled as he strode toward them and seized his daughter's arm. "And what in tarnation are you doing with this jezebel? I told you to stay away from her." As he spoke, he ripped the borrowed cloak from Gertie's shoulders and cast it to the ground.

Amelia drew herself up to speak over him, but he pulled his daughter back up the steps to Stonehouse amid such a violent stream of words, no one had a chance to interrupt—though his wife had seen the truth of the matter and seemed to want to address her daughter. Minerva moved as if she would reach out, then thought better of it. That aborted gesture was what made Amelia mount the steps and throw out an arm as Salter slapped the door to shove it closed. She stopped it, though the impact with the heel of her hand jarred her arm up to the shoulder socket.

"What do you think you're doing?" he said.

She forced herself to speak calmly. "In case you haven't noticed, your daughter needs her mother's help right now, and your compassion, if you can muster any, would be kinder and far more useful than quoting scripture at her."

Salter's eyes flashed. "'I suffer not a woman to teach, nor to usurp authority over the man, but to be in silence.'"

"I suffer no obligation to obey you in any way," Amelia answered. Part of her yearned for him to hit her, to try.

Instead, he slammed the door in her face, so hard it ruffled her hair and the collar of her dress. Had she been standing a fraction of an inch closer, it would have broken her nose; as it was, it did not quite graze her.

Amelia wanted to charge inside after them. The lock was flimsy enough that she could have, but she'd already been too brash. Even if Salter wouldn't dare raise a hand against her, what might he do to his family, his property? If she heard anything like a shout or a slap, then she would force her way in, Amelia told herself. But though she stood outside with her ear to the door, she heard nothing but a faint murmur of voices that moved away and faded out. From her back, the droning of the fog signal rose and fell and rose again.

$$\sim$$

Her damp cloak bundled in her arms, Amelia continued to the keepers' quarters and stole upstairs without waking anyone, as far as she could tell. Too electrified to sleep but too numb to do anything else, she fell into a trance.

She went to her trunk, where she'd stowed the cyclopean elephant seal skull from Stonehouse. She lifted it out and placed it reverently upon her washstand, since it was far too big to sit in the center of the mantel, then lit a candle on either side of it so the shadows danced and glorified its grotesquerie.

Amelia had no herbs to burn and knew no other languages in which to utter unhallowed invocations, but she had hatred enough. She poured it into the gaping abyss in the center of the fanged skull until she imagined it glowed.

For good measure, she took a hatpin from one of her trinket boxes and pricked her finger, dabbed the beaded blood on the ivory bones. An animating potion, a mixture of the same life force that had flowed through her mother's veins, and her father's. It couldn't hurt, Amelia thought. After all, what were spells but prayers, and how often did those go unanswered? Maybe all gods were ineffectual, or imaginary, or simply immune to the beseeching of meager human hearts and tongues.

Thirty-Seven

Offerings

A few days after their meeting in the chapel, Gertie slipped away from Stonehouse and came to the keepers' house during school hours.

Mrs. Clifford brought her upstairs, took the children down so Amelia and Gertie could speak in private. The girl seemed too nervous to sit but went to study the bird skulls on the mantel. "These are pretty," she said, which wasn't what Amelia expected, but before she could reply, Gertrude rushed more words together. "Thank you for giving me your coat and being so nice to me the other night. I think you are. Nice, I mean. I don't know why my father doesn't."

Amelia offered a smile when the girl turned to face her. "Well, I suppose I'm a bit . . . too independent for his tastes."

"He's mean to all my friends. I think he just doesn't like you because I do. And I like the Cliffords and Mr. Sisson too. And his dog. So, I'm sorry."

"Sweetheart, it isn't your fault if your father dislikes someone. It doesn't make us like you any less."

Gertie quirked her lips at the floor, twisted her fingers together.

Amelia's heart tugged toward the girl. "Are you feeling better now? Than you were the other day?"

A surge of passion lifted Gertie's voice, and eyes, and shoulders. "I don't want that to happen again, but Mother says it will now, every month. It's *awful*."

"It's not so bad once you get used to it," Amelia said, without as much conviction as she might have mustered. She missed Mrs. Pollard; perhaps she would have needed a few glasses of cider in her, but she would have handled this conversation far better.

As gingerly as she could, Amelia said, "Your father seemed quite angry."

"I was disobedient," Gertie answered.

"Is he unkind to you?"

Gertie looked up at her with wide eyes. "He provides for us and guides us. We would be lost without him. We would have nothing then. I must pray to be more deserving."

Amelia clenched her fists, nails scoring her palms. She couldn't possibly tell Gertie her father was a liar and a thief—she knew the girl wouldn't listen—but Amelia wanted at least to speak to her of the beliefs imparted during her own childhood in the Quaker meeting-house. That no person was any better or any less worthy than another. That each man and woman had a breath of God within them, a divine light that could not be extinguished and did not dim for lack of prayer or penance. That she was loved unconditionally by her true creator.

But she wasn't sure what danger lay in that, if Gertrude were to repeat such things to her father, let alone come to believe them. Besides, Amelia wasn't entirely sure she still did. And while she was supposed to love her enemies and abhor violence against them, she'd never truly managed that herself. In her vulnerable, vicious heart, she'd killed numerous times.

All she said, then, was, "I am certain you are perfectly deserving of all the love and kindness in this world, just as you are. Whatever he says."

Gertie smiled at her, even held her gaze for a moment before she glanced away again. The way she nudged the carpet with her toe made tears sting Amelia's eyes; it was Finn's gesture, and it was in almost the same spot she was now convinced he'd worn away before her time on the island.

"I had a friend in Crescent City," Gertie said. "Hannah. Daddy didn't like her either. In fact, I think he hated her. Which is a sin, but I think he did. Because I loved her. That's why he brought us here, away from temptation. Because my spirit is weak, just like my flesh. He delivered us. Now we watch and we pray. But I got all bloody anyway."

Amelia had to stop herself from gathering the girl in her arms. She spoke carefully, softly. "Does he punish you? Or your mother?"

"God?"

"Your father. Does he hurt you?"

She shook her head without looking up from the rug. Amelia weighed the wisdom of her next words. Though her gut told her not to speak them, her lips did not obey. "What would he do if he found you here right now?"

Gertie's eyes grew wider. "He wouldn't like that."

Despite Amelia's best efforts to detain the girl, she'd spooked her, and Gertie fled.

Since then, she hadn't returned to the keepers' house. Amelia couldn't very well go to Stonehouse again and was furious with herself.

All she could do was rehash her suspicions and her fears with Will. Though equally troubled, he was also at a loss as to what they could do. Amelia didn't tell him about her makeshift altar, how she stared into that sea elephant skull every night until she fell asleep, awaiting the flicker of an augury within that black pit of shadow.

She shouldn't dabble in such dark things, which seemed by turns dangerous and simply stupid. There should be no place in her heart for ill will, nor any space in her mind for the possibility of magic in any shade. Yet if sanity was a matter of resisting the impossible, would fully embracing madness effect true faith? She *was* delusional, or at least desperate—but perhaps not quite enough?

At any rate, Amelia continued to light her candles and fix her eyes on the skull as if it might speak to her, night after night. And though nothing happened, she found some small measure of comfort in the ritual itself.

⁓

When the *Shubrick* came in early September, along with the usual quarterly delivery of oil and food and maintenance supplies, all it brought for Amelia was some new clothing she'd ordered since her hems were worn ragged, salt-stained and guano-spattered. The wind and rocks and insidious saline spray of the Farallones ate at fabric as if the island itself sought to unravel a person, or at least to strip them to their essential self. Amelia checked her reinforced inner petticoat hem several times each day to ensure the necklace was still there.

There was no letter from New York, only one from the Board for Mr. Clifford, but the news wasn't what he and his wife had hoped for.

"Everything they want to offer him is in Maryland, or Virginia, or Florida, or the Carolinas," Mrs. Clifford said over coffee after the tender departed. "I'd rather be up north if we have to go back east. In Maine or someplace like that. With everything that's going on, I don't know . . . maybe we'd be better just sticking it out here. At least Mr. Salter mostly leaves him be now."

"Small mercies," Amelia mused, dandling Jacob in her arms.

For the first time, as the *Shubrick* blew its keening whistle and steamed away, Amelia almost wished she were on board. The Farallones' allure had become tarnished, although it felt both sad and traitorous to think so. But she still had her obligations there.

She had the sense of something coming. It was not something lurking far off in the dreadful distance, nor something barreling at breakneck speed toward her, but a slow gathering right on the horizon where Amelia could plainly see it. Clouds massing and swelling, sure to burst as they hung over her head, something she might in fact move away from if she cared to try, if she felt she had the choice.

She hadn't forgotten about Miss Price and Giancarlo Ricci, but they seemed suddenly nebulous threats. So did Amelia's father—because Salter, after all, was right there. And he was a monster too, Amelia was certain now. A flesh-and-blood fiend. That made him more dangerous than any phantom, but it also made him mortal.

~

On Sundays, when she walked to Will's for tea and whatever else the afternoon might offer, she was frequently distant, disturbed. They went upstairs less often and lapsed into silences that were less comfortable than they used to be. Yet he always seemed glad to see Amelia, and when he kissed her goodbye, it pulled her back into the present moment so she wanted to hold it still, stay suspended.

In mid-September, on her way around Tower Hill, a hundred yards distant on the marine terrace, she spotted a huge sea elephant in tatters. It was only molting, but though she'd seen the creatures in the process of shedding their skin before, it still startled Amelia to catch a first glimpse. This one looked to be rotting, with great shreds of paler coat hanging from its massive frame, a rubber slop boot covered with velour that was separating in patchy flakes.

It was late in the season for the animal to be there, and it was all alone, but before Amelia could allow herself to entertain the notion that she might have conjured it, she hurried past.

As she neared Will's door and heard the now familiar sound of Salter preaching from the chapel, she spared a wish that the roof might fall in on him, just the piece above the altar.

Amelia vaguely noticed that Will seemed preoccupied himself; she bent to greet Banquo while his master finished in the kitchen. Then they sat in the parlor, and sipped, and said little. The companionable quiet was tinged with tension. It seemed, like the sensation of general portentousness that dogged Amelia now, to balloon, but rather than burst, it was carefully pierced to allow a slow leak.

"I need to show you something," Will said, and put his empty cup aside. He fetched the ledger from his bookshelf, removed a loose sheet of paper, reluctant to hand it to Amelia, which made her hesitant to reach out and take it. Even before her fingertips closed on the parchment, her stomach flipped, and the tea inside it sloshed.

Thirty-Eight

ANSWERED PRAYERS

The unexpected names in the missive triggered a twinge of confusion followed by a pulse of shock.

Dear Mr. Smith,

I regret to inform you that Captain Barzillai Osborne passed away on December 10, 1855, of complications from pneumonia, though quietly, in his own bed. He was in fact injured in the Great Fire of 1846 and did not return to his captaincy following that event, but he was much admired on this island until the time of his death and I extend my deepest condolences to you, as his friend. I unfortunately have no information on his wife or children, as they separated from him many years ago and could not be located. He left no will and had few possessions at the time of his demise, but what remained of his property was bequeathed to his closest living relatives in Boston, who sold the house he rebuilt in brick on Orange Street to Mr. Benjamin Coffin and his family.

I wish that I had happier news to share but hope that you will be soothed to know he did not suffer and is missed by many. His former home bears a plaque commemorating his life's work and miraculous survival, at sea and on land. It may be said he was both blessed and cursed, and was truly a giant of a man, who has now gone to his much-deserved rest. Please let me know if I may be of any further assistance in this or any other matters. Should you ever visit Nantucket, do pay a visit, as any friend of Captain Osborne's is also a friend of mine.
    Sincerely,
    Wickliffe Gardner, Esq.

Amelia scanned the letter several times over, and still the words refused to become real to her. Her body quivered, and her eyes dried from her failure to blink. Everything beyond the paper darkened to an indistinct blur; Will hovered at the edge of her vision. She put the letter down on the table beside her and stood, walked stiffly toward the far side of the room, though she had not chosen a particular direction.

"Amelia . . ."

Her voice seemed to come from someplace far outside her throat, as if someone else asked on her behalf: "What did you do? How could you?"

"I'm sorry I didn't tell you, but I promise, I was careful—"

"What if he had been alive?"

"I used a different name, sent it through a friend's address in the city—a business, so if anyone had come round, they would have claimed not to know anything; true enough. And I didn't mention you, of course. I only said I was an old acquaintance and wondered if there was any information on his current whereabouts or his family, since we'd lost touch. I sent it to a general address, the town clerk; they must have passed it to his solicitor."

She shook her head, though she found it difficult to maintain the spark of outrage that had flared in her for a moment. "When?"

"In January, just after you told me about the fire. I had to know. Managed to get it on a clipper, too. I didn't expect a reply so soon, but a fishing boat brought it just the other day."

She kept her back turned as Will approached. "You and your letters . . ."

"Is it not a relief? To know he's no threat?"

Now Amelia stepped away from him. She couldn't quite believe it, couldn't wholly trust it, couldn't fathom she'd been free for so many years and hadn't even known it—nor could she say any of that, as her breath became jagged and tears crowded her eyes. She let them fall, and turned and let Will hold her, and managed to scrape out a few words: "It doesn't mean . . . It doesn't mean the past is done with me."

"The past is never done with any of us," he said. "But you're safe from that beast. He can't hurt you anymore, my love."

Amelia could not speak to say that didn't matter either—because he already had, and that would never entirely diminish. But even as she thought it, she did feel better, lighter, safer, there in Will's arms, with the overwhelming knowledge her father was nothing but moldering bones buried far away. And still stunned by the fact he had been dead for nearly five years now; all that time she'd spent carrying the fear and worry with her, when she could have let it fall away.

Once her crying subsided and her breathing calmed, she squeezed Will tighter. He kissed her temple, and she drew a deep breath that convulsed through her, then melted against him. She would have stayed like that forever.

But a sharp crack made them both start.

"Christ, what now?"

Amelia knew at once: the sea elephant. And while she didn't condone Mr. Salter's wanton slaughter of whatever animals caught his fancy, she didn't feel any particularly deep stab of disgust, or sadness, or surprise. Dull curiosity, perhaps, as to why he'd chosen to pick off this one at last; maybe he'd finally decided to try his hand at rendering blubber for personal use or profit, or the bull had simply lumbered too close to Stonehouse for his liking.

She followed Will, who made Banquo stay inside. As they rounded the base of the hill, there was another shot, followed by shouts, which quickened their pace.

Gertie and Minerva stood screaming twenty feet from Mr. Salter, who was sprawled on the ground, struggling beneath the gigantic, thrashing elephant seal.

Judging by the bleeding gouge on his cheek, Amelia surmised Salter had walked close enough to shoot the animal a second time point-blank, yet still failed to kill it, so it lashed out and knocked the repeating rifle from his hands as it knocked him to the ground.

Now Salter's leg was pinned under several thousand pounds of fury. He was trying to scramble back and grab for the Root carbine, shouting garbled words Amelia couldn't make out.

Before she could attempt to stop him, Will dashed forward. Amelia watched him pick up the gun and level it, but the echoing report still made her flinch. The second shot, only a little. The third, not at all.

As the defeated elephant seal finally collapsed, Will laid the rifle down, lowered his shoulder to shove the molting bull's velvet-scaled head aside. He needed help to move it enough for Mr. Salter to drag himself free. Luckily, Mr. Clifford had come out to see what was happening and added his muscle.

As the men shoved, Minerva and Gertrude helped pull Elijah out from under the dead weight of the animal. The friction of Salter's injured leg against the ground made him shriek even louder. Then they each fitted a shoulder under one of his arms and helped him stand. He could bear no weight upon the broken leg, but supported in that way—a yoke upon his wife and daughter—they helped him hop to Stonehouse and inside.

As Amelia approached the hulking carcass, she heard Will say, "Can't leave this to rot right in the middle of the terrace. God knows how we'll manage to drag the bloody thing off, though. Might need Mary's help."

"And I reckon he'll need to go to the hospital," Mr. Clifford said. "We'll have to hail a ship if we can. Row him in ourselves if we can't. I'd wager that leg's crushed; can't mess around with that kind of thing. He might need it amputated. Liable to get infected if he doesn't get it seen to right away."

"Be a damn shame," Will muttered. Mr. Clifford looked taken aback at the remark.

Amelia wished—just for a moment—that Will had aimed at Salter's unholy heart.

~

He refused to be moved to the mainland or receive any treatment beyond what his family could provide. He trusted God would heal him. Amelia thought He might. Perhaps He was in fact jealous and vengeful and had truly made some men in His own image—in which case, she should have cast off her last allegiances long ago and begged her mother to introduce her to other deities. But they hadn't helped either. Not enough. Best to rely on oneself in the end.

Gertie said he prayed at all hours when he was awake, made them join him; indeed, her voice was hoarse. She tended to him at night while her mother took his watches in the tower.

It wasn't uncommon for widows of lighthouse keepers to inherit their posts after they died. Why shouldn't Mrs. Salter stand in for her husband while he was temporarily incapacitated? Amelia assumed he loathed the idea of his wife in his place. But what could he possibly do? The thought gave her some satisfaction.

Gertrude, with her father confined to his bed, finally moved freely about the island. She visited the keepers' quarters most days, sat in on classes. She could read—though the only book she'd ever perused was the Bible—but she could only write her own name and a few other words.

Phyllis was astounded that this much older girl was so much less capable than herself, and though Amelia tried to gently redirect her energies to ward off embarrassment, Gertie evinced none. Instead, she asked her younger counterpart to show her what she knew. Soon, Joy was chipping in on subjects closer to her own heart. Samuel, still in mourning for Finn, didn't speak much at all, but Gertie earned a smile now and then when she addressed him. "Samuel—you must be in favor both with the Lord and with men. And with women too."

The girl evidently kept a lookout for Amelia, often popped up and tagged along when she went on walks. On Sundays, the Salters listened to Elijah preach from his mound of pillows—so Amelia was still able to rendezvous with Will—but she frequently found Gertie waiting nearby when she took her leave.

When they launched Will's boat in October, they had no choice but to invite Gertrude along, though neither of them minded. Joy came too, and told Gertie all about whales, which seemed to help the older girl relax a little when they breached close by. Phyllis rode tucked between the benches, cackling as the noisome spray of cetacean exhalations rained down on her, but Samuel stayed with their parents and baby brother. Finn's fall from the rocks had made him afraid to venture far from the terrace.

The first time they returned to shore after such a crowded dory excursion, Will and Amelia hung back at the landing and watched the children pelt home.

"Well, that was exhausting," Will said, and she gave him a narrow-eyed smile that made his grin widen. "But nice," he added, and slipped an arm around her waist, since no one was there to see. "I could get used to it. Having little ones around."

That evening, Amelia put the sea elephant skull away. She lined up Will's precious carvings on the bedroom mantel so she could gaze at them while she fell asleep instead.

Thirty-Nine

THE RECKONING

Nine weeks passed with no sign of any danger. No sign of Elijah Salter either.

Amelia only knew he was still alive because Mr. Clifford reported to him daily. The Board had yet to appoint another assistant keeper, and although Mr. Clifford said Mrs. Salter performed the duties admirably, this sustained period of upheaval didn't sit right with him.

He said Elijah looked awful, eyes and tongue the only lively things about him. "Like a hunk of old cheese possessed by some evil spirit."

The shock of such words from Mr. Clifford occasioned a profound silence at the table, shattered by helpless laughter from the rest of them a second later.

"Percy!" Mrs. Clifford cried.

Amelia said, "I thought your wife was the poet!" The women both snorted, which further delighted the children. Mr. Clifford only looked embarrassed.

～

When Amelia asked Gertie about her father, the girl always said he was doing better, by the grace of God, getting stronger every day. Sometimes she sounded less than glad about it, but if Amelia gently prodded, Gertie said little else. What she did was often confounding.

"He fears for me," she confessed one day.

"Why?"

Gertrude shook her head, searched for the right words to explain. "I don't mean to be . . . bad."

"You're not bad."

"But it lives within me. Evil. Temptation. I try to root it out like he says, but I don't know how. Prayers should work, shouldn't they? If you mean them? And I *do*—I think I do—but if they don't work to change me, then my heart must not be pure. Not true. I deceive myself. I can't cast the devil out because I must want him there."

Amelia struggled for an appropriate response. "People are complicated. Even good people don't have perfectly good thoughts all the time. And some thoughts—and even actions—that are perfectly fine, and good, are judged to be . . . bad, by certain other people. Immoral, even. Your father has very specific ideas about right and wrong, but that doesn't mean he's right about you. Or anything else, for that matter. At least not about everything. You shouldn't be afraid to think for yourself. But I know it must be difficult if you're afraid of him."

Gertie tensed but shook her head again. "It isn't his fault. He's only trying to save me. I have a wicked nature, but he—"

"What isn't his fault?" When Gertie didn't answer, Amelia softened her tone. "Let me ask you this: Does he think I'm wicked too? You can tell the truth."

The girl nodded.

"And do you think I am?"

"Of course not. You're kind, and good."

"Then consider the fact that he's wrong about you too. And consider why he wants you to think otherwise. If he keeps you believing there's something wrong with you and he's the only one who knows how to fix it, then he keeps you in thrall to him, you understand? He wants to control you, but you are your own person. You are allowed to be. You are meant to be."

"But the Bible says to honor thy father and thy mother."

"Yes, and I don't mean you should disrespect them, or stop listening to them entirely. Just . . . don't mistake your father for more than he is: a man. You look for God within yourself, and I think you'll find Him there. Because you are a lovely girl and there is nothing wicked in you."

Gertie looked less than certain but after a moment darted closer and hugged Amelia—hard, and so quickly she could barely return the gesture before the girl drew back.

∽

Amelia should have been more careful, she supposed, but failing to address Gertrude's father's lies and misinformation would have meant failing the girl herself. And she felt an urgency to do everything she could while Mr. Salter was out of commission. Once he was back on his feet, he wouldn't tolerate his daughter scampering off to the schoolroom or joining Amelia for walks, much less climbing aboard Will's boat.

In early November, Amelia lent Gertie a novel. "I was never quite so self-assured, but I've always felt an affinity for Miss Eyre. I think you'll like her too."

Every day, Gertie found a moment to recount the latest pages she'd read and how she loved them, though she sometimes needed clarification on certain words and concepts.

As her father began to exercise his mended leg, she confessed she hid the book and read it in bed by the light of a lantern. Gertie was eager for him to return to his tower duties so she could spend whole nights at Thornfield Hall. Amelia smiled and said they were kindred spirits, but a ripple of disquiet went through her at the notion that she had given Gertie something to hide.

~

Mr. Salter appeared outside again, an ersatz crutch under one arm, gait slower and stiffer, glower more intense from the effort of hobbling about. He wasn't yet fit to climb the hill, but he stumped about the island, ranging farther all the time.

The weather soon turned against him. But with her father able to move about the house while the cold rain and dense fog shrouded it, Gertie was trapped again too.

When she could steal a few moments to visit, she flashed quick smiles and gave flitting hugs, but the bright sheen in her eyes and dark smudges beneath them troubled Amelia. Yet no matter how gently or persistently she asked if anything was wrong, Gertie shook her head and changed the subject, willing to speak only of books and boats, the Holy Spirit and the ghostly fog.

One afternoon, she chewed her lip for a moment before she said, "I lie to him all the time now and I don't feel guilty for it—but I know I *should*. Isn't that bad?"

"Some lies are necessary," Amelia said, without thinking. "Some lies you have to tell to keep yourself safe." She took encouragement from Gertie's consideration and confidence and added, "But other lies will destroy you. And you know you can always tell me the truth. Is there anything the matter, at home? Anything you need help with?"

Gertie hesitated so long Amelia held her breath, but then she shook her head and scurried off. Amelia was frustrated, and frightened, but knew that you could not force someone to share their secrets.

~

The last night she lay in Will's bed was cold and rainy. December blew closer with every gust. She was loath to leave the comfort beneath the covers. She curled closer to Will's body for a moment, brushed a kiss across his shoulder before she slid into the prickling air.

She pulled on her chemise and drawers and one petticoat—she'd carry her corset—and was stepping into her cage crinoline when Banquo cocked his head before the dying hearth. Amelia paused and listened too, heard nothing over the wind and rain and sea.

But then Banquo jumped up and began to bark.

Will groaned, propped himself up and shushed Banquo, saw Amelia still there. She felt it, that distended mass of clouds, about to rupture at last. She tried to steel herself for what was to come. Her veins were a mass of ice-encrusted branches, breath frozen too.

Downstairs, the front door burst open. A tremulous voice called, "Miss Riley?"

Amelia let the cage of cotton strips and whalebone hoops collapse around her feet and kicked clear of it. Gertie didn't call again, but scrapes and thumps came from below. As Amelia reached the threshold of the bedroom, the girl's feet slapped up the stairs.

She stepped into the shadowy hall and pulled the door shut, since Will hadn't yet fumbled on any clothes. She opened her arms to Gertie. "What is it? Come here. Tell me what's wrong."

Gertrude was soaked, nightgown clinging to her frail frame, hair plastered to her skull and shoulders. Her body shook from cold and shuddered with sobs, so it was hard to make out her words. "I wouldn't do it. I told him *no* and that he's a liar and a false prophet and I *hate* him, and I think I hurt him, but he's coming after me. I blocked the door with a chair—but it won't be enough. He'll be here any minute!"

Will, having pulled on trousers and a wool sweater, opened the bedroom door.

"Load your gun," Amelia said, and drew Gertrude inside. She grabbed another of Will's knitted pullovers to put on Gertie. Its sleeves hung past her fingertips; the collar drooped on her chest.

No time to waste getting all her own outer garments on, so Amelia took a cardigan for herself, fastened a few buttons in the middle. All the while, she tried to calm Gertie, work out exactly what had happened, but the girl became less coherent, babbled fragments of phrases, bubbled with panic.

As Will finished checking his pistol, a thunderous crash below made them all start.

"He's here!" Gertie cried, and locked her arms around Amelia's waist as her father battered at the door again.

"Stay here," Will said. He stepped out of the room with gun in hand, closing the door behind him. The rhythmic pounding of a body against the front entrance of the house put Amelia in mind again of sea elephants. How could a recently injured man have such strength?

With a final crunching splinter, the barrier was breached. Banquo would not stop barking, and Gertie would not loosen her grip, and Amelia felt dizzy, faint with fear.

"Where is she?" Salter shouted. "Miserable Goddamned girl!"

Amelia smelled smoke but wasn't sure if it was drifting from downstairs or out of her past. Gertie whimpered and squeezed her closer.

"You're not going to hurt her," Will said, voice muffled by the closed door.

"I'll do what must be done, by God! She's *mine*."

"Put that down. *Now*."

A sharp bang made them gasp. A harsh "Fuck!" and another crack in quick succession, an answering report from much closer, in the hall—Will's pistol.

A bitten-off cry and a clatter, and then he flung the door open, motioned them out. "Come on, hurry."

311

Amelia saw two bullet holes in the wall as they passed, but Will appeared unscathed. She wanted to look closer, to be sure, but her attention was snared by flames lapping across the floor by the front entrance—a broken lantern lay beside a smashed chair. Gertie must have carried the light with her from her bedside table and set it down when she came in, to clap the door shut and wedge one of the ladder-back mermaid chairs beneath the knob.

When her father had broken through, the impact had upset the lamp. Rather than smother the wick, the oil glutted it, and the woven seat of the chair had caught, as had the nearby rug. The lace curtains would be next, the chaise, the bookshelves.

Amelia's legs were shaky on the stairs, heart unsteady in her chest, a pale flicker like a moth about to sizzle into oblivion. Her vision was crazed by the bright orange flames, but she saw Elijah Salter where he'd fallen. A crimson blot spread upon the abdomen of his sopping night-shirt where his robe gaped open. Will herded them out the back door, into the howling wind and needling rain. "Go to the Cliffords; I'll be right behind you!"

Amelia faltered as he darted back inside—to what end? To attempt to douse the flames, to drag Salter's body clear, to grab the company ledger or some other valuables? She wanted to yank him back, but Gertie still had a hand around her waist, so after a moment's hesitation, they began to totter over the sharp, slippery rocks in their bare feet, heads bent into the weather, Banquo prancing and barking by their side. Their progress was painstakingly slow, and Amelia imagined she could feel heat on their backs.

When another shot rang out, she immediately pried Gertie's arm off her. "Go on! Don't wait for me! Take him with you! *Go!*"

The girl reached for Banquo, but the dog bounded after Amelia. Before she could reach the house, the treacherous footing and the wind snapping her petticoat about her ankles tripped her up. She fell hard, scraping the heels of her hands, jarring her teeth. As she pushed herself to her knees, a dark bulk filled the doorway, backlit by flames.

Amelia's feeble heart quaked again in her chest.

That stentorian voice, so like her father's, boomed above the shrieking wind as he walked forward. "*You*, perverse rebellious woman! Corrupter! I can smell the stink of you from here!"

Behind his shoulder, Amelia could swear she saw a shadow emerge, a shape that could have been a woman in a cloak, or a dark fold of fog mixed with the black smoke pouring from the house. She was transfixed. Before she could stand or make sense of what she saw, Salter raised the rifle and fired.

Amelia sucked in a breath and shut her eyes. Nothing hit her save a deep shock of terror—and in the split second before her lids closed, she saw a flash of bright orange where Salter gripped the barrel. In the split second after, she heard him shout.

A misfire. He dropped the gun and doubled over, clutched at his left hand, pocked with burning lead.

Amelia didn't think; her fingers closed around a rock as she shoved herself to her feet. She rushed toward him, raised her arm, and, screeching, brought the chunk of granite down upon his dripping head. He cried out and staggered sideways, raised his forearms to cover his face, but she hit him again, hard enough to crack his ulna. When Amelia kneed his injured leg, Salter crumpled to the unforgiving earth. She dropped down upon him and drove the stone into his temple, then his face.

It was like a murre egg—tough, but hardly indestructible. Cartilage and bone shifted beneath his skin. One eye ran like a yolk in the rain.

Even as Amelia screamed, her gorge rose. A fingernail snapped. Blood spattered her face, lashes of heat among the cold rain, bitter salt and metal in her mouth. When another nail split and her hand went numb, she stopped.

Water pooled in the broken shell of Salter's skull even as it washed the gelatinous fluid and oozing blood away. Amelia let go of the rock but couldn't move. She slumped over the corpse as oddly quiet sobs wrenched themselves up from her frozen core.

The rain beat down. The fire still spread inside. She had to go get Will. Even if he was dead too, she couldn't leave him to the flames. But once again, Amelia's body failed her. She wished the bullet had found its mark.

"We should burn him," a flat voice said. She looked over her shoulder and saw Gertie gazing down at her defaced father.

Amelia tried to summon her own voice, to apologize, to explain, to beg forgiveness, to tell her not to look, but someone else spoke first.

"No; we should throw him over."

Amelia swiveled her neck to behold Will and felt a rush of annihilating relief. She pushed herself up and swept toward him as he stepped closer. There was a dark patch of blood down his right sleeve, and the left shoulder of his sweater was singed black, burned through.

"Oh *God*," she said, hands darting toward him but hesitating over his injuries.

"We need to do it now," he said, breathing labored, voice halting. "Before Percy comes round. We can say he slipped. Running after us. But we should weigh him down, make sure he disappears. Hitting the rocks wouldn't account for the hole in his chest. Better if there's no body to recover."

"It was self-defense," Amelia said, but even she couldn't bring herself to look again at what she'd done to the man's mutilated head.

Gertie was trembling now, not just from the cold; her jaw was clattering, but she didn't cry. "S-some lies are n-necessary," she said, and bent to stuff a handful of stones into her father's robe pocket.

Forty

RETRIBUTION

They pitched Elijah Salter's corpse over the edge of the island and heard it hit the water, but it was difficult to see through the rain-slashed dark and the spray of the pounding surf. They'd have to trust the undertow, the voracious carnivores that swam beneath it.

Mr. Clifford met them halfway around Tower Hill, pulled up short, eyes wide as if he beheld a group of ghosts. When they finally got inside the keepers' quarters, the children peeped out from behind their bedroom door but did not emerge, even to see Banquo.

Amelia glimpsed herself in the hall mirror, rusty streaks of blood all over her white underclothes where the cardigan left them exposed. The rain had mostly washed it off her skin, but only rinsed some of the pigment from the thirsty fabric, made it spread like diluted dye. She wanted to peel the chemise and petticoat off right there, but first they were obliged to tell their lie in three-part harmony.

Like the best falsehoods, it was built on truth: Salter attacked them, chased Gertie with a gun, and shot at them all multiple times, though only one bullet hit. Will wounded him in return, but Salter still pursued when they fled the fire he'd started. In the dark and the wind and the rain, he'd slipped, fallen down the rocks and into the sea.

They should have thrown his rifle in too, Amelia thought.

The Cliffords exchanged a look but said nothing to indicate doubt. They helped Will upstairs, into the room Finn once slept in. Mrs. Clifford gathered supplies to treat his wounds, and Mr. Clifford said he'd find some clothes for Will to change into.

"I should go fetch you something too," Amelia said to Gertie. "And leave your mother a note so she knows where you are come morning."

She wondered if Minerva had heard the gunshots, if she could see the flames from the tower—but if so, Amelia imagined her fixed to the spot by fear as much as duty. Since she was already dripping, she dashed off a few lines and went back out at once. She made her way to Stonehouse, tried not to look at anything as she walked into the kitchen to place her note upon the table. Then up the stairs to her old room—Gertie's now—to find a dress and underthings in the armoire, a flannel nightgown.

There were no lamps or candles or fires burning, so it was easy to imagine shadowy figures in the corners, though they dissolved when Amelia looked directly at them. Other things were clearer: sheets pulled half off Gertie's bed; *Jane Eyre* splayed open on the floor among shards of the shattered mirror by the nightstand; the wash pitcher in fragments on the ground by the door, a smudge of blood on one porcelain jigsaw piece.

Amelia blinked away a flurry of images—her splintered cider glass before the fire in Nantucket; Miss Price's razor; Salter's fractured face—and hurried back to her new home.

In her own room, she gave Gertie her clothes and said she'd be back to check on her in a moment, then went to find Will shivering beneath a double layer of blankets, though Mrs. Clifford had also laid a fire.

She set aside the cloth she'd been holding to his bare shoulder and came to the door to meet Amelia. "It looks like the bullet only grazed him, but it's still deep. Not bleeding too much, at least. But the burn on his other shoulder and his back . . . We need to get him to a hospital as soon as we can."

Amelia looked to the window, pummeled by blowing rain, and nodded. "It should clear up soon." Astounding how certain her voice sounded when she felt no such thing beneath the bravado.

"Are you hurt?"

She looked down at her bloodstained clothes and shook her head, then turned up her abraded palms. "I just took a tumble. Nothing worse. Gertie's fine too, I think."

"I'll go check on her," Mrs. Clifford said, and left the room.

Amelia went to Will's side, took in the bloody tunnel the bullet had grooved into his bicep, the blistered, peeling burn that spread across his opposite shoulder and up the side of his neck. She gripped the nightstand to steady herself.

"I'm fine," he said, but Amelia couldn't stop the tears from spilling down her cheeks as she gently touched his face, softly kissed his cheek and lips and forehead.

"I'm sorry," she said, again, and again, even as Will shushed her.

~

Amelia gave Gertie her own bed and spent a little while with her to gauge how she was doing.

"He would have killed me," the girl murmured, tucked under the covers in her flannel gown. "He said I couldn't be saved. But I was."

Amelia smoothed Gertie's damp hair until her eyelids batted closed. Then she got a nightgown of her own and slipped back across the hall to Will. He was awake, but barely; she guessed only the pain kept him conscious.

From the rug before the hearth, Banquo looked up, head on his paws, eyebrows twitching. Amelia shut the door and finally pulled off the sodden cardigan, her rain-heavy petticoat, her bloody chemise. Mrs.

317

Clifford had filled the ewer and left fresh linens, so she swiped at her chill, damp skin until it felt slightly less grimy, then pulled on her gown and carefully settled beside Will.

"Are you all right?" he croaked.

"I'm fine. We'll get you out of here tomorrow. But all your things; I'm so sorry . . ."

"All that matters is right here."

As Amelia nestled closer, something struck her. She shot up and retrieved her petticoat, felt around the hem with mounting panic. She picked at the stitches and, when a section loosened, ripped the fabric open all the way around.

"What are you doing?"

"I left my other petticoat in your room."

"So?"

Amelia laughed, a little madly. "The necklace!"

"That *sodding* thing—" Will broke off in a fit of coughing that frightened her into dropping the ruined garment and returning to his side. "I have enough," he said.

She laced her fingers with his, murmured, "It was the principle of the thing."

Eventually, he drifted off, but Amelia couldn't sleep. The rain and wind did not relent, nor did the harrowing images in her mind. The ones that caught in the topmost swirl of the maelstrom that night were less well-worn than others, and still had a hard shine to them that burned Amelia's eyes.

～

Only days before her father came home for the last time, Amelia's mother slipped into her room with a sewing kit and a velvet box entombing a necklace of emeralds and pearls, a breathtaking thing she'd never seen.

"This was a wedding present," her mother said, and pressed it into Amelia's hands. "It's worth a fortune. Of course I could never wear it. He knew that, but he wanted me to have it. To be chained to it, and to him."

While Amelia marveled at the depth and clarity of the gems and the soft luster of the pearls, the way they warmed in her hands, her mother took out a petticoat and unpicked part of its hem, then tucked the necklace inside, sewed the garment up again with impeccable stitches.

"I want thee to wear this from now on. Sleep in it, even. If anything should happen, if thou should need to run, this will keep thee from ruin. Sell it, so thou never need sell thyself. Not to a husband nor to an innkeeper nor to anyone. Use the money to get as far away as thou can. Never let thy father find thee."

She'd fended off Amelia's protests and questions. It was always easier to accept, to say, "Yes, Mother," and give her a soothing look and smooth her hands. So she did, and because her mother checked, Amelia took to wearing the petticoat with its uneven weight against one ankle even when she went to bed.

She'd been wearing it the night she escaped the fire, but she hadn't followed the rest of her mother's directive for a long while, too afraid to take it out and hand it over, no matter how much money she might have gotten. It was the only thing Amelia had left. The small hamlets she passed through seemed unlikely places to exchange it, besides.

Eventually, she grew brave enough—desperate enough—to separate a single emerald or pearl at a time, take it to a jeweler or a pawnbroker, to buy a train ticket and a few weeks in a hotel room while she looked for work or her next destination. It could have lasted her a lifetime.

But when she'd been ready to leave Chicago, she'd presented a single stone to a loupe-wielding man with muttonchops. His gold watch chain glinted in his dim but spotless shop, bedecked with taxidermy owls, crows, even sparrows, the door guarded by a sentient slab of beef with obsidian eyes. She'd almost turned and left the minute she saw him but stepped inside instead.

The jeweler wanted to know where she'd gotten the stone, if it was stolen, as it was clearly pried from a larger piece. She'd lied, but she wasn't good at that yet, and he'd sidled out from behind the counter as Amelia took a few steps back. When she decided to leave, despite the fact that he had the gem and hadn't paid for it, he grabbed her, ordered the lackey to lock the door and close the curtain while he wrestled her back toward his station. He picked up a scalpel from beside a half-skinned hummingbird.

"Let's play a game of hide and seek," he breathed, and pressed his hand to Amelia's stomach. "For your sake, I hope you haven't swallowed it. Tell me where it is and you'll still have your pretty dress, at least." She squirmed and tried to elbow him, but he stilled her with a hard-knuckled jab to the kidney, motioned the larger man over to hold her steady.

The jeweler sliced open the front of Amelia's bodice, reached into her corset, found nothing but flesh, slashed her skirt into ribbons beneath the pockets, which held only a change purse. He patted her outer petticoat, then tugged it down and untied her crinoline so it sank into a heap at her feet. Pinioned, it was useless to struggle, yet Amelia tried to kick him as his hands went straight to the sagging side of her inner petticoat, the telltale weight of the necklace.

He cut it free and held it up to the gaslight. "My, *my*. Wherever did you get this magnificent piece? You must have stolen it—I should call the police."

"It was my mother's! Give it back!"

He only laughed and carried the necklace behind the counter. "Shame what you've done to it, but it can be salvaged. Incredible."

"It's *mine!*"

"Possession is eleven points in the law, my dear. And I am in possession of it now." He gave Amelia an appraising look as well, then flicked his eyes up to his man. "Put her out. If she tries to get back in, then by all means, call the police. Or break her neck; makes no difference to me."

Amelia might have been sea-foam, so easily did he push her toward the door, though she resisted, tried to. He shoved her into the street so hard she pitched forward and stumbled to the opposite sidewalk, where she sprawled. Few people passed at that hour; those who did averted their eyes. The giant tossed her crinoline and petticoat out. After a bottomless moment of incomprehensible fury—and shame—that made her hate herself and everyone in the whole execrable world, Amelia snatched them up and began blundering back to her hotel.

Blind with tears, she was bumped out of the way by several passersby—the ones who did not step wide to avoid her, whether they curled their lips in disgust or pretended not to see her at all. A few catcalled her; one tried to grab her but laughed and pulled away when she snarled at him through her sobs.

And then a soft hand touched Amelia's elbow, and a gentle voice calmed her when she spun away. "Hey, hey. Easy, darling. What's the matter? Come now, love. Let me help you, eh? I'm Lucy. What's your name?"

∼

Lying beside Will, Amelia squeezed shut her eyes and seeped silent tears onto the pillow.

Forty-One

FLIGHT

When she woke, the wind still clattered the glass as rain pelted it. Amelia jerked up and looked to Will, still asleep, still breathing steadily. She heard voices downstairs and put her feet on the floor, peeked into the hall.

Mrs. Salter's tones, more identifiable for their strangeness, as she'd barely ever heard them before, and Gertie's. Amelia padded halfway down the stairs and saw them, the girl wrapped in her mother's arms, Minerva clad in trousers and sweater and cap. Amelia was surprised to see her out of a dress, but she must have dispensed with such frippery for the sake of tending the light. She looked up at the creak of a tread and met Amelia's eyes. Minerva gave a slight nod that might have meant nothing in particular but felt like one small weight lifted from Amelia's chest.

~

She borrowed Mrs. Clifford's raincoat and went to search the shell of Will's house. The stone walls stood firm, but everything inside was ruined. Stairs and second floor collapsed, roof fallen in, charred timbers and furniture like jumbled bones, a skeleton in disarray. Amelia picked her way through the debris, and in the warm, rain-spattered ashes below the place where his room had been, she found Lucy's necklace, soot-smoked but otherwise intact. The silver watch survived too. Amelia wiped both clean on her damp skirt and slipped them into her pocket. She stood still and attuned herself to any possible presence, whatever figure she might have glimpsed over Salter's shoulder the night before, but she was alone.

Before she went back, she ventured to the edge of the shore where they had thrown Salter over, expecting nothing but churning sea—and the ground slid beneath Amelia's feet when she jerked back from the sight of the upper half of Salter's bloodless body snagged on the rocks. The rest appeared to have been bitten off, a ragged margin of bleached pink meat and tattered clothes, a mess to match his ruined head. She pictured the massive shark tooth she'd taken from Stonehouse and suppressed a shudder.

She wouldn't say anything, would trust the storm tide to carry the remains away.

Back at the Cliffords' house, she nibbled at bacon and biscuits, her stomach even more unsettled by the way Will couldn't manage more than a few bites. He barely made it out of bed, though he said he was fine even through agonizing coughs.

They couldn't launch the boat in that weather; no one had to say so because they all knew it. But Amelia went repeatedly to the window to stare at the snarl of surf in the near distance, the sheets of water blowing in the gale, spray exploding against the rocks.

It had to clear sometime. In her head, she repeated two simple words like a prayer: *Soon. Please. Soon.*

Will went back to bed and sipped a little water, slept off and on. He had a fever and was clearly still in pain, likely far more than he showed. His burn wept, skin like a furnace. Amelia felt her heart skipping every other beat. Her eyes leaked tears perpetually, as she paced, as she stared out the window, as she gazed at him.

In the early evening, he woke and weakly held her hand. "Do you think she would have forgiven me?" he murmured.

Amelia's face crumpled, and she was glad Will's eyes had closed. "I know she did. She loved you. She must have missed you so much."

"I wonder if she would have ever introduced us."

A terrible, traitorous truth flashed through Amelia's heart. That if Lucy—Cathy—had, then nothing ever would have grown between her and Will but friendship. Amelia might have loved him after a fashion, but she never would have left his sister. Yet she was grateful there was no way to trade one for the other, because if offered the awful chance now, she could not do it, could never make such a choice.

She closed her eyes, placed her other hand over both of theirs, and held on for dear life.

~

Will took a few spoonfuls of broth at dinner. His breathing changed as night fell. Ragged, punctuated by deeper inhalations as if he'd just come up from underwater. He sweated and shivered, his forehead clammy.

Gertie came to see them and knelt by the bed while Amelia sat on its edge. The girl prayed. Amelia did too, but with only one word now: *Please. Please. Please.*

The wind wailed and shook the house all night. The hours seemed endless, like Amelia's tears. She knelt again until she couldn't feel her legs, bent her head over her hand clasped with Will's, let her heartbeat be her supplication.

Again, she fell asleep and woke with a jolt of surprise, a sense of consummate terror, certain someone was in the room with them, but there was no one she could see.

The next day passed with so little variation Amelia was almost convinced it was the very same one, somehow wound back and begun again; she was trapped in limbo. Will barely stirred, didn't eat or drink.

But the burn was brighter, and ran more freely, the fluid taking on a yellow cast. She saw Salter's ruined eye and feared they were both being made to pay for her crime.

"How long can it go on?" she demanded of the storm when Mrs. Clifford came to check on them. "It has to break. It *has* to."

"It will."

"But *when?*"

Not that night, yet somehow Amelia managed to doze for several hours. The cycle repeated. The storm had no eye, no end, no mercy.

~

When next she woke—she had no concept anymore of time, what hour or day it might be—Will's breath was too loud in the room. But Amelia realized that was partly because it was quiet outside.

At last, the wind had died, the rain abated. The sun had risen, but the light was pearly and diffuse, a thick mantle of fog muffling the world without. She sprinted downstairs and found the parlor deserted. A glance at the clock told her it was only five thirty.

She hesitated just a moment before she pounded on the Cliffords' bedroom door. They came shambling and blinking in trepidation.

"The storm stopped—we have to go!"

They both looked at Amelia strangely, which unsettled her; was she mistaking things? Was the south wind still howling but she'd gone deaf to it? Or was she invisible, one of those ghosts who rattled doors but didn't materialize when they were opened?

"Did you hear me?"

They exchanged another of their inscrutable looks, and Mr. Clifford went to the window, pulled back the curtain. "Miss Riley . . . we're socked in."

"But it's calm. Finally."

Another maddening glance between husband and wife before he said, "We couldn't see a thing out there. We'd run up on the rocks—"

"No! I won't. I'll take him myself—just, please, help me get him in the boat, help me get it launched—"

"We need to wait for it to clear."

"We *can't*. It's been too long already. *Please*."

"Honey," Mrs. Clifford said, "Percy's right. It's too dangerous in this soup. Let's just wait a few hours and see if it doesn't lift."

Amelia opened her mouth to argue, but only a sob emerged. Mrs. Clifford stepped closer and embraced her, swirled her fingertips in a motherly circle on Amelia's back. "He'll be all right."

"You don't know that."

"But I have to believe it."

Amelia couldn't—it was too dangerous—yet she held fast to Mrs. Clifford and the woman's own conviction for another long moment.

When she returned to Will, Amelia watched the window for any intimation of a thinning of the veil beyond. She realized, with an electric spike of horror, why the Cliffords had regarded her strangely. She'd forgotten to put on Lucy's voice, spoke with her own. Perhaps they'd put it down to shock. It didn't matter.

Gertrude came round again, but Amelia stopped her from praying, even as she felt hateful for it.

"We need to get him out of here," she told the girl.

"I'll help you."

Gertie was too frail, of course, but Amelia squeezed her hand in thanks. "Could you go see if there's any tea?"

Alone again with Will, she tried to wake him and could get no more than vague groans. Even in the grips of her frantic despair, Amelia knew she wouldn't die the instant Will took his last breath, that she couldn't perish from a broken heart. That itself was what would be unbearable.

She flew back downstairs and grabbed her cloak from its hook, fastened it as she marched into the parlor and appealed to Mr. Clifford again, this time in the voice he expected.

"I need you to help me get Will in the boat right now. I can handle it myself if you just get us in the water. But we have no more time to waste."

"I can't do that, Miss Riley."

"You must. I insist."

He shook his head. "We won't make it in this weather."

"*I* might!"

"The sea's still rough. Can't see twenty feet ahead of you. Storm's liable to pick up again too. I can't be responsible—"

"You won't be! My God, I have to *try*. He won't make it another night. And I will not just sit and watch him die. Please. *Please.*"

After a moment of crushing silence, Mrs. Clifford stood and laid Jacob in his basket. "I can handle Mary and the derrick." She nodded at Gertie, who stood as if she wanted to dissolve into the bookcase. "Between the three of us, we can probably get him situated."

"Abigail."

She looked at her husband. "If it was me?"

So he rose, told Joy to keep an eye on her brothers and sister, and went to grab his rain gear. The women pulled a sweater and an oilskin over Will, who should have cried out at the pain but only whimpered. They carried him down the stairs and through the swollen fog to the boathouse, settled him in a nest of blankets at the bottom of the dory, and attached the winch. Amelia sat on one of the benches, and Mr. Clifford made as if to join her, but his wife grabbed his arm, gave a slight shake of her head.

"It's my job," he said, and her fingers tightened.

"I'm not asking you to come with me," Amelia said.

"I have to," said Mr. Clifford, eyes still on his wife.

Amelia thought Mrs. Clifford wanted to argue, wanted to cry, but instead she crushed her husband close and said, "You come back to me, you hear? Come back to me or else."

"Yes, ma'am." He kissed her, and Amelia looked away as grief pulverized her chest, a rogue wave pounding a fragile reef.

And then Mr. Clifford got into the boat and his wife coaxed Mary into motion. The world swung away as the dory rose in the air and canted over the side of the cliff. The surrounding outcroppings were mere suggestions of shadows lost in the swirling fog. Even in the cove, the waves were turbulent, scummed with foam, the spray blinding. The shore lunged for them as they touched the water and broke their last tether to the island.

With the concerted effort to keep from crashing into the rocks, Amelia was only half aware of sudden shouts and a blur of movement, a louder splash. Then she realized: Banquo had run out after them—perhaps the children had opened the door to peek out—and he'd tripped down the ladder stairs, hit the water, and struggled to swim.

She let go of her oars—stupid, but it was pure reflex—and leaned over the gunwale, stretched her arms. "You idiot dog! Come *on!*" And then she had him. She hauled his wriggling body on board, picked up the oars—miraculously, neither slipped nor torn free—and helped Mr. Clifford fight against the ocean. They propelled themselves away from the gnashing rocks running with spume and spindrift, saliva sluicing down sharp teeth.

Banquo pitched and shifted on stiff legs as he whined and nosed Will's head. *"Sit,"* Amelia told him. "Lie down." He did, the look on his face as close to regret as a dog could ever manage.

They pulled hard and held their breath as they waited for the Eye of the Needle or Sugarloaf to rear up at them; they were bound to get turned around in the fog, sideswiped by stones, or swamped by a wave. The boat went almost vertical as they climbed the glassy granite faces of mountainous swells before they plunged down their backs. Amelia should have refused Mr. Clifford's help. But she knew what it was to strike out alone and was glad he was with her.

By God's grace or dumb luck, they avoided colliding with any rocks. Amelia felt the Farallones slip away behind them, yet the sea remained daunting as it yawned around the boat. The sky darkened above, and rain began to fall.

Cold, fat drops, hard as dimes crashing down. She covered Will and Banquo with another oilskin as best she could, but everything was sopping wet and freezing cold. Will's burn went white and puckered. The horizon lurched in another direction every second; the sibilant rain changed to even harder hail, icy buckshot that clattered in the bottom of the boat and bounced off their lowered heads. They put their hands up to protect their skulls, and a wave hit them broadside. Water slopped into the spinning dory; they bailed, and Banquo cried.

It won't ever be the water kills thee. Amelia heard her mother's voice in the lee of the waves, but it was no solace—even if the prophecy, the promise, still held true, that innate protection did not extend to Amelia's shipmates. Besides, fire had already claimed her in some sense, twice. Perhaps she'd worked some counterfeit magic and escaped her fate only to perish the way she'd first thought she would die, consigned to a watery mass grave with its undertaking fish and crabs.

She imagined eyeless faces rolling in the waves, their chalk-white fingers reaching from the foam: little Finn, long-lost Nathaniel, vanquished Salter. Insatiable as the very sea.

She imagined leviathan sharks and lurking whales as well, other creatures she had never seen but feared existed. A mass of mile-long tentacles undulating beneath them, waiting for the right moment to shoot up and tug them down. Several times, Amelia thought she saw sharp black fins slicing through the waves toward them.

But there was only the fanged, flinty, heaving sea itself, and the driving rain, and the banshee wind that came to drown out even her mother's ghostly voice.

~

They struggled on for hours. The compass indicated they were still headed in the right direction, but for all they could see, they might have been no more than a hundred feet from the Farallones.

At last, the rain relented to a cold drizzle and the sky smudged a darker gray as afternoon gave way to evening.

Perhaps it was the pewter light cast down on him, the sheen of the rain and spray that slicked him, but the driftwood pallor of Will's face made Amelia's insides seize like hot wax dropped in water.

Another silent prayer prickled within her, but the single word was different now: *No. No. No.*

Forty-Two

PHANTASM

They must have battled through the ocean for nine hours or more, yet it was a timeless interlude in its way; it felt like an eternity and a mere blink of an eye, at least once they finally came in sight of the pier. Amelia knew then that she could never deny the existence of miracles, or salvation.

The next hours were an ecstatic, exhausted blur in her mind. Several men who saw their boat came to help them; somehow, they made it to the hospital. Mr. Clifford refused to stay, though a nurse tried to make him. Amelia gripped his hand in both of hers and thanked him as deeply as she could. He wished her luck and said he had to get back to Abby as soon as the weather cleared, must go see to the boat. She let go and was guided away.

Amelia had a vague sense of cold air and warm blankets—marvelously dry—and hot liquid. She shivered so hard her muscles hurt. She blinked and was in a strange bed, staggered out of it. Blinked again and was in a chair beside Will's cot, back in her own clothes, though without her crinoline. For a moment, Amelia thought she'd woken in the room on the island again, but the too-close, windowless walls resolved into filmy sheets of fabric, and snatches of memory flooded her head as she tried to work out how many days she'd been on the mainland.

A nurse came in and seemed to know her, though she called her Miss Riley, in a gentle Irish lilt. When Amelia corrected her, the woman frowned and asked if she knew where she was, what year it was. Agitated, Amelia asked her own questions: Would Will be all right; how long had they been there?

"Just two days now. You were disorientated at first, but you insisted on getting up to see him yesterday. He's fighting. He seems strong. Lord knows you are. You're in the paper, too. Why don't you go get a bite to eat and take a look—we've copies all over the place. Just go to the nurses' station out in the hall; they won't let any journalists through, and they'll take care of you. I need to tend his wounds."

She didn't want to leave, but the nurse insisted. Before Amelia stepped through the part in the curtains, she turned. "Where's Banquo?"

The woman frowned again. "Ah, the *madigan*? The custodians are taking care of him. He's not allowed on the ward, of course, but you can go visit."

⁓

It felt horrible to eat when Will still hadn't opened his eyes, yet when another nurse brought Amelia a bowl of soup and a sandwich, her stomach growled. She gobbled down the food as she read.

The newspaper story was bereft of quotes from its subjects but recounted the gripping ordeal of the rescue from the forbidding Farallones in detail.

Mr. Clifford had given their names upon admission, she supposed, but someone from the hospital, or perhaps one of the dockhands who'd helped pull them ashore, must have furnished the other particulars: Will's burn—no mention of the gunshot, but then it wasn't obvious if you didn't know how that wound had happened; the faithful mutt along for the ride; the harrowing storm; the beautiful, intrepid heroine intent on saving her lover, regardless of the perils of the sea. There was nothing about Mr. Clifford at all, but Amelia was certain he'd been there. She only entertained the notion she'd imagined him for a moment.

She returned to Will, spoke to him, chafed his hand, kissed his cheek. He stirred, but only fluttered his eyelids, made inarticulate sounds beneath his breath. When next Amelia was ejected from the room, she asked to be taken to Banquo, and crouched to ruffle his fur while he jumped up with his paws on her shoulders. They showed her out a back entrance to walk him on a lead they'd procured.

She was stunned to find the day clear, bright, blue.

∾

Even if she'd had someplace else to go, Amelia wouldn't have left Will for more than a few moments at a time. The next day, his eyes stayed open long enough to focus on her face, and he smiled. She dripped happy tears onto his cheeks and, in snatches, answered the fragmentary questions he was able to formulate as she kissed him.

She took Banquo out again, ventured around the front of the building. From Stockton Street, she looked out toward the wharf, the gleaming bay studded with boats of all descriptions. There was still a Nantucket whaler rotting on the mudflats, abandoned by fellow island-ers who'd come to get in on the Gold Rush. The first time she'd seen it, such fear had struck Amelia's heart. Now, she let her eyes skim over the decrepit hulk for brighter prospects.

As she strolled down the block, a man approached, his gaze so fixed Amelia felt a riffle of unease, but the notepad in his hand explained his interest. She turned and quickened her step, even as he called out, "Lucy Riley? A word, miss, please—everyone's dying to know more about your valiant escape! In your own words, please! Tell your story!"

Amelia reached the safety of St. Mary's and decided not to go out again until darkness fell, though she wasn't sure journalists slept. She felt she wouldn't either.

∾

Will sat up and ate but was still weak, in pain. They spoke only of easy things for the time being, mostly where they'd go when he was better. Back to the island to get their things and say proper goodbyes, of course, pay the place due respect. Then north. "But first," Will said, "we have to make a stop at the Sanford."

At Amelia's quizzical look, he clarified: "They have the most glorious copper tubs you've ever seen."

She laughed—the sound itself surprised her, doubled her delight— and kissed him again. She knew she could live with anything—with everything—now that Will was all right.

That night, she took Banquo out and spied a few stars, the rest obscured by low clouds. But still there, she knew, still uncountable. Tendrils of fog rolled in off the water. A tiny ember glowed off to her left, some other stargazer out for a smoke.

"Lucy Riley?"

Reflex made Amelia turn toward the voice, brows raised in expectation, but then she smiled and shook her head. "No."

The man, neatly mustached, mercury-and-iron hair gleaming with pomade, narrowed his eyes. "You didn't just come in from the Farallones?"

A slight waver of misgiving moved through her, but she replied readily enough. "Well, yes, but—the papers made a little mistake. My name is Amelia Osborne." It was so shockingly easy to say, it almost made her giddy.

He extended a hand and said around his cigar, "Giancarlo Ricci."

Forty-Three

REQUIEM

Amelia gasped, danced back.

He grinned. "You're familiar with the name, I see. Kitty tell you all about me?"

When Amelia made to turn, Giancarlo nodded, and another man appeared behind her, stopped her with his sheer size, though the gun that nearly disappeared in his palm gave her equal pause. "Don't scream."

"Come and talk," Giancarlo said, and gestured to a waiting carriage.

When Amelia didn't move or speak, he grimaced. "I won't hurt you, all right? But I will lose my patience if you make me repeat myself."

In a trance, she stepped toward the carriage. The man behind her ripped Banquo's lead from her so violently he nearly lashed his boss. Ricci launched the burning stub of his cigar at the man, called him an idiot followed by a string of Italian as he shoved Amelia the rest of the way inside. She protested, then cried out when Giancarlo kicked Banquo back from the carriage.

"He'll be fine," Ricci said, and pushed Amelia back against the seat as he climbed in behind her. He slammed the door, and his henchman mounted the driver's seat.

As they lurched forth, Amelia began to plead, but Giancarlo winced and held up a hand to stop her. "I can't stand tryin' to jaw over all this clatter. We're not going far. It can wait." A thin smile hung on his face, but the cold fire in his eyes made her decide to sit still, and be silent.

They rattled down the rutted street in an intolerable tension. When the carriage stopped ten minutes later, Ricci guided Amelia out, steered her through the door of a grand gambling parlor, not one she'd ever been to, though she recognized the area. The few people who glanced at them—men in suits, men in threadbare work shirts, women in fine, low-cut dresses and feathers and twinkling gems—showed little interest as he marched her through the main floor and up the stairs.

They entered an opulent room, a fire roaring in a huge marble hearth with a mahogany mantel, overstuffed chairs arranged before it, carpet thick as several seasons' fallen leaves beneath their feet.

"Sit."

Amelia walked obediently toward the chairs, but stopped short, distracted by a small, gold-framed photograph on the mantel: this man, though over a decade younger, and Lucy, stone-faced behind a wedding veil.

As Giancarlo poured a glass of whiskey, Amelia leaned closer, struck by that stoic beauty, so different from the laughing vibrancy she had known; even when Lucy had been solemn, a sympathetic smile touched her eyes. You knew a laugh was never far behind.

"So where exactly is my wife?" Giancarlo said. "Still on the island? Or has she run someplace else by now? I heard a lot of crazy shit from Eva, so I don't know what to believe."

Amelia assumed Will's last letter, in which he'd decided to tell the Riccis of his sister's death himself, hadn't reached New York in time. Or Gianni had chosen to reject the truth. So she had to say it yet again.

The words still weighed as much as ever, had to be dredged up out of her body as Amelia finally lowered herself into a chair.

"She's dead. She's been dead almost two years now. I took her name because I thought someone was after me. It's caused quite a bit of confusion."

Gianni sank into his chair and stared into the fire, upper lip sucked between his teeth, already half-empty glass in his fingers. When he whipped the tumbler into the hearth, Amelia jumped at the explosion of glass and alcohol.

"How do I know you're not lying too, huh? Not just covering for Kitty 'cause she has you thinking I'm the fucking devil when I've only ever been a slave to her!"

Amelia tried to sound reasonably calm. "Because if she were alive, I would be with her right now. I don't know what Miss Price told you about how she died, but the fact that she's gone is true."

Ricci stood and paced the rug. "Eva thought she was so slick. Thought she could throw me a bone and I wouldn't ask any follow-up questions, I'd be so grateful she had news for me, wouldn't find out she'd sat on it for so long. I didn't mind that shit in New York, so long as Kitty came back home to me—or, hell, let me watch. But behind my back? And carrying on for all that time, when I was the one who sent Eva out here? And she *knew* I wanted Kitty back. She knew she belonged to me."

Ricci poured a new glass of whiskey from the service on the table between their chairs. "I just wanted a little foothold out here on the Barbary Coast. Better late than never, I figured. I sent Eva 'cause she was . . . *formidable*. But like most formidable women, she vastly over-estimated her own abilities. And her value to me."

He gulped from his glass, filled it again. "I thought I might have made a bit of a rash decision, but she's where she belongs. On the bottom of the fuckin' bay. *Puttana*."

Amelia fought to keep herself from shaking.

Ricci nodded at her. "What are you worried for, huh? You haven't done anything to me, personally. I don't think Eva was telling the truth about you hurtin' Kitty. See, I got a feeling about people. You sure as hell ain't a killer. Still, I had to come do my due diligence. Which was proving difficult, let me tell you. Until you rowed yourself back here, thirty miles of open ocean in a son-of-a-bitchin' storm. Saved me the hassle of trying to find a couple assholes to go out and get you—nobody wants to sail out there in the winter, even with a lot of money on the line. Oughta thank you for saving me a hell of a payday too. Shit, I oughta offer you a job—you're tenacious, clearly. Formidable, even. And Eva left an opening . . ."

He gulped again, shook his head. "Still, I can't deny, I am a bit *disappointed* at this particular turn of events. I'm a bit disappointed I killed that bitch already. Frankly, I'd like to have her here right now." His grip looked tight enough to shatter the glass. "So, tell me." When Amelia hesitated, he added, "Everything."

She was surprised to feel a sense of calm suffuse her as she recounted her story, as it intersected with Lucy's—Cathy's, Kitty's. She went through their meeting, their moves, their last day together. She left Will out of it, and the notebooks too. But when she looked up at Ricci, he wanted more.

"You're editing. You're redacting. You ain't sayin' how you managed to end up on that same Christ-forsaken island as her brother." The first gleam of pleasure came into his eyes at Amelia's trepidation. "Oh, she was all torn up when Billy wasn't there in Brooklyn. Poor Kitty came all that way for nothing. She was inconsolable—but I did my best. And then she ran out on me anyway. Will knew she was here all that time? In San Francisco? He help her hide from me?"

Amelia swallowed with some difficulty. "No. He didn't know. And I didn't know about him when I went out there, either—I didn't know he existed. But when I found out, we made a truce. We decided she must have been coming to him for help getting rid of Miss Price."

"Shit. Well, too little, too late. And what, then you fell in love with him? How 'bout that. And then what happened? Papers said a fire. Another one?"

Amelia summoned the composure with which she'd once spoken of the conflagration that obliterated her first life. "A lamp got knocked over. Will went back in . . . to save me, and he got burned. I couldn't lose him too."

"Well, what're the fuckin' odds, huh?" Ricci swirled his glass. "I ain't sayin' I changed my mind about Eva's story, but it does seem a little queer to me. Two fires. One Sisson dead, one just about. You there both times . . ."

But, of course, she wasn't there for Lucy; that was the point where so much went so terribly wrong. Amelia took a breath and went through it all again. Gianni tossed back the remainder of his drink and peered at her until she finished, then drained the decanter and rose to look at his wedding portrait. Amelia imagined it was a totem to him, which he'd carried all the way across the country. Yet his faith had gone unrewarded.

"And Kitty really never mentioned me?" he asked.

"No."

"You never saw her ring?"

"Never." But Amelia thought of how the inaugural entry in Lucy's first notebook had simply been a large sum, her starting balance. She must have sold the wedding jewelry, used it to finance her escape. Amelia shifted her feet and felt Miss Price's necklace tap against her ankle. She'd sewn it back into her hem by Will's bedside while praying for the tempest to relent. "I have something else that belonged to her, though."

Ricci turned and watched Amelia bend to pick at the stitches. It took some time with only her broken fingernails, but finally, the necklace slithered free. She raised her scabbed palm, the diamonds and rubies sparkling with refracted firelight. Ricci slugged down half his drink, blew a puff of air between his lips. "Never seen it before. Means nothin' to me."

"But it's real—it's worth a lot of money." Amelia set it on the whiskey-splashed side table, hands shaking.

Giancarlo laughed. "Tryin' to buy your way outa here? I have more money than I'll ever be able to spend in this lifetime, or the next. And no use for pretty little baubles, genuine or otherwise."

"Then what do you want? I thought—"

"I want. My *wife*. I want that bright-eyed, sweet little liar who snuck off from me like I was some common *coglione*! Who took years off my life. You can't give me that, can you? All you can give me is a story—a good one, to be fair, but it doesn't have a very satisfying fuckin' ending, so I wonder what that's even worth."

Amelia trembled in her chair, leaned sideways and fumbled in her pocket, which caused Gianni to reach behind him and pull a stiletto from beneath his vest. She shrank back but held out her hand again, this time full of a familiar silver weight that ticked like her own heart in her palm. It ached as much to offer it up, but it was the only other thing she had.

The man's whole face slumped; he set the dagger and his glass on the mantel and stepped forward, lifted the pocket watch from Amelia's hand as tenderly as he might a downy chick. He was so absorbed she entertained a wild thought of grabbing a tumbler and staving his head in. But just because she'd done it once didn't mean she could ever do it again. So she stayed still and focused on drawing air past the swelling lump in her throat.

"This fuckin' thing," Ricci murmured, and turned the watch over to run a thumb across the engraving; Amelia could feel the faint grooves as if she brushed them herself.

"She was late to her own wedding, you know that? She came rushin' into the church holdin' this up in front of her like a Goddamn Roman medallion for the emperor. Had to find her 'somethin' old,' she said. Couldn't ever stay mad at her. That smile. That face. All spun gold and sunstruck glass."

Ricci's sigh slid into something like a laugh. He slipped the watch into his pocket, finished his drink, contemplated the glazed facets of the tumbler, the flicker of fire through its base.

"I guess, on balance, I'm glad I finally got to see Frisco, at least. Different world out west. I bet Kitty liked it here."

"She did."

"And how about you, Miss—?"

"Osborne. Amelia." It felt strangely powerless to say aloud this time.

"You plan to stick around? Interested in a new line of work?"

"No, thank you."

He smirked and set down his glass, plunged his hand into his pocket to finger the watch again. Amelia knew that gesture in her muscles and bones; she would repeat it for the rest of her life, she suspected. And though her fingers would never close on that silver weight again, and her throat ached to think so, she had tiny wooden whales and a boat to carry with her. She had the hand that made them to clasp instead. If she was only allowed to leave this stifling, elegant, awful room. If fate would see fit to deliver her once more.

"Well," Ricci mused, "I suppose you can go, then."

Amelia couldn't help but infer some joke, some trick, some false promise. She stared at him, lips parted, neck taut as a violin string about to snap.

"Havin' second thoughts?"

She shook her head, pushed herself up from the chair. She barely heard her own voice when she said, "That's all?"

Ricci shrugged. "That's all."

Amelia backed toward the door, too afraid to lose sight of him, groped behind her for the knob. When she turned it, he said, "You tell Will Carmelo would be glad to hear from him again, if he was ever inclined to strike up an old friendship. I'd pay him a visit, but—I don't think he ever cared much for me. Even before we was brothers-in-law."

He winked at Amelia as she backed into the hall and finally turned, heart careening in her chest. She expected the huge man from before to be stationed there, but the corridor was empty. The dissonance of laughter and singing and shouting filtered up from below, like the cacophony of the birds, underscored by off-kilter music.

She paused a moment, torn between the urge to flee and the knowledge that once she did, she would look over her shoulder for Giancarlo Ricci for the rest of her time in the city, if not the rest of her life. It occurred to Amelia that she could go back into the room, ask him to talk with her about Kitty, spin stories of the woman he knew. She could encourage him to pour more drinks. Watch him swill another decanter of whiskey and wait for him to pass out with his head tipped back against his chair. Then she could take his stiletto and stand behind his body as she pressed the blade into his neck and drew it fast across his throat.

That way she wouldn't end up covered in blood, and it might look credibly self-inflicted. People could surely be persuaded that he'd been so distraught at the news of his wife's death he'd decided to end himself. Once Amelia was sure Gianni was beyond salvation, she could put the knife in his hand and run downstairs for help, to make it seem more believable.

If his enforcer showed the slightest suspicion, she could slip him the necklace. Amelia suspected he'd be happy enough to keep any misgivings quiet in exchange.

But even if she managed to execute such a desperate and dangerous plan, she would be a murderer twice over. She would be haunted by that fact instead of by the fear of Ricci himself. And even if he deserved to die, Amelia couldn't be the one to make it happen.

She hurried toward the stairs and dashed down them, plunged through the smoke-wreathed, booze-soaked, boisterous crowd on the main floor, and tripped through the doorway into the cold December night.

The fog had thickened, but Amelia knew well enough where she was. She raced down the street, glanced back behind her every few seconds, certain someone would appear to stop her. It couldn't possibly be that easy to get away. Yet she remained unhounded by anything save her own fear.

Forty-Four

At Last

When Amelia came in sight of St. Mary's, she felt a joyous sob well up in her chest. She ran inside and hastened through the corridor to Will's ward. But as she started down the row of beds her ebullience churned over again into distress.

His spot was empty, the covers rumpled as if they'd been thrown off, the wheeled curtains shoved wide.

"Where is he?" She turned in a tight circle, addressing anyone and everyone within earshot. "Where is he? The man who was in this bed?"

An old fellow two places down the line coughed and strained to lift his stringy neck from the pillow; a bandage covered half his head, but he fixed his good eye on Amelia. "Left up out of here maybe an hour ago. Was bothering the nurses, all in a lather, wanted to know where *you* went. Ships in the night, eh?" He emitted a phlegmy laugh that turned into another cough, and Amelia rushed back down the aisle, toward the main entry and the front desk.

"Will Sisson, the patient from the Farallones, where did he go? Did you see him leave?"

The admitting nurse shook her head. "He was in no fit state to be up and about, but he wouldn't be handled, no. Strode out of here some time ago. I can't go chasing after patients who won't listen to reason and good sense. But if you find him, you'd best bring him back here. He's not healed yet. Hardheaded men, all of them. They break a leg and they want to run a race, but let them catch a little cold and they'll moan your ear off like they were dying . . ."

Her brogue faded behind Amelia as she barreled to the door and pushed her way once more into the night. She went north by instinct, called for Will and called for Banquo too.

The last time she'd wandered the streets of San Francisco alone in the dark, she'd unwittingly walked away from everything she knew and loved and took for granted; upon her return, as the sun climbed above the hill, she'd arrived at an abominable scene.

Determined as she was to push that away, it pushed back. There could be nothing good waiting for her, wherever she might end up. She understood why she'd been allowed out of that opulent room: to find out what worse fate was in store.

Amelia's voice was hoarse, lashes thick with tears, breath weak and rasping in her chest. Her feet ached from running, her cheeks from the cold. She found herself passing the bakery where she'd first met Mr. Pollard for their interview. The day he was due, she'd stood outside the boardinghouse and intercepted him on the sidewalk, said she was afraid a rather noisy birthday party was going on, and would he mind terribly much if they went somewhere else to talk?

He'd been delighted to saunter with her down the street and tuck into pastries while they chatted, and she'd been relieved to be far from the attention of Mrs. McGowan. A lifetime ago. A distant dream. If only the present moment were a nightmare.

Now she retraced her steps. When Amelia turned the next corner, she would be in sight of her old home. Her eyes slid up, but only chimney smoke stained the sky, while fog stirred at her feet. Morning was still a long way off.

She heard a sound that made her heart leap in her chest, though there was a stutter of fear as well—that she'd only imagined it, that it was some other dog barking—but as she swung round the corner, Banquo came racing toward her, and she nearly crashed to her knees. She ruffled his ears and drew in a deep breath as she straightened up.

"Will!"

He turned in time to see Amelia flying at him, and she slowed enough not to knock him over, but he still staggered back a step, even as he wrapped his arms around her, unmindful of his injuries. Amelia's frenzied sobs were full of a wild relief, a ragged joy—she sounded like Mrs. Clifford the first time she held Jacob.

"Where were you?" Will said, voice muffled by Amelia's neck as he pressed his face close. "Where did you go?"

All she could say at that moment was, "It's over. It's all right. It's all over. I love you. My God, I love you."

∼

She told him, briefly, about her meeting with Giancarlo Ricci. Will was aghast, despite Amelia's reassurances that the man had no further interest in them. She hoped that was true. She understood that leniency did not unmake the monster, but she didn't believe either of them were destined to slay him. They'd do best to try and forget he existed.

When Will wondered why Cathy had repeatedly been punished for his own sins, Amelia gripped his elbows, looked into his eyes.

"She wasn't. Bad things happen. But good things, too. She got away from him. And she was happy."

"With you."

At least for a while, Amelia thought. But that was all anyone ever got. She tucked Will's arm beneath her own and led him back to the hospital, hauled them both toward the future.

That morning, sunrise inflamed the sky and stained the bay crimson, but it meant nothing, Amelia decided. Only that a new day had come at last.

~

While Will recuperated, she sent a brief letter by pilot boat to the island, to let them know all was well and they would be back to settle affairs as soon as possible—but she didn't pretend they would stay. Friends deserved time to prepare for parting.

She granted an interview, too, mostly to clear the record, but only on the points she wanted known: her real name (which she would have to explain on her return to Southeast Farallon), and Mr. Clifford's involvement, without which Amelia was certain she would never have made it. She mailed a copy of the article to the Lighthouse Board with a handwritten note in hopes they would finally see fit to make him head keeper.

~

When Will was discharged, they stopped at a bank. Amelia stayed outside with Banquo, whose presence made her less uneasy among so many bustling people and rushing horses and carts and carriages.

At the Sanford, Will bribed a porter to sneak the dog in through the back way and registered at the front under "Mr. and Mrs. Sisson." The red-nosed desk clerk studied them over the tops of his spectacles. Amelia tensed for some cutting remark or a refusal to admit them, but then recognition sparked a grin.

"Are you the ones from the Farallones? My sisters can't stop squealing about you all! Can I get your autographs for them?"

"If you promise not to tell anyone else we're here."

"No, sir! Deal." He passed them a hotel business card, flipped it over for them to sign the back.

As Will took the fountain pen, he said, "You do realize I did nothing but lie unconscious in the bottom of a boat?"

"But golly, what a ride!" The clerk looked at Amelia as if he were a little afraid of her and blurted out, "Sure hope I get myself a gal like you someday."

She laughed as Will passed her the pen and she started to write, stopped midstroke; without thinking, she'd penned *Amelia Sis*—

She looked at Will, who glanced down and smiled as he met her eyes again. "Well, I like the sound of that."

So she finished signing her new name—the last one she'd ever have—and pushed the card back across the desk. Wished the boy good luck.

Their corner suite on the top floor had a separate washroom, the deep slipper tub glorious indeed. It was filled with warm water posthaste, and they submerged themselves, heads leaned back at either sloping end. Steam rose, beaded the windows. Banquo lay on the tiled floor where he could soak up some of the radiant heat. They sighed, and the dog heaved his own deep, luxuriant breath a moment later, which set them laughing again.

There would be no complete and lasting reprieve, Amelia knew. The past would always be with them, and not always behind them; recent events would no doubt work their way into her dreams and reoccur as long as she drew breath. Wounds she'd rather pretend had closed, smoothed over with the pinkest scar tissue, would reopen because time did not, in fact, heal all things. It could also let them fester, but Amelia believed she'd learned to air and tend the memories that marred her, not to keep them smothered under wraps for the dangerous comfort of not looking.

She would not hide from anyone else or from herself again; the stories she told would all be true. She would acknowledge where she'd come from and what she'd done and who she'd been, so she could go forward in honesty and know just who she was.

Amelia moved from her end of the tub, water gently sloshing as she resettled herself with her head on Will's shoulder. She closed her eyes and let the hush of breath and the beat of blood wash through her, his chest a seamless shell through which she heard an ocean of time. In her own breast was the answering echo of a consubstantial sea.

But her hope, her happiness, was not foolhardy. She realized there would be new hardships too, for some danger always lay ahead. Love itself would guarantee the pain of loss. Yet Amelia would never live again without it.

Even with such clarity, there was no fragment of fear anywhere in her, no shade of sadness or regret. What she felt was sanctified: warm and quiet and content, at rest, at peace, at last.

~

Soon it would be another memory, those things and times and places and people one could never reclaim, yet never be rid of either. A feeling that would fade and flicker back to brightness, subject to her will and otherwise, but that could never be undone or erased.

And this feeling—this moment—was beautiful.

In the end, Amelia hoped, most of her life would be.

AUTHOR'S NOTE

This book was inspired by a real place and strives to capture as many period-accurate details as possible—but it is also a work of fiction. As such, and because the Farallon Islands seem so timelessly otherworldly, I have freely twisted some facts and completely invented other things. For instance, there has never been a chapel on the islands. There *was* a longtime resident mule, but his name was Jack. Stonehouse was real, as were the keepers' homes (which, in fact, still stand), but the latter weren't built until the 1870s. Some of the strangest events, including the rebuilding of the lighthouse, the murre-egg harvests, and the red aurora of 1859, actually happened—and are barely exaggerated for effect. If you're interested in a straightforward history of the Farallones, I recommend both *The Farallon Islands: Sentinels of the Golden Gate* by Peter White and *Farallon Islands: The Devil's Teeth (Images of America)* by Marla Daily as excellent resources to start.

ACKNOWLEDGMENTS

My deepest thanks:

To my mom for reading to me from a time before I can even remember—and for always being my first reader and greatest champion. (Pretend this is an auditorium stage and I'm whispering, "I love you, Mommy" into the microphone.)

To Neil Tierney for providing unwavering support in all things, including this journey, just one of many I'm glad to have gotten to take with you.

To Abby Saul for so much, not least of all helping strengthen my story and finding it a home—and for being a fabulous guide into and through the world of publishing. I couldn't have asked for a better agent and still can't believe I got so lucky.

To Danielle Marshall and Erin Adair-Hodges for loving this story too, understanding it so well, and making it become a real live book. Erin, your insights and edits further refined the manuscript, and your enthusiasm and support have made for an ideal debut experience.

To Jodi Warshaw for being another absolute dream of an editor and human being and having such wonderful questions and suggestions. This book is immeasurably better for your input—and you made the process a pleasure too.

To everyone else I've come into contact with via Lake Union, including Erica Mena for invaluable insights and exceedingly kind feedback; Elizabeth Cameron for careful copyedits; Patty Economos for precision proofreading; Abi Pollokoff for additional comments and production work I probably can't even fathom; Jen Bentham and Lauren Grange for keeping everything on schedule; and Shasti O'Leary Soudant for a flat-out gorgeous cover. And to everyone else behind the scenes who I certainly missed for doing the incredible amount of work it takes to bring a book into being.

To all the librarians and teachers I've known and adored, especially Mary Sands, for nurturing my love of literature and general curiosity about the wide world, to which books are windows and doors.

To all my friends and family who have encouraged and believed in me through the years, including those who are no longer here to see their faith finally rewarded but would be so proud.

To Joey Skladany for correctly predicting I'd write the next book (probably not the one you thought, but hey, there's still some food in it).

To Susan Casey for writing *The Devil's Teeth* and Nathaniel Philbrick for writing *In the Heart of the Sea*, two fascinating books that stirred my soul and fired my imagination. Ditto Peter White, Marla Daily, and the Point Blue Los Farallones bloggers; their accounts of the islands were all indispensable resources and sources of inspiration (but, of course, any mistakes and inaccuracies in this manuscript, intentional and otherwise, are mine alone).

To every reader who made the voyage into this book and took part in making my wildest and deepest-held dream come true.

Thank you.

ABOUT THE AUTHOR

Photo © 2022 Neil Tierney

Jen Wheeler is a former managing editor of Chowhound and lives in Oregon. *The Light on Farallon Island* is her first novel.